D0536653

SOUR GRAPES

by
Dan Rhodes

Lightning
Books

Published in 2021
by Lightning Books Ltd
Imprint of Eye Books Ltd
29A Barrow Street
Much Wenlock
Shropshire
TF13 6EN

www.lightning-books.com

Cover design by Nell Wood
Original artwork, illustrations and lettering by Andrea Joseph
Typeset in Book Antiqua

British Library Cataloguing in Publication Data
A catalogue record for this book is available from the British Library.

Printed by CPI Group (UK) Ltd, Croydon CR0 4YY

ISBN: 9781785632921

MIX
Paper from
responsible sources
FSC® C020471

Preamble

Spare a moment to feel sorry for literary gossip columnists. We writers are, by and large, aggressively dreary, and we don't give them a great deal to work with. The gruel is so thin that even I have made appearances over the years – once when I revamped my bathroom, and another time when a publicist returned to the office refreshed after a Christmas party and sent out a press release trumpeting how my work had been compared to that of my teenage hero 'Ivor Cutlet'. In that item I was described as a 'luckless fabulist', words which I expect to be carved into my headstone. Another dismal appearance occurred several years ago, shortly after I had won a prize. There had been a grand ceremony, and I was up against some big names so hadn't expected to win. I'd had a few drinks by that point, and got up to give a short acceptance speech.

It was off the cuff, and I don't remember much about it apart from telling a story about how I had recently had some warts cauterised, and complaining about how my publisher had invited me out for dinner earlier in the evening, and when the bill arrived had broken with protocol and insisted we split it. The audience roundly booed them for this, which, of course, they deserved. I made some quips, and said my thank yous, and got a friendly response, but all the while I was aware of a pair of glassy eyes boring into me.

At the table directly in front of the lectern sat a mid-profile restaurant critic, radio essayist and occasional novelist. This person seemed determined to remain conspicuously uninterested, right in my eyeline. I didn't think too much about it at the time; after all, good times are hard to come by in the writing racket and I had just won some money. I was enjoying myself, and you can't please everybody. I subsequently found out, though, about the dark thoughts that had been going on behind those gimlet eyes – this person was making plans to, as he might put it, micturate upon one's *pommes frites*.

After the event, the mid-profile restaurant critic, *Evening Standard* columnist and occasional novelist had gone on to the Internet and written up his impressions of the evening. All he had to say about it was that while note had been made of my having been the youngest author on the shortlist, my hair was starting to turn grey. 'Hmmm,' he cattily concluded. Quite what his point was I couldn't work out, and I still can't. There was no question, though, that he was being snarky.

I wouldn't have known about any of this were it not for his sardonic observation being picked up on by a literary gossip columnist, who, desperate to make up their word count, repeated it in a national newspaper.

A week or two had passed by the time this all reached me, so it was too late for a lightning comeback. I wasn't sure what to do, but I knew I had to do something. Every day when I was growing up my mother would impress upon me that I had Robertson blood, and that our motto is *Garg'n uair dhuis gear*: Fierce When Raised. One thing was clear – I would be letting my ancestors down if I didn't get my revenge.

Many years later, here it is.

I have, though, granted the mid-profile restaurant critic, current affairs pundit and occasional novelist a cloak of anonymity, and I will never reveal his true identity. Just as Carly Simon has spent decades being evasive about the subject of her song 'You're So Vain', so shall I discreetly draw a veil over this matter. Please don't ask.

It is perhaps worth emphasising that what follows is meant as light entertainment. It's a pantomime. To clarify: none of it really happened*. If you think this is a true story, please seek professional help. It contains coarse language, and due to its content it should not be read by anybody.

---

*Apart from the bit about piles of money going AWOL at a Scottish publishing house. That really happened.

Thursday

Chapter 1

Not very long ago, in the heart of England, some cleaning took place, and an alarming sight was beheld

When viewed from the village green, as it tended to be, the parsonage stood to the right-hand side of St. Peter's church, a yew tree and a grave-spattered lawn separating the two. A handsome brick building of three storeys, it had been built on the site of a previous, smaller church house and had been accommodating parsons for more than two hundred years. A list of their names could be found engraved on a wooden board inside the church. Its fortunes had declined though, and its latest incumbent had been the first to suffer its new incarnation as a semi-detached dwelling. A few years earlier, for reasons to do with money, the third of the building closest to the church had, with some internal bricking-up, been discreetly separated from the rest. It continued to fulfil its job of sheltering its parson from the elements, while the other two-thirds had been sold off. In spite of its greater size (five bedrooms and two bathrooms, according to the estate agent's particulars), the part now in private ownership had been given the modest name of Parsonage Cottage.

Though the parson was not at home, his third of the building was neither empty nor quiet. His housekeeper, a Mrs Rosemary Chapman, was going about her business in the guest bedroom on the top floor – wiping surfaces, vacuuming, and humming as she went. This room wasn't used very often so she didn't always attend to it, but the parson had made a special request for her to get it looking extra nice, and she had taken to the task with her customary diligence. She had worked in this building for years, the current parson being her fourth, and though she liked to feel that she had always given her best, she couldn't help but wonder whether she worked a little bit harder for, and took a little more care of, Reverend Jacobs than she had his predecessors. After all, he had *been through so much*, and *needed her more than ever*. She had known his wife, with her big earrings and her big laugh, and her cigarette always on the go, and at first she hadn't known what to make of her, but as the illness moved in and took over she decided that she liked her very much. As she tended to her in that last, long year, those eyes had shone up at her and she had said *thank you, dear Rosie*, and *you are so kind*, and *When I'm gone, you will look after him, won't you?* And now she was gone, and that was that, and it was down to Mrs Chapman to make sure the parsonage's surfaces were shiny, and the parson's clothes – clerical and secular – free of shaming creases.

She had more or less finished the guest bedroom, and was just giving its carpet a lucky final vacuum when the machine lost power. This moment had become a part of her routine. Though her build was powerful, she wasn't getting any younger, and the parson, shamed by the sight of her lugging a heavy old Henry up and down the stairs, had upgraded to the modern, cordless type of cleaner. This had been a great improvement, but it came with the downside of always needing to be mounted on its charger at some point during a shift, requiring her to get on with other things while she waited for its battery to recharge. It seemed to give up at a different part of the house each week, and it was just bad luck that she now had two flights of stairs between her and the kitchen cupboard, where the charger was. She hummed the tune of a favourite hymn, 'Praise For The Fountain Opened', as she went down the first flight, and on the landing she stopped dead. She looked around, and listened. Things seemed different. She couldn't work out how they were different, but something was not quite as it ought to have been. No longer humming, she carried on. Halfway down the next flight, she felt a draught on her legs. This was odd. She was sure the external doors were closed, and the windows open only a crack. Her sense of unease escalated. *Don't be silly, Rosemary*, she told herself.

Still, she walked cautiously through the hall and towards the kitchen. There was now no denying that there was a draught – a breeze even – and from the clear sound of a wren's song she knew that the back door must be open, the door that led into the garden and to the flagged path to the churchyard. She tried to tell herself that she mustn't have closed it properly, but it was no use; she always left the kitchen until last, and had only been in there to get the vacuum cleaner. She hadn't been near the back door all morning. It would have been the parson, that was all. He must have absent-mindedly left it ajar, and it would have opened by itself. Again, she told herself there was nothing to worry about.

She walked through the doorway, gasped, and put a hand to her thumping chest. The door was indeed open, and a man, if such a sight could be called a man, was standing beside the kitchen table, facing her. She had never seen anybody quite like him. His eyes were open, but blank, as if made of glass, or perhaps plastic, seeming to stare at a point far beyond the walls of the house. He was tall and thin, and though he was several feet away he still seemed to loom over her, and she noticed with horror that he appeared to be carrying in his hand a shrunken, severed head that looked as though it was a miniature version of his own. Perhaps even worse than that, she saw that behind him hung a long, thin tail. He began to talk but she couldn't understand what she was hearing; though the sounds he made were something like words, they were not words she had ever heard. She began to shake, and felt her legs weaken. The new, and quite expensive, vacuum cleaner clattered to the floor, and she steadied herself against the door frame. She knew she ought to be screaming in the hope that help would arrive, but she was frozen in terror. The strange, droning language went on and on, and the world seemed to swim around her. Just as time was losing all meaning, the sounds stopped.

The visitor, now silent, seemed to look not into the distance but straight into her eyes. As she trembled, Mrs Chapman took in some more details. He was wearing black trousers, a dark grey shirt and a black blazer, his face was a greyish white, and he was covered in mud and leaves, as though he had risen from the earth. She wanted to call God to protect her, to bring something holy into this tableau. She tried to sing the hymn she had been humming: *There is a fountain filled with blood...* but it was no use. Her voice would not cooperate.

The visitor raised a thin hand – the one that was not holding the shrunken head – and slowly ran his long fingers through his hair, where they seemed to find what they had been looking for. Something that was almost a smile, yet at the same time was not a smile at all, passed over his face, and as he withdrew his hand from his hair Mrs Chapman could see that between his forefinger and thumb was a large and brownish-grey slug, curling and uncurling as if desperately trying to get away. With quite some vigour the man rubbed it between his fingers for a while, then took a long look at it, seeming to appraise and appreciate it, then put it, whole, into his mouth. After what seemed like an eternity, he began to chew.

The soft squelches of the chewing knocked her out of her catatonic state, and she thought about how desperately the slug had tried to save itself, right up to the last. Taking inspiration from it, Mrs Chapman raced past the black-clad figure, out of the open door, and toward the laurel hedge that separated The Parsonage from Parsonage Cottage. She had not run a step since her school days, but with all the speed she had within her she thundered into the leaves. There was no pathway, not even a handy gap, but that didn't stop her. With all her strength she forced her way through the branches, and it was only when she was on the other side, safely in the garden of Parsonage Cottage, that she let out the scream she had been holding back for so long.

Chapter 2

Wedding arrangements are made, a mystery is solved, and a spectral face appears at a window

As the battery on Mrs Chapman's vacuum cleaner had been giving up, Reverend Jacobs hadn't been far away. He was only next door, in the back garden of Parsonage Cottage, discussing the wedding of the resident family's daughter that was due to take place at St. Peter's in a few weeks' time. This was an unusual event for the parson, as the family, including the bride, were genuine churchgoers. Normally the couples he married only attended in order to secure the venue for their wedding. They wanted the old stone building, with its low tower, its stained-glass windows, its medieval font and its yew tree, and they simpered their way through the bare minimum of services in the run-up to the big day, attempting to convince him that they were God People, and failing completely.

Sometimes they were local, and sometimes they came in from the cities. Either way, after the ceremony he rarely saw or heard from them again. Some of the more straight-laced couples would be put off by the church's full name – The Church of St. Peter in the Bottoms – while others were positively encouraged by it. The idea of being married in a scattering of villages known as *The Bottoms*, and specifically in a village called Green Bottom, held a certain puerile charm, and there had been a lot of big beards, and tattoos, and brides arriving in Citroën 2CVs or split-screen VW Campervans, as well as two-camera *cinéma vérité* crews trying to get into the vestry to film him changing into his cassock. He didn't mind any of this too much. They all seemed to enjoy it, and it made a change.

This family though, the Bells, had been regulars in the pews for as long as they had lived in the house. 'We really are church Bells,' Mrs Bell would joke, in her low, soothing voice. Even though their daughter had moved away to university and to work, whenever she came back to the village she joined them on Sunday mornings. Reverend Jacobs liked their daughter a lot, and a few years earlier he had gone through a phase of hoping she and his son would end up together, but both had too much imagination to marry the girl or the boy next door. Still, they were great friends, and his son would be coming home for the big day. For the first time in a long while, Reverend Jacobs found himself really looking forward to a wedding rather than regarding it as a duty to be good-naturedly endured. He had high hopes for the reception too, which was taking place in a marquee on the lawn; the Bells were always good hosts, and he planned to get pleasantly drunk. He would even dance. There had been a time, before he had heard his calling, when he had danced a great deal. Now, when opportunities arose for him to take to the floor, he would embrace them with enthusiasm, to the wonderment of his flock.

While not quite open to charges of being a trendy cleric – there was no earring, for one thing – he was considered to have a youthful demeanour and outlook. His grey hair often grew, more from neglect than by design, into a shaggy mop, and he only wore his dog collar when it was called for. Anybody who had seen him for the first time that day in the Bells' garden, in his jeans and open-neck shirt, would have been surprised to learn that he was a man of the cloth. Sometimes he even surprised himself at the thought that he was a man of the cloth.

And so they sat at a garden table, the parson and Mr and Mrs Bell, and they talked about the service, and sipped iced lemonade; not the clear, fizzy kind, but the English garden kind – still and yellow. A light breeze kept them cool in the warm mid-morning air, a bumble bee made its way around the buddleia, an elderly chocolate Labrador called Bevis lazed in the shade of a pear tree, and a wren sang as it flew from branch to branch.

'My mother used to have a rhyme,' said Mrs Bell, as she refilled Reverend Jacobs' glass, 'Lemonade is from lemons m...'

But before Mrs Bell could finish her rhyme, she was startled by the unexpected sound of cracking branches. Her eyes widened as it became clear that something was charging towards them through the laurel. After a little more rustling and snapping, the thing emerged, revealing itself to be Mrs Chapman, her face white with terror and lined with fresh red scratches. When she made it through to the lawn she stopped, opened her mouth, and screamed.

For all the years of their acquaintance, and for all the familiarity that had grown between them, Mrs Chapman had never been able to move beyond the knowledge that Reverend Jacobs was the parson and she was his housekeeper, and the feeling that because of the nature of this relationship she must always be deferential in her manner. Though the parson did all he could to disabuse her of this old-fashioned notion, she was keenly aware of a very clear and historically established hierarchy that it was not her place to question, and so there was always a formality between them. Over the years *Reverend Jacobs* had softened to simply *Reverend*, and she had grown accustomed to him calling her *Mrs C*, but first names were a world away.

Mrs Chapman made sure that when she spoke to the parson, her choice of words was very precise, as though his ear would be offended by any deviation from what she considered to be proper usage. A bus was never a bus, but an omnibus; a fridge not a fridge, but a refrigerator; and a piano was always a pianoforte. And so it was that as Mr and Mrs Bell and Reverend Jacobs dashed over to find out what on earth was going on, she pointed at the gap she had made in the hedge and said, her eyes wild, 'Personage.'

'Personage, Mrs C?' asked the parson. 'Which personage?'

She pointed again. 'Parsonage.'

'I'm sorry, I misheard. I thought you said *personage*. Tell us, what's wrong? What's happened at the parsonage?'

'Personage,' she said again, looking from one concerned face to another.

'What is it, Mrs Chapman?' asked Mrs Bell. 'Please tell us.'

Something about Mrs Bell's kind and restful voice must have had an effect on her, because she was at last able to tell them what she had been trying to say ever since she had burst through the hedge.

'There is a personage at the parsonage.'

Mrs Chapman had been brought over to the garden table by the parson and Mr Bell, who had lowered her into a chair and plied her with lemonade while Mrs Bell had gone inside for some antiseptic. On her return she gently dabbed the fresh scratches with dampened cotton wool, as Mrs Chapman winced.

'I wonder whether I imagined it all,' said Mrs Chapman, as she finished her description of the visitor to the house next door, and told them about what she had seen him do. 'I must be going potty, imagining monsters that have risen from the grave.'

'I'm sure you're not going potty, Mrs C,' said the

parson. 'Did you catch any of what this person, or thing, said?'

'No, Reverend. It really was just as I described. It was these strange sounds that weren't really words at all.'

'What were the sounds like? Perhaps he was speaking in a foreign language. Could you give us an idea of what you heard?'

She looked very serious as she cast her mind back. '*Sblongambamnulent,*' she said, in a low monotone. 'Yes, that was one, or something like it, anyway. *Twumplastitude. Lyxbambulationarically.* Oh, and there was one sound he made several times. It was almost like a real sentence, but not quite.' She closed her eyes as she tried to recall it. 'It was something like... *Systematic in a brown cordial mayonnaise.*'

Reverend Jacobs tilted his head a little. 'That sounds familiar. Was it, in fact, *Symptomatic of a broad cultural malaise?*'

'That's it,' she cried, amazed. 'Those were the exact sounds. Do you...do you know the creature, Reverend?'

'Don't worry, Mrs C. That wasn't a creature, it was just one of our visiting authors. I've been reading up on him, and that's his catchphrase; he says it all the time. He's up here for the book festival – it's starting this evening, you know.' Mrs Chapman had heard about this festival, and couldn't have missed the enormous marquee that had swallowed up half the expansive village green across the road. 'You remember when I asked you to pay special attention to the guest bedroom? That was for him. I'm putting him up while he's here, but I wasn't expecting him to arrive until later on. Not to worry, there's room at the inn.'

'An author? So...' she looked relieved as this news sank in, '...he's not a zombie after all. Oh, I do feel silly. I'm ashamed, as well; I should have known that zombies aren't real, and even if they were, they wouldn't have tails, would they?' Her troubled look returned. 'But *people* don't have tails either. And what about the shrunken head?'

'I'm sure there will be a perfectly reasonable explanation, and we'll all have a good laugh about it later on. Writers are an eccentric bunch, Mrs C.'

'Eccentric, yes... Do they *all* eat slugs, Reverend?'

'I'm not sure. Perhaps they do. Let's go and say hello. I'll introduce you properly this time. His name is Wilberforce Selfram.'

Aided by Mrs Bell, Mrs Chapman rose from her seat. Even though there was now a navigable route through the hedge, they decided not to use it, and to go around the more conventional way instead. As they walked across the lawn and around to the front garden, Mrs Chapman looked at the blue sky, and over to a pair of pied wagtails that had landed nearby. She was being cared for, and she had nothing to worry about. She looked at the house, at its old bricks that shone red in the sunshine, and the wisteria growing up the wall. It was all so reassuring; her world was returning to normal.

Something at one of the top-floor windows caught

her eye. From behind leaded panes, a featureless and brilliant white face was staring down at her. She wondered whether it was a tailor's dummy; maybe they were using it for wedding dress fittings. But the face seemed to move, very slightly, as though it were following them as they walked through the garden.

It was all too much for one day, and down she went – arms out, and flat on her back.

It wasn't long before she had been revived with smelling salts and lemonade. She was carefully helped to her feet, and the world came back into focus. She looked up at the window.

The face had gone.

Chapter 3

We go back in time to the preceding summer. A committee
is formed, a meeting is held, and two letters are read out

Within a few hours of moving in to Honeysuckle
Nook, a tile-hung house set behind a mature garden
on the quiet main street of Broad Bottom, Mrs Angelica
Bruschini had established a committee. The idea had
come to her as she stood behind her low front gate,
poised like an opera singer about to launch into an
aria, and watched as village life unfolded before her.
A Royal Mail van drove past; a cat jumped up on to a
nearby wall, then down the other side and out of view;
an elderly couple walked towards the village shop and
looked at the notice board for a while before going
inside.

She concluded that this was all very well, but that
something had to be done. She went back indoors,
unpacked a pashmina shawl – a real one – from a

cardboard box, threw it artfully over her shoulders and, chin aloft, left Honeysuckle Nook behind her and glided into the streets, like an ocean liner on its maiden voyage.

To her astonishment, her door-knocking recruitment drive for the All Bottoms Cultural Committee was not the triumph she had anticipated. The Bottoms already had its fair share of committees, and nobody could quite see the need for another one. While everybody who came to their door was very polite to her as she explained that she had recently moved to the village and was determined to *breathe new life into the area*, on every doorstep she failed to strike a chord. Everybody she spoke to was, it seemed, *all booked up*. It was as if they didn't want new life breathed into the area, that they were content with the life it already had – vans driving past; cats jumping on to walls; pensioners going, somewhat gradually, into shops.

Since early childhood, she had set up committee after committee, leading each one herself, and by sheer force of personality she had ensured her meetings were well attended and her goals, whatever they had been, were reached. Here, though, instead of a full complement of supporters, she had a handbag full of flyers for local groups that her new neighbours had kindly suggested she try out. Bell ringers. Steam traction enthusiasts. Naturalists. *Why don't you pop along?* they had said. *We're a friendly bunch, and we're always looking for new people to join the committee.* Her belief that joining an existing committee was a sign of weakness was so deeply held that popping along to any of these groups was out of the question. This level of resistance was new to her, and she faced it as a challenge. Without knowing it, she very slightly adjusted the set of her jaw, changing her mien from imperious to defiant, and resolved that before nightfall she would have secured the services of, at the very least, a secretary and a treasurer.

On a war footing now, she carried on until her aim was achieved. Broad Bottom wasn't a large village, and she was close to running out of front doors to knock on when at last she found her two committee members, a young man and a young woman who lived at opposite ends of the same street. Both had just come home from work, and had answered the doors of their parents' houses where, in their mid-twenties, they still lived. Both had always suffered from a crippling difficulty when it came to saying no to forceful people, and faced with a determined Mrs Bruschini they were quite flattened. The young man she anointed treasurer, telling him in her extraordinarily loud voice that it would have been ridiculous to offer him the other available position because *Who has ever heard of a male secretary?* The young woman, though, was informed that she was fully qualified to fulfil this role, and that it was her job to arrange the date, time and venue for their inaugural meeting. Each of her recruits, their appointments set in stone, went straight back indoors and on to the Internet, where they looked up books with titles like *How to Say NO!*, *Learn to Say NO!*, and *Saying NO!*.

This sort of thing, they resolved, *has to stop*.

Her core team in place, Mrs Bruschini returned to Honeysuckle Nook satisfied with her progress, and ready to settle down with a bottle of sherry. She very much enjoyed drinking sherry, and several cases had come up with the removal van. She thought about Mr Bruschini, and soon she had drunk a bit too much. *I've found you a lovely little place in the country*, he had said, very kindly.

She had prepared what she was going to tell people when they asked after him. *He's ever so busy in town. Ever so busy. He is very high up, you know.* It wasn't only other people she was going to say this to; she was going to keep on saying it to herself as well. 'Very, very busy,' she said, the sound of her voice dulled a little by the cardboard boxes that surrounded her. 'Very high up indeed.'

Their third weekly meeting was held, like its predecessors, in the Broad Bottom Village Hall. The committee hadn't grown at all in that time. Having been entrusted with the key, the secretary arrived first, ten minutes early as per Mrs Bruschini's instructions. This gave her time to unfold the table and set out the chairs to ensure a punctual start. The treasurer turned up with two minutes to spare. Avoiding eye contact, they had greeted each other with a brief *hello*, after which they sat in silence as they waited for Mrs Bruschini to arrive.

Unbeknown to one another, in their houses at

opposite ends of their street, they had been making their way through the same reading list, and each had decided that this was the evening when they would put everything from the books into practice. Both planned to tell her, politely but with no ambiguity, that while they would see this meeting through they would not be returning. It seemed a little cruel to leave her, to see her already threadbare committee reduced further still, but it was something they had to do. Neither felt any reason to be there. The previous two meetings had been little more than monologues from the chair, and in spite of these they still had no real grasp of what their committee was trying to achieve. They were leaving, and if she asked them why, they would say that they had other commitments. It was none of her business what those commitments were, and they would not be drawn to elucidate. They waited for the right moment, and as Mrs Bruschini swept in at seven o'clock on the dot it was clear to both of them that this wasn't it.

Some of this hesitancy could be put down to a nervous failure to reach the required pitch of courage expected of them by their books, and some to the way their invocation of *other commitments* rang hollow; they had no other commitments besides staying in their rooms and wondering when their lives were going to get better. As she rose before them, a mountain in pearls, they sensed she would know this, and see through their exaggerations, and ask them questions that they couldn't answer. Another difficulty was the structure of the sentence that they needed. It had been hard to pin down, and now the words swam in their minds. Both vaguely recalled it being something along the lines of *I can no longer commit to the committee because I am committed to other commitments*, but that wasn't quite right...

Without a word of greeting, Mrs Bruschini started the meeting. She never left the house without a mahogany gavel and sound block, and she withdrew them from her handbag, placed them before her, and gave a solid thump to announce the commencement of business.

Mrs Bruschini's style as chair was to make no use at all of her actual chair, this one being a generic stackable metal and plastic specimen that had profoundly disappointed her. Even if she wasn't ever going to use it to sit on, she liked her chair to have some craftsmanship to it. She resolved to deal with this another day, and for now she got on with the urgent business of standing in position and addressing the room without let-up, and at such volume that it was as though she was having to project to be heard by people squashed up against the back wall. Her audience, though, was immediately below her and consisted of just two timid young people who didn't know quite where to look, and who were only half-listening anyway, so preoccupied were they by plotting their escape.

For the preceding fifty minutes, Mrs Bruschini had outlined her renewed vision for the group. She had decided that the committee's focus would be on turning The Bottoms into an international epicentre of culture, rather than developing the culture it already had – amateur dramatics, bands playing in beer gardens, folk nights and painting groups; that was the sort of thing that could be found anywhere, and Mrs Bruschini had written it off. She was in pursuit of only the very highest culture. 'Ballet. Opera. That sort of thing,' she roared, and she recounted various visits to Glyndebourne, Sadler's Wells, Vienna and Berlin. When, at last, her monologue was complete she looked to her audience. 'So, we are all in agreement that what this area needs is a symphony hall.'

Both the secretary and the treasurer thought that this was a ridiculous idea. The Bottoms was a collection of villages and hamlets set in rolling countryside and connected by narrow lanes; there would be nowhere to put a symphony hall, and even if there was there would barely be enough B&Bs to accommodate a percussion section, let alone the strings, and the ballerinas, and whoever else she had in mind. A quiet fell over the room. A moment for rebellion had finally come, and they thought back to their deep-breathing exercises. It was no good. They let their chance slip away. They both decided they would wait until *any other business*, at the end of the meeting. Previously they had just silently shaken their heads when asked if they had anything to add, but today would be different. They would grasp the opportunity. For now though, she took their silence for assent. 'At our next meeting we shall address the practicalities of building such a structure. Trap doors and the like.' Mrs Bruschini now turned to her treasurer. 'Your summary, treasurer.'

The treasurer noted their outgoings. Stationery had been dealt with after their first meeting, and no pens or paper had been bought since, so he only had to report the cost of renting the room. He then moved on to their income. Six pounds had been collected at the last meeting. And then the moment came, perhaps the worst moment of all. Furious with themselves, the treasurer and the secretary reached into their pockets. Each produced a two-pound coin: their subs. Not only were they putting themselves through all this, they were paying for the experience. At least it was going to be the last time. No way were they coming back here to help a madwoman plan an imaginary auditorium in a field. The treasurer put the coins, along with the one proffered by Mrs Bruschini, into a small metal box, and logged the amount in his ledger.

The chair turned to the secretary. 'To correspondence,' she said.

The secretary took out two letters and, shaking a little, read out the first one. It was from the local MP, patiently declining their invitation to attend a meeting of the committee, citing time constraints. She had, though, asked for clarification of their aims, as well as their attendance figures. Mrs Bruschini harrumphed, and told the secretary to reply with the idea about the symphony hall, but to gloss over the attendance figures: '*Rather well attended* should be adequate.'

Then came the second letter, the one that was to lead to Mrs Chapman being startled in the parson's kitchen.

It was on headed notepaper, from an organisation that had written to them from an address in London's WC2 postcode. On hearing this, Mrs Bruschini gasped.

London! WC2! In a flash she was back in her finery on St Martin's Lane, with Mr Bruschini by her side, and they were being dropped off outside the Coliseum before going in to find their box. She was jolted back to the Broad Bottom Village Hall by the voice of her secretary. 'They are called,' the secretary said, 'The Literary Festival People.'

Literary! This just got better and better. 'What do they say?' she asked, ravenous for news from home.

In her quiet voice, the secretary read the letter.

Dear cultural committee,

I very much hope you will allow me to introduce my organisation. We are a small team devoted to scouring the country in search of homes for new literary festivals. Just this morning we put all the relevant data into our computer, and it came back with the opinion that your area, The Bottoms, is perfectly placed to be the next location for a rather prestigious event of this sort. We felt you would be the best people to approach about taking this idea further. We do so hope to hear from you, and that we might be able to provide you with the support and expertise you will need to make this event the enormous success that we are sure it would be.

If you feel this venture would not be to your taste, I wonder whether you would kindly put us in touch with other local organisations that may be interested.

With literary regards,
Florence Peters

Suddenly everything was clear to Mrs Bruschini. The symphony hall was forgotten, trap doors and all. 'Other local organisations?' she bellowed. 'I think not. This, lady and gentleman, is no longer the All Bottoms Cultural Committee. No, from this moment forward we are the All Bottoms *Literary* Committee.' Without bothering to put it to the vote, she turned to the secretary. 'Make a note of that, and see to all the necessary paperwork.'

The secretary made a note.

'I shall reply to Ms Peters personally,' said Mrs Bruschini. 'There is no further business, so we shall disperse forthwith and prepare for the next chapter of my glorious committee.' She had begun their meeting with a resonant thud, and she concluded it the same way before putting her gavel and sound block back into her handbag and sweeping away.

As they gathered their bits and pieces, the treasurer and the secretary exchanged a glance. Until now shame had led them to avoid looking directly at one another, but their eyes met for a moment, and it was then that the treasurer knew he would keep returning to these diabolical meetings. It wasn't the book festival that interested him: he liked books well enough, but didn't have the faintest interest in listening to authors reading aloud and answering questions about where they get their ideas from. It was something else entirely. Suddenly that two pounds seemed like money very well spent.

The secretary was also resigned to returning the following week as she folded the table and moved it into the side room, while the treasurer stacked the chairs and put them away too. With the lights off and the door locked, they stood outside the hall. The treasurer turned to the secretary in the mellowing late summer light and didn't know what to say. He wondered whether he should tell her how much he liked her cardigan. He decided against it, but with a courage he didn't know he had, he spoke. 'Shall we walk back together?'

All the books she had read crowded to the forefront of her mind. The deep breathing exercises she had worked on so hard suddenly took effect and she said, simply, 'No.'

He watched her walk away. He knew she lived on the same street as he did, and that their route home was the same, so he leant against the wall of the village hall for a few minutes to make sure he had no chance of catching up with her, or seeming as if he was following her. He had been rejected, and he wondered whether there was anything he could do about it. It was a shame. That cardigan really did suit her. As he thought about what lay beneath it, he knew he wasn't ready to give up.

Chapter 4

We return to the parsonage, where another slug is eaten
and a novelty drinking vessel is misnamed

They were in the kitchen – the parson, Mrs Chapman, and Mr and Mrs Bell, as well as Wilberforce Selfram, who displayed no sign of a tail or a shrunken head. His backpack, grubby and damp, was leaning against a kitchen cabinet. Introductions had been made, but hands were not shaken, because the visitor had between his fingers another living slug, a jet-black specimen this time, that he had pulled from beneath his lapel and was rubbing between his fingers. 'Do excuse one,' he said, in a low monotone, then he stopped rubbing the animal and put it in his mouth. They looked on, simultaneously repulsed and enthralled, as he slowly chewed it. They wondered what the texture would be like. The longer the chewing went on the more rubbery, perhaps even leathery, they supposed it to be.

They tried to tell themselves that it must have been a bit like eating snails, and the French did that all the time, so it wasn't really all that strange if you looked at it that way.

Having already witnessed a similar display, and become accustomed to it, Mrs Chapman's mind wandered. She was ill at ease. Because of all the drama of the morning, the parson had insisted on taking over the tea-making duties, which were normally her domain when they had visitors, and as the kettle boiled and mugs clinked in the background she wasn't sure what to do with herself. The unfortunate circumstances of her first meeting with Mr Selfram had not been mentioned, but she knew she had to say something. She didn't want the visitor to think she had been rude by screaming and running away from him. She could have said, *I'm sorry, but I mistook you for a burglar*, but this wouldn't have been true, and she couldn't possibly tell a lie, no matter how white, within earshot of a parson. She decided that the best thing would be to stop standing there like a lemon, and get it over with.

'Mr Selfram,' she said, clutching her apron in her writhing fists, 'I'm very sorry about what happened earlier. I'm afraid I rather thought...' At the sound of her voice the visitor turned to Mrs Chapman, and swallowed the last of his snack. She swallowed too, as she felt those unblinking eyes bore into her. '...I rather thought you were a zombie.' His expression did not change, and in the silence that followed she felt flattened by the gravity of what she had just said. She had admitted that she had thought he was a corpse that had come back to life, risen from its grave, and wandered into the kitchen. She felt she had to go on. 'It's just, well, you were all covered in leaves and mud, and you seemed to have a tail, and you were carrying what looked like a shrunken severed head, and I hope you don't mind me saying, but all those things seem quite zombielike. I feel silly now, because I'm sure you're a very nice man and not a zombie at all.'

Showing no emotion, his voice a now familiar drone, he replied. 'One becomes accustomed to such misapprehensions. However, were such a creature in existence, the zonbi – one prefers to employ the Haitian Creole – being the reanimated cadaver of an example of the effectively acaudal species *Homo sapiens*, would not, Mrs Chapman, be in possession of a tail.'

Mrs Chapman was just about able to unravel the gist of all this. 'Yes, I had wondered about that. I was a little flustered at the time…but I couldn't have imagined it, could I?'

'One suspects you failed to correctly identify one's portable misericord.' He withdrew from a side pocket of his blazer something that looked like a truncheon, then he telescopically extended it, flipped the top so it made a sort of seat, and gave a brief demonstration of it holding him upright, before folding it away again. 'It is bespoke, hand-crafted to reach precisely the optimum point of repose upon one's posterior; one abhors the mass-produced portable misericords to be found at supermarkets, betwixt J-cloth and sprout. One never leaves one's home without it – it maintains one's erectitude.' He paused, considering for a moment what he had just said. 'And there is nothing amusing about that.'

'But the severed head, Mr Selfram…what about the severed head?' He reached into the other side-pocket of his blazer and placed on the table what she could now see was a porcelain jug that had been cast in the shape of a face. There was an uncanny likeness to its owner, but she was relieved to see, at these close quarters, that it was a piece of pottery.

'So you're not going barmy after all, Mrs Chapman,' said Mr Bell, 'there *was* a little head.'

She was lost for words, but the parson came to her rescue, carrying the teapot. 'I see you've got a Toby jug,' he exclaimed, addressing Wilberforce Selfram.

'Where?' asked the visitor.

'There,' said the parson, putting down the teapot and pointing to the ceramic head.

'Where?'

'Just there.' This time the parson's pointing finger almost touched the jug's nose.

'One remains incognisant of a Toby jug in the vicinity.'

'This thing here, that I'm pointing at.'

'Allow one to correct you. That is not a Toby jug, as it depicts merely the head, rather than a full seated figure. The proper nomenclature is *character jug*.'

'I see. Either way, it's missing its handle.' There were two clear breaks where the handle had become detached from the body of the jug. The parson put two and two together, and smiled. 'Did you by any chance meet Margaret Thatcher on your way here?'

On the very edge of the village was an antiques shop run by a tiny and extremely elderly woman of that name. She didn't have a great aptitude for stocking interesting items, and she sold very little in the usual way, but she was kept in business by a sign on the door that stated, very clearly, that *All breakages must be paid for*. The shop's aisles were so narrow, and its shelves and tables so overfilled, that it was hard to navigate it without knocking something delicate on to the flagstoned floor. The locals knew to avoid going in, but there were always passers-by, and through them she made several sales a day and her business ticked over well enough. There was no criminal design behind this – her stock was fairly priced for what it was, and she dealt with all her unfortunate customers with a genuine sympathy that made it impossible to dispute her demand for the full price. She always made sure they got what they paid for, gathering together the shattered ruins of their purchase, and giving an assurance, in the tiny voice that matched her build, that it would fix up nicely with a spot of glue. Whenever a customer had bought something, broken or not, Margaret Thatcher rewarded them by holding open the door as they left, and singing them out of the shop with the opening lines of 'We'll Meet Again'. As a quavering soprano emerged from this frail bark, so unexpectedly and at an almost deafening volume, even people who had managed to get their purchases this far without mishap would often drop them in shock.

Wilberforce Selfram removed the broken-off handle from his pocket, and placed it beside the mug. 'One only entered the premises because of one's notoriously insatiable curiosity, and before one knew it one's ganderbag had caught this wretched exhibit with a glancing blow. Duly the monstrosity descended and, seven-pounds-twenty later, one finds oneself encumbered with it. And yet…' A solution flashed into his mind, and he passed both pieces to Mrs Chapman. 'A memento of our encounter,' he said. 'The monstrosity is yours: one's severed and shrunken auxiliary head. Place it high upon your mantel. One shall present you with a certificate of provenance in due course.'

She accepted her new encumbrance. 'Thank you, Mr Selfram,' she said, quietly. 'That is very kind of you.'

The parson returned to his tea making, and it was Mrs Bell who, sensitive to Mrs Chapman's suffering, came to her rescue this time, with an attempt to change the subject. 'So, Mr Selfram,' she said, 'you're an author. You must be frightfully clever.'

'Affirmative.'

The conversation faltered. The parson was still sorting out the mugs, and Mrs Bell, her voice as calm as ever, soldiered on. 'How did you get here? Did you drive?'

'Negative. One mounted *le petit cheval de Shanks,* and sallied forth.' This drew blank looks. 'One ambulated; indeed perambulated.' They were still unsure. Wilberforce Selfram sighed through his nose, as he always did when accepting that he would have to simplify his vocabulary for the comprehension of the people around him. 'One walked.'

'Walked? From the train station?' The nearest station was miles away.

'Negative.'

'Oh…'

'*Oh* indeed. One commenced one's peregrinations

from a settlement in the southeast of this fractured isle; a conurbation known commonly as *London*. Perhaps you have heard of it, perhaps not.'

'Oh yes, we've heard of it. We've even been there quite a few times. We normally take the train, though. It must have taken you an awfully long time to walk.'

'Very little time. A mere eight nights.'

'Eight nights? Gosh. *Nights*, Mr Selfram?'

'One travelled primarily through the hours of darkness. One made full use of the gloaming to locate foodstuffs, after which one would fade into the forest dim and continue upon one's odyssey until cockcrow.'

'Didn't you keep tripping over things?'

'Every few paces one stumbled and fell to the ground, but this was to be expected. One merely righted oneself and continued upon one's way.'

'What did you do during the day? Did you check into a hotel?'

'One begs your pardon. Check into what?'

'A hotel.'

'What is *a hotel*?'

'Oh.' Mrs Bell was a little stuck for a moment, but soon she had her answer. 'It's a big building, and it's got lots of bedrooms, and you walk in through the front door, and there's a desk, or counter, and a nice lady behind the counter...'

'Or man,' put in Mr Bell. 'Sometimes it's a chap.'

'Yes, you're absolutely right, darling, sometimes it is a man. So, there's a nice lady, or man, there, and you say, *Do you have a room for the night?* and they say...'

Wilberforce Selfram raised a hand, signalling her to stop. 'You appear,' he said, 'to be describing *an hôtel*.'

'Oh. Yes. That is what I meant.'

Wilberforce Selfram looked to the side, as though he were gazing into the lens of a film camera, and breaking the fourth wall to communicate with an audience who understood him in a way these people never would. 'One despairs,' he sighed. He returned his gaze to Mrs Bell. 'One's rejoinder is an unequivocal *negative*.'

It was the parson's turn to come to the rescue. He had finally found enough mugs, and filled a jug with milk, and a bowl with sugar lumps. 'Let's all sit down and have a cup of tea, and Mr Selfram can tell us about his journey. It sounds fascinating.'

They took their seats around the kitchen table. There was something of a false start as Wilberforce Selfram pointed out that they weren't having a *cup* of tea because they were drinking from mugs, but once this was over with, his account began.

'In all that time you never stayed in a B&B, or ate in a restaurant, or bought food from a shop?' asked the parson.

'Affirmative. One left one's home, ganderbag upon one's back, and picked whatever sustenance one required from hedgerow and greensward; from cliff face and fosse.'

'A bit like that nice man on the television,' put in Mrs Bell. 'Ray Mears; that's his name. He's always going into the woods and eating things he finds.'

'One despairs,' monotoned Wilberforce Selfram, again looking into the imaginary camera before returning his stare to Mrs Bell. 'That your mind would immediately fix upon an ephemeral celebrity of our modern age is symptomatic of a broad cultural malaise; one is walking in the footsteps not of a transient televisular personality, but in those of an immortal: Beoffrey of Biddenden, no less. You will, surely, have heard of Beoffrey of Biddenden.'

'I think I have,' said the parson, who listened to Radio 4 a fair amount. 'Didn't they recently find those fragments of his writings on old bits of paper?'

'Affirmative. The material has only lately been released for public consumption. However, one has absorbed them and acted upon them with what has been described as almost preternatural alacrity.' Wilberforce Selfram chose not to explain how he had in fact gained access to these documents long before they were widely available.

Chapter 5

A young professor fathers a child, falls from favour,
and spends quite a long time at a distant vending machine

Eighteen months earlier, Wilberforce Selfram had set himself the task of spending an entire year conversing exclusively in Middle English. It is not a widely spoken tongue, and his social circle was limited to a young professor from the University of Rutland who had taken on the same challenge. Around this time the academic had, in collaboration with his wife, embarked on a programme of procreation. Before the new-born had come along he had held a broad range of interests, but as fatherhood consumed him he found himself able only to talk about baby monitors, and Calpol, and pushchairs, and muslin squares, and how tired he was. As his focus narrowed, their acquaintanceship fell apart. Exasperated by his companion's limited conversational scope, Wilberforce Selfram told him, in exemplary Middle English and no uncertain terms, that in spite of his academic credentials he had proved himself to have the intellect of a hogge's turd.

With several weeks of the experiment left to run, Wilberforce Selfram had completed it alone, talking only to himself and his mystified tobacconist. When the year was at last over, he had written a long article about the experience for a highly regarded periodical, in which the young professor, while not being explicitly named, could easily be identified by anybody in such circles. The hogge's turd line was used once again, and the author had also made a comment about how, in professorial terms, his rejected compatriot was considered young, but the hair on his temples was turning grey. He followed this misjudged and ultimately pointless personal observation with a lofty *Hmmm*.

Not long after this article's publication, Wilberforce Selfram had been surprised to receive a letter from the professor, cordially inviting him to his office to share an extraordinary find: what had since become known as *The Beoffrey Papers*, a slim ream of writings from the thirteenth century that, the professor explained, had been found inside an old cider jug after it was ploughed up by a farmer in a field in Kent. On their reunion the men had fallen straight back into their medieval dialogue. Wearing special gloves, the professor took the entire ream from his safe. He allowed his guest to read the first page, telling him there was a strict embargo in place, and there was no way he could show him the rest at this point.

That top page alone, on browning paper with jagged

edges, was incredible; written in diary form, and seemingly with an eye on it becoming an instructional guide, it offered an unprecedented insight into day-to-day life in the Dark Ages. Beoffrey was clearly something of a wayfarer, and what intrigued the reader most of all were the descriptions of his travels, and, particularly, the food he had eaten along the way. On just this first page Beoffrey lifted a stone and snacked on some millipedes that had been living underneath it; wrapped a worm around a stick and toasted it over a fire; and strangled a weasel. Wilberforce Selfram was, silently, desperate to read on. The professor suddenly announced, maintaining his impeccable Middle English, that he was off to get some packets of Flamin' Hot Monster Munch and cans of Tango from a vending machine in the building's basement, and that it would be at least ten minutes before he was back. The moment he left the room, his visitor used the opportunity to take out his phone and capture clear photographs of every page of The Beoffrey Papers before returning to his seat.

The professor came back with two bags of Monster Munch and two cans of Fanta, which he shared with his visitor, who gave every impression of not having moved an inch since he had left. The professor explained that the machine hadn't had Tango after all, but that Fanta was much the same sort of thing.

'One doth wyshhe one coulde reidde the ressed o' the payperrs,' said Wilberforce Selfram, all innocence.

'Out o' the quesstionne, auld chappe,' said the professor, casually opening his can with a *pfzzz*, and taking a long drink. 'Out o' the quesstionne.'

*

With his secret knowledge, Wilberforce Selfram was able to plan ahead. He knew there was no way that such an old manuscript could be subject to copyright, and that the moment The Beoffrey Papers were made public his rivals would clamour to read them and mine them for all they were worth; after all, this was the most significant find of medieval writings for centuries. They would pore over them, and try to decode their meaning and, having ruminated upon what it all meant, they would begin to pitch articles about it: *What Beoffrey Can Teach Us; What Beoffrey Saw; If Beoffrey Were Here Today; De-clutter Your Life the Beoffrey Way*, and so on. But all this would take time. There was a lot of material to digest, and it had been Wilberforce Selfram's aim to ensure that his enemies would not be in the vanguard, because the vanguard would consist of one writer alone: Wilberforce Selfram. With his advance knowledge he had been able to untangle the Beoffrey Papers long before anybody else, and would be out of the starting pen the moment they were released, while the others were still getting to grips with it all. They would be swept aside in his wake, and he would become the go-to authority for all Beoffrey-related media appearances. Once his amazing affinity with the material was established, he would use his profile to eclipse even the young professor, who had told him he had been the first person to be contacted by the farmer, and had consequently been invited to head up the academic end of the Beoffrey Project. He, Wilberforce Selfram, would be the public face of Beoffrey though: the one to sell Beoffrey articles, to write and read radio essays on the subject, and even – he dared to dream – present a television series.

He had known that the first thing he must do was to write about moving through the English landscape as Beoffrey had done, travelling only on foot and grazing on whatever came to hand. Just a week earlier the papers had been published, to great interest from broadsheet newspapers and Radio 4, and Wilberforce Selfram had already had two pieces commissioned for substantial fees. The first article, *Why One Intends to Walk in the Footsteps of Beoffrey*, had already been written; in it he decried what he considered to be a broad cultural malaise, lamented what we had lost since Beoffrey's day, and expounded on what could be regained from reading him closely. Advocating a readjustment to the old ways of eating grubs, while simultaneously positioning Beoffrey as the first true Modernist, it was due out in a travel supplement on the coming Sunday. The second article, *In the Footsteps of Beoffrey*, had been commissioned, and was set to detail Wilberforce Selfram's journey from London to Green Bottom, and would be written and published not long after this jaunt was over. It was all going very well. Editors were amazed by the speed with which he was able to read, digest and act upon this new discovery. He could even quote long passages verbatim. Their cheque books were open.

Already, he had left everybody standing.

Chapter 6

*An angler is startled, and something unusual happens
as night falls over Hampstead Heath*

'*Lyffte th' logge and fynde beneethe foode fytte forr a kyng,*'
quoted Wilberforce Selfram, still sitting at the kitchen
table in the parsonage. 'While one eschews the very
notion of royalty, one is compelled to view this line
within its sociohistorical context and to exonerate
its author of charges of monarchist inclinations.
Centuries on, there remains a good deal of veracity
in these words of Beoffrey's – with so much natural
abundance in every crevice there is scant need for
the supermarket. One doubts whether one will enter
a grocery establishment again in one's lifetime; such
merchants seem superfluous when so many morsels
more delicious than those purchased from even the
most highly regarded delicatessen await one beneath
boulder and fallen branch. Often one deviated from

one's winding mossy way in order to tear an edible fungus from the trunk of a tree, or dig in a field for a mangelwurzel or, if you prefer, *mangold wurzel*, or perhaps you would rather one referred to it as *the root of scarcity.*'

'How fascinating,' said Mrs Bell. 'But something I've been wondering is how did you…?'

Before she had a chance to finish her question, Wilberforce Selfram cut in. 'One defecated in the manner of our kin the wild animal – crouching amid the foliage, or beneath the forest canopy. And before you pose your inevitable subsequent question, the answer is "with a leaf". *Wyppe wyth a leaffe and a cleene anus ye shalle havve.* One intends to write a lengthy paragraph on this topic for one's forthcoming article, in which one shall make mention of how one's faeces, being unusually long and thin, blended with the twigs of the forest.'

'That's very interesting, Mr Selfram,' said Mrs Bell, 'but I was actually going to ask how you managed to sleep through the day. I always find it quite tricky to drop off when the sun's still up – and that's indoors; it must be even harder outside.'

'In the mornings one covered oneself in a layer of whichever natural materials came to hand: primarily the stick and the frond, with perhaps a handful of mulch upon each of one's organs of optical vision. Once mummified thus, one was able to enter a state of torpidity until the day began to turn to dusk. Cometh the crepuscule, riseth the man.'

'That's rather poetic,' said the parson. 'Beoffrey of Biddenden again?'

The visitor pointed a long thumb at himself. 'Selfram, Wilberforce. There was one day when one attempted another of Beoffrey's methods, and slumbered beneath the surface of a waterway.'

'Really? You slept in a river? Underwater?' the parson was amazed. 'However did you manage that?'

'When the luminescence of the o'erarching welkin began its metamorphosis into daylight, one took to the shallows, weighed oneself down with rocks and submerged oneself amid the bulrushes. *Wyth reede as pype may ye breethe the ayre abovve.*'

'Incredible,' said the parson. 'But how did you stop the water from getting up your nose?'

'One stuffed pebbles up one's nostrils.'

There was quite a long silence while his audience took all this in.

'Did you sleep well?' asked Mrs Chapman. It was one of her favourite questions, and she was glad to be able to contribute to the conversation.

'One slept, amid tench and bream, as soundly as one does on *terra firma*, though one's slumber was somewhat truncated by a hapless angler whose barbéd hook embedded itself in one's raiments. Labouring under the misapprehension that he had caught a fish, he reeled his prey out of the shallows and to the opposite bank, whereupon one found a foothold on the river bed, rose from below the surface of the water, and fixed him with one's gaze.'

'A true fisher of men,' put in the parson. 'Was he a little surprised?'

'The yokel screamed, dropped his rod, and fled. One becomes accustomed to such responses to one's appearance. One unhooked oneself, waded back to the opposite bank, retrieved one's ganderbag from the rushes and, since the day's light was expiring, continued in embalméd darkness upon one's way.'

'Your bag was underwater too?' asked Mrs Bell. 'Didn't it get rather wet?'

'Though one abhors the machinery of conflict, one's ganderbag has been fabricated to a military specification, and its rubberlike double inner lining ensured its contents remained unenmoistened throughout one's tenure 'neath the rippléd surface of the e'er-flowing stream.'

Wilberforce Selfram's already glassy eyes glazed over further still as he thought of the contents of his bag. For the sake of authenticity he had been determined not to open it for the duration of his journey, except to take out and return his notepad and pencil, and he had stuck to this up until the moment he had been obliged by Margaret Thatcher to dig out his wallet and hand over seven-pounds-twenty for the broken jug. He was looking forward to becoming reacquainted with its contents, and one item in particular. There was something in there that would have left Beoffrey amazed: his computer. Before setting out on his journey he had drained the battery in order to avoid the temptation to turn it on. Soon he would be able to power it up and, at last, reconnect with the modern world. He wished he could have shown this machine to Beoffrey, to introduce his medieval mentor to the technology of his own age. There were some things on the hard drive, though, that he would not wish Beoffrey to see; that he would not wish anybody to see.

The silence that fell as Wilberforce Selfram pondered the contents of his hard drive was broken by Mrs Bell who, feeling that the conversation was reaching a natural end and ought to be wrapped up, offered up what she thought would be a bookend. 'Well,' she said. 'That was all terribly interesting. To think you've come all the way from Hampstead on foot.'

'Hampstead, you say?' replied Wilberforce Selfram. 'One did not commence one's journey in Hampstead; one resides in a more paradigmatically urban locale.'

'Oh, I'm sorry,' said Mrs Bell. 'I thought all you famous writers lived in Hampstead.'

'While the overwhelming majority of scribes certainly dwell in the verdant suburb you name, one parades to the cadence of one's own tympanic membrane. Quite by happenstance, however, on the first day of one's journey, before one had crossed the boundary of our principal cosmopolis, one spent one's first period of rest recumbent beneath a pile of twigs on Hampstead Heath. Something rather singular occurred as one awoke in the gloaming, though one is sure you have no wish to hear of the extraordinary event that came to pass that evening, as the cloak of darkness fell.' He stared, unblinking, ahead.

Though moments earlier his audience had been relieved that Mrs Bell had seemed to be skilfully steering the conversation to a close, they now found themselves wanting to know what had happened in the dusk on Hampstead Heath.

'Do tell,' said Mrs Bell.

Chapter 7

The committee grows, a meeting is held,
and we hear one side of an enigmatic phone call

The change of name, from the somewhat vague *All Bottoms Cultural Committee* to the focused *All Bottoms Literary Committee*, made a swift and profound difference to the trajectory of Mrs Bruschini's enterprise. With her new mission in mind, she returned to knocking on doors, and the news that there was going to be a literary festival in the area was greeted with warmth and enthusiasm. A lot of people, it seemed, enjoyed books, and would welcome the opportunity to hear authors reading aloud from them and answering questions about them. On their arrival at the next meeting, the treasurer and the secretary were amazed to find a dozen new faces quietly waiting to find out what it was all about, and whether they could do anything to help.

Mrs Bruschini swept in at precisely seven o'clock and banged her gavel, and an hour later everybody had a position, and responsibilities, and a list of tasks to accomplish before their next meeting. For her own part, the chair of the committee announced that she had booked a train to London, where she was due to visit their potential associate, Florence Peters, at the offices of The Literary Festival People. 'I had thought about sending a delegation,' she explained, 'but decided to go myself as I am very familiar with WC2, very familiar indeed, and if any of you were to go, you would probably get lost.' This was met with a murmur of agreement. They probably would get lost.

Mrs Bruschini hammered her gavel again at exactly eight o'clock and swept away, leaving the treasurer and the secretary to pack away more folding tables than usual, and to stack more chairs. Both had had a hectic hour; many more notes than usual had been taken, and more subs collected. There were also mounting expenses to log, not least Mrs Bruschini's train fare. Both were quite dazed as they left the building and locked up.

With a casual 'See you next time,' which was met with a half-smile and a nod, the treasurer let the secretary walk away without further interaction. Last week's resolute *NO* still rang in his ears. He loitered for a couple of minutes, pretending to himself that he needed to tighten a shoe lace before beginning his own journey home. He wasn't ready to give up. He knew he had to do something. Something big, that would make her see him in a new light.

The answer came like a piano landing on him: he

would throw himself into the book festival, and the secretary would see him shine. He would do this by getting as close as he could to Mrs Bruschini. He would be Chancellor of the Exchequer to her Prime Minister. He would visit her at Honeysuckle Nook to go through the accounts, and before long she would find him indispensable, and he would have power within the committee. He had read on the Internet that power is an irresistible aphrodisiac. This, he decided, was how he was going to get the secretary's cardigan off and a ring on her finger. He loved her, he was certain of that. *I love the secretary*, he said to himself, as he walked home in the evening light. He caught a glimpse of her up ahead, as she turned into their street, and once again he felt the stabbing pain of rejection.

The nearest railway station was in the town of Market Horton, and the treasurer had offered to drive Mrs Bruschini there. He called his work to tell them he would be in late, and would make up the time at the end of the day, then he borrowed his dad's Volvo, which he had carefully valeted and fitted with a fresh-cut pine deodoriser, and picked her up at precisely the agreed time. He waited with her on the station platform, and helped her find her seat. It was, of course, in first class, so she would be well-rested and alert for the meeting. Wishing her well, he waved her off, and so it was that she began a journey that ended in a room above an Italian restaurant on St Martin's Lane. She set her jaw at just the correct angle; an angle at which she would not inadvertently reveal, not even to herself, that butterflies were flapping around inside her.

The office occupied by The Literary Festival People was, as would be expected, lined with books, and behind a large antique oak desk sat a rather squat woman in late middle age, wearing tweeds, and sensible shoes, and enormous glasses that magnified her eyes, giving the impression of an illustration come to life. Her grey hair sat on her head in a messy bun. The welcome she gave to Mrs Bruschini was warm, and a cup of coffee was offered. She seemed to be the only person in the office that day, and rather than buzz through to an assistant to bring it, she made it herself from a machine in the corner of the room. Coffee dispensed, and pleasantries exchanged, the meeting proper began.

Florence Peters pulled out a ream of graphs and charts which, she explained in her soft and slightly breathy voice, their computer had produced. She showed them to Mrs Bruschini, each one passing before her eyes so quickly that it was all a bit too much to take in. 'So, we can clearly see,' said Florence Peters, finishing by pointing to a printout showing a map with a big circle around The Bottoms, 'that the whole Bottoms area is, geographically and demographically, uniquely positioned to be the perfect location for a high-profile late-summer book festival.' This print-out, at least, was clear. There was The Bottoms, and there was the big circle around it. The computer had identified her new home as a national literary sweet spot, and she wasn't about to start arguing with a computer, particularly not one that had told her exactly what she wanted to hear. She asked for, and was given, that last sheet of paper. She would present it to the committee at their next meeting. None of them could take issue with a plan that was based upon a map with a circle on it.

'You'll need to start preparing everything straightaway if you're to get this up and running by late summer next year,' said Florence Peters. 'Venues have to be secured, and events programmed. There's a lot to consider.' Behind her thick lenses, her eyes narrowed. 'Are you up to the job, Mrs Bruschini?'

There was an air of challenge to this, and Mrs Bruschini rose to it. There had never been a job that she had not been up to, and she told her as much.

'Glad to hear it,' smiled Florence Peters. They were friends again. 'With you at the helm, I'm sure this festival will be a triumph. Now, we need to consider, of course, the expense of it all. A good deal of money will be needed.'

'I suppose it will. We'll have to pay the writers, of course.'

Florence Peters had been sipping her coffee as Mrs Bruschini said this, and in her surprise she spluttered, spraying out a fine mist. Fortunately, none of it hit her visitor, and she swiftly mopped up the mess with a tissue. 'My dear Mrs Bruschini,' she said. 'Authors are not to be paid in anything as vulgar as money; they will be glad of the honour. Just imagine it – having a book published, and being invited to speak about it at a prestigious literary event. That is reward enough. They are artists, and if anything it would be insulting to offer them money, as it means so little to them. You will, of course, give them a memento to take away with them – a bottle of something perhaps, and a pencil case. That sort of thing.'

Mrs Bruschini was starting to realise that she had entered a world about which she knew very little, and her face must have shown it. She was relieved when Florence Peters opened her arms wide and said, with great warmth, 'The Literary Festival People will be here to help you every step of the way. All these trifling details will iron themselves out as we go along.'

'So how much do you think we'll need to get things going?'

'We'll need to consider hiring venues, pitching marquees, shuttling people from village to village in buses – we'll call them Book Buses, that way people won't mind using shared transport – and printing the programme, and hiring technical people to sort out the microphones, etc. etc.. All this will require deposits, so we'll need a pretty full kitty from the off. In all I would estimate the amount you would need, to be sure of setting everything up to a high standard, would be in the region of…' She jotted a figure on a piece of paper and slid it across the desk to Mrs Bruschini.

Mrs Bruschini couldn't quite believe what she was being asked to look at. There were six digits. 'Is this…' she said, trying to get her mind around why it would cost so much to have some people come and talk about their books '…is this pounds or pence?'

'Pounds, Mrs Bruschini,' replied Florence Peters. 'Very much pounds.'

'Isn't that a little on the expensive side?'

'Ah. I see. I'm terribly sorry Mrs Bruschini,' she said, a light chuckle in her voice. 'This has all been a huge misunderstanding. It's my fault, and mine alone, and I apologise for dragging you all this way. You see, I had been under the impression that you wanted to run your book festival in a professional manner. Had I known you would want to do this on a low budget – having some local poets read from their chapbooks in the back room of a pub, perhaps – I would never have contacted you. However, you must have the festival you want, and I wish you all the very best with it.' She extended a valedictory hand across the desk. 'Do have a safe journey home.'

'No!' Mrs Bruschini did not take the extended hand. 'No, I can see, now, that there are costs to consider. You must forgive me.' Humility did not sit easily with her, but she soldiered on. 'It's all rather new to me, and I understand that it will be quite pricey, but...' She faltered.

'Yes, Mrs Bruschini?'

'I'm afraid we're a new committee, and though we have a very high class of membership I'm not sure we will be able to raise quite that much.'

'That oughtn't be a problem.'

'No?'

'You just need to find a sponsor. Now, I wonder who might be able to stump up this sort of money. This is where we come in handy, you know. We have all sorts of contacts. Let me have a little ponder about who would be the best fit for you...' She pursed her lips, and her brow furrowed as she appeared to drift into a state of deep thought.

Mrs Bruschini didn't know what to say, but she felt she should contribute something. 'How about Colgate?'

'The toothpaste people?'

'Yes. Why not? They must have an awful lot of money, and I'm sure they would jump at the chance to sponsor a literary festival.'

'A few years ago maybe they would have done, but they had a bad experience in Devon. They sponsored a book festival in Totnes, only to find that the locals had taken against toothpaste for ethical reasons; they'd come to the conclusion that everybody should be brushing their teeth with foraged moss, and there were placards everywhere, and pickets outside the events, and it all turned into a bit of a drama. Rather tragically, the ringleaders have all since died from moss poisoning; they might have survived if they'd gone to their GPs when they fell ill, but instead they tried to heal themselves with magic crystals rather than antibiotics. Anyway, the publicity wasn't quite what Colgate had been hoping for, and I have a feeling they'll be keeping out of the literary festival scene for some time to come.'

Mrs Bruschini could feel her book festival slipping through her fingers. She shuddered as she pictured the next meeting, at which she would have to tell her committee that their festival was going to be little more than some local poets – mad people in second-hand clothes – expressing their feelings in the back room of a pub. She doubted their poems would even rhyme. She couldn't allow that to happen, and her mind clutched desperately at potential sponsors. Fortnum & Mason?

Jammie Dodgers? Stannah Stairlifts?

'Hold on,' said Florence Peters. She opened a drawer, and pulled out a haphazard pile of papers. 'I did have an enquiry a few days ago from a possible lead. Let… me…see…' She found what she'd been looking for, and squinted at it over her glasses. 'Ah, yes, this is it. One of those clean electricity set-ups. Solar panels and windmills and all that. *Très maintenant.*' She handed a letter to Mrs Bruschini, who read it aloud.

'Dear Literary Festival People, I do hope this finds you well. We here at the Happy Smile Energy Company are all great readers, and we were wondering whether you would be able to put us in touch with a book festival that may be looking for a sponsor. We would be able to put up around…' Mrs Bruschini couldn't believe what she was reading. The amount they were offering was very similar to the amount that Florence Peters had written on the scrap of paper. *'Do let us know if anybody drifts by. With energetic regards…'*

'So there we are,' said Florence Peters. 'Very encouraging, I'm sure you'll agree. I'll give them a tinkle, and see if I can get them on board. I'll let you know what they say – I think you two would make a perfect match.'

Mrs Bruschini had never felt so relieved. The chilling moment when it had looked as if she was going to have to return from her trip to London empty-handed was over. 'Thank you so much,' she said, as if she had just been pulled into a lifeboat from the icy sea. 'You must tell me about your fee. How do we repay you?'

'I hadn't really thought about that. I do all this for the love of books, you see, and the sheer joy of facilitating the exchange of ideas.'

'We have to give you *something* for all your help.'

'How about...oh, I don't know, shall we say a hundred pounds?'

'I'll pay it now.' She made to open her bag, but Florence Peters gestured for her not to.

'We'll settle up at the end of the festival. I want to make sure it all goes according to plan.'

Mrs Bruschini was dumbfounded.

'Now,' said Florence Peters, 'we need to think about which authors you're going to invite. We can help you here too; we have all sorts of contacts and can secure some very big names. Who do you read?'

'I'm rather keen on Anthony Trollope,' said Mrs Bruschini.

'Aren't we all?' sighed Florence Peters. 'The sad thing is, I don't think he's available to give talks at the moment. How about any authors who are, broadly speaking, alive?'

For a moment Mrs Bruschini came close to panic as she realised that while she defined herself as a great lover of books, she actually didn't read very much at all. A Trollope or two a year, and a couple of others along the way – usually books she had heard about on Radio 4, most of which had been written by regular contributors to Radio 4. She quickly composed herself. 'I have quite the wish list, as a matter of fact, and we are discussing potential speakers at our meetings. I shall send you their names in a few days' time.'

'Wonderful.'

After a brief flurry of shaking hands and gathering of papers, Mrs Bruschini found herself standing in the sunshine on St Martin's Lane. She was at last able to admit to herself that she had been apprehensive about this visit, and that she had not been operating at her highest level. But with the result she had just procured she would be able to return to The Bottoms with her chin more aloft than ever. With a swish of her shawl she made her way towards the National Portrait Gallery, to take in some grand faces before catching the train back to her new home. She thought for a moment about taking the opportunity to see how Mr Bruschini was getting along, but decided against it. Better to leave him be.

Florence Peters stood at her window, her eyes following Mrs Bruschini as she walked away. Her enormous glasses were off now, and without them her appearance was remarkably different. As she watched Mrs Bruschini disappear from view she shook out her bun, and let her hair fall. She sat down, picked up the big old-fashioned phone on her desk, and dialled. 'It's the Silver Eagle,' she said, in a steady, steely voice that Mrs Bruschini would not have recognised. 'Target Number One has left the building.'

[...]

'I had to make up a load of crap about people in Devon brushing their teeth with moss, but apart from that it all went precisely according to the script. The bait was swallowed, and the Big Bottoms Book Festival will be taking place late summer next year.'

[...]

'We'll expect a cheque from Happy Smile to reach them in the coming days. And just so you don't forget, we agreed a guaranteed initial payment to me of a hundred thousand on conclusion of the festival, and when it all comes together and we get the result we're hoping for, I'll receive my shares and be on the next plane to Umbria, scouting farmhouses for a gently alcoholic retirement.'

[…]

'I believe it was Roland Barthes who said *I love it when a plan comes together.*'

[…]

'I've got to get out of these horrible tweeds. They itch, and make me look squat.'

[…]

'Ciao indeed.'

She put down the phone, stood up, and wriggled out of her thick skirt and jacket. She bundled them into a drawer, and a minute later she was dressed in a slim-fitting trouser suit and skilfully touching up her face with make-up. Her clumpy shoes had been replaced by notably unsensible high heels. Anybody seeing her now would describe her as petite rather than squat, and her hair not so much grey as ash blonde. She seemed a different person altogether, as if the Florence Peters that Mrs Bruschini had just met had never really existed.

Chapter 8

*We find out what happened as dusk fell on Hampstead Heath,
and a familiar face visits the parsonage*

Mrs Chapman was still in a state of shock, and so
mystified by everything that was going on around her
that she hadn't been able to follow the story. Everybody
else in the kitchen, though, was aghast at what they
had just heard. Wilberforce Selfram had reached the
end of his account of his stay on Hampstead Heath,
and none of them knew quite what to say. It had started
straightforwardly enough, with him entering a copse
and making his bed beneath a pile of leaves as, in his
words, the rosy-fingered dawn disrupted the night's
gloomy passage. He had slept well, and as the daylight
began to fade, he had woken up.

Wilberforce Selfram, they learned, is inclined to
wake slowly, and when going through a phase of
living as Beoffrey did, he likes to find himself a snack

before rising and starting his night's walk. He will reach out a hand from the cover of his nest, and feel around for any grubs or lice that might be going about their business nearby, and pop them in his mouth. This particular nightfall, his hand had reached out and he had been lucky enough, or so he had at first thought, to find a moderately-sized slug. He had pulled at it, but had struggled to get a grip; it seemed to be stuck to something. He kept pulling and pulling at it, and as he did, something strange happened – the slug seemed to expand, and stiffen. Still he pulled and pulled, and still the slug was stuck fast, until things took an even more unexpected turn when it seemed to issue a secretion, before shrinking again and, slimy now, wriggling from his grasp.

At this point Wilberforce Selfram had brought his hand back into his hideaway, and tasted the lukewarm, gooey liquid that had been left behind. Deciding to be content with this as a snack, and licking his fingers clean, he rose from his pile of twigs, and there in the twilight, he found himself face to face with somebody he knew rather well, whom he had met a number of times in the green rooms of various television studios while both were waiting to offer their political insights on current affairs shows. 'Evening Selfram,' the man had said, 'What a surprise. I didn't know you were into this sort of thing.'

Wilberforce Selfram had, to his parsonage kitchen audience, expressed his dismay at this greeting, explaining that he had given this person, on many occasions, detailed accounts of his psychogeographical excursions to obscure corners of the metropolis, so he oughtn't have been at all surprised to find him under a pile of twigs on Hampstead Heath. 'Of course one is into this sort of thing,' he had asserted, before asking the man whether he had seen an unusual slug in the area, one with a curious rigidity about it, and prone to a degree of oozing.

'No, I can't say I've spotted any slugs today,' the man had said. 'I come here to look for badgers.' He had winked, repeatedly, as though he had something in his eye. 'I'm all about the badgers, Selfram old boy,' he had said. 'I'm so glad we understand one another. Perhaps I'll see you here again one day?'

'One has every intention of returning,' Wilberforce Selfram had said. He meant it, too. It had struck him that if he could catch the creature, he might be able to present it to some academy or other. He pictured himself in a wood-panelled lecture theatre, telling an audience of distinguished men with large whiskers all about this extraordinary slug, with its hardening qualities and its ability to shoot out a gooey liquid. He would be lauded the world over for his discovery of a previously unknown species of gastropod. Perhaps it would not stop there. He had found the liquid quite palatable – what if it turned out be the perfect accompaniment to meat? Not commonplace meat, but cheval tartare, perhaps, or bob veal? He would corner the market with his global chain of slug farms. Or perhaps its goo would have medicinal properties, and he would be hailed as a pharmaceutical pioneer. He saw himself, grand and solemn, on the front cover of *The Lancet*. Doubtless the whiskered men would name this new slug after him. *Selframia*, they would wish to call it. *Selframia magnifica*. To his already extensive list of careers – Restaurant Critic, Radio Essayist, Occasional Novelist – he would be able to add Great Naturalist. Prior to eating them, he had been assiduously rubbing all the slugs he had hunted on his travels, in the hope that they too would harden and ooze. He had not had any luck, and he intended, on his return to London, to make a beeline for the same spot on the Heath and, armed with a jam jar, keep an eye out for the mighty specimen.

'At this point one's interlocutor abruptly turned and vanished through a nearby shrubbery,' he said, concluding his anecdote. 'One found this to be markedly unconventional behaviour for a gentleman of his rank – a member of the House of Lords no less, and a rather prominent one at that.'

And so they stood in the kitchen of the parsonage, not one of them knowing what to say. Fortunately, the silence was broken by the ring of the doorbell. The parson went to answer it, and Mrs Chapman busied herself with the kettle, in case whoever it was wanted a cup of tea.

The parson returned from answering the door, and before him sailed Mrs Bruschini.

'Oh hello, Mrs Bruschini,' exclaimed Mrs Bell who, being a committee member, had discreetly sent her a text message alerting her to the author's arrival. 'Mr Selfram was just telling us all about an encounter he had with a prominent member on Hampstead Heath.'

'A *very* prominent mem… Oh.' There was something about Mrs Bell's choice of words that made Wilberforce Selfram realise at last what had really happened that evening. His mind reeled at the thought of what he had done, and his glassy eyes widened at the memory of licking the goo from his fingers. In that moment the dream was over. There would be no return visit with a jam jar, and no wood-panelled auditorium. He had been rubbing all those slugs for nothing, and *Selframia magnifica* was dead. 'One senses that one's visage,' he mumbled to himself, 'has become encrimsoned.' His face had indeed turned from its previous deathly grey to a deathly grey with a very slight pinkish tinge around its sunken cheeks.

He was relieved when the newcomer displayed no interest in this story, and his pallor soon returned to its normal level of deathly greyness. 'Fascinating,' she said, in an offhand way that showed she hadn't been listening, stopping the line of conversation dead. 'Now, you are Mr Selfram…' She held a clipboard, and looked down a list until she found his name. She put a tick in a box. Another confirmed arrival. 'I am Mrs Bruschini. May I welcome you to the Big Bottoms Book Festival.' She handed him a plastic bag.

Wilberforce Selfram opened it and looked inside. 'A bottle of Cinzano,' he said, 'and a pencil case. How thoughtful.'

Mrs Bell did her best to keep the conversation flowing. 'Mr Selfram has been telling us about how he walked all the way here, and slept rough, just like they would have done centuries ago. He didn't use anything modern at all for the whole journey, not even a toothbrush.'

'Then how did he clean his teeth?'

Mrs Bell was at a loss, so Wilberforce Selfram answered. 'One rubbed them with moss.'

'That was rather foolish, Mr Selfram – didn't you hear about what happened to all those silly people in Totnes?'

'Negative.'

'We don't have time for that now; I have a literary festival to direct. Just remember to brush your teeth properly from now on. No more moss. We'll also need you to clean yourself up. We can't have you looking like a scarecrow in front of the primary school children. What sort of example would that set?'

'Why the Ballard would one be in front of primary school children?'

'Mr Selfram, today is Thursday, your main event is on Saturday, and tomorrow, which is Friday...' she leafed through the papers on her clipboard, '...at nine forty-five in the morning you will be giving a talk to the children of Lower Bottom Primary School. It's all here in the agreement. Look.' She removed a piece of paper from her clipboard, and waved it in front of him. 'It was part of our funding arrangement with Happy Smile Energy. Community outreach, you understand.'

'One despairs,' he sighed. He had intended to spend the day starting to write up his journey. Mrs Bruschini, he had noted, was of a type, and he knew from bitter experience that while resistance might not be entirely futile when faced with examples of this type, it was rarely worth the effort. He made a mental note to remind his publicist to vet all festival contracts for small print, and resigned himself to the inevitability of this school visit. 'Allow one to cogitate. Which of one's talks shall one bestow upon the assembled infants? One had best keep it elementary. An introduction to psychogeography, perhaps?'

'I'm not sure what you mean, Mr Selfram.'

'One is not surprised. Allow one to enlighten you – the heart of psychogeography lies in the visiting of variegated locales, principally, though by no means exclusively, within a cityscape, and ruminating upon them – flyovers, charabanc termini, pedestrian underpasses and the like.'

'I sometimes read an author called Iain Sinclair,' put in the parson. 'He does that sort of thing. He's very good at it, too. Do you know him, Mr Selfram?'

Wilberforce Selfram carried on as if he hadn't heard what the parson had said. 'One shall offer the assembled juveniles a soupçon of this, along with, perhaps, a straightforward career retrospective.'

'I'm sure that will be fine. Just so long as you inspire them. And no swearing.' The clipboard came into play once again. 'And at one o'clock tomorrow you will be running your Writing Workshop.'

'One's what?'

'Writing workshop. I believe it's where people come along and read out their work and you offer them words of encouragement. I'm told authors thrive on this sort of thing. Quite a few people have signed up for it, so we mustn't disappoint them.'

'All for a bottle of Cinzano and a pencil case. Again, one despairs.'

Ignoring his complaint, Mrs Bruschini carried on.

'To accommodation. You are staying here with the Reverend Jacobs, and your publicist will be billeted next door, with Mr and Mrs Bell.'

'Affirmative. As one understands the situation, she will be arriving tomorrow behind the steering wheel of a pantechnicon containing one's lexica.'

'Yes,' said Mr Bell. 'We've spoken on the phone. She seems a very pleasant young lady; her voice has something of a Croydon twang to it. We're also putting up someone from *The Guardian* who's writing an article about the festival. It's all rather exciting.'

Mrs Bruschini made a point of never taking *The Guardian*, and she merely raised an eyebrow, while Mrs Chapman, hearing all this, wondered whether she should warn the newcomers about the ghostly face that had appeared at the window.

'Your event on the Saturday will be in the Upper Bottom village hall. We've even sold some tickets,' said Mrs Bruschini. 'We're all quite relieved about that, because when we booked you, we had no idea who you were. Absolutely none at all.'

Chapter 9

The festival's programme takes shape,
and an attempt is made to bag a big name

It was Mrs Bell who had pointed out a notable absence in the ranks of the writers secured for the festival. The committee had been busy, the programme was almost full, and in the Broad Bottom village hall they were going through the array of talent that had been booked. 'There's just one tiny thing,' said Mrs Bell. 'We haven't got any authors.'

'What?' foghorned Mrs Bruschini. 'Can you not see the names on the list?'

'Well, yes, there are a good amount of names there, and it's all going very well, but none of them are really, you know...authors. We've got actors with books out, and rugby players with books out, and cooks with books, and pop stars, and game-show hosts, and alternative comedians, and people from Radio 2, and people from Radio 4, but no real authors. I mean the ones who just do books. As this is a literary festival, I thought it might be an idea to fill the last few slots with people who aren't so much celebrities-with-books-out, as just, well, writers.'

The idea was not met with great enthusiasm. Everybody on the committee was very much looking forward to meeting all the famous people, and the thought of having to accommodate some obscure and serious writer types didn't interest them at all. At the same time, though, they saw Mrs Bell's point, and the topic was thrown open for discussion.

The room was quiet for a long time, as they all tried to think of some actual writers they could invite. Mrs Bell had a few ideas, but she didn't want to appear pushy so decided to keep them to herself for the time being. The committee had continued to grow, and it was one of the newer members who piped up with what was to be a fateful suggestion: 'What about that nice Harry Potter lady?'

Mrs Bruschini pounced on this idea. 'Excellent. We shall book her. Secretary, I place you in charge of this. Work out who to call, and meet me at Honeysuckle Nook on your lunch break tomorrow. Treasurer, you come too; if she asks for a fee it will be down to you to tactfully explain why this is simply impossible.'

Everybody was intoxicated by the Harry Potter plan, apart from Mrs Bell, who suggested it might be a bit ambitious, that the Harry Potter lady, nice as she was, might not want to appear at an untested book festival, and their energies might be better spent concentrating on considering some more realistic guests.

'Stuff and nonsense,' roared Mrs Bruschini. 'She will be honoured to be invited, and I am sure she will jump at the chance. Her inclusion will give our festival just the profile it needs.'

As the room seemed to be in full agreement with the chair, Mrs Bell gracefully stepped back and left them to their excited chatter, as they drew up lists of nieces and nephews to get autographs for. Mrs Bruschini brought them back to order with a bang of her gavel before winding up the evening's business, ending another productive meeting.

The next day, Mrs Bruschini and her two lieutenants sat in the dining room of Honeysuckle Nook, which had become the book festival's command centre. Weeks earlier Mrs Bruschini had telephoned both their bosses, and bulldozed them into agreeing to let their employees out for extended lunch breaks to engage in festival business. As their duties increased, these meetings had become longer and more frequent, but their bosses didn't dare to dispute them for fear of another phone call. While the secretary flicked through her notebook to find the phone number, the treasurer took the opportunity to take a good look at her. She seemed nervous about the task she had been assigned, and he thought that somehow made her extra attractive. He also took the opportunity to steal glances at Mrs Bruschini. He had been stealing a lot of glances at Mrs Bruschini lately. He knew she was at least twice his age, and that somewhere very high up there was a Mr Bruschini, and that because of this he ought not to look at her in this way, but ever since she had come back from London, her control of the committee had been consolidated and she had carried herself with such supreme confidence that he had begun to find her quite mesmerising. His eyes moved from one woman to the other. He tried to tell himself he still loved the secretary, but doubt had begun to appear in his heart. He remembered her adamant *NO*. Perhaps he was on the rebound. Either way, it seemed to be true what he had read – power really was an aphrodisiac.

The secretary had done her research the night before by looking at the Harry Potter books on her shelf, finding out who they were published by, and searching for a phone number on the Internet. Using Mrs Bruschini's home phone, she dialled.

'It's ringing,' she said. Mrs Bruschini could faintly hear the sound of the tone coming from the earpiece, and her nervous anticipation reached a crescendo. Suddenly the tone stopped. The call had been answered. Mrs Bruschini and the treasurer listened to the half of the conversation they could hear.

[…]

'Oh. Hello. I'm the secretary of the Big Bottoms Book Festival.'

[…]

'Yes, we're from a place called The Bottoms. It's in the countryside. We're quite new; in fact it's our first year, and it's on next September, and we were wondering whether JK Rowling would be available to come along and do a talk for us.'

[…]

'Oh, I see.'

[…]

'Oh really?'

[…]

'And he definitely writes books?'

[…]

'Are they any good?'

[…]

'Well, I suppose so.'

[…]

'OK.'

[…]

'Drugs?'

[…]

'Oh.'

[…]

'Elton John?'

[…]

'Would he sing a few songs for us? Will he play *Rocket Man*?'

[…]

'I see. I think for now we'll just stick with the first one.'

[…]

'It's secretary@bigbottomsbookfestival.org.uk.'

[…]

'Bye.'

'That,' said Mrs Bruschini, 'Did not sound encouraging.'

'I'm afraid not, no. The Harry Potter lady is pretending to be a man now, and she writes detective books.'

Mrs Bruschini pulled a face. 'We'll have none of that.'

'But it's not all bad news. We've booked another writer. He writes books with lots of long words.'

'Very well. What is his name?'

She checked her notes. 'Wilberforce Selfram.'

'Have you heard of him?' She looked to her secretary and her treasurer and they both shook their heads. 'Nor I, but I suppose he will do. If nothing else, Mrs Bell will get one of her precious "proper" writers. Return to your places of work, and I shall contact Florence Peters and see if she can advise on the last few available slots.'

Chapter 10

*We meet the future driver of the pantechnicon,
and hear the other side of the telephone conversation*

When she had started her new job the previous Monday, Ayanna had been amazed to be given her own office. It wasn't much of an office – just a small and architecturally inexplicable windowless space jutting off a corridor and screened from passers-by with a folding divider – but even so it was her own domain. She had a desk, with a phone and a computer, a chair for herself, and two other folding chairs that she could bring into use whenever she had visitors. At first she wasn't sure how often that would be, but she was soon to find out that these chairs would be occupied quite often, and always by the same two people. She quickly deduced the reason why she, an entry-level recruit, had been given her own space – it was to keep these two corralled, so everybody else could get on with their jobs. She also realised she had been given her own phone number, the one listed on the Internet, to deal solely with low-grade Harry Potter-related enquiries. All the more regular calls went through another number, one given out more cautiously and only to contacts in the business.

Her visitors sat across the desk from her on their folding chairs, and looked intently at the phone, waiting for it to ring again. Sure enough it did, as if they had willed it into life. She answered, and they listened closely, waiting for their chance.

'Hello, Bloomsbury Publicity Department, Ayanna speaking.'

[...]

'Big Bottoms? Really?'

[...]

She glanced at the index card on her desk. It was her fifth day in the job, and she had read it so many times that she now turned it over, hiding the words and challenging herself to remember them by heart. On her first day she had been handed this card and told that most people started this way, and that there would be little respite until she moved to a new role. To begin with, Ayanna had kept count of these calls, but she had given up after her first day. She estimated that this must have been the sixth or seventh such enquiry so far this day alone. They tended to come from schools, from libraries, and from parents wanting an entertainer for their child's party, and occasionally they came from fledgling book festivals where they hadn't quite got the hang of things. To amuse herself, she held her free hand over her eyes, and spoke the words printed on the other side of the card: *'I'm afraid Ms Rowling has finished with her Harry Potter books and has decided to take her future titles to a rival publishing house. We wish her all the very best. She is currently writing detective fiction under a man's name, and we suggest you contact her new publisher should you wish to invite her to an event.'*

[...]

Ayanna flipped the card over and checked. She had got it word-perfect and she punched the air as the people in the folding chairs gave her a silent round of applause, then started pointing at themselves. Their moment had arrived. These two were also something her predecessor had told her about. They came into the offices most days, and sat there, sometimes for hours at a time, poised for opportunities just like this one. This was also something she would have to deal with until she moved to a new position. Whenever the phone rang, they took turns in getting her to pitch for them. Last time it had been the disgraced journalist Harry Johannes' turn, and she had successfully landed him his first booking of the day, filling in for a cancellation at the Durness Book Bonanza in three weeks' time, so it was the other one who would get first dibs this time around.

'We do have another author who might interest you, though.'

[...]

'Yes, he's called Wilberforce Selfram. He's reasonably well known. He's been in the newspapers a fair bit.'

'And on television,' monotoned the author.

Ayanna ignored this, which was probably just as well as it may have made him seem like too much of a celebrity for this final recruitment drive.

[...]

'Yes, he's written quite a few books.'

[...]

'He uses a lot of long words.' The author nodded his approval of this description of his output. 'Does that sound like something that would interest you?'

[...]

'Great, so that's agreed.'

Wilberforce Selfram, his booking secure, put his hands behind his head, settling back as Harry Johannes took his turn to muscle in on the opportunity before the door slammed shut. An established rule was that once a firm booking had been made, the other writer was allowed to have a go, and he started pointing to himself again. Ayanna went through the motions.

'We've got another author too. He's written a book about drugs.'

[...]

'Yes, it's non-fiction, all about the war on drugs.'

[...]

Harry Johannes spoke in a single breath: 'Tell them it's all true tell them I don't make things up any more and I've been on a special course all about how it's best to tell the truth.' Ayanna chose not to pass this on, but undaunted, he continued his pitch. 'Tell them Elton John likes it.'

She sighed. 'Elton John likes it.'

[...]

'Yes, he's very keen on it.'

[...]

'No, I don't think Sir Elton will be available for the

event.'

[...]

'That's fine. Just give me your email address so we can be in touch about the details.'

[...]

'We'll sort out the exact date in the next week or two then. Bye for now.'

[...]

The call over, the men settled down. Harry Johannes folded his arms in a sulk, while Wilberforce Selfram looked, glassy-eyed, ahead of him. 'One abhors literary festivals,' he said. 'They are Nuremberg Rallies for the blue-rinse brigade. Ghastly occurrences.'

'I could call right back and cancel,' said Ayanna.

'Negative, negative; one shall suffer for one's art.'

They went through this charade every time: Wilberforce Selfram decrying the ignominy of the promotional circuit, while simultaneously waiting for the phone to ring and grasping at every opportunity for publicity that came his way. Deciding to quit while they were tied at one booking each, the authors stood up and folded away their chairs.

'One shall catapult oneself into the cityscape and engage in a spot of the old psychogeography,' said Wilberforce Selfram. 'Perhaps one shall find a decommissioned gasometer that catches one's eye, and proceed to write an essay about it for a leading journal.'

'I'm off to do some true writing, sticking only to the

facts,' said Harry Johannes, 'and then I'll start planning my trip to Durness. I've always wanted to visit Derek Jarman's garden.'

Ayanna smiled, but said nothing. She would let him find out his mistake for himself. She waved them off, and shortly after they left the phone rang. 'Bloomsbury Publicity Department, Ayanna speaking.' Once again she found she didn't need her index card. She put it in a drawer, ready for her successor. She wondered how long it would be before she had a successor. It was only the Friday of her first week, but already she was hoping for better days.

Chapter 11

Mrs Bruschini is won over by a cocktail, and Wilberforce
Selfram senses a deterioration in his vocabulary

Mrs Bruschini handed Wilberforce Selfram a copy of the Big Bottoms Book Festival's programme. It was a high-quality production, bankrolled by their sponsor, whose name was emblazoned across the front page. A delegation of young men and women from Happy Smile Energy, all dreadlocks and patchwork dungarees, had arrived in the area a few days earlier and set about getting ready for the festivities. Their main centre of operations was to be the big marquee on the village green that lay across the road from the church and the parsonage. This marquee was due to host events in a four-hundred-seat auditorium, as well as operating as the main green room and box office. Local objections to the size of this temporary edifice were becalmed when it became known that they would be offering free drinks throughout the festival, that anybody could turn up and grab a cocktail in a reusable cup that had been recycled from recovered ocean plastic.

Wilberforce Selfram had a cursory leaf through the programme. 'One despairs,' he said, 'at the stultifying parade of the usual faces; dismal celebrities and authors of…' he pulled a face, '…genre fiction. That this line-up is what passes for acceptable at a so-called literary festival is symptomatic of a broad cultural malaise. There is so little of true merit here; one wishes you provincial programmers would have a little more ambition. More, at least, than the almost-none-at-all currently on display. Were it not for one's presence, this line-up would be an unmitigated catastrophe.'

Neither Mrs Bruschini nor anybody else in the room heard a word of this, since the moment he had started talking, the Happy Smile Energy people had switched on their machine. A loud rumble pierced the air and shook the building. By the time it had finished, Wilberforce Selfram, who had apparently been oblivious throughout, had finished too.

'That confounded ice grinder again,' said Mrs Bruschini. Two days before, when she had first heard it, she had gone over to see what all the noise was about. She had found a bearded and tattooed helper, who explained that they were making some practice cocktails and had been crushing ice for them, and asked whether she would like to try one of their efforts. She decided there would be no harm in a little margarita, and he had disappeared behind a canvas flap and returned a minute later with a beautifully mixed drink. Thus, like so many of the villagers who had also been over to complain about it, had she reached an uneasy truce with the machine.

Wilberforce Selfram closed the programme, largely unread. Since they had booked him, Florence Peters had helped them to flesh out the empty slots and had added a wider range of attractions by including a couple of heavy-hitting Booker Prize types, an author of light romantic fiction, and a handful of supposedly promising new writers. They had also secured a big name for the opening night, which was that very evening.

'You will, I hope, be joining us for our inaugural event, Mr Selfram.'

'May one enquire who is on the bill?'

Mrs Bruschini puffed up to the outer reaches of her *embonpoint*, and declared that their very special guest was to be the famous author Nick Hornby.

'Oh, he's very good, Mr Selfram,' said Mrs Bell. 'I'm sure you won't want to miss that.'

'Hmph,' said Wilberforce Selfram. 'You say *Nick Hornby*; one says *Nick Yawnby*. One abhors his dismal scribblings. One has even appeared upon the nation's television receivers to say so, and tonight one shall prove that one would not even cross the road to listen to what that intellectual microbe has to say. He hardly uses any long words at all.'

'Very well Mr Selfram,' said Mrs Bruschini, bristling. 'We shall sell the seat we had put aside for you. His event is set to be a full house, and there is quite the list for returns.'

'That,' sighed Wilberforce Selfram, 'is symptomatic of a broad cultural malaise. Now tell me, Mrs Bruschini, where would one go to purchase heroin around here?'

Mrs Bruschini, along with everybody else, was quite taken aback by this. 'Heroin?'

'Skag. Horse. Brown sugar. Smack. One is referring to the infamous opiate.'

'We don't take heroin in The Bottoms, Mr Selfram, and I would thank you to keep your filthy habits away from my festival.'

'You misunderstand. One does not wish to purchase the drug; one wishes to avoid places – back alleys and the like – where it may be procured. One no longer indulges in excesses of narcotica, and wishes to place oneself beyond the chill grasp of temptation.'

'I'm very glad to hear it. You can rest assured that you will find no such nonsense around here. Heroin indeed.'

'I would stay away from Market Horten if I were you,' interjected the parson, who was heavily involved in the local rehabilitation scheme, 'particularly the street behind the railway station. It's our nearest town, and it's peaceful enough but I don't think anywhere gets away from that sort of thing entirely.'

Mrs Bruschini gave him an icy stare.

'Market Horten, you say?' monotoned Wilberforce Selfram. 'The street to the rear of the railway station? So that is where beats the dark heart of this locale.'

'But I think you'll be fine in the Bottoms,' said the parson, reacting to the icy stare. 'There really isn't anything like that going on as far as I know.'

'More's the pity. This neighbourhood could do with an injection of urban grit, of metropolitan, er...roughness. No, there must be a better word. There must...' Wilberforce

Selfram began to look panicked. 'One's vocabulary... since arriving in this backwater...gone downhill... descended...descendified...descendificated...no...it's no use...'

'I think you've been using a lot of super words, Mr Selfram,' said Mrs Bell. 'Don't you worry.'

Her reassuring tones were not enough to quell his anxiety. 'One does worry, though. One often finds oneself obliged to simplify one's vocabulary when conversing with one's cerebral inferiors, yet one feels that while within the confines of this country kitchen one has descended to such depths that one may never rise once again to one's previous powers. There have been flashes of competence: *paradigmatically*, and *peregrinations*, and perhaps two or three others, yet there have been frightful lapses, even unto the realm of floridity: *the rippléd surface of the e'er-flowing stream*, to provide just one example. Though high poetry of the classical style, and worthy of a place within the leaves of Herr Palgrave's *Golden Treasury*, it is in no way in keeping with the Selfram brand. It is not Modernist, and one is Modernist to one's very giblets. Even when speaking Middle English and following in the footsteps of Beoffrey of Biddenden one does so in a way that is indubitably Modernist. One can feel oneself becoming decreasingly articulate with each dread tick of time's e'er-tocking clock. There one goes again... When one thinks of the words one could have used since one arrived in this kitchen...*emunctory*... *antiphrasis*...perhaps even,' he said, looking at Mrs Bruschini, *'embonpoint*. What else? Oh, how the letters swim and blur before one's eyes. Parson,' he urgently droned, 'is there a thesaurus in the house? And if so will you fetch it with celerity?'

As if he had been asked to go for warm water and towels to aid the delivery of an unexpectedly emerging litter of kittens, the parson dashed off to his study and raced back moments later with the family thesaurus, which he gravely presented to the author. At the same time Mrs Chapman, who had made a mad dash for the fridge, gravely presented the author with a stick of celery. Wilberforce Selfram greeted both with a sigh through his nose. 'This,' he said, pointing at the vegetable, 'was inevitable. Even as the words were being formed in one's larynx one knew that such an umbelliferae would appear before one.' His attention turned to the thesaurus. 'A paperback *Roget's*. One supposes one is unlikely to find anything superior in a cultural hinterland such as this. It will have to suffice.'

Sitting at the head of the kitchen table, Wilberforce Selfram looked up at the parson. 'May one?' he asked.

'Be my guest,' said the parson, thinking that his visitor was just asking permission to leaf through the book and look up a few choice words.

This was not the case. With permission granted, Wilberforce Selfram appeared to enter a trance. He placed his hands on the book's cover, and looked to the ceiling. As he did so, his eyeballs rolled back, their irises completely hidden and only the whites visible. A guttural moan escaped him, and he opened the thesaurus at what seemed to be a random point. This was strange enough, but what he did next surprised them all, and their surprise soon turned to discomfort, and then concern. It was quite extraordinary, and they all knew straightaway that however it was to end, this was something they would be talking about for many years to come.

Not for the first time that day, poor Mrs Chapman fainted clean away. Mr Bell caught her, and made her comfortable on the floor, while his wife reached once again for the smelling salts, all the while keeping one eye on her patient and the other on the extraordinary scene that was unfolding at the kitchen table.

Chapter 12

Ayanna gives up on her new job,
and receives an imperial visit

Six weeks into her publishing career, nothing much had changed for Ayanna, and she had decided to leave. Her uncle had always told her that if she could handle a large vehicle she would never be out of work, and so far he'd been proven right. He was more of a father to her than his brother, her father, had ever been, and he had treated her to a light goods vehicle course for her twenty-first birthday. It turned out she was a natural behind the wheel. She had passed first time, and had spent the following four years driving a lorry around London, mainly delivering pallets of building materials, or goods for wholesalers. She had enjoyed the work, and when she left to take her job in the book trade, they had wished her well and told her she would always be welcome back. The weekend was coming, and her old boss was always in the yard on a Saturday morning. She decided to go and see him the next day. There would be a bit of ribbing as they'd all had a big night out when she'd left just a few weeks earlier. It had been quite an event, and she'd had one too many and ended up kissing someone she shouldn't have kissed, and had been quite glad that she wouldn't have to face him at work. Still, she would get past that. She would make more money, and be able to get back to saving up for her own place.

She was dismayed by how things had worked out in her new job. She had always been a mad reader, and it was the books that had lured her to it. When she was small, she would go to the public library after school and wait for her mum to finish work and pick her up. As she made her way through piles of books, she would sometimes find herself appraising them as objects, and wondering about the people who had printed them, and picked the covers, and as she grew older this fascination had remained until finally, after endless applications, she had managed to get herself this job. It was just a shame, she thought, that it hadn't been up to much. Still, she'd tried.

Her decision had been hastened by the exhaustingly familiar sight of Wilberforce Selfram and Harry Johannes in their folding chairs. Wilberforce Selfram was coming to the end of a speech she had heard many times already, in various forms, about how on a personal level he defied simple categorisation. 'One is an Englishman, yet one's mother was born and indeed raised within the United States of America; one is a Londoner; a European; of Jewish heritage yet of a secular bent; an academic; a drug addict. One could go on. The textures and contradictions are as scintillating to the lay person as they are manifold.'

'Manifold?' she asked, barely bothering to engage with the conversation.

'Manifold. One may at any moment sense one's transatlantic side coming to the fore, and find oneself wearing a backward baseball cap and saying *oh boy*, and *short pants*, and *fanny pack*, and *hide-and-go-seek*. The subsequent instant one may instead be inclined to dust off one's kippah and consume a pile of latkes. Being, perhaps above all things, a European, until recently one was often to be found playing the alpenhorn. The mouthpiece was at a top floor window of one's house and the instrument extended into the garden far below. When one was feeling particularly European, one would play it for hours on end, and one received not a single word of appreciation from one's neighbours, so morbidly opposed are the denizens of this fractured isle to the European project. When one's house fell down, taking several of one's neighbours' abodes with it, the vibrations from one's instrument were blamed. Legal complications are ongoing. As for one's Englishness, one never travels without one's full Morris dancing accoutrementalia: sticks, bells and all.'

'Are you part of a Morris-dancing troupe?' asked Ayanna, semi-successfully stifling a yawn.

'Negative. Though one reveres the tradition of the dance, one cannot abide Morris dancers; it is all one can do to stop oneself from sending them letter bombs. As an immutable rule, when finding oneself garbed in the same habiliments as a personage with whom one is ideologically at odds, one has no choice but to immolate one's own clothing. At one's only attempt to dance with a Morris troupe, one found oneself in political discord with the uniformed membership to such an extent that before long one found oneself stark Dallas naked upon a village green, one's garments a smouldering heap at one's feet and one's modesty preserved only by virtue of one having brought with one a pewter tankard. One was escorted from the scene by the local constabulary; consequently, since that day one has danced the Morris alone.'

'How about you, Harry? Do you ever do any Morris dancing?'

'Of course. I belong to a number of Morris-dancing troupes, and know everything there is to...' Remembering the special course he had been on, he stopped himself. 'No. No, I don't.'

Ayanna cleared her throat, and Wilberforce Selfram stared at her. 'One hopes you are not suffering from pneumonoultramicroscopicsilicovolcanoconiosis,' he said.

'No, I was just clearing my throat.'

'You should consult a physician nonetheless.'

At that moment the folding screen suddenly opened, and there in the corridor, dramatically backlit by a strip light, stood a pair of evidently very grand people – a dazed-looking man with wiry white hair who was wearing tweeds and offering the world no discernible chin; and a vital woman in her sixties, dressed in what was most likely a Chanel suit. At this sight, Wilberforce Selfram threw himself to the ground and lay prostrate before them. 'Duke and Duchess of Bloomsbury, to what do we owe this most gracious of visitations?'

'Oh do get up, Selfram,' said the Duchess of Bloomsbury. He dusted himself down as he obeyed her instructions. 'And how are you, Mr Johannes? Behaving yourself, I hope.'

He pouted and shrugged. 'Why should I tell you?'

'That's the spirit. And whom do we have here?'

Ayanna felt the Duchess of Bloomsbury's steely eyes upon her. She rose from her seat and extended a hand. 'I'm Ayanna,' she said. 'I'm quite new.'

'The Duchess of Bloomsbury,' said the Duchess of Bloomsbury, offering a noncommittal hand in return, and smiling with only half her mouth. 'How nice to meet you.' Her husband was apparently staring at a piece of lint that was caught in a ray of light, his eyes following it as a light breeze blew it back and forth. 'Don't mind the Duke of Bloomsbury,' she said. 'We're just down from the country. He bagged a skylark this morning, and can't stop thinking about it.'

On cue, the Duke of Bloomsbury cocked an imaginary shotgun, aimed it at the floating lint, and fired. This was evidently an imaginary direct hit, as he gave a little leap for joy.'

'And how are you finding the job?'

'It's fine thanks,' she said, deciding not to mention her plan to hand in her notice.

'Do I detect an accent? A little cockney, perhaps?'

She found it jarring that here, in the epicentre of the M25, her accent would be a talking point. 'I'm from Croydon.'

'Of course, the famous Croydon twang. How…nice.' Her eyes narrowed. 'And what did you do before you came to us?'

'I drove a lorry.'

She smiled again, this time with her whole mouth. 'Good. Good. Splendid to meet you, but we must be off.' Once again Wilberforce Selfram threw himself to the ground. She shook her head, but said nothing this time. 'Come along,' she called to her husband, who seemed not to hear her. 'Here, boy.' He scampered after her.

Wilberforce Selfram clambered back into his chair, brushing himself down.

'That,' said Ayanna, pointing to the spot on the floor where he had lain, so there would be no doubt about what she was referring to, 'was the most pathetic thing I have ever seen.'

'One is not unaware of the display's disheartening properties. This hearkens back, however, to our earlier conversation. When the regal visitors arrived, one was in Englishman mode, and one of the many dispiriting aspects of such a state is an unfortunate servility when faced with those of a titled disposition. Had one been in a transatlantic frame of mind, one would have said, *Howdy! Gee whizz, it sure is swell to see you. Say, are you a real Duke and Dukess?* and so forth. Alas, one was not.'

'Well I'm English, and it didn't cross my mind to roll around on the floor. How about you, Harry?'

'I'm not English, as it goes. I'm as Scottish as Nessie and as Swiss as Toblerone, so to see an Englishman crumble in the face of ill-gotten status is a cause of no little amusement. You wouldn't catch me doing that; I just sat there and sulked.'

'How very predictable of you,' said Wilberforce

Selfram. 'When dealing with a character as complex as one's own, the lay onlooker must anticipate surprise and contradiction. As a great public intellectual and *de facto* figurehead of what might, unhappily perhaps, be termed *the counterculture*, one of course eschews such subservience, and yet when reduced to one's basest component – mere Englishman – one finds oneself entranced and enfeebled by nobility. One's reason abhors the royal honours system, for example, and yet those words – *Arise, Sir Wilberforce* – stir something deep within one's identity. Have they not beauty? Have they not fragrance?'

'Pah,' said Harry Johannes. 'Royal honours are a ridiculous anachronism, and only a snivelling cretin would accept one. Except for Sir Elton John, of course; he doesn't count. Did I tell you he liked my book?'

'Hold on,' said Wilberforce Selfram, addressing Ayanna. 'Did one hear you say that you used to drive a large vehicle?'

It was the first time Wilberforce Selfram had ever asked her about herself, but having decided she would be leaving the company, she had tuned out. She neither replied nor bothered stifling her next yawn. She wondered what she was doing there. The phone rang again. Who was going to be disappointed this time?

Chapter 13

There is an unexpected dried-fruit crisis

Wilberforce Selfram had begun by tearing a page from the thesaurus, stuffing it in his mouth, chewing it, and swallowing, all the while maintaining the unsettling guttural moan. Then another page, and another. His pace picked up until it became quite frenzied, and before long hundreds of pages had gone, and all that remained was the book's paperback cover.

At last his irises reappeared, the moan subsided, and he stared straight ahead. In his familiar low monotone, he tried out a few words: 'Incommensurable. Bursectomy. Sustentative. Parasymbiotic. Zymogenous. The wordbook appears to have taken effect. Some of those cannot even be found within the pages of this rather humdrum tome; much as a car may be jump-started, it is not its mere electrical storage device which is reincarnated, but its whole – wheels, pistons, windscreen wipers and so forth, and so it is with one's vocabulary. When it begins to falter, one simply swallows a thesaurus, and everything, as it were, clatters back into gear. This exercise will go some way towards keeping one's conversation free of the commonplace. Our cleric's *Roget's* has not perished in vain, as one shall henceforth be able once again to pepper one's speech with extraordinary wordage. One is an author, and it is an author's duty – duty, no less – to educate and improve his, or indeed *her*, audience by the employment of words that lie beyond the boundary of the everyday. Lesser writers evade and/or eschew circumlocution; not one, however – one positively embraces, indeed enfolds, indeed enclasps it.' He tried a few more words, and they were all quite long and nobody knew what they meant. 'This is a source of substantial relief. One had been feeling increasingly microcephalous by the moment.' He pointed a long, grey finger at the casualty on the floor. 'Why is Mrs Chapman in a state of repose?'

Mrs Chapman had begun to come to, but the sight of those gimlet eyes and the finger put her straight back under. Mrs Bell got the smelling salts out again.

'A soupçon more,' said Wilberforce Selfram. 'Senectitude. Ptygma. Concupiscence. Exalbuminous. Sbamnimnulent.'

'What was that last one?' asked the parson, who felt there was something not quite right about it.

'Sbamnimnulent.'

'What does it mean?'

'It means nothing yet. It is a word of one's own

devising. Often one will coin a word and add it to a personal lexicon which one shall, upon one's passing, hand down to future generations. When wishing to find a name for a new discovery or invention, or means to describe such, our descendants shall turn to one's list, and pick a neologism which they feel appropriate for the denotation at hand, thus saving themselves the trouble of thinking one up themselves. How grateful they shall be. Though we be separated by the decades, perhaps even the centuries, they shall regard one as a most munificent friend and benefactor. They shall erect statues in one's likeness, and refer to one, with no little affection, as just *Selfram*, or perhaps *Selfram of Yore.*'

Even Mrs Bruschini had been dumbfounded by the last few minutes in the kitchen, and though she opened her mouth in an attempt to contribute something to this scene, no sound came out. It was not often that the cat got her tongue.

Wilberforce Selfram continued. 'One is inclined to begin these words with the nineteenth and second letters of the conventional English alphabet, as this combination is in scant employment. *Sblont. Sbractanicafal. Sbifundificationally.* When one's words are absorbed into the dictionaries of the future – space dictionaries, perhaps – they shall coagulate within their leaves and be found with ease by historians researching what shall doubtless become known as *The Selfram Pages.*'

Mrs Bruschini finally found her voice. 'Mr Selfram,' she said. 'Never mind space dictionaries, I have just seen you consume an earthly dictionary...'

'A thesaurus,' he cut in.

'There is no need to be pedantic.'

'There is every need. It is one's duty to correct...'

She cut him off with a raised palm. 'Mr Selfram, I demand to know what will happen to all that paper. You have a school hall to address tomorrow morning at a quarter to ten, and you will not be able to do so if your bowels are playing merry hell with you. It has gone in – we all saw that – but how ever are you going to get it out?'

'Mrs Bruschini,' he said, 'this is a commonplace occurrence, and one has taken medical advice from the very finest physicians. One's interior tends towards the eupeptic in nature, and requires very little in the way of assistance. One shall follow the pages of the thesaurus with five kilogrammes of prunes. The prune, as one is sure you are sensible, is renowned for its laxative properties, and its consequent ability to assist the movement of foodstuffs and their associated waste through the human bowel. Once ensconced within one's gut, the mass of dried fruit will merge with the pages and result in an excretion which resembles, though not entirely, the mainstream stool. It will be firm yet perfectly passable. Parson, bring one your prunes.'

'I don't have any. I'm not really a prune person.'

'Not a single prune?' Wilberforce Selfram's pallor reached a hitherto unreached shade of deathly grey.

'No. I've got about a quarter of a bag of raisins, if that's any use.'

'Raisins will not suffice.'

The parson found the bag anyway. 'Actually they aren't raisins, they're currants.'

'Though the differences between the raisin and the currant are myriad, neither is suitable for the emergency at hand. Who among you can bring one prunes?' He stared imploringly from one member of the party to the next. They all looked blankly at one another. Between them they could have amassed a fair amount of sultanas, and even a few dried cranberries, but none of them was a prune person.

Mrs Chapman had come to again. 'You could try that stick of celerity,' she said, weakly from her makeshift sickbed on the kitchen floor. The unfortunate vegetable had been in front of him on the table throughout this episode.

'Negative, that will not do. One requires five kilogrammes of prunes.' For the first time since his arrival his voice left its monotonous register and began to waver, as his eyes, though still blank, also somehow seemed to burn with mortal dread. 'One must have prunes,' he cried. 'Bring one prunes.'

'We could try the village shop,' said Mrs Bell, 'though I don't think they carry prunes, and I think they'll be closing for lunch about now anyway.'

'Then the supermarket. Where is your nearest expansive retail grocery emporium? There is a likelihood that the dried fruit one requires can be found in such an establishment, betwixt J-cloth and sprout.'

'There's the Morrison's in Market Horton,' said Mrs Bell.

'That's certainly our nearest one,' said Mr Bell. 'We could be there and back in about an hour, depending on the queues.'

'An hour? That will be too late. One must commence

the consumption of prunes within thirty minutes of eating the final leaf of paper, otherwise the resultant pulp will form an impenetrable bolus within one's stomach. The aforesaid bolus will swiftly reach the stage where it cannot be softened at all, and it will form a lethal, nay fatal, intestinal blockage. If you do not bring one prunes, in less than an hour one will be quite, quite dead. One's life shall reach its denouement here, in this very kitchen.'

'We can't have that,' said Mrs Bruschini. 'You have three engagements to fulfil, and I'm told the schoolchildren are very excited. They've all drawn pictures of you.'

'I have an idea,' said Mr Bell. 'If we could contact somebody who was already in Morrison's, then they could buy the prunes and be back here in half the time. Now, my pal Anthony told me he was going there to do the weekly shop. He's been under the thumb ever since his wife caught him sending photos to that poor young lady. He was lucky she didn't press charges, you know. The young lady that is – not his wife; he would be on the register if she had done. He was very apologetic, and said he thought that was just how young people did things these days. He would never have got off if it had gone to court; apparently it's *very* distinctive and there would have been no mistaking it for anybody else's. But never mind that, if we call him now, we might just catch him at the right moment. If he's in the shop he could grab the prunes and race straight here, and we would be in with a chance of saving Mr Selfram's life.'

'Hitherto you have been a rather blank character,'

said Wilberforce Selfram, 'just standing around and occasionally exchanging a bland pleasantry with your spouse. One has, at times, wondered what purpose you serve in all this. However, one concedes that your idea is viable. Your moment at the centre of this drama has come: let us pursue your plan, and with celerity.'

'I thought it was prunes you were after.'

Wilberforce Selfram sighed through his nose. 'Affirmative, one is desirous of prunes. By *celerity* one means, to employ the commonplace, *speed*. With each dread tick of time's aforementioned e'er-tocking clock, one inches toward an untimely sepulchre.'

'I understand. Time is of the essence.'

'Indubitably so.'

Mr Bell took his phone from his pocket, and appraised it for a while. 'Now,' he said, 'which way round does this thing go?'

'It's that way,' said his wife, pointing. 'With the bit you listen to at the top.'

'So it is.' The screen lit up, and he looked at it. 'It's asking for a code. What is it again?'

'It's your sister's birthday, I think. Or Bevis's. Try one, and if that doesn't work, try the other.'

'One had not anticipated one's expiration to unfold thus,' said Wilberforce Selfram, to himself. 'Encircled by Bœotians as they struggle to operate a simple telephone. What will one's legacy be? Will one's obituaries be favourable? Oh, one had so much left to give.'

'No, it's not my sister's... Let's...try...the...dog's... There. I'm in. Now, how do I make a call? I hardly ever use this thing,' he explained to the visitor.

'Pull up your address book and find Anthony's name,' said Mrs Bell.

Mr Bell looked quizzically at the screen. 'I've done this before… I think I remember how…' He scrolled around for a while. 'No, that's the weather forecast… Ah, here…contacts. Anthony, Anthony, Anthony… No, he doesn't seem to be here. I could have sworn I had his number because I called him when we met up with him and Sheila at the garden centre. It was the time we talked them out of buying that village-pump water feature. It would have dominated their front garden.'

'Did you call him, or did he call you?'

'I definitely called him, because I remember pulling into that lay-by, the one just past the Royal Oak. I always pull over to use the phone – it makes my blood boil when I see people using them at the wheel. He's got to be in here somewhere…'

'Celerity, if you please. Already one can feel the paper beginning to congeal within one's viscera.'

Mrs Bell remained as calm as ever. 'Are you looking under his first name or his surname?'

'I only list my pals by their first names, and he's not there under the *A*s.'

'Don't you sometimes call him Tony?'

'Sometimes. About 60/40, I would say.'

'Try the *T*s then.'

'OK…and…here we go… P… Q… R… S… U… I've gone right past it. Hang on… I'll go back… Here we are. T. *Terry*. *Thomas*. That's not Terry Thomas the famous actor, it's just Terry and Thomas, a couple of my badminton pals. *Tim*. *Tom*. Thomas and Tom are two different people. Tom's not a badminton pal, he's cricket. *Tony.* Here he is. I've found him.'

'Call him,' said Mrs Bell. 'With celerity. I mean quickly.'

'OK.'

'We'll put him on speakerphone so we can all hear,' said Mrs Bell. To speed things along she took the phone from her husband, and pressed the appropriate parts of the screen. The phone sat in the middle of the kitchen table, and they all gravitated around it, taking seats. Even Mrs Chapman, blinking in the light, rose from the floor and joined them. They stared at it as it rang. And rang. And rang. And then it stopped. At last, the call had been answered.

'Anthony,' said Mr Bell. 'Thank God.'

'Hello, you're through to Anthony Stapleton. I'm afraid I'm not able to take your call at the moment. Please leave your message after the tone, with your name and number, and I'll get back to you. They waited for the tone. And waited. *Hang on,* said the recorded voice. *Am I supposed to press something… Ah, there.*

At last the tone sounded, and Mr Bell started his message. 'Hi Anthony, it's David. I wonder if you could give me a ring back on… What's my number?'

'I can't remember it off the top of my head. It'll show up on his phone though.'

'If you could return this call as soon as you can it would be really helpful. It's actually urge...'

The phone began to ring. It was an incoming call from Anthony. 'He must have just missed it, and called straight back,' said Mrs Bell. 'That happens sometimes.'

Mr Bell accepted the call, and they were through to their potential saviour. 'Hello.'

'Is that David?'

'Yes. Hi, Anthony.'

'I just missed your call. Well, I tried to answer it, but I think I must have pressed the reject button by mistake. I can't get the hang of these bloody things.'

'It's easily done. I was just leaving you a message when you called back, so just ignore it when you get it. So what can I do for you?' asked Mr Bell.

'I don't know. It was you who called me. First time round, at any rate.'

'Was it? Oh yes, of course. Tell me, where are you right now?'

'I'm in Morrison's, worse luck. Sheila's had me doing the weekly shop, ever since…the episode. I come here straight from the counselling they're making me do. Honestly, one little *faux pas*…' Everybody's eyes widened at this ray of hope, while at the same time they tried not to think too much about what Anthony had done, and what it was that might have made the subject of the photograph so very distinctive.

'I'm afraid I need a favour from you. It's really quite urgent. It would take too long to explain, but could you buy five kilos of prunes and bring them to the parsonage as quickly as possible?'

'Prunes?'

'Yes, prunes.'

'I could have a look. Do you know which aisle they're in?'

'I'm not sure. How about you, darling, do you know?'

'Ah, Susan,' said Anthony. 'She's there too?'

'Yes, she's here. We're on speakerphone.'

'How are you, Anthony?' asked Mrs Bell.

'I'm fine, thanks, Susan. Or at least I was until your old man started forcing me to make a mad dash for the prune aisle. Do you know where I can find them?'

'I'm trying to picture it. They've just rejigged the whole shop, haven't they?'

'I know, it's driving me mad. I can't find anything. I feel like a lab rat.'

'I think dried fruit tends to be next to the baking section. Either that or the bit with the lentils and that sort of thing.'

'You wouldn't catch me eating lentils. No fear. Hippy rubbish. I'll try the baking aisle first. I think I know where that is. I'm at the freezers now, but I was there a minute ago to get some of those cake decorations that look like ball bearings. I always feel a bit on edge eating them, to be honest, but they're on the list, and who am I to question She-Who-Must-Be-Obeyed? OK, here we are…'

'One can feel it pressing ever downwards,' moaned Wilberforce Selfram, gripping the table and staring at the kitchen clock. Six minutes had passed since he had finished the final page.

'OK. Baking. Let me see. Prunes. Prunes prunes prunes prunes prunes.'

'This is not helping,' whimpered Wilberforce Selfram.

'I can hear all sorts of voices,' said Anthony. 'How many of you are there?'

'Quite a few,' said Mrs Bell, who had taken command of the call in case the men were to start talking about golf. 'We're at the parsonage. As in the real parsonage, next door. There's no time to explain, I'm afraid, but we do need these prunes straightaway.'

'There are quite long queues at the checkouts today,' he said, 'and I've got a full trolley so it'll probably be at least an hour before I can get to you. Will that be OK?'

'I'm afraid not,' said Mrs Bell. 'You see we've got someone here who's just eaten a bellyful of paper, and he needs prunes to flush it out. If he doesn't get the prunes within half an hour – well, about twenty-five minutes now – the paper will start turning to rock in his tummy and it'll be the end of him, I'm afraid.'

'Paper? Why's he been eating paper?'

'I'll explain everything when you get here, but please hurry.'

'OK, I'll leave the trolley here for now, and come back for it later. And I'll try the self-service checkout for the prunes. I've not used it before though. Is it difficult?'

'I won't use them,' said Mrs Bell, 'they take people's jobs. Honestly, when I see people using those things I lose all hope for humanity. There usually seems to be someone standing there though, and I'm sure they'll help you if you get stuck.'

'That's a relief. I'd better put all the cold stuff back in the cabinets - if it starts to defrost then goes back in the freezer it all clumps together.'

'You won't have time. We'll cover the cost of anything that gets spoiled.'

'Fair enough. Now, I still can't see any prunes. I can see raisins. Are they any use?'

'No,' cried everybody in the kitchen.

'What about sultanas?'

This was greeted with an identical chorus.

'Excuse me,' said Anthony to a passing staff member. 'Where can I find the prunes?'

[…]

'Oh.'

[…]

'I see.'

[…]

'Yes, my wife watches that. It's got whatsisname in it, hasn't it? I can't stand him myself. I usually go out and water the hanging baskets whenever he comes on.'

[…]

'Thanks anyway.' He addressed the phone again. 'I'm afraid they've sold out. They were making prune crumble on the BBC last night, and first thing this morning everyone came in and cleared the shelves. Dried and tinned. They won't be in again until tomorrow at the earliest, and I suppose that'll be too late for you. They've got dates, though. They look more or less the same.'

'No,' said Wilberforce Selfram, 'it must be prunes. Nothing else has comparable laxative properties, and since prunes are not forthcoming one shall lie upon the kitchen floor, and stray no farther.'

Wilberforce Selfram duly lowered himself, taking the place of the recently risen Mrs Chapman. 'So this is the end,' he said. 'One is again for Cydnus, to meet Uncle Jim.' He crossed his arms over his chest, and his eyes, though open, fell absolutely still.

Chapter 14

*An initiative to encourage social diversity
in publishing is launched*

In its panic the fawn had put up a frantic struggle, the desperation showing in its big, beautiful eyes as many hands held it and pinned it down. It had never stood a chance, and now it lay still on the oak altar, its throat slit, its mouth slightly open, and those same eyes, now blind, reflecting the flicker of candlelight. Its blood had been drained into a chalice, which was being passed from hand to hand, each person present taking their turn to drink from it. *We drink the blood of the fawn*, they chanted. *We drink the blood of the fawn.*

Nothing had ever been written down, so there was no way of knowing for certain just how long the

Brotherhood of Darkness (Publishing Division) had been meeting, but its rituals and traditions were so convoluted that everybody involved knew that they were continuing something that reached far back in time. Once every season, and only when the moon was full, they came together. This time it was the turn of the ancient house of Faber & Faber to host. They had done so in a large brick-lined vault deep underneath their central London office. Lady Faber had provided the fawn from her own herd, and she had been the one to slit its throat, and to take the first draught of blood from the chalice.

When everybody had drunk their share, Lady Faber rang a large bell three times, its low note rippling the flesh beneath the robes of those present. The figures fell silent.

The overriding purpose of this convocation was to reinforce the boundaries of their trade, to keep its borders iron-clad, and to remind its members that on no account must their position be compromised by outsiders. It was time for business to commence. Standing in a circle, with the altar and the body of the young deer at its centre, the chanting resumed, led by Lady Faber.

'What do we do to those who oppose us?'

Destroy them. Destroy them. Destroy, destroy, destroy.

'What do we do to those who betray us?'

Crush them. Crush them. Crush, crush, crush.

They continued in this vein for a long while, and when at last it was over, the time came for them to discuss recent developments. The floor was taken by the Brotherhood's current president, Lord Barnstable of Barnstable & Barnstaple. A relative newcomer to the position, this was only his fourth meeting at the helm, but with his penetrating eyes and George V beard he had a naturally presidential bearing that served him well.

'As we all know,' he said, 'the world is changing at a rapid pace, and we must be seen to change with it. Questions are being asked of us, and sadly we find ourselves obliged to respond to them. There are those who are saying, rather volubly, that the publishing industry is run by a shadowy cabal of upper-class cronies. What do we do when we hear this?'

Deny it. Deny it. Deny, deny, deny.

'Indeed. As ever we shall brush it off it with a half-chuckle, while subtly suggesting that the accuser is an inverted snob. And if these suggestions persist?'

Ridicule them. Ridicule them. Ridicule, ridicule, ridicule.

'Correct. We must make it seem as if those who are making these accusations are potty conspiracy theorists, deserving more of pity than of censure, even though we know that what they are saying…' he paused for a moment, and made eye contact with several members of the group, '…is true.' He let this hang in the air for a moment. 'Our core strategy shall remain as it has been for many years: denial and ridicule. We need, however, to bolster our defences. What do we need to build?'

A wall. A wall. We need to build a wall.

'Precisely. Fortification remains key to our future. We must appear to be moving away from the aristocentric business model we have sustained, and which has sustained us, for so many years. It has never been more important to give the impression that we are embracing these changes in a significant way while, of course, ensuring that fundamentally everything stays the same and our citadel remains secure. For this reason, I am implementing a revival of Operation Great Unwashed.'

This was met with an involuntary communal groan, which was quickly extinguished with a presidential glare. They knew what was coming. Every few years a light from outside would be shone on the industry's lack of social diversity. Articles would be written about how publishing was overbearingly upper-class, and whenever this happened they found themselves launching a scheme to get people from other backgrounds into the field. These would run for a while before quietly fizzling out, but while they lasted, they gave publishers the opportunity to point at this junior publicist, or that marketing trainee, and declare that their workforce was inclusive, conveying the impression that the grandees of the business were indeed committed to social modernisation, and taking an enthusiastic role in its implementation.

'Every house must play its part and employ a proportion of people who can be held up as examples of progressive recruitment strategies. We deny, we ridicule, and we flag up somebody behind one of our desks who perhaps did not go to boarding school.' This was met with a shudder. 'Or who doesn't have any relatives or family friends high up in the industry.' More shuddering. 'Somebody who, perhaps, attended a former polytechnic, or doesn't have a degree at all.' Had he continued along these lines, the shuddering would have become convulsing. 'Thus,' he concluded, 'will our fortress remain impregnable. As you all know, we have been running such initiatives on-and-off for a long time, and at the top of the industry, where the important work is done, nothing really changes; this one will be no different.'

There was still a palpable lack of enthusiasm in the room.

'I realise that this is a bit of a chore for everybody, but even with our new scheme in place we shall be able to continue to discreetly sort out jobs for one another's godsons and goddaughters, and nieces and nephews, and so on. And you needn't worry; our complex system of impenetrable glass ceilings will remain in place. Sometimes one of these recruits may be permitted to rise through the ranks, even, in some rare cases, to a minor seat on a board of directors. They will believe they are dining at the top table, but they are not. This,' he pointed at the altar, 'is the top table, and they will never even know it exists. They will not walk among us. Does anybody have anything to say?'

At a meeting a few years earlier, when a similar plan had been discussed, one of the publishers had piped up and said that allowing more people from outside into the industry, as an ongoing recruitment strategy and not just because of a box-ticking gimmick, might be to their benefit, that they could bring with them new approaches, and ideas that would refresh the business. Perhaps, it was ventured, the time had come for them to stop merely paying lip service to modernisation and progressive recruitment but to really look beyond their own narrow gene pool and traditional modes of operation. This liberal attitude had not been well received, and a few days later that same publisher had been found face-down in the River Thames, their body fished out of the water by a police patrol boat at Rotherhithe. It had been declared by the coroner to have been a tragic accident, and was reported as such in the trade journal *The Bookseller,* in an article which contained apparently sincere tributes from a number of people now at the gathering, Lord Barnstable among them. His question hung in the air.

He acknowledged the silence, and continued. 'We are going to call this latest effort The Kaleidoscope Scheme, which we believe sounds rather friendly, and I am sure that I can count on all of you to cooperate with boundless enthusiasm. And what do we say to the inevitable cynics who will ask us why we feel the need to sign up to a scheme in order to be persuaded to recruit beyond our own social milieu?'

He cupped a hand to his ear, but was met with yet more silence.

'No, we've still not quite worked out an answer to that one, have we? Get your thinking caps on, and return with ideas next time. On a lighter note we shall, as ever, be playing Common People Bingo.'

This cheered everybody up. *Bingo. Bingo. Common People Bingo,* they chanted.

They were familiar with the rules: points would be awarded to houses for recruits who came from comically unfashionable towns, or who had identifiably proletarian names or accents. There was to be a special prize for the publisher who was to find the single recruit who embodied the highest number of relevant traits. This was why, a few weeks after this meeting of the Brotherhood of Darkness (Publishing Division), the Duchess of Bloomsbury would leave her first encounter with Ayanna with a smile and a spring in her step.

Bingo, the Duchess of Bloomsbury thought to herself after her first meeting with the girl with the Croydon twang. With the news that she had previously driven a lorry for a living, there was now a very good chance of her winning the grand prize. Before she concluded the tour of the offices that day she had visited the Human Resources office and spoken to the manager. 'That new girl,' she said. 'The one in the cupboard with Selfram and Johannes – could I have a look at her CV?'

She was handed a sheet of paper, and it was even better than she had hoped. She had feared a scholarship to a private school, but there was just a comprehensive, followed by no degree; although she had aced her English literature A Level she hadn't been triumphant in her other subjects, and apart from driving tests she had clearly given up on formal education at that point. 'A forklift-truck certificate,' she read. 'How adorable. Tell me, did she come to us through Kaleidoscope?'

'Yes, your grace.'

The Duchess of Bloomsbury smiled with one side of her mouth. 'She seemed a little elbows-on-the-table, but this is pure gold. We must make sure she doesn't leave.' *At least not until after the competition,* she thought. All entrants in Common People Bingo had to be still on their publishers' payroll when the results were announced. 'We'll employ everything in our armoury.

Oh, and we should find out whether or not she's a lesbian, or from a broken home. It helps to know these sorts of things.' She was already confident that she had the top prize in the bag, but presidents past had used this sort of information if a tie-breaker was needed. She had learned on the hockey fields of Roedean that it was never a bad idea to consolidate a lead.

Just at that moment the potential source of her prize had walked in to the HR office, a letter of resignation in her hand...

Lord Barnstable allowed the assembled hooded publishers to enjoy the Common People Bingo announcement, and let the torchlit hubbub continue for a couple of minutes as they recalled past competitions, boasting of triumphs and bemoaning perceived injustices. Then, with an authoritative cough, he brought the room to silence. 'To other business. We have gathered intelligence that an author with an axe to grind has chosen to depict our humble community in a novel he is writing. The word from our contacts suggests that our activities have been described to an extraordinary degree of accuracy – the oak altar is mentioned, the candlelight, the three strikes of the low bell, our robes, and even, I am afraid to say, Operation Great Unwashed.' He paused while he made momentary eye contact with every attendee. 'If I ever find he has been getting information from a source within our ranks I shall act swiftly, and without mercy.'

A chilling silence fell over the room.

'The author in question is a notably marginal figure, by the name of…' he checked his notes, 'Dan Rhodes. Has anybody heard of him?'

Heads were shaken.

'I thought as much. He is, I am informed, one of that ghastly legion of superannuated *enfant terrible* types, yet for all his obscurity the threat to our way of life from this novel must not be understated. It will be called, perhaps inevitably, *Sour Grapes*. So far, he is only up to chapter fourteen, but is writing with some speed and we expect it to be completed before very long. You may, however, rest assured that I have the matter in hand.'

There came a burst of cries from the floor. *Burn him. Poison him. Bury him alive.*

This was calmed by a raised presidential hand. 'We shall allow him to finish work on the book, and then…' he paused, for dramatic effect, '…we will stage a bidding war for it, starting at five hundred thousand pounds and finishing somewhere comfortably above a million, perhaps one point three. It will be published with great fanfare, and I have already received an assurance from my contacts in the television industry that it will be turned into a long-running series. Edward Tudor-Pole is on standby to take the lead role.' This was too much for his audience, all of whom now displayed textbook symptoms of confusion. Though the president's strategy seemed odd, his mien throughout had been so presidential that, as baffled as they were, their confidence in him remained. 'Are there any questions?'

There was silence for a while, but the president didn't move the meeting along. He knew they all had the same question, and he waited, presidentially, for it.

At last, a hand rose.

'President, why are you allowing this?'

'It's simple. If the business is seen to embrace the book, the strength of any revelations within it will be diluted into pointlessness. If we sought to suppress it, and news of its suppression were to leak out, it would only fuel speculation about our harmless little order, and lead to intolerable exposure. If, on the other hand, we jovially cheer it into the world it will pass as a piece of ephemeral entertainment, too far-fetched to be believed. A million or two is a small price to pay when we consider what we have to lose. And besides, we'll make it back through sales; rather surprisingly we've found the book to have enormous commercial potential. Our focus groups, which as you know have never been wrong, have reported that the three runaway trends in fiction in the coming eighteen months are set to be heritage bottom jokes, penis-based misunderstandings, and longueurs concerning the absence of prunes. This book is perfectly placed to be in the vanguard of all of these. It will be unstoppable – one of the biggest titles of the year; possibly of all time. And the bigger it gets, the safer we are.'

His logic was accepted.

'The publication will be undertaken by you, Lady Chatsworthy. I've already secured prominent reviews in all the papers; you will only have to provide the money up-front and coordinate a blanket advertising campaign. Oh, and factor in around half a million for his backlist. Most of it used to be handled by a miserable little bindery north of the border. Our sources tell us they had a good deal of difficulty when it came to keeping on top of their accounts, and managed to lose substantial amounts of his wages down the back of their sofa. He spent several years fighting a long and ugly battle to get the pay he was due, and when the discrepancies were at last confirmed he took the opportunity to pull the relevant titles out of print. In the current draft he goes on about this squalid debacle somewhat interminably, throwing his toys out of the pram for a full seventy pages; hopefully this will be reined in prior to publication, as I can't see it sitting too well with the book clubs. There evidently remains a dossier of unanswered questions – all of them pertinent, I am sorry to say, and the conflict remains very much active. It is a smouldering tyre fire that could easily have been avoided with a bit of common sense and capability on the part of the publisher, and it goes a long way towards explaining his bitterness and his desire for revenge against the entire industry.' He addressed Lady Chatsworthy. 'See to it that this work is printed on high-quality paper. It will earn out in weeks.'

'Very well, President,' said Lady Chatsworthy. Though notably unenthusiastic about being obliged to add this title to the Chatsworthy Editions catalogue, she was resigned to her duty.

A supplementary question was raised. 'But this author, President…he sounds like a tiresome upstart, so why are we letting him get away with it?'

'We're not. He will die suddenly in the countryside shortly after the book comes out. We'll employ the same chap Tony Blair used when he needed to get rid of David Kelly and Robin Cook. He's very discreet, and his rates are surprisingly reasonable considering his track record. You wouldn't think so to see him presenting that gardening show on the BBC, but apparently he does it for the thrill of the kill.'

The president thus strengthened his reputation as a safe pair of hands for the Brotherhood of Darkness (Publishing Division), and relief in the room was palpable as the meeting moved on to the next item on the agenda. When business was concluded, the attendees let their robes fall to the ground, and smeared their naked bodies with the remaining blood of the fawn, which had been hoisted up by its hind legs, and decapitated. In the midst of all this, Lord Barnstable took the Duchess of Bloomsbury to one side.

'I had my annual meeting with my contact from MI7 the other day,' he said, rubbing the thickening red gunge across his belly, up his chest and into his beard, 'on a bench in St James's Park, of course. He told me that he is most satisfied with your work on The Selfram Project. The Palace too, I'm happy to report.'

'Good,' she said, smudging streaks up and down her arms. 'It's hard work, so I'm glad it's appreciated.'

'I'm starting to worry, though, that his sales figures are a little low. Even with our operatives going around the bookshops bumping things up, they are still not quite where they could be. My concern is that people might begin to suspect that something's not quite right, that his profile is wildly disproportionate to his popularity.'

'I've discussed this with some close contacts,' she said, 'and we've arranged to get him on the Booker Prize shortlist. That should keep us covered for a year or two.'

'The Booker, eh? Excellent work. But will he play ball?'

'Oh yes. He likes to think of himself as this great hero of the underworld, but give him the chance to turn up at an award ceremony in a dickie bow and he'll bite your hand off. Needless to say he won't be winning; that would be too audacious.'

'And you're sure he's not getting suspicious?'

'Not a bit of it, bless his heart. He hasn't got a clue.'

'You really are running this perfectly.'

'Yes, I rather am. I do wonder, though, why I've been saddled with both Selfram *and* Johannes. One or the other would be bad enough, but both?' She fixed him with a steely glare, and though his expression remained as presidential as ever, one of his testicles visibly retracted. He had felt it happen, and he knew that she had caught it from the corner of her eye.

'You're right, of course. I suppose you're a victim of your own success; you've shown yourself to be too capable in these situations. It is rather a lot to expect you to deal with the pair of them indefinitely; I'll contact MI7 and see if they will allow you to release one of them in due course. I'll keep you posted. In the meantime, after everything you've done for them I'm sure they would be more than happy to do you a favour, should you ever feel the need for one.'

Her eyes narrowed at this, and she smiled with both sides of her mouth.

The opening strains of the national anthem began, played on the order's antique harmonium by Lord Macmillan. This signalled the end of the meeting, and they all stopped rubbing themselves with blood, stood to attention in a circle around the altar, and sang along with extraordinary fervour.

Chapter 15

As Wilberforce Selfram's life ebbs away,
Mrs Chapman has a thought

They all stood around him, looking down. 'We should call an ambulance,' said Mrs Bell.

'Negative,' whimpered the dying man. 'It would be of no assistance. One has campaigned for such vehicles to carry prunes, but to scant avail. Cutbacks are to blame. One would sooner perish in relative peace than spend one's final moments enduring futile attempts to extract the bolus.' He pointed before him with a long, grey finger. 'What is that one sees? Is it a vision, or a waking dream?' His eyes, already glassy, glazed over further still as he pawed the air before him. 'Is it a rainbow, or is it a bridge? Perhaps it is both. And what is that music one can hear? One always thought that in extremis one's cerebral cortices would generate perhaps *Density 21.5* by Edgard Varèse, or a selection of pieces from Karlheinz Stockhausen's *Stimmung*, yet this is not the case; one can hear instead the more mainstream strains of Antonín Dvořák's *Symphony Number 9: From the New World.'*

'Oh, I do like that,' said Mrs Bell. 'They used it in that Hovis advert, the one with the boy pushing his bike up the hill.'

'The symphony was composed in 1893,' explained Wilberforce Selfram. 'Though the brand you mentioned had been extant for some three years at this juncture, it was long before the widespread adoption of the television receiver and its eventual, some might say inevitable, descent into commercial broadcasting. You will extend the courtesy of allowing one to appreciate one's last ever earthly experience of music without having to think about sliced bread. Now, please, some peace for one's final moments upon this ever-revolving spheroid.'

'Would you like me to say a prayer?' asked the parson.

'Negative, parson,' droned Wilberforce Selfram. 'One is of a Hebrew persuasion, and irreligious to boot. Your Anglican wafflings would be inappropriate, and serve only to irritate; one is half in love with easeful death, and requests only quietude as one slips away.'

They stopped talking, all of them keenly aware of the ticking of what they had all now come to think of as *time's e'er-tocking clock*. In less than ten minutes it would be too late, and they tried to think of something they could do. Mrs Chapman was close to tears. She whispered something in Mrs Bell's ear.

'Brilliant, Rosemary,' said Mrs Bell. 'You're a genius.'

'Am I?'

'Yes.' Overriding the dying man's plea for silence, she continued. 'Mrs Chapman just said that it was all very sad, a bit like… What was it you said?'

'It's a bit like when someone's in hospital and there's a sign that says *Do not regurgitate.*'

'The word for which you are grasping,' corrected Wilberforce Selfram, 'is resuscitate.'

'Yes, it is,' said Mrs Bell, 'but Mrs Chapman's mix-up gave me the idea that if the thesaurus can't come out the conventional way, perhaps…well, perhaps you could sick it back up. Do you think you could try, Mr Selfram?'

He pondered for a while. 'One supposes one could make an attempt. Bring one a befitting receptacle.'

The parson dashed off to the cupboard under the stairs and returned with an orange B&Q bucket. Wilberforce Selfram was propped up, and the bucket was placed in his lap. He tried a bit of dry heaving, and with the encouragement of the others he stuck his fingers down his throat, but in spite of some dramatic retching nothing came up. After a few tries it became clear that the paper had gone too deep into his belly. He lay down once again.

'That's it, I'm calling an ambulance,' said the parson.

'You would deny a man his dying wish?'

The parson stayed where he was, and the room fell silent.

Again, it was Mrs Chapman who broke the silence. 'I've just had a thought,' she said, in a whisper. 'An idea that may save this poor man's life.'

'Tell us, Mrs Chapman,' whispered Mrs Bruschini

as quietly as she could, which was still considerably louder than the average voice, 'for the schoolchildren's sake.'

'It's rather delicate I'm afraid, and I wouldn't have dreamt of mentioning it if there wasn't a crisis happening, but you know Mr and Mrs Preston who live in that nice white cottage on the other side of the village green?'

'Yes, I know them very well,' said Mrs Bell, who was involved in every community initiative going. 'They're a lovely couple.'

'Yes, they are, but I've noticed something lately, which is that Mr Preston has been walking a bit funny, and wincing a lot.'

'I've noticed that too, but just like you I've not wanted to say anything. It doesn't do to ask personal questions.'

'It's crossed my mind that he might have...you know... Oh, I don't like to say the word.'

'Could you write it down for us?'

She nodded.

The parson opened a drawer, found a pen and a sheet of paper, and laid them in front of Mrs Chapman. She took the pen in a trembling hand.

'Take your time, Mrs Chapman,' said Mrs Bell.

A moan came from the makeshift death bed.

'Perhaps not too much time. What would the first letter be?'

Mrs Chapman slowly formed the letter H.

'Very good, Mrs C. Now what comes next?' urged the parson.

A while later the H had been joined by an E, an M,

another E, and an R. 'I'm not sure I'm spelling this correctly,' she said, blushing bright red. 'There is a shorter word for it, but I prefer to use the longer one. It sounds more decent.'

'Under the circumstances do you think you might use the shorter word?' asked Mrs Bell.

'I still would rather not,' said Mrs Chapman.

'A woman after one's own heart,' piped up the patient. 'A rule of thumb by which one has written since one's young manhood is that *a longer word is a better word*. One is now less than seven minutes from reaching the banks of the River Styx and pressing a pound coin into the palm of the nearest psychopomp, and one does not wish to spend one's final moments bearing witness to the slipping of Mrs Chapman's hitherto exemplary standards.'

A few more letters were written down, and the parson worked it out. 'Haemorrhoids!' he cried.

'That's it I'm afraid,' said Mrs Chapman. 'And if he has…those unfortunate things that the parson said… then perhaps he's been on a special diet to keep things soft.'

'Mrs Chapman, you've done it again. I'll call Mrs Preston right away.' Mrs Bell pulled her phone from her bag, and quickly found the number. She put it on speaker so everyone could hear. After a long time the call was answered. 'Oh? Hello? Is that you, Susan?'

'Hello Iris, yes it's me, Susan.'

'Hello Susan. I thought it might be you because your name came up on the screen. Aren't these things clever?'

'They really are. Now, I'm going to ask you a

question, and it may seem a little blunt, but it's very important and I'll explain everything later.'

'Very well.'

'Does Malcolm have piles?'

'Oh dear, yes I'm afraid he does.'

'Good.'

'Oh no, it's not good. Poor Malcolm.'

'I'm sorry Iris, I didn't mean it like that. It must be awful for him. I'd better explain after all…' She told Mrs Preston about the paper, and how they only had a few minutes before it would be too late. 'And we were wondering, well it was Mrs Chapman who thought of it, whether you happened to have five kilogrammes of prunes?'

'Five?' cried Mrs Preston. 'Five hundred, more like. We buy them from bulkbuyprunesonline.com. Or, now I come to think of it, maybe it's bulkbuyprunesonline. co.uk.'

'Oh Iris, whichever it is, could we have some?'

'Of course you can. I'll measure them out right away.'

'I'll go and fetch them,' said Mr Bell, glad that again he had something to do, and that he could now consolidate his role in the unfolding drama.

Mrs Bell accompanied him to the front door and told him to run like the wind. 'Think of the theme from *Chariots of Fire*,' she said. The music played in her mind as she watched him running heroically across the village green, just missing the guy ropes of the big marquee. His regular badminton sessions had stood him in good stead. Bursting with pride, she returned to the kitchen and joined the others as they watched the clock. There were just four minutes left.

'You hang in there, Mr Selfram,' said Mrs Bell. 'We're not going to let you die there on the ground.'

'One is not dying on the ground, one is dying on the floor.'

'Either way, David is going to get you your prunes, so keep your spirits up.'

'One is beginning to wonder whether the floor really was the optimal location for one's final breath. Perhaps one should have ventured outside and perished as Beoffrey might have done, amid crowflowers, nettles, daisies and long purples.'

The clock continued to tick, and with only twenty seconds left before it would have been too late, Mr Bell returned, puffed-out but elated, and carrying a different orange B&Q bucket, this one half-filled with prunes.

Wilberforce Selfram found himself being propped up by the parson and Mr Bell, and the bucket was set on his lap. In went his long, grey fingers, and they picked out a prune. He appraised it, and must have found it met his standards, as he put it in his mouth, chewed, and swallowed. He did this again, and again, and soon he was eating them with the same level of frenzy with which he had eaten the thesaurus. In a few minutes they were all gone.

Something returned to his cheeks; something that could not quite be described as colour, but whatever it was signalled the passing of a crisis. 'One can sense the commencement of agglutination,' he said. 'One is at last confident that one's bowels will regain their equilibrium, and that one shall not expire.'

'Excellent,' said Mrs Bruschini. 'A car will be here to collect you at nine o'clock sharp tomorrow morning. Be ready and presentable. Good day to you all.' And with that she swept away.

Wilberforce Selfram rose to his feet and loomed over them once again. 'Not for the first time, one has narrowly escaped the clutches of the Grim Reaper, or *Śmierć* if you prefer. Above all, one owes one's life to…' They all held their breath; it was as if he was about to reveal the identity of a murderer. His long, grey finger pointed first at the ceiling, and then directly at his saviour. '…Mrs Chapman.'

And down she went. As she was made comfortable, and smelling salts were once again administered, Wilberforce Selfram continued. 'Since she appears to be unconscious, one shall tell you of her surprise reward. When back in civilisation, one shall send her a John Cale CD and a bunch of Lebanese grapes; in show business this is the standard bounty proffered when one's life has been plucked from the ravening jaws of doom. You may be surprised, perhaps even shocked, by one's declaration that one is engaged in "show business", when you know only too well that one's oeuvre is held in such extraordinarily high regard that it has been translated into numerous foreign languages, and has been the subject of many a doctoral thesis. Rival authors have even been known to write novels with a character clearly based on oneself at their core. Though they decry one, one's nemeses are unable to tear their eyes away – one is the maypole around which they frolic. Further to this, one's wordsmithery is also often to be found in the broadsheet newspaper and the journal of note, and one frequently broadcasts to the nation on any number of serious topics through the dual media of television and radio. Alongside one's higher pursuits, however, one has also appeared as a much-requested wireless panellist upon BBC Light Programme broadcasts, and as an extremely successful comedian upon the stand-up circuit. One informs, educates and entertains.' Wilberforce Selfram carried on with this speech, though nobody heard the rest of it. The thunder of the machine in the marquee had started up again, rendering him inaudible. Not that they minded; they hadn't really been listening anyway.

Chapter 16

Ayanna hands in her notice, but hits a snag before
almost getting into a fight and missing her bus

When Wilberforce Selfram and Harry Johannes had finally left her office, Ayanna typed her resignation, printed it, signed it, and took it to Human Resources.

The manager was there, but so were the Duke and Duchess of Bloomsbury. While her husband stood at the window with an invisible machine gun, imagining he was slaughtering pigeons on nearby rooftops, the Duchess of Bloomsbury took over proceedings. She was greeted with a smile. 'Hello. It's Ariana, isn't it?'

'Ayanna.'

'Close enough. What can we do for you?'

'I've decided I'm leaving,' she said, and handed over the letter.

The letter was brief and polite. The Duchess of Bloomsbury read it, and made a sad face. 'I'm so sorry,' she said. 'Have you found another position?'

'I'm going back to my old job. I'm just not happy here. To be honest I feel like I've been stuffed in a cupboard to do things no one else wants to do.'

'That's exactly right. Most people start in the Rowling Room. All entry-level positions across the industry are similar to yours; some great careers have begun in cupboards.'

Ayanna hadn't heard it called *the Rowling Room* before. 'Maybe, but it's not just that. I don't think I fit in here. It's nothing personal; it's the whole industry, not just you lot. If I thought it was for me, I might put up with it, but it's not. And the money's not great; I can hardly afford to eat.'

She had taken a forty per cent pay cut to do this job, and had to pay peak prices for the commute. After her wages went in, all she had to show for her labours was a terrifyingly expanding overdraft. She had formed the impression that most people in the business had money coming in from elsewhere, on top of their salaries.

On work nights out, when the employees of various publishing houses had mingled, she had found herself in groups containing men with floppy hair and tailored suits, who looked like they belonged, slightly blurry, in the background of a Merchant-Ivory film, and women who looked as though they had stepped out of a Toast catalogue; she could picture them, angular and impatient, wearing linen on a jetty. She had overheard talk of cottages in Southwold, weekends in Paris, and dinners at restaurants with expensive-sounding names; there was no way all this could have been funded on the low wages that she had been primed to expect if she was to stay in the business.

She had kept quiet; she didn't think anyone needed to know that she was struggling to maintain a small and dark room in an unhappy flat share in an inconvenient part of an unfashionable suburb. If she'd loved the work she would have felt differently, but she didn't love the work. She'd had a try, but it wasn't what she'd thought it would be, and it was time to move on. Books were for reading, not for…whatever this was.

'It's a tremendous pity, but if you're sure.'

'Yeah.' Earlier in the day she would have carefully said *yes*, but she didn't care any more. Fuck it. She was going back to Croydon. 'I'll work my notice if you want, but I'd be just as happy not to come back on Monday.'

'We can wrap all this up now. Better to get it over with. I'll just sort out the paperwork.' The Human Resources manager looked awkward as the Duchess of Bloomsbury commandeered her computer, tapped away for a while, and printed off a sheet of paper. 'Just sign here to say you won't be back,' she said. Ayanna signed. 'And how would you like to pay?'

'Pay?'

'Of course,' said the Duchess of Bloomsbury, looking surprised. 'Cash, cheque, banker's draft. Whichever suits you.'

'What do you mean *pay*?'

'The early severance supplement. It covers our costs. Recruitment is a pricey business these days, and if people won't stay…'

'How much…?'

'Let me see…' She looked at the computer screen.

'Eight thousand four hundred and thirty-nine pounds and seven pence. We can waive the seven pence.'

'Eight and a half grand? I ain't got that kind of money.'

'Then that puts us in a bit of a spot, doesn't it? You did read the contract, didn't you?'

It had been thirty pages long, and although she had read it, she hadn't been sure what all of it had meant. They'd assured her that it was all very standard. Ayanna wished she had read it more thoroughly, and asked questions, but it was too late now.

'I'm not sure there's anything we can do,' said the Duchess of Bloomsbury, looking at the form Ayanna had just signed.

There was a long silence as Ayanna tried to work out how she was ever going to be able to raise so much money. Even if she could, somehow, borrow it, it would take years to pay back. She felt like beating herself up for having been so stupid as to sign something without properly understanding it.

'I suppose I could…' said the Duchess of Bloomsbury. Instead of finishing her sentence she took hold of Ayanna's letter of resignation and the signed severance form between manicured forefinger and thumb, then walked across the room to the shredder and held the papers over its mouth.

Ayanna couldn't see another way out. She nodded. The Duchess of Bloomsbury let the papers go, and the machine whirred. Ayanna watched as her mistake was sliced into thousands of tiny pieces.

'Have a super weekend,' smiled the Duchess of Bloomsbury. 'Anything planned? Meeting your boyfriend, perhaps? Or girlfriend?'

Ayanna would not be drawn. She didn't feel it was any of her boss's business what she did in her free time. 'I'll take it as it comes.'

'Good, good. I'll be sure to look in on you next time I'm in the office.'

Ayanna left the room. The HR manager was ashen. 'I've not heard of an early severance supplement before. I'm not entirely sure that was quite in line with industry protocol, your grace,' she said.

'Industry protocol? Oh please.'

Ayanna went back to her nook. If she was going to be stuck here, she was going to make some changes. The first thing she did was take the folding chairs and hide them in a cleaning cupboard a long way away. If those two were going to come into her office and stare at the phone for hours they would have to do it standing up.

She picked up her bag, and left. As she walked towards the bus stop, she felt a tugging at her arm. She was in a bad enough mood already, and now someone was trying to mug her. She clenched her fist and turned, ready to flatten them, but it was only the Human Resources manager, looking terrified. 'You didn't hear this from me,' she whispered, 'but the severance supplement is a load of crap. Your contract's completely normal. You're free to go, you don't have to pay anything. Just don't come in on Monday, and I'll sort out the paperwork.'

'Thanks,' said Ayanna, lowering her fist. 'But you know what? I am coming back on Monday.'

'OK… I'm glad. But don't feel alone. There are others like you. Like…us. I live above a kebab shop in Catford. I'm subletting off a friend, and the landlord doesn't know. We're here in the business – at every publishing house there are a few of us. Normally we're not at the glamorous end of things, but we're here. We've learned to blend into the background; it's the only way to survive.

'I've worked at a few publishers now, and I've learned things. Things about *them*, the ones at the top who waft around. I can tell you stories you wouldn't believe. They're all in this weird club; they think it's a big secret, but we all know about it. They take their clothes off and smear…' She looked panicked. 'We never had this conversation.' She turned, and quickly walked away.

Ayanna watched her go, wondering what sort of world she'd got herself into. Why had the Duchess of Bloomsbury been so keen to keep her on? Things were going to get a lot more interesting from now on; she would see to it. And now she knew the severance supplement was a load of bollocks, she had nothing to lose.

She walked on towards the bus stop. She decided she would still call in at the yard the next day. Her old boss might even give her some work straightaway. He always had trouble covering shifts on weekends, and it was helpful for him to have a few people around who weren't particularly interested in football. She didn't want to stay so long away from the LGVs that she forgot how to drive one, and the extra money would be a big help.

She reached the bus stop, and took out her book as she waited. She was so engrossed in it that she missed the first bus that came by, and had to wait fifteen minutes for the next one. She missed that too.

Chapter 17

*Wilberforce Selfram responds strangely to some watercolours,
and at last the festival begins*

The crowd in the kitchen had broken up. It hadn't
been much more than an hour since Mrs Chapman
had first been startled by the stranger in the kitchen,
but she had been through an awful lot in that time,
and it was generally decided that it would be best for
her to be seen home by Mr and Mrs Bell. Now only the
host and his guest remained. 'Parson,' said Wilberforce
Selfram, 'one believes you to be the proprietor of this
xenodochium. One wonders whether this moment
might present an apposite opportunity for you to play
Tenzing to one's Hillary and guide one upward, to
one's quarters.'

'Absolutely,' said the parson. 'I suppose you'll be
wanting to sleep until dusk.'

'Negative. One's journey has now reached its

conclusion, so one shall endeavour to realign one's circadian rhythm with that of the more conventional habitants of this fractured isle. One shall unpack one's ganderbag, encharge one's computer and re-join the contemporary epoch.'

'I'll show you to your room.'

Wilberforce Selfram's room was on the top floor; his head nearly touched the sloping ceiling even at its highest point, so he had to stoop as he moved around. The parson enquired of his meal plans. 'Let me know when you fancy a bite to eat. How long does it take to build up an appetite after scoffing a thesaurus and a gallon of prunes?'

'One's onomasiological culinary activities customarily see one replete for a number of hours. One is doubtful that one shall be requiring sustenance until one breaks one's fast upon the morningtide.'

'I'll get something ready at about eight. I've got the usual sort of stuff: toast; cereal; nothing fancy. We have a hedgehog come to the garden some nights; I could wait in the dark and see if I can get it with a cricket bat, and you can have it on toast.'

Wilberforce Selfram's eyes grew wide, and his face lightened to the very palest of greys. 'Negative,' he said. 'One shall never consume a hedgehog.'

'I was only joking,' said the parson, dismayed to have caused what seemed to be genuine alarm. 'I wasn't really going to hunt a hedgehog for your breakfast. Anyway, if you get peckish there's plenty in the fridge. There's no shortage of slugs in the garden too. Just help yourself.'

*

With the parson gone, Wilberforce Selfram looked around the room. Hanging on the walls were watercolours of countryside scenes. His reaction to such paintings was always the same, and he tried to suppress it. *Negative,* he thought to himself, *one must not think this way.* But it was too late. He *had* thought that way.

He had been given the Wi-Fi password, and he plugged in his laptop and sat it on the antique bureau near the socket. As he waited for it to charge enough to start up, he crossed the landing and ran a bath. Soon the water was covered in a film of dirt, and a layer of grit lined the bottom of the tub. As he got out, he noticed a woodlouse floating on the surface of the water, but he didn't pluck it out and eat it; instead, he watched it flailing on its back as it circled the plughole before disappearing into the pipework. He rinsed himself under the shower, towelled himself dry and, having made the decision to remain in the parsonage until the morning, changed into his nightgown and nightcap.

Back in his room he approached his computer with some trepidation. As much as he had missed it, he knew it contained things it really shouldn't; things that he sometimes felt he ought to expel from his life for fear of the consequences if news of them was ever to get out. With the watercolours on the wall, and the talk of hedgehogs, it was almost becoming too much to bear. He faced the inevitable, closed the curtains, opened the computer, and switched it on. It whirred, and the screen lit up. He knew there would be a lot waiting for him. He typed an unusually long row of asterisks into the password box, and the modern world was open to him again.

As the afternoon went by, the machine in the marquee juddered a few more times, and the leaded panes rattled. When at last the computer was fully charged, Wilberforce Selfram unplugged it and took it with him to the bed.

For the first time since leaving his home he felt the softness of a mattress and freshly laundered cotton sheets, and though he tried to fight it he couldn't help but accept that the feeling was preferable to lying on mud under some sticks, with decaying leaves pressed over his eyes. He was going to sleep incredibly well. He looked forward to breakfast, too. The parson had mentioned cereal and toast, and for a long time he was lost in the thought as he fantasised about marmalade and Frosties.

Earlier, in the kitchen, he had really thought that he had meant everything he had said about continuing his diet of slugs, but at last he began to admit to himself that he had not enjoyed the food he had eaten on his journey. He would be returning to fairly normal eating habits, and giving lice, centipedes and raw mangelwurzels a wide berth for some time to come. The slugs, in particular, had been a trial.

'Beoffrey, forgive one,' he mumbled, then he turned his attention to the urgent business he had found in his inbox on his return to the twenty-first century. He had a lot to catch up with.

As the afternoon went on there came the chatter of a crowd as the village green filled with revellers waiting for the festival to begin. At two minutes past seven there was a roar of applause, and a compère took to the microphone. The windows in Wilberforce Selfram's attic were original, and single-glazed, and the sound carried so clearly that the compère might as well have been in the room with him. 'Ladies and gentlemen,' boomed the voice, 'will you please welcome to the stage, for the inaugural event of this, the first ever Big Bottoms Book Festival, the author of numerous bestsellers, many of which have been adapted into popular films and television shows...'

Wilberforce Selfram looked into the lens of the imaginary camera. 'One despairs,' he said. He pulled his nightcap down over his ears. He didn't want to hear any of this.

Friday

Chapter 18

*Wilberforce Selfram's primary school visit
goes surprisingly well*

The engagement at Lower Bottom Primary School had got off to an uncomfortable start when Wilberforce Selfram was ushered into a corridor and shown a gallery of portraits of himself that the children had been working on as their art project for the week. In some he was just a stick figure, and in others he was nothing more than a head with arms and legs jutting out in apparently random directions. In most he was smiling, a broad grin bisecting a plump pink face, and in one he appeared to have a blond bubble perm. True likenesses were thin on the ground.

'One despairs,' he had said, looking away from Ms Dmochowski, the deputy head teacher who had been giving him the tour, and into the lens of the imaginary camera.

Irked by his reaction, Ms Dmochowski tersely showed him through to the staff room, and asked him whether he would like a cup of tea. Rather than give a straightforward *yes*, or even a slightly less straightforward *affirmative*, Wilberforce Selfram decided to deliver a grand declaration: 'Even this fractured isle's pre-eminent psychogeographer requires, on occasion, liquid sustenance.'

'Yes,' said Ms Dmochowski, her eyes narrowing. She read the Sunday culture pages often enough, and in light of his response to the children's artwork she decided to administer a low blow. 'I suppose Iain Sinclair must get a little thirsty from time to time. But how about you, Mr Selfram? Would *you* like a cup of tea?'

Wilberforce Selfram stared at Ms Dmochowski, who stared back.

'I'll come and get you when it's time to go through,' she said, before leaving him alone in the staff room, where he sat on a padded vinyl chair and wished he had said, simply, *That would be very nice. Thank you.*

It had been a frosty start, but thirty minutes later he was on stage, the children were rapt, and he was drenched in sweat as he declaimed and proclaimed. He had turned the morning into a triumph.

The day had begun with him waking refreshed after a long sleep in the attic of the parsonage, his first amid fresh linen for what seemed like aeons. He had showered, dressed, and gone downstairs for a hearty breakfast without a slug in sight. While he ate, he had treated his dining companion, the parson, to an unsolicited lecture about the differences and similarities between jams, jellies, marmalades, preserves and conserves. 'One's preference,' he declared, 'is for marmalade, as its name contains more letters than that of any of its rivals, and is consequently longer.' He had backed this up by getting through an entire jar of olde-English thick-cut.

At nine o'clock a car had come to pick him up. It had *Dave's Taxi* emblazoned on the side, and for the entirety of the seventeen-minute journey, Wilberforce Selfram had delivered his second monologue of the day, in which he told the driver about a novel he had written which starred a taxi driver by the name of Dave. 'That the sales were modest is not a reflection of its quality,' he explained, 'it is merely symptomatic of a broad cultural malaise.'

'Righto boy,' Dave had said, as he drew to a stop in front of a brick Victorian building. 'It sounds like a belter – I'll put it on me list. Here's the school. I'll stay put and take you back after.'

The event was in the hall. The school was a small one, and all sixty of the pupils, aged between four and eleven, were in situ and, just like their teachers, none of them quite knew what to expect. The visit had been set up in a single phone call from Mrs Bruschini, to whom the school secretary had found it impossible to say no, and now, after quite some dread, here it was.

When the long and glowering star attraction walked into the hall at precisely a quarter to ten, some of the younger children burst into tears and fled to the teaching assistants for a hug. The more adventurous ones, though, were intrigued by what they saw, and wondered what was going to happen next.

'Good morning boys and girls,' said Ms Dmochowski.

Good morning Ms Dmochowski, they trilled in return.

'This morning we've got a very special assembly because an interesting man is going to give us a talk. He's a writer called Wilberforce Selfram, and he's come all the way from London. Who here has been to London?'

A smattering of hands shot up, and one little girl, bobbing up and down with excitement, announced that when she was there, she had seen Big Ben.

'Lucky you,' said Ms Dmochowski.

'Allow one to interject,' said Wilberforce Selfram. He addressed the child who had just spoken. 'You say you saw Big Ben. Could you please describe precisely what you observed.'

The child looked confused, but Ms Dmochowski helped out. 'Tell us all about Big Ben, Ella.'

'Ooh, it's very high,' she said, 'and there's a big clock.'

'That,' said Wilberforce Selfram, 'is the most unusual description of a bell one has ever heard.'

There followed a good deal of confusion as Wilberforce Selfram explained to the child that Big Ben was merely the nickname of the Great Bell, which was situated within the Clock Tower of the Palace of Westminster. 'Though,' he expounded, 'the structure has recently been saddled with the somewhat unfortunate appellation *The Elizabeth Tower*. In order to see the bell from outside you would require X-ray vision. Do you have X-ray vision?'

Ella looked close to tears at the news that she hadn't really seen Big Ben. She shook her head, but other hands shot up, and a number of declarations of X-ray vision were made.

'It is imperative,' said Wilberforce Selfram, 'that today you all learn the first rule of psychogeography, which is to get the facts right. Carry this with you through life.'

Ms Dmochowski bristled. 'Children,' she said, though she was looking directly at her guest with her hands on her hips, 'Mr Selfram is just being silly. It's fine to call it Big Ben. Over the years it's become so well-established as the nickname for the whole building – tower, clock, bell and all – that it has become its *de facto* name. To correct somebody for calling it Big Ben would make you a…' She walked over to a whiteboard at the side of the stage and wrote on it: PEDANT. She underlined the word three times, then explained to the children what it meant.

'Standards in mainstream education,' Wilberforce Selfram sighed, 'are indubitably slipping. By any name, the structure is one of London town's gaudier sights. Perhaps, children, the next time you are in the great metropolis you might ask your parents and guardians to avoid the more obvious tourist locations, and to take you instead to see parts of the city that do not appear in the guide books; the, if you will, *real* London. One suggests you start with…' He went over to the whiteboard, erased Ms Dmochowski's *PEDANT*, and replaced it with *SPRINGBRIDGE MULTI-STOREY CAR PARK, EALING*. 'Visit this edifice, and evaluate its architecture – the expanse of external brick wall, blank but for graffiti and stains from ill-considered drainage outlets; its security fencing; its height barrier, which is almost Soviet in its utilitarian design, or rather lack of. You must go, children, and allow your young minds to drift as you absorb its presence; indeed as its presence absorbs you. Write an essay detailing your impressions of it, and your intellectual and emotional response to it, then junior psychogeographers you all shall be.'

Thus, the event began. Biting her tongue, Ms Dmochowski withdrew, and Wilberforce Selfram established himself on the centre of the stage, from where he began to tell the children about his early work, giving them an overview of a number of his publications. As things went along, his audience became quite mesmerised; even the ones who had been sobbing quietened down, lifted their faces and began to listen to the peculiar and oddly hypnotic droning sounds. The tall man had given them a few lines of their own so they could join in, and they listened out for their cues, ready to shout them out. For the last couple of minutes, he had been telling them all about how he had once been contractually obliged to deliver a novel, but having no ideas of his own had opted to rewrite Oscar Wilde's *A Picture of Dorian Gray*. His version, he explained, had not sold as many copies as he felt it should have done. 'One's book has substantially more pages than Wilde's, but why is this so? Does it contain more words? Negative. However, the words one employed were, on average, considerably longer than those used by Oscar Wilde. And as we all know, children, a longer word is...' He cupped an ear.

Well primed and practised by this point, the children knew exactly what to say. '...*a better word*,' they cried in unison. Even Ella was smiling again, and bouncing up and down as she shouted out.

'Correct. And better words make for better books; ergo one's book is better than Oscar Wilde's. There were some critics,' he monotoned, 'who concluded that anybody who had read and enjoyed the original would hardly be inclined to read a reworking of it, just as anybody who had *not* enjoyed the original would likewise give one's book a wide berth. Those critics were wrong. That it failed to strike a chord with the general reading public was symptomatic of...' Again he cupped his ear.

'...*a broad cultural malaise*,' the children chirruped, joyfully.

Dave was taken aback by the sight of his passenger as he flopped into the back seat. 'Caress me with a cauliflower,' he said. 'They been throwing buckets of water over you?'

'Negative. This is the perspiration of performance.' The applause was still ringing in Wilberforce Selfram's ears. 'One was, metaphorically, you understand, aflame. The symbiosis twixt speaker and audience was, certainly in one's own experience, unprecedented. Though they knew remarkably little, those children were perhaps the most receptive listeners to whom one has ever expiated. With young minds like these in maturation there is even hope for the future; hope that the wider populace will one day come out of the fug that envelops it, and that literary Modernism shall once again reign supreme, just as it did in times long past. One shall, of course, be at the very helm of this revival.'

'I'm glad it seemed to go well. Buckle up and we'll get you back to the parsonage.'

'As we traverse this bucolic locale one shall regale you once again with details relating to the novel one wrote about a taxi driver who went by the shortened version of the name David, videlicet *Dave*. Time constraints dictated that there was much one was obliged to omit on our journey hither, so one shall furnish you with further points of interest as we proceed upon our passage thither.'

'Fair enough,' said Dave. Wilberforce Selfram launched into another monologue, but Dave didn't really listen. He was too busy wondering what he was going to have for lunch.

Spotting a sign that told him Green Bottom was two miles away, Wilberforce Selfram made a sudden decision. Needing to know that he was not completely putting the ways of Beoffrey behind him, he asked Dave to pull over. 'One shall ambulate, indeed perambulate, through pasture and boscage for the remainder of one's journey. One feels a pressing requirement to interfuse oneself with the world outwith the confines of this vehicle.'

'Righto, boy,' said Dave. He let his passenger out and drove away, grateful for the peace and quiet.

Chapter 19

Ayanna stops caring, then starts caring again,
and makes her journey to Parsonage Cottage

On her return to the office, Ayanna made sure things changed. She had walked straight into Saturday work, and her boss had told her he was tearing his hair out, not that he had any hair, and wanted her back full-time. It was liberating to no longer care whether or not she got the sack at the publishing house. Back in the Rowling Room she lost her self-consciousness about her accent and let it sing out; she tore up the index card, and spoke to the people who called as though they were real human beings, which she supposed they were; she rigged up an answerphone message so she could be away from her desk for long periods, which she spent on the wander, sometimes answering other people's ringing phones to see what was going on, or picking up random manuscripts and taking them back

154

to her office, where she read them with her feet on her desk.

Through all this she noted the silent responses from her colleagues to her new modus operandi, and from that she gauged who were her allies and who weren't. Some were evidently big-eyes appalled, while others gave subtle signals with the corners of their mouths that they were willing her on.

Something else that had changed were the daily visits from Wilberforce Selfram and Harry Johannes. For the first couple of days, she felt the blessed relief of their absence, and she hoped they had found other interests to keep them busy, but halfway through the Wednesday morning they returned. After noting that the folding chairs were gone, Wilberforce Selfram pulled from an inside pocket something that looked like a truncheon, which he unfolded into a long stick with a small crossbar before propping himself up on it. Harry Johannes did the same. Wilberforce Selfram looked disparagingly at the other man's portable misericord. 'No doubt you found that mass-produced embarrassment at the supermarket, betwixt J-cloth and sprout.'

'Argos. Nine pounds ninety-five. They offered me a further twelve months' misericord cover for an additional one forty-nine, but I decided against it.'

Wilberforce Selfram scoffed. 'One's portable misericord was handmade in the Bulgarian city of Targovishte which, as one is sure you are cognisant, is the global capital of such items. One used the most highly regarded of that settlement's handcraftsfolk in order to ensure that it melded impeccably with one's anatomy. There was quite the waiting list. One reveres the misericordier above all other artisans, with the exception, perhaps, of the mighty cooper – one never ceases to be astonished by the way in which a wooden barrel does not leak.'

Ayanna hadn't really thought about the construction of old-fashioned barrels before, and had to admit to herself that she was pretty amazed by this too. She made a mental note to look up the technique on Wikipedia on her way home.

'Were one a manual craftsperson,' Wilberforce Selfram continued, 'one would be one or perhaps both of these; one is instead a cerebral craftsperson – an, if you will, artisan of words.'

'My portable misericord was made in a factory in Taiwan,' said Harry Johannes. 'I am of the people; I'm not bourgeois like you.'

'One is hesitant to stoop to rebut such accusations, though in this instance one feels compelled to point out that an appreciation of quality craftspersonship is not a bourgeois trait. One is substantially more *du prolétariat* than you are; let it be noted that one is considered, by ditching boy and baronet alike, to be a National Treasure.'

'No you're not.'

'One is. Just ask…'

'That's enough,' snapped Ayanna. She wasn't going to have this sort of bickering in her office. 'How was Durness, Harry?' she asked. 'Did you see that garden you were all excited about?'

'There was a bit of a mix-up there, but even so it felt invigorating to be back among my people, the Scots.'

'One has spent substantial swathes of time amid our Caledonian brethren,' put in Wilberforce Selfram. 'Unusually for one of a substantially English disposition, one finds oneself accepted by the inhabitants of the northernmost portion of this fractured isle. They are, to employ their own vernacular, muckle fond of one.'

'You will only ever be a visitor to that proudest of lands, Selfram,' put in Harry Johannes. 'Cut me, though, and I bleed shortbread. In fact, just last night I painted my face blue, and listened to The Proclaimers.'

Having lost patience with this, Ayanna decided to go for a wander. 'Don't you dare touch anything,' she said, and left the room.

Her wandering took her to the slush pile, the mountain of unsolicited manuscripts that had been sent in by people who didn't have an agent to plug their work on their behalf. Authors without agents are, she had learned, considered quite beyond the pale, and across the trade this pile is spoken of with exasperation, which attracted her to it all the more. She pulled out three random reams, and took them out of the office and on to the street. The morning was warm, and she sat on a bench in Soho Square.

The first one started with a couple, a lawyer and another lawyer, having an argument. There seemed to be some sort of affair going on. Thirty pages in, she knew the brand name of every appliance in their kitchen, but nothing else was clear so she gave up on it. The second one was basically *Jaws* but with an abominable snowman instead of a shark, and a ski resort instead of a beach. It was pretty good, but Peter Benchley's estate would probably have quite a lot to say about it, so she abandoned that one too. The third, though, a short novel called *Out of the Strong Came Forth Sweetness*, grabbed her by the throat and wouldn't let her go. She took it with her to a café, and finished it in the middle of the afternoon. Shaken by having read something so brilliant, she went back to the office.

Wilberforce Selfram and Harry Johannes were still there, perched on their telescopic misericords.

'You haven't touched anything have you?'

They shook their heads.

'You'd better not've done.' She looked around the room, as if checking to see whether any item of stationery had shifted position. Ignoring her visitors, she checked her messages and returned the calls she had received, disappointing the six people who had hoped to add a little star quality to their Harry Potter-themed events. Her visitors left without bookings.

She couldn't stop thinking about what she had just read, and wondering what she could do about it. This was why she had spent all those evenings typing up letters and sending them off to publishers in the hope that she could somehow get involved. Her time of being past caring was over. She mentioned the manuscript to her ally in HR, who told her there was going to be an acquisitions meeting the next day, and maybe she could wheedle her way in and mention it. She took the manuscript home with her and read it again, to make sure it was as good as she'd thought it was.

If anything, it was even better.

The next day the Duke and Duchess of Bloomsbury arrived at the offices shortly after lunch, and went straight through to the room where the acquisitions meeting was to be held. Everybody else was already there, waiting for it to begin. The Duke of Bloomsbury was put in the corner with some horse brasses, a cloth and a bottle of polish, and he got on with that while everybody else sat around the big table. Various titles were brought out and discussed, and in the midst of this the door opened. Ayanna walked in, put the manuscript on the big table and said, 'We've got to publish this. I've read over five thousand books, and this is one of the best ones yet. Top five.' At the age of eight she had started listing everything she read, and she hadn't stopped. She had completed five thousand two hundred and forty-one books, and abandoned eight hundred and seven for the crime of not being up her street.

'Well well, if it isn't our friend from Croydon,' said an icy Duchess of Bloomsbury. 'How nice to see you again. Well, I say *nice*, but this isn't how we behave in acquisition meetings.' Ayanna's face heated up. She imagined this was how being told off by a headteacher would feel, but she didn't know for sure because she had always been so well behaved at school – at least up until the sixth form, when her dad had been around a lot more than usual and, as tended to happen when he was in the picture, everything had gone wrong. Even then she hadn't got in trouble because her teachers had known what was going on and didn't want to add to her woes. 'Since you're still relatively new we'll let it pass. Good day to you.'

Ayanna pointed at the manuscript and tried to say *Read it*, but she couldn't make a sound. She turned and left. She had made a note of the author's details, so she could contact her. If nothing else she would be getting a fan letter.

Back in her office she sent Wilberforce Selfram and Harry Johannes away, and threw a stapler at the wall. The staples went everywhere, and she spent the next few minutes picking them up and putting them back in. The Duchess of Bloomsbury, on her way out of the building, put her head around the partition. 'I've had a look at your CV. It seems you're quite the driver. Would you mind doing a little of that sort of thing for us?'

Ayanna just stared at her.

'Splendid.'

And so it was that she had ended up transporting Wilberforce Selfram's personal collection of dictionaries and thesauruses, along with the reinforced trestle tables needed to house them alongside him on stage, to various stops on his endless tour of literary festivals. Sometimes he joined her in the cab, but this time he had gone ahead on foot. Something about some old papers that someone had found in a jug, or something.

She tended not to listen very closely. She had been planning on sneaking her boyfriend along with her, but one or two things had happened and suddenly he wasn't her boyfriend any more, so she travelled alone. Her heart, she had noticed with relief, had not broken. Not this time.

It had been a smooth journey on a warm, late summer day. She had set off early to beat the rush hour, and had stopped a couple of times along the way. Just before noon she was in the village, and scanning the houses along the green, trying to work out which of them was to be her home for the next two nights.

Chapter 20

The treasurer wakes up in an unexpected location,
Wilberforce Selfram (understandably for once) despairs,
and Ayanna meets a wild-eyed stranger on a garden path

The treasurer awoke from a night of broken sleep with a feeling of dread. He hadn't opened his eyes yet, and he hoped that when he did he would find that the last few days had been a terrible dream. At last, he dared to look, and there he was, in Mrs Bruschini's bed, and there she was, beside him – naked, wide awake, and looking at him. 'Good morning,' she said. 'I'll fetch you a coffee, my brave little gardener.'

It had all really happened.

The seduction had taken place a few weeks earlier, as they had sat side by side at the dining table in Honeysuckle Nook. It hadn't taken a great deal of effort. They had been going over the relative costs of various seating options when she had reached across the desk to get a pen, pressing her body into his as she did. He had not backed off, but had allowed the pressing to go ahead. A few minutes later she had reached for a pencil, and this time he also leaned his own body a little way in towards hers. And thus, it had been sealed.

'But what about Mr Bruschini?' he had asked, in a break from their long first kiss.

'Don't worry about him,' she said. 'Things are a little complicated between us, but you needn't concern yourself.'

He had done as he was told, and pushed her husband out of his mind as much as he could. He told himself that his love for the secretary was ancient history to him now; her chance had come and gone. Over the next few weeks, he and Mrs Bruschini had held a number of important book festival meetings together, just the two of them, and they had all ended in the same way. It was a kind of heaven for him to have this large, handsome and strident woman melt in his arms, and one night, as they lay together in the aftermath, he told her he would do anything for her.

'Anything?'

'Anything, Mrs Bruschini.'

He realised now that he must have meant it. The day before, he had returned from a trip to London that she had sent him on, a trip that had lasted several days, and to have done what he did while he was there proved that he was indeed ready to do anything for her. He was picturing himself in her garden, starring in a slow-motion horror movie. It was awful.

She could see the fear in his face. 'Don't worry,' she said. 'It'll be our little secret.' She kissed him, and the feelings came back. Again he felt as if he really would do anything for her. He only hoped that next time her request would be something a lot more hygienic, and less exhausting, and, above all, nowhere near as petrifying.

Back from his walk, Wilberforce Selfram strode into the big marquee on the village green to find Mrs Bruschini at the box office window, checking the sales for various events. They were going well. For the preceding few weeks she had, at Florence Peters' suggestion, been using the local shopkeepers as ticket agents. They were, by nature and necessity, extraordinarily persuasive; a customer at Brown Bottom Hardware Supplies, for example, might be hoping to find a replacement chain for their bathplug, and they would leave Brown Bottom Hardware Supplies with not only the exact chain they had been hoping for, but also clutching a pair of tickets to a talk by somebody they knew from the television, or, if they hadn't been so lucky, a writer of whom they had never heard. This way, most of the main-stage events had already sold out, and those that hadn't were close enough to count as a full house. 'Mr Selfram, how nice to see you,' Mrs Bruschini smiled. 'I hear from the school that your event passed without major incident.'

'If, Mrs Bruschini, by *without major incident* they

mean *with innumerable young minds opened to the power of long words and the possibilities of psychogeography*, then one can only affirm their statement.'

'I heard there was no swearing, which was my primary concern. What a pity, though, that you chose not to attend our inaugural event. It was a great success.' Nick Hornby's publisher had had the foresight to supply some nearby book groups with tickets, along with copies of his latest novel, thus ensuring questions that were mostly relevant. They also provided their own chair for the event, and made sure there were a couple of plants in the audience to steer things back on course when the questioning started to go adrift. 'Mr Hornby stayed on afterwards, chatting to people, and signing books and so on. He was ever so gracious.'

'This is not the Graciousness Olympics.'

'Evidently not. So how can I help you, Mr Selfram?'

'One felt one ought to scrutinise the venue in order to prepare oneself for one's address upon the morrowtide.'

'Mr Selfram, your event is not here, it is at the Upper Bottom Village Hall. We thought it would be best to hold it there so the children would have more room to run around.'

'Why, Mrs Bruschini, would children be running around?'

'They always get very excited when they're in costume.'

'Costume, Mrs Bruschini?'

'Come with me.' She guided him to a pin board that carried posters for a number of the festival's events. She proudly pointed one out:

****

FROM THE PEOPLE WHO BROUGHT YOU

HARRY

POTTER

WE PRESENT
BLOOMSBURY BOOKS AUTHOR

Wilberforce Selfram

PRIZE FOR BEST COSTUME
CAKES
TOMBOLA
SURPRISES
BOUNCY 'HOGWARTS' CASTLE

**Saturday 22nd September, 3-4.30pm: £5
(£3 children)**

****

'One despairs.'

'Don't forget your Writing Workshop at one o'clock,' she said. 'It's in the church hall; Mrs Bell will meet you at the parsonage and walk you there.'

'One can barely contain oneself,' he drawled. He left the marquee, and noticed Ayanna's vehicle pulling into the driveway of Parsonage Cottage. He almost smiled. 'One's pantechnicon of lexica,' he sighed. 'At last, civilisation.'

Though Wilberforce Selfram had styled it as a pantechnicon, it was really just a van. Ayanna had been entrusted to book it herself, and she had gone upscale, choosing a silver Mercedes from a firm that didn't splash their logo on the side panels. It had been a smooth ride, and a space had been left for her on the driveway, as the Bells had told her to expect.

She jumped out of the cab and was walking along the path to the front door to announce her arrival when a figure suddenly appeared, apparently from behind a bush, and stood in her way. It was a wild-eyed woman with scratches on her face and a feather duster in her hand. 'Beware,' she said, trembling and barely able to get her words out. 'Beware the white face.'

'Which one?' asked Ayanna. 'There's quite a lot to choose from.' She had seen nothing but white faces for the final fifty miles of her journey.

The woman pointed towards the top of the building, then, as if she had said too much, she vanished back in to the greenery. 'Interesting welcome,' Ayanna said to herself. She walked up to the house and knocked on the Bells' door. She would only have time to drop off her bag before leaving to get ready for the event.

She was greeted warmly and shown to her room.

It was on the top floor.

Chapter 21

Wilberforce Selfram meets the local writing community

Ayanna had set up Wilberforce Selfram's personal trestle tables in the church hall, a small room without a raised stage. Not wanting to risk coming into contact with Formica in a professional setting, he always eschewed his host venues' tables, and provided his own vintage wooden ones instead. They had once belonged to the Czech literary theorist Vratislav Effenberger, who had mainly used them for wallpapering but, according to the auctioneer, had written some essays at them too. They were heavy and awkward, but Ayanna handled them with ease. When they were set up, she laid out Wilberforce Selfram's books on them. Because this wasn't his main event, he was only using a fraction of his mobile library; even so, the display looked impressive as the author stood behind the centre of the row of tables, flanked by around a dozen volumes on each side, among them a Shorter Oxford, a Hobson-Jobson, an English to Kazakh, and some leather-bound tomes, including a set of antiquarian medical dictionaries. Their spines faced the audience.

At this personal appearance he was using the books mainly for aesthetic reasons, to underline that he was very much the gentleman of language, but he was ready to open one if need be, to find an obscure and probably longer synonym for a commonplace word. On his journeys in the passenger seat of Ayanna's van he had often told her how, when he was writing, he would reach for his thesaurus in order to expand the vocabulary of his readership. 'It is one's duty – duty, no less – to increase their knowledge,' he had explained, 'and as a custodian of the lexicon it is one's duty unto the words themselves to maintain their extant status.'

'But aren't these words underused because they're only for specialists, or because they've just not caught on?' she asked. 'It's natural selection, isn't it? Some words just fizzle out. And you know a lot of words already, so if even you have to look them up in a thesaurus, your readers will have to look them up in a dictionary to find out what you're gibbering on about.'

'One does not *gibber on*; one informs, educates and entertains.'

'You do gibber on a bit. Either way, even if they find out what it means they'll never remember it, and even if they do happen to remember it, they won't be able to use it without everyone thinking they're pretentious. And half the long words you use in your novels wouldn't even be in a normal dictionary, so they have to go on the Internet every other sentence just to work out what they're reading. Don't you think that makes it all a bit fussy? It's not so much enlightening as wilfully annoying. Wouldn't it be better to tell your stories using normal words? You might even sell more books that way.'

'One writes not to sell books, but to astonish.'

'You should try it one day, Selfram. Write a book using normal words; you might even enjoy it.'

This conversation had happened, in very slightly different forms, a number of times, and each time it reached this point, Wilberforce Selfram pretended he hadn't heard. If she carried on, he would say, 'One is, at this juncture, absorbed in the world of psychogeography, and requests the quiet of the catacombs.'

Though she would drop the subject, she wouldn't stay quiet. She had often wondered why, at his advanced age, he still felt the need to posture like a rebellious teenager, to always be so self-consciously outré. It seemed a little sad, and she had a feeling that there was another side to him, just out of reach, maybe even out of reach to him too. Sometimes she tried to lure it to the surface. She tried to interest him in things they saw; not the concrete footbridges, overgrown escape lanes and electricity substations that usually caught his attention, but things that normal people might like to see. If she ever spotted a hot-air balloon, which she often did, she would point it out to him, and she noticed he would drop his guard and gaze at it until it was out of view. One time he was so busy following a balloon's progress that they drove right past a cluster of decommissioned cooling towers without his even noticing. Another time they found themselves going at the same speed as a steam train as it ran along a heritage railway line parallel to the road. For a full minute they kept pace with the engine, and Ayanna, glancing over, was sure she could see childlike wonder in his eyes. She resolved to bring this out of him as often as she could.

There were plenty of times, though, when her patience snapped, and she would turn up the radio, drive on, and leave him to it. Even so, she quite enjoyed it when they bickered like an old married couple, and she suspected he did too.

Five minutes before the event, Wilberforce Selfram arrived, accompanied by Mrs Bell. He looked around at the audience: seven people had applied for the opportunity to read from their work and have it critiqued. They sat to one side, in a row, waiting their turn. Friends and other onlookers were allowed to buy tickets too, and with around three dozen people in the audience, the room felt quite full. Wilberforce Selfram was shown to his spot behind his table. Refusing the offer of a seat, he unfolded his misericord and assumed his position, extremely still and very much looming. Beside the tables was a lectern for the people reading their work; it was set at an angle so they could address both author and audience. Mrs Bell had volunteered to run the event, and as soon as the church bell had finished chiming one, she offered a warm welcome to all who had turned up, and gave a brief introduction to Wilberforce Selfram, telling the impressed attendees that he had published a number of books, and had walked all the way from London.

'Without further ado,' she said, 'please welcome Mrs Halcrow, who I'm sure a lot of you will know from her having run Select Attire, the clothes shop in Middle Bottom, until she retired last year.'

Shaking, Mrs Halcrow made her way to the lectern, and leaned into the microphone. 'Oh dear,' she said.

'Don't you worry Mrs Halcrow,' said Mrs Bell. 'There's no need to be nervous. Just take your time.'

'I know I'm being silly,' said Mrs Halcrow, 'but I've never spoken into one of these before, and there are so many people here.'

'We're all friends,' said Mrs Bell, desperately hoping that Wilberforce Selfram would be kind to her.

Mrs Bell's calming tones put her at her ease. 'Now,' started Mrs Halcrow, 'ever since I retired, I've been spending a lot of time on my sewing machine making wimples, and even designing my own patterns for them. I've brought one with me.' She reached into her bag, brought out a wimple, and put it on. There were murmurs of approval through the room. It was generally agreed that as wimples go, this was quite the specimen. 'I've decided to share everything I've learned, so I've written an instruction book for anyone who might be interested in taking up the hobby. A beginner's guide, if you like.'

Wilberforce Selfram stared at her, his face giving nothing away.

'It's almost finished, so I don't need any help with

the words, but I was wondering whether the writing expert – that's you Mr Selfram – would help me to pick a name for it. I would like it to be a bestseller, you see, and I realise you have to get the title right. Would you be kind enough to let me know what I should call it?'

'You must, surely, have ideas of your own?' he monotoned.

'Yes, I do have a few. *Straightforward Wimples* is one of them, and *Uncomplicated Wimples* is another. But I can't help thinking there's a catchier title out there, just beyond my reach.'

Wilberforce Selfram fixed her with a still gaze. 'You must call your book…' No stranger to stagecraft, he left a long pause before revealing his idea. Mrs Bell willed him to give the obvious answer. 'Ssssssss….' He strung out the first letter of his suggested title for a long time prior to launching into the word proper.

Good for you, Mr Selfram, thought Mrs Bell, on hearing the long s. *That's exactly what I was thinking.*

'…*Sblomtamgungulous Wimples*,' he said.

Oh, thought Mrs Bell. *Perhaps not.*

'I beg your pardon?' said Mrs Halcrow.

'*Sblomtamgungulous Wimples.*'

'Could you write that down for me?'

'With pleasure.' He did so, and held out the piece of paper for her to take.

Mrs Halcrow looked at it for a while. 'But what does it mean?'

'It means whatever you want it to mean, Mrs Halcrow. That is the beauty of it. Next.'

A mystified Mrs Halcrow took her seat, and she was soon replaced at the lectern by one Mr Fish, who presented a children's book called *Samuel Spaniel*, which was about a spaniel called Samuel. Wilberforce Selfram expressed interest in the way the title almost rhymed, but didn't quite. 'Rather Modernist,' he said. 'One is surprised to find oneself looking forward to learning of the antics of this hound.' In the event, though, the book really wasn't very Modernist at all. The dog just did a few cheeky things, and briefly got into trouble before being forgiven.

'Perhaps you could put in some longer words,' he said, by way of advice. 'Next.'

Wilberforce Selfram had failed to be enlivened by the following three writers, and he stood behind his table with a deathly face, complete with glassy eyes, as the penultimate entrant was signalled forward by Mrs Bell. The entrant took to the lectern. 'I'm going to read a little poem,' she said. 'I do hope you all enjoy it.'

'Poetry,' put in Wilberforce Selfram. 'The gay science. In this context the word *gay* is, of course, used in the archaic fashion, meaning *merry*, though throughout the annals of history, there have been many avidly homosexual poets. One is very much of a heterosexual persuasion, repeatedly so, yet one eschews the heterocracy and supports and applauds the same-sex fraternity, or indeed sorority. One hopes the verse we are about to hear will be Modernist in tone, or maybe Surrealist, perhaps after the influence of José Maria Hinojosa Lasarte, or Étienne Léro. Local poet: you may proceed.'

The poem began. It rhymed, it scanned, and it was about the poet tending her garden through the seasons. After a minute or two of *frost on the compost*, and *there I go, carrying my hoe*, she finished with a flourish:

"*As I walk back up the garden path,*
I am looking forward to my bath.
Then with my eye,
I do espy,
A butterfly,
As it flutters by."

Wilberforce Selfram's corpselike expression had not changed throughout.

There was a warm round of applause, and when it died down Mrs Bell took the floor, her face red. 'I'm very sorry everybody,' she said, 'but I forgot to give our poet a proper introduction. A lot of you know her already, but for those who don't, she is Miss Cooper. I'm so sorry Miss Cooper.'

'That's quite all right,' said Miss Cooper, looking anxiously towards the forbidding figure amid the books. She noticed a change in him.

'Cooper, you say?'

Miss Cooper nodded.

'*Miss* Cooper?'

Another nod.

'A spinster of this parish?'

'Yes, I suppose I am.'

'Read your verse again.'

Miss Cooper ran through her poem once more, and this time Wilberforce Selfram was rapt. When she finished it, he applauded. He was joined by the rest of the attendees.

'That,' said Wilberforce Selfram, 'was extraordinary. Your poem is clearly a metaphor for the bleak condition of this fractured isle. The compost needs, of course, no further explanation, likewise the hoe. And oh, how you end it with the image of a butterfly, giving us all hope, and yet…it flutters by, and all hope is lost.'

'Really?' she said. 'I had no idea.'

Wilberforce Selfram's eyes widened. 'An *idiot savant*. This is even better than one had thought. Miss Cooper, on Monday morning one shall telephone Roger Daltrey and tell him all about you. Herr Daltrey, as one is sure you are aware, maintains the position of editor at the ancient publishing house of Faber and Faber. With one's recommendation, he will snap you up. *And,*' he mumbled, inaudibly to those around him, '*furnish one with a six-figure finder's fee.*'

'Really, Mr Selfram? Do you think Mr Daltrey will like my little poems?'

'Like them, Miss Cooper? They will transport him. Come, stand before one.'

She shuffled forwards and stood before the table, her back to the audience.

'Present your hands for inspection,' he droned, and she held them out, palms upward.

'Affirmative. It is here: the cooper's crease.' He pointed at a distinct mark going across her fingers. 'Ladies and gentlemen,' he intoned, 'We have before us not only an unacknowledged legislator of the world, but a scion of noble barrel-makers of yore. The very finest of craftspeople, the cooper, in bending all that metal into circles and wood into curves, finds himself with a permanent crease across his fingers, thus. Show them, Miss Cooper.'

She self-consciously turned and held up her hands, to a chorus of gasps.

'So deeply ingrained is this crease that it is handed down from generation to generation. Truly, the blood of epochs of mighty artisanship courses through your veins, Miss Cooper, and your poetry reflects this.'

She stood in silence for a moment, looking bewildered. 'I'm afraid there's been a bit of a mix-up,' she said. 'You see I'm not really a Cooper.'

'Not a Cooper?'

'No. Well, I *am* a Cooper, but when I was a baby I was adopted by a nice family called the Coopers. When I grew up I found out what my name would have been if I'd stayed with my birth family.'

'Tell one.'

'Baxter.'

'Baxter?'

She nodded.

'Baxter. Baxter.' Wilberforce Selfram was thinking aloud. 'If coopers make barrels, bakers make bread, fletchers make arrows, and so forth, then baxters make...' his eyes widened further still as the realisation struck him, '...soup. You are the descendent of simple potagiers.'

'Perhaps I am,' she said. 'I'd not really given it much thought.'

'But what of the cooper's crease?'

'I'm in the middle of an embroidery project, and I was spooling some thread while I was waiting for my slot. At one point I got into quite a tangle and I suppose it must have left these marks.'

Wilberforce Selfram sighed through his nose. 'Upon reflection, one has decided to withdraw one's support for the publication of your work. One has decided one did not like your poem after all. Good day to you, madam. Next.'

Miss Baxter was ashen as she returned to her seat. Mrs Bell put an arm around her. 'You take no notice,' she whispered. 'You send your poems to Roger Daltrey anyway; I'm sure he'll think they're super.'

There was one more writer to go, but everybody in the room had somewhat lost heart with the event, and just wanted it to be over. This entrant was from Ireland, and was in The Bottoms visiting her aunt, who had persuaded her to read the opening chapter of a novel she had written, called 'Attacked by Jellyfish!!!'.

Wilberforce Selfram was not impressed. 'It lacks literary ambition,' he said. 'By which one means the words are too short. One despairs of the younger generation.'

The writer looked daggers at him as she returned to her seat, and with that the event was over. Mrs Bell thanked the writers and the audience for coming, and Wilberforce Selfram for his insights, and the crowd began to disperse.

The Irish writer's aunt was fuming. 'You ignore him,' she said. 'You can tell he feels threatened by younger people coming along and writing well, and potentially being given attention that he believes is due to him, so he tries to sharp-elbow them out of the picture by making catty comments. You send it to the Roger Daltrey people – they'll publish it, mark my words.'

'Maybe I will, auntie,' she said.

'Just one thing,' said the aunt. 'I'm not sure about you calling it 'Attacked by Jellyfish!!!'. I mean, it doesn't have much to do with the book; as far as I can see there aren't any jellyfish in it at all, let alone aggressive ones. Why don't you call it, oh I don't know, *Ordinary People*, or something like that?'

'I'll have a good think about it, auntie.'

As people filed out, Wilberforce Selfram continued to stand behind the table, propped up by his misericord. His mind was on the event, and it kept returning to some of the work he had heard; Samuel Spaniel in particular, and the poem about the garden. In the time that had elapsed since dismissing them they had evoked certain feelings in him, feelings that he wished he could suppress, but was unable to do so.

Ayanna loaded the books and the tables into the van, and drove the short distance back to Parsonage Cottage. She parked up and went indoors, hoping her duties were over until the next day. She'd spotted the village pub, The White Horse, and hoped to spend some time in there later on. After a minute of bonding with Bevis in the hall, she went up to the top floor. As she turned on to the landing, she stopped. There, in her path, was a man. His face was white, brilliant white, and featureless. He was moving swiftly towards her, and she remembered the words of the strange, scratched woman with the feather duster.

Beware the white face.

Chapter 22

*Ayanna has little patience
for the figure with the white face*

On seeing the man racing towards her, Ayanna knew exactly what to do. From a young age her uncle had taken her along to his boxing gym, and she still went from time to time. Though she had never got into the sport as a competitor, she appreciated the training, and over the years she had fine-tuned her reflexes and built a solid repertoire of hooks and jabs. On her bad days at work, she had always taken comfort in the belief that if it came to it, she could beat the shit out of any one of her colleagues. This, though, was the only time she had ever had cause to use her skills outside the gym.

Just at this moment the machine in the main marquee chugged into life, and though there were people in the house none of them heard the *Oof* that came out of the man's mouth as Ayanna's fist pounded into his solar plexus, nor the next two punches, one to his chest and the other to his left shoulder, nor the thump as he fell to the floor. She could see now that the white face was a bare plastic mask. For a long time he lay there, holding his belly while he tried to get his breath back. She stood over him, poised to renew her defence if he tried anything funny. The machine stopped, the room fell quiet, and from behind the mask came a wheezing voice. 'I was just going to the toilet,' he explained. 'I'm desperate. Let me past and I'll explain everything when I've finished.'

She stood aside as he got up and, bent over, walked down the steps to the shower room on the half-landing. She heard a powerful stream through the door. It went on for ages, so if nothing else that part of his story checked out.

While she was waiting, she looked out of the landing window and over to the village green and the marquee. It was busy; Book Buses were dropping off their passengers outside the tent, and lots of people were standing around with a programme in one hand and a complimentary cocktail in the other. She had a running order in her pocket, and checked it. Salman Rushdie was due on in a few minutes, and security had been beefed up accordingly. There was a police presence, and everybody filing into the tent had to do so past uniformed security guards, who were checking bags. She recognised the familiar tweedy and squat figure of Florence Peters, who often seemed to be lurking around these events. Ayanna's eyes followed her as she walked down the side of the tent and in through an unmarked flap. She seemed to know her way around. Ayanna spotted Wilberforce Selfram there too, loitering on the periphery.

'Sorry I startled you,' said the voice from behind the mask. 'I can't see very well through this thing. The eye holes are quite small, and I didn't know you were there.'

'You know I'm here now, so why don't you take it off?'

'I'd rather keep it on, if that's OK. I always wear it.'

'How do you eat?'

'I sort of lift it out a bit at the bottom.' He demonstrated.

'Oh.' It was hard to know how to continue the conversation after that. She certainly wasn't going to apologise for having thumped him; she would do the same again. 'Who are you?'

'I'm Richard. I live here. I'm their son.'

'OK. So what's with the mask?'

'I'm part of a group called Incognito. We do things on the Internet, activism and stuff, and we all wear these masks.'

She shook her head in disbelief. She was about to say something, but thought better of it. There was a sadness about him, and she didn't want to make things worse. 'Why don't you take it off?' she asked.

'I can't.'

'Yes you can. Just try.'

'But why?'

'For one thing it gives me the willies. I'm staying

here for the next couple of nights and I don't want to share a landing with…*that*.' He still didn't move to take off his mask. 'It's up to you. If you want to be another white-faced "freedom fighter" on the Internet, I'll leave you to it.'

She walked past him to her room.

'Wait,' he said.

She turned and looked at him. Slowly he put a hand to his face and lifted the mask.

Ayanna had not thought about what would be behind it, but when she looked back on this moment, she admitted to herself that if she had been expecting anything it would have been a sallow face, a salad of bumfluff and pimples. It certainly wouldn't have been what she saw. His mask was in his hand now, and before her was a quite beautiful sight – full lips, and soulful brown eyes set in clear, smooth skin. She noticed how his shaggy brown hair had a curl to it, and the light that was streaming through the leaded landing window revealed it to have a hint of chestnut.

'Hello Richard,' she said, unclenching her right fist and extending her hand. 'I'm Ayanna.' As the hand came towards him, he flinched. Then, nervously, he reached forward, and shook it. 'Now,' said Ayanna, finally letting her left fist unclench too, 'let's get to the bottom of this.' She cracked her knuckles.

She decided she needed some caffeine to get her through her interrogation of the unmasked boy, and went down to the kitchen. Richard had offered to do the honours, but Ayanna had found she liked the adventure of walking around this lovely big old house by herself, so she insisted he stay put. Mrs Bell was there. 'Hello Ayanna,' she said. 'Do you have everything you need?'

'I just came down to get a coffee.'

'I'll show you where all the bits and pieces are.' She lowered her voice as she reached for the cafetière. 'There's something I'd better tell you,' she said, 'because I don't want you to be alarmed. It's our son, Richard. He's had a bit of a difficult time, and...'

'It's fine Mrs B,' said Ayanna. 'I've met him.' She wondered how much to tell Mrs Bell about their encounter. She chose not to mention that she had beaten him up, but in the liberating spirit of openness that had entered her life since her spat with the Duchess of Bloomsbury, she thought there would be no harm in sharing her positive impressions. 'He's very good-looking, isn't he?'

'You mean he...' She mimed lifting a mask.

Ayanna nodded, and Mrs Bell was delighted.

Seeing that Mrs Bell had only taken one mug from the rack, Ayanna said, 'We'd better make that two coffees, Mrs B.'

'Of course.' She took down a second mug, for Richard. 'And you *must* call me Susan.'

Mrs Bell was in a trance. She could hear the sound of church bells, and was picturing another marquee on the lawn, and Ayanna, in a white dress, making her boy happy again.

Ayanna hadn't got quite that far ahead, but that's not to say she didn't have plans of her own.

Chapter 23

*Wilberforce Selfram's visit to an event
by another author hits a snag*

Wilberforce Selfram waited until the rest of the audience was in situ before entering the marquee to watch Salman Rushdie's event. The house lights had just gone down, and as he made his way along the side aisle to his reserved seat towards the front of the auditorium, he heard a whisper in the dark: 'We've got a live one.'

Suddenly he felt an intense pain, followed by a strange numbness, across his whole body. He collapsed, and lay still. A pair of burly figures rose over him. A torch shone in his face, and he heard a familiar voice. It was one of Salman Rushdie's bodyguards. 'Sorry Mr Selfram,' he said. 'We didn't know it was you.'

'You never do,' he moaned, slowly regaining the power of speech. 'On how many occasions have you erred thus?'

'I lose count, but it must be six or seven by now. I do wish you wouldn't lurk so suspiciously, sir,' he said, tenderly removing two small barbs from Wilberforce Selfram's neck, and dabbing the wound with TCP.

'One does not lurk. One merely attends public appearances by one's occasional compatriot Sir Salman, and every time, one finds oneself Tasered by you and your colleagues.'

'Would you like us to carry you to your seat, sir?'

'Negative. One knows from experience that one's body has been temporarily paralysed into a stiff board, and one will be unable to assume a sitting position for some time to come. One shall, as usual, listen to the talk from ground level. If you would be so good as to move one clockwise by sixty degrees one will at least have a partial view of the festivities from one's rather unfortunate vantage point.'

The security guards did as they were asked, sliding him around on the plywood floor, and just as they got him into place a round of applause signalled the start of the talk.

Salman Rushdie's publishers had entrusted the event to a chair provided by the festival committee, so the author was accompanied on stage by Sallicent Summers who, along with her husband, ran a popular local garden centre. Her appearance garnered quite the reaction. There were lots of *Oooh*s of recognition. This was Sallicent Summers' first time at a book event, both onstage and as an attendee, so she wasn't quite sure how they were supposed to go. She had given it a good deal of preparation though, as evidenced by the ream of papers in her hand.

Twenty minutes into the event, Salman Rushdie still hadn't been called upon to say anything. He sat patiently, though; had the Graciousness Olympics been running, he would have been giving Nick Hornby some serious competition for his place on the podium. He was quite used to smiling politely through book festival introductions, but they rarely lasted longer than a couple of minutes. In Green Bottom, though, close observers might have noticed that he was finding his smile hard to maintain, that his facial muscles were under enormous strain. It was not only the length of time he was sat there grinning that was the problem, but also the material to which he was obliged to listen. His early life had been covered – his place of birth, his school days, and his time at university. Only now was he heading out into the world of work.

'It was at this point that Salman Rushdie decided to become an advertising person,' Sallicent Summers read from her sheet. 'He was behind a lot of very famous slogans, not least one that I'm sure we all remember. It was for the cream cake people. Who can remember the cream cake slogan?'

She looked out at the audience, who all seemed a little shy, but after a while somebody shouted out, tentatively, 'Was it *Naughty But Nice*?'

'That's right,' said Sallicent Summers. 'Well done. Salman Rushdie,' she pointed at him, 'thought that up.' There was a spontaneous burst of applause, and the author puffed up a little with pride. 'And shortly after this, the grapefruit juice people got in touch. They had accidentally ordered a lot more grapefruits than they should have done, and asked him to come up with a slogan so they could sell all the juice before it went off. I'm sure you all remember what that was.'

There was a mass intake of breath, and as one the audience chanted: *Grapefruit juice – it's a great fruit juice.*

'That's right. And it was such a success that the entire grapefruit juice surplus was gone in just a few weeks.' Again the audience applauded. 'The very next year Salman Rushdie was contacted by the pineapple juice people, who had made the same mistake as the grapefruit juice people. The slogan he came up with for them was...' She looked out at the audience. 'Can anyone remember?' They were silent this time. 'Anyone?' Again, nothing. 'It was *Pineapple juice – it's like a fine apple juice.*' Heads were shaken. 'This one wasn't such a success, I'm afraid to say. In fact, it had the opposite effect, as everybody rushed out to buy fine apple juice instead. While shares in orchards skyrocketed,' she read, 'an estimated ten million gallons of unsold pineapple juice were pumped into the North Sea, and it is said that for the next few weeks any fish caught in the area had a pineappley flavour to them. Citation needed,' she continued, looking down at her sheet, 'this claim needs a reliable source.'

Salman Rushdie didn't want to think about so much fruit juice going to waste, and he yearned for the introduction to end so he could start talking about his latest novel. A seasoned book-festival crowd would have noticed from the desperation in his eyes that he was dying on the inside, but this was not a seasoned book-festival crowd, and they were so busy reminiscing about television advertisements from years ago that they had more or less forgotten he was there.

'After this,' continued Sallicent Summers, 'Salman Rushdie decided not to do adverts any more, but to become a book writer instead. Now, I must confess that I've not read any of his books, but I've looked them up on the Internet, so I can tell you a little bit about each one. His first novel, *Grimus*, and I'm quoting here, *nosedived into oblivion amid almost universal critical derision...*'

And so she went on. While the author's mouth remained locked in its smile, his eyes blazed with fury.

With only ten minutes of his allotted hour left, Salman Rushdie still hadn't spoken. His smile had stayed in place, but the anger had left his eyes, which now registered only resignation. Sallicent Summers, on the other hand, hadn't stopped talking. When she had finished précising all his books, she moved on the fatwah, which was dealt with in two sentences, and elicited some tuts of dismay from the audience. Then it was time to catch up with developments in his personal life.

'It was around this time that Salman Rushdie married the actress and model Padma Lakshmi,' she read. At this point, an enormous screen behind her lit up, and on it was a photograph of a strikingly beautiful woman, dressed in what appeared to be a small amount of kitchen foil. As one, the audience went *Oooh*. This picture was replaced by another one of her, this time on a beach in a tiny bikini, then another, where she smouldered in a formal gown. The slideshow continued for three minutes, a fresh *Oooh* or *Aaah* greeting each new photograph, as though it were the fifth of November and this was a firework display. When at last the pictures came to an end and the screen switched off, there was a fulsome round of applause.

'Now,' said Sallicent Summers. 'I was just checking my watch, and I see we've only got a few minutes left. The organisers have told me to allow some time for the audience to ask some questions, so we'd better get on with that.'

The author's eyes unglazed.

'Who would like to start?'

Again, the audience seemed gripped by a collective bashfulness.

'Come along now.'

After a long silence, a hand was raised, and Sallicent Summers gestured for the man to speak.

'We lost some fence panels in those winds we had a few weeks ago,' said the audience member, 'and we couldn't see any for sale when we were in the garden centre a couple of days ago. It's just those six-foot-by-three-foot lap panels we're after. Do you know when you'll be getting them back in stock? I was going to ask your husband, but he was busy with a customer and I was in a bit of a hurry, you see.'

'We had quite a run on them after all that weather,' she said, 'and we've sold out. We're expecting a delivery on Tuesday, but make sure you call ahead because I don't want you making a special journey if they don't come in. We'll be offering free delivery if you buy five or more, as well.'

'That's great, I'll call on Tuesday then.'

'Looking forward to it. Anyone else?'

Another hand went up. 'I hope you don't mind me asking, but something I've wondered for a long time is why are you called Sallicent? It's quite an unusual name, isn't it?'

Time ticked by as she explained that her mother had always wanted a little girl called Sally. Her father, though, felt the name was a little frivolous, so as a compromise they had called her Sallicent, with the intention of shortening it in informal situations, but when she came along, they found they always used the long version. 'And it just stuck. I always find it funny that before I was married my name was Sallicent Winters, but now it's Sallicent Summers.' This got a big chortle. 'But that's enough about me, does anybody have a question for our special guest Salman Rushdie?'

His face became ultra-gracious as he awaited his big moment. A trembling hand in the audience went up. 'Oh, look, it's Mr Wrafter from the kennels,' said Sallicent Summers. 'What would you like to ask, Mr Wrafter?'

'I've always wondered,' said Mr Wrafter, 'about that song *Bridge Over Troubled Water* - where is the actual bridge that he's singing about?'

Sallicent Summers looked at Salman Rushdie, who

looked baffled.

'I don't think we know,' said Sallicent Summers. 'But,' she said, throwing it out to the audience, 'does anybody else?'

A few people shouted out names of bridges that they thought it might be about.

'Food for thought there,' she said. 'I suppose we'll all be able to look it up on the Internet when we get home. I think, though, that the idea is that you ask Salman Rushdie questions that are to do with him, rather than Simon and Garfunkel.'

'I'm sorry,' said Mr Wrafter. 'I'm new to this, and I thought it was general knowledge.'

'Not to worry. But can you think of something to ask our guest?'

There was a long silence, then at last Mr Wrafter spoke. 'I've got one now,' he said. 'What's it like to have such a pretty wife?'

A general murmur along the theme of *Oooh, yes, I was wondering that too*, passed through the marquee, and everybody eagerly awaited the answer.

The author looked at his hands. 'I'm sorry to tell you that the lady you saw in the photographs and I have... somewhat...separated.'

There was a sympathetic *Aaah*, and Sallicent Summers again checked her watch. 'It's time for us to wrap things up,' she said, 'but not without saying a big thank you to our special guest Salman Rushdie for coming all this way. We do hope he will come back and see us again one day. With that in mind, we've got a special treat to end on. Will you all please clap very loudly for Margaret Thatcher.'

To a roar of applause, frail little Margaret Thatcher appeared from the side of the stage, stood facing a mystified Salman Rushdie, and began her signature tune. As *We'll Meet Again* boomed from her ancient lungs, the author was visibly startled. Normally she would only sing a fragment of the song, but today she sang it all the way through. The words were projected on to the big screen, and the audience joined in. When it finally finished, there was a standing ovation. The house lights went up, Salman Rushdie, Sallicent Summers and Margaret Thatcher walked off stage, and the marquee began to empty. The event was considered a success; the audience members saw nothing untoward with the way things had gone, and they were glad to know that when they were asked what they did at the weekend, they would be able to say that they had gone to the book festival and seen the *Naughty but Nice* man.

Still paralysed, Wilberforce Selfram had no option but to continue lying in the aisle. The festival committee's secretary had been mobilised to stand beside him in a high-visibility vest, and issue a warning to passers-by: 'Please don't trip over the gentleman.'

After the audience had filed out and dispersed, Salman Rushdie emerged from backstage and walked through the auditorium on his way to the blacked-out Range Rover that was waiting for him outside, its engine running.

The secretary remained in place. 'Please don't trip

over the gentleman,' she said, as they approached.

Salman Rushdie looked at the gentleman in question. 'Selfram,' he said, recognising the prostrate figure as he stepped over it. 'What a pleasant surprise. What are you doing on the ground?'

'One is not on the ground, one is on the floor. Though the structure be impermanent, that does not prevent the hardboard surface beneath one from being categorised as flooring.'

'As you wish. My chaps didn't Taser you again, did they?'

'As has become customary, they laboured under the delusion that one was up to no good.'

'I'll have strong words with them when we get back to the Range Rover. It must have been quite the ordeal.'

'One becomes accustomed.'

Salman Rushdie sighed. 'Look at you down there. I wish there was something I could do to get you up and about again,' he said, thoughtfully stroking his beard. 'I seem to recall a time when I was in a low posture and someone encouraged me to stand up. Now, let me get the details clear in my mind, because the story might just help. Who was it again...? Oh yes, it was that nice lady. Let me try and remember the words she used. Ah, that's right, she said, *Arise Sir Salman*. Would you like me to give it a try? We could stage a mock knighting, and pretend that you're being elevated to a senior position within the British Empire. It might just get you back on those feet of yours.' He lifted the plastic bag he was holding. 'They just gave me a bottle. I could use it in place of a sword.'

'One hardly thinks one could be convincingly

knighted with a bottle of Cinzano.'

Salman Rushdie pulled a confused face. 'Cinzano, Selfram? Oh no. No Cinzano for me.' He reached into the bag, pulled out a bottle and displayed the label for Wilberforce Selfram to read.

Wilberforce Selfram's eyes widened, and before he was able to stop himself, he spoke admiringly of what he saw. 'Rougemont Castle '83 – universally regarded as the finest wine ever to have existed.'

'So I've heard,' said Salman Rushdie. 'Julian Barnes certainly speaks very highly of it. You know, it's quite remarkable the way doors open when you've got a knighthood and a Booker Prize or two under your belt. Just imagine how things will be when the Nobel comes in.' He gazed at the bottle, and stroked it. 'I'll put it in one of my wine cellars. Still, I'm sure you'll enjoy your Cinzano. One of my wives, I don't remember which, used to drink it with a splash of Vimto and a cherry on a stick.'

Wilberforce Selfram seethed.

'So what do you say?' asked Salman Rushdie. 'A tap on the shoulder from a bottle of the very finest wine this galaxy has to offer?'

'Negative. It is unscientific and would not work. And besides, one abhors the royal honours system.'

'No word from the Palace yet, then?'

'One is not at liberty to say; however, as a National Treasure it can only be matter of time before one is called before the throne.' Remembering that he had a reputation to maintain as a prominent countercultural figure, he added, 'One shall, of course, reject their overtures.'

'Of course you will, Selfram,' said Salman Rushdie, flamboyantly unconvinced. 'Now, I would love to stop and chat, but I've got to keep moving. Security reasons, you understand. Back to the old Range Rover,' he sighed, and with that he was off. Wilberforce Selfram watched him as he jovially slapped his guards on the back and, after a flurry of fist-bumping, took out his wallet and handed them each a twenty-pound note. It was a ritual that they always seemed to perform on these occasions, and he wondered what it was all about.

A significant part of the festival's infrastructure was its battalion of reluctant teenage volunteers, all of whom had been encouraged to take part by their parents in the belief that it would be character-building. Just such a reluctant teenage volunteer arrived with some orange traffic cones, having been given instructions to place them around the immobile writer, which she did without a word. With their health-and-safety duty done, the volunteer and the secretary walked away, leaving Wilberforce Selfram alone in the empty marquee.

Another event was due to start in a while, and he could hear the audience milling around outside in anticipation, no doubt enjoying their complimentary cocktails. The machine started up again, with just a canvas wall between it and his ears. The floor shook violently beneath him. As the rumble continued, he felt sure it seemed too loud to be a conventional ice crusher. *One is beginning to wonder what is going on*, he thought. Immobile, coned off, and vibrating just feet away from a mysterious and deafening machine, he looked into the lens of his imaginary camera.

'One despairs.'

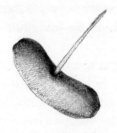

Chapter 24

*Ayanna and Richard continue to get acquainted,
and another overnight guest arrives*

Richard's window was open, and he and Ayanna could hear the crowd noise from the Salman Rushdie event. There had been a fair amount of applause, and for some time the audience had been making *Oooh*ing and *Aaah*ing sounds. It seemed to be going very well. Their coffee was finished, and Ayanna moved closer to him. Seeing he was quite comfortable with this, she looked into his eyes, and he looked back into hers. The connection was indisputable, and she put her hands on his shoulders, and kissed him. She had decided to do this as soon as he had lifted his mask, and nothing had happened since to put her off the idea. With some trepidation she had glanced over his bookshelves, and finding their contents to be just about acceptable, she had seen no obstacle. She wasn't going to be in Green

Bottom for very long, and didn't want to waste any time.

Surprised, and extremely pleased, he returned the kiss. When it was over, he said, 'Really? After knowing what you know?'

She had managed to get a small amount of his life story out of him. She had heard how he'd had an unrequited love go disastrously wrong, had taken comfort in the outer reaches of the Internet, and had retreated back to his family home, where he had lived in seclusion for the last four years.

'All the best people are at least a bit nuts. Would it surprise you to learn that I've had first-hand experience of a shitty non-romance too? I've got at least a bit of an idea of what you've gone through.'

It did surprise him, because he couldn't imagine anybody not wanting to be with her.

'Anyway, I'm glad you've decided to stop all the creepy mask stuff. You're moving on.'

'I like to think I was starting to drift away from it anyway,' he said. 'I've not even logged on for a couple of d… Oh no.'

He had spotted something out of the window, and Ayanna craned her neck to see what he was looking at. A group of about fifteen people of an extraordinary range of shapes and sizes, all young men as far as she could tell, were walking up the garden path. Every one of them was wearing a blank white mask.

The doorbell rang, and a minute later Mrs Bell called upstairs. 'Richard,' she said, 'your Incognito friends are here to see you.'

He looked at Ayanna. She didn't say a word, but

he knew what she was thinking. It was time to make a firm break. He walked over to the door. She smiled encouragement at him, and watched him leave the room. Unable to resist, she quietly followed him down, and sat on the stairs leading to the hall, peering through the bannisters. He stood in the doorway.

'Hi,' he said. 'How are you all doing?'

The masked men stared blankly at him. One, who seemed to have been appointed spokesman, stepped on to the doorstep. 'This is an intervention,' he said. 'You've not logged on for forty-eight hours, and we're concerned about you.'

'Thanks,' he said. 'I appreciate that. But I'm fine. I've just decided...' He stopped, and Ayanna willed him on. 'I've decided to move on. It's been great knowing you all...but I'm making a few changes, and I'm not going to be around any more.'

'They've got to you, haven't they?' said the spokesman.

'Who has?'

'The Illuminati. They've brainwashed you. You always were our best man, and they knew it. They've taken you out. Can't you see?'

'No, really, it's just...'

'It's just what?'

Ayanna wanted them all to go away, and she had a fair idea of what would make them scatter. She walked down the stairs, crept up behind Richard, and rested her chin on his shoulder. She just knew the spokesman's eyes were saucers behind their pinprick holes. He pointed at her. 'You've...you've got a girlfriend,' he spluttered.

Ayanna twirled one of Richard's curls around her finger as she waited to see what he would say in response.

'I wouldn't say she was my girlfriend,' he said, quite casually. 'That would be presumptuous. But...we hang out.'

Ayanna thought that was nicely played, and she briefly nibbled his ear, to make it clear what they got up to when they were hanging out.

The spokesman backed away. 'This is worse than the Illuminati. One day she'll leave you,' he said, his voice wavering, 'and you'll come crawling back. But we won't have you. You're tainted; how can we ever trust you now?' Soundtracked by Margaret Thatcher singing her song, they all started to retreat, walking backwards towards the gate. One of them lost his balance and fell over, taking some of the others with him, a couple of whom momentarily lost their masks.

When, at last, they were all out of the garden, Ayanna whispered in Richard's ear. 'Let's hang out,' she said.

This had all been observed not only by the apparently indifferent Bevis, but also by an ecstatic Mrs Bell, who had been peeping through a gap in the kitchen door. The young people went back upstairs, where they hung out for quite a while.

'So what exactly happened with this girl, then?' asked Ayanna, finally showered after her journey, and in fresh clothes. She wanted to know more than the outline she had been given.

'Oh Christ. I just really fancied her. I was at university in Bristol – not the actual Bristol University, but Bristol Gerard Langley University, an old Poly that got promoted; they've got one of the country's best computer science departments. Anyway, she was the Ents officer there, and I was on the committee.'

'Most of that was white noise. I never went to uni.'

'Oh, right. Sorry. I was at college doing computers, and she was in charge of booking bands and DJs and comedians for the Union bar, and I helped out. Anyway, I had this big thing for her, and one day I plucked up the courage to ask her out.'

'Don't tell me: it went really well?'

'She told me I'd made an inappropriate approach and that I would have to leave the committee and the Union. She said that if I'd wanted to ask her out, I should have filled in a DSI form.'

'What does DSI stand for?'

'Declaration of Sexual Interest. They were piloting a Union scheme to put an end to the analogue initiation of romance, and move everything online. Apparently I was supposed to have filled in one of these things on my phone, and sent it to the Sexual Activity Committee for appraisal, and if they had deemed it an acceptable application, they would have electronically passed notice of my intentions on to her, and it would have been up to her whether or not to sanction a romantic approach. I hadn't done that, and so...I was out.'

'Seems a bit harsh.'

'I'm glad you think so. The trouble was, nobody would stand up to her. Everyone took her side, and I was ostracised. Nobody would sit next to me in lectures, and I lost my social life. I was frozen out of the running club; the Society of Vegans held a silent vigil for the pig; my flatmates snubbed me; even some of my lecturers went frosty on me.'

'So you were completely ostraci... Hang on... What pig?' It seemed as though there was more to this story than he was letting on.

'Oh, I'd asked her if she'd like to go to Pork on a Pole, a sausage-on-a-stick place near the campus.'

'But if you never went, no pigs were harmed.'

'Yes, it was only ever a notional pig – I think they just wanted an excuse to hold a silent vigil; you know what that lot are like. Anyway, I spent my last year there by myself. When I wasn't at the back of a lecture hall I just stayed in my room, on the computer, and got sucked into a bit of a black hole. It seemed exciting at first. I felt a sense of community, and it was as if we could really make things better through online activism, but lately some of the wackier conspiracy theories have started creeping in, and there's been infighting, and... well, suddenly you've turned up.'

'And I'm completely un-virtual. Old-fashioned, I know.'

For a moment neither knew what to say. They sat in silence, until it was broken by the throaty growl of a large motorbike pulling up nearby.

'But you still like her, after all this time,' said Ayanna. 'You've obviously not been able to get her out of your system.'

'This morning I'd have had trouble denying it. I'd clung to this idea that deep down she was really nice, that maybe she'd been brainwashed into being mean.'

'Like in *Zoolander*?'

He turned red. 'A bit like in *Zoolander*, yes. Now, though…well, a lot's changed today; suddenly she's ancient history. Look,' he said. 'I know this is a strange story, and I don't want doubt in your mind. I don't want you wondering whether I really am a stalker, or whatever. All this is public knowledge now.' He opened his computer, and navigated to an article on the BBC website about the DSI scheme, and how it had ultimately failed. The conclusion was that most of the student body had secretly thought it was a ridiculous idea, but hadn't said anything against it because it had been presented to them as a leap forward for equality, and to oppose it would have made it seem as if they were somehow cheering on sex pests. Only the Young Conservative society had spoken out against it, and this dampened opposition further still, because nobody outside their ranks wanted to be seen to align with them on account of their general weirdness, as well as their propensity to speak out against anything that might help to make the world a fairer place. The Ents officer herself had not been interviewed for the piece; apparently she had left, and the reporter could find no trace of her.

Ayanna read it through. Richard had spoken to them, and his story was there, anonymised. There was no need for him to have told her any of this, and she had a feeling that doing so was a great release for him. She would have struggled with the idea that maybe this handsome and endearingly awkward boy really was a sex case of some sort, and now she was sure it was just a dodgy crush combined with some woeful and counter-productive student politics; so woeful and counter-productive that she wondered whether there might be more to the story. It was certainly odd that the principal player had seemed to vanish into thin air. She embraced Richard. 'Things are going to get better for you. So where is she now, this mysterious former love interest of yours?'

Just at this moment, the door opened. Richard's face turned pale, and he answered her question. 'She's behind you,' he whispered.

Ayanna hadn't had high hopes for her stay in Green Bottom, and had even expected it to be a little dull. She'd been proven wrong. Not only had she found herself an unlikely romantic lead, but right there was his former crush and tormentor. She was wearing motorbike leathers, and sporting an immaculate blonde bob and an icily furious face. 'What are you spods doing in my room?' she snarled.

For the second time that afternoon, Ayanna felt her hands ball into fists. She felt an overwhelming instinct to protect this dorky and damaged but good-looking boy she had only just met, and she was ready to use them again.

Chapter 25

*A gameshow host feels aggrieved, money is raised for a good cause,
and Wilberforce Selfram, still coned off, continues to despair*

Wilberforce Selfram could feel movement beginning to return to one of his arms. If he had chosen to, he could have utilised all the strength in that arm to roll himself over on to his front and lie face down on the marquee's wooden floor. He had decided not to do so though, and remained on his back as the audience for the next event began to file in. People looked at him as they walked by, but because of the cones they assumed, correctly, that everything was being dealt with, so they left him alone.

Mrs Bruschini, who had so far spent the day being driven from venue to venue by her treasurer, had heard of the episode and visited him to find out whether he had changed his mind about having an ambulance called.

'One shall deport oneself in a supine manner until one's limbs begin once more to function to an adequate degree,' he said, in reply to her enquiry. 'Were this a novel, one would begin to have one's suspicions that one had been stranded thus as an anchor around which the author has chosen to write a sequence of increasingly exhausting and indistinguishable set pieces. This cannot be a novel, however, for the novel is – as one points out with extraordinary regularity in articles for respected journals and suchlike – dead. The only contemporary novels of any worth are those one writes oneself, though these go largely unheeded by the greater reading public. This is, of course, symptomatic of a broad cultural malaise; were one writing in a more enlightened era, when Modernism was appreciated by crossing sweeper and crown prince alike – the 1950s, let us say – one's work would have sold extraordinarily well, and one's standing would be substantially higher than it is in these dismal times.'

'So is that a *yes* or a *no* to the ambulance?' she asked.

'Negative.'

'So no ambulance?'

'Affirmative.'

'That means *yes*?'

'Affirmative.'

'To be clear, is that yes to an ambulance or yes to *no* ambulance?'

'One despairs.'

'If you want an ambulance, Mr Selfram, say *ambulance*. If you don't want an ambulance, don't say anything.'

The author stared at Mrs Bruschini, who after a long

wait said, 'Have it your way Mr Selfram, but if you
should pass away, or cause an accident, I will not be
held liable.' She told him that a car would be collecting
him from the parsonage the next day at half past
two, and that he mustn't be late. With a swish of her
pashmina, she went away, and as she did, the house
lights went down.

This was to be the third consecutive event that
Wilberforce Selfram had watched from the floor of the
aisle of the main auditorium. Salman Rushdie's effort
had been followed by a talk so unsuccessful that it even
rivalled the earlier writing workshop as a contender for
the crown of the least satisfactory event of the festival.
The popular quiz show host Alexander Armstrong had
taken to the stage in front of an excited sell-out crowd,
but in spite of the warmth of his reception things had
gone downhill, and he had ended up storming off
stage to the sound of his own footsteps. The main
difficulty was that the audience had been expecting
affable behind-the-scenes anecdotes from the various
TV shows he had appeared on, but instead of this
he had insisted on aggressively promoting his latest
book, *It's Just Not Fair*, in which he railed against what
he believed to be the many obstacles with which the
upper classes were confronted as they made their way
through life. Purple-faced with fury, he read chapter
after chapter about the setbacks he was convinced he
had suffered just because he was a direct descendant
of William the Conqueror, and his family historically

owned most of Northumberland. 'It's social injustice,' he concluded, spluttering with indignation. 'I have said it before, in numerous interviews with major newspapers, and I say it again: I am Britain's top light entertainer and singer, and I got where I am today by working bloody hard and being bloody good at what I do, not just because I'm the great-great-great-grandson of St Andrew St John, Fifteenth Baron St John of Bletso. And that,' he thundered, 'is final. Now who has a question?'

A hand went up, and an audience member attempted to get at least a little bit of value for money. 'You know Richard Osmond, who you do that quiz show with?'

'Yes, yes, what about him?'

'Is he that tall in real life?' This question was well-received by the audience, who fidgeted in anticipation of the answer.

'There are urgent matters of social injustice to address, and I didn't come here to talk about how tall people are. However, out of graciousness I shall answer. He is exactly as tall as he looks. There. More questions please,' he snapped, 'preferably ones that are relevant to my book. This is a book festival after all.'

Another hand went up. 'My question isn't exactly about your book, but could you sing us a song? If you're taking requests, I really like it when you sing *Fly Me to the Moon*.' This was met with a round of applause.

For a full minute, Alexander Armstrong stood silently on stage, his eyes bulging and his chest heaving as he breathed heavily through his nose. At last, he spoke. 'Very well,' he said, 'if that is what you came here for,' and he launched into a note-perfect *a cappella* rendition of the popular song, smiling throughout, his eyes twinkling as he did a little dance. The audience clapped along, and when he finished, he was greeted with a warm ovation.

His face turned purple again. 'There,' he hissed. 'You got what you wanted. Congratulations – I hope you're happy now.' He checked his watch. 'That's it, my contractual obligations have been discharged. I would have hated to have forfeited my fee: a pencil case and a bottle of Pimm's. Pimm's, for God's sake. I'll be at the signing table for twenty minutes,' he huffed, 'and twenty minutes only. I have some friends nearby who are hosting a straightforward shooting weekend, and I might just catch the end of the first day's sport. I'll be there, shotgun in hand, blasting living creatures out of the air for fun, and if you have a problem with that it says more about you than it does about me. Good day to you.'

With that, he had left the stage. It wasn't until he was in the wings that the mystified audience realised that his talk really was at an end, and a smattering of applause broke out.

Wilberforce Selfram had enjoyed Alexander Armstrong's event more than he had expected to. It had reminded him of the work of the Romanian underground absurdist Theatre of Rage movement of the 1970s. As he watched Alexander Armstrong thump into the wings, he wondered who the next attraction was going to be.

*

Alexander Armstrong walked straight into the green room, and sat on a sofa opposite the next author in line, Morag MacLochness, the writer of upbeat romance stories who was promoting her seventh novel so far that year. 'Good God,' he said. 'I try to enlighten the populace about social justice, and all they want to do is talk about how tall people are, and hear songs they've heard a thousand times before.'

'Ah didnae ken ye were intae aw that, Sandy,' said Morag MacLochness. 'Me and a few pals are setting up a wee group called Castle Dwellers for Social Justice – Rankin, McCall Smith, Vettriano, Lorraine Kelly – that crowd. Mibbie ye'd care tae join us? Hands across the border, ken?'

'Where do I sign?' he said, taking a solid-gold fountain pen from his inside pocket. 'We've been at the sharp end for too long – it's about time we castle dwellers had our share of social justice.'

'Ach naw, it's no that way roond. Oor group is all aboot the castle people being nice to the poor folk, no demanding that the poor folk be nice to the castle people.'

'Well stuff that,' said Alexander Armstrong. Clutching his plastic gift bag, with its Pimm's and its pencil case, he got up and thundered towards the signing table, leaving Morag MacLochness alone as she waited to be called for her talk. She used the time to check inside her own plastic bag. Along with the pencil case she found a bottle of Buckfast Tonic Wine. They certainly knew how to make their authors feel at home.

*

Mrs Bell had agreed to host this event too, and now that her son had taken off his mask and met a really nice girl, she was smiling broadly as she took to the stage and introduced Morag MacLochness.

'Genre nonsense,' muttered Wilberforce Selfram to himself, as he heard that the book to be discussed was a light romantic comedy. 'One wishes one had accepted the offer of ambulancification; one would sooner be deep within the bowels of an hôspital, attached to an iron lung while enduring a simultaneous colonoscopy and cystoscopy, *sans anaesthésie*, than listen to such enervating piffle. It shall not – indeed, *will* not – be countenanced.' With all the strength in his recovering arm, he flipped himself on to his front and began to claw his way towards the exit. Movement had returned to three of his toes, two on one foot and one on the other, and they joined the effort as he inched himself along the plywood floor in his attempt to get away from being exposed to genre fiction.

His attempt failed.

An hour later, as Mrs Bell and Morag MacLochness were wrapping things up, he was still less than halfway along the aisle. In that time, he had listened to some extracts from the novel, as well as a lively Q&A about the book, and the genre in general. The final question was related to the novel. The scatter-brained main character, Chamomile, had met an apparently gruff man called Bruno. They had got off to a bad start, but after a series of unexpected events they had begun to see one another in a different light. 'Please tell us,' the audience member asked, 'Will Chamomile and Bruno get together? I think they would make a lovely couple.'

Wilberforce Selfram stopped slithering for a moment. This was what he had feared, and this fear had been the real reason for his attempted escape from the marquee. He was angry with himself for it, but he had become absorbed in the story, and wanted to know the answer to this question.

'Yous'll huv to buy the book to find oot,' said Morag MacLochness.

Ballard's bodkins, thought Wilberforce Selfram. *That is a stroke of genius. One shall employ that strategy at one's next event.* Annoyed by not having thought of it first, and having to learn it from an author of genre fiction, he resumed his journey along the floor. As he did, he also resigned himself to secretly buying the book at the first opportunity.

'That's all we have time for,' said Mrs Bell, 'but you can get your copy signed in a few minutes. As you leave the marquee there are going to be some volunteers with buckets collecting for Morag MacLochness's charity, Castle Dwellers for Social Justice, so do feel free to throw in a few coins on your way out. Morag will just tell us a little bit about it.'

'We're a new group, and oor motto is *Just cos we live in muckle big hooses, it disnae mean we dinnae remember the poor folk.* If you could throw any spare siller in ma bucket I'd be richt glad o it.' She carried on, but as the event reached its final furlong she became demob happy; the moderation she had been showing in her vocabulary vanished, and nobody could understand a word she was saying. There was, perhaps, something about a tappit hen, and getting blootered, but to the Green Bottom audience it was mainly just sounds. They all decided it must be a good cause though, and rummaged in purses and pockets for change. Eventually she stopped, and Mrs Bell realised it was her turn to speak.

'If you're leaving via the side aisle,' she said, having witnessed what had been going on, 'please don't trip over the gentleman on the ground.'

'One is not on the ground,' he monotoned. 'One is on the fl... Never mind.' Nobody heard him, because they were all clapping loudly, having had a nice time at the talk.

Chapter 26

Wilberforce Selfram is given a special meal,
and Mara expounds on her sexuality

Wilberforce Selfram had managed to free both his arms and four more of his toes, and he was now able to bend a little at the knees. From the window of Richard's bedroom, Ayanna saw him crawling slowly up the front path of the house next door; there had clearly been a drama of some sort. She wasn't surprised. On the trips she had made with him he had been variously swept out to sea, trampled by cows, arrested for a bank robbery in a case of mistaken identity, and at least twice he had been Tasered by... She realised what must have happened. He seemed to be allergic to Tasers, and they always stiffened him out for hours afterwards. She called down to him. 'Selfram, do you need a doctor?'

'Negative,' he replied. 'One is in the very rudest of health.'

She closed the window and left him to it. She was going to be driving him back to London on Sunday, and he would doubtless give her a full account of his experiences. She looked at the business card that Richard's nemesis had left.

Mara
Journalist – Activist – Millennial

mail@millennialmara.com

Below that was a list of social media platforms that she could be found on, some of which Ayanna hadn't even heard of. She put the card down. It wasn't that there was something about Mara that she didn't like, it was more that she couldn't think of *anything* about her that was even slightly likeable. Her hair was good, she would give her that, but not in a likeable way. She was also slim, with flawless alabaster skin and piercing blue eyes, and she could understand why Richard had developed something of a bee in his bonnet over her, but again it didn't make her likeable. After her sudden appearance it had been established that someone must have got their lefts and rights mixed up, and the newcomer's room was in fact the one across the landing, which was usually used as a study. She hadn't gone to find it, though. She had stood there staring at Richard.

'You look familiar,' she said. 'Where do I know you from?'

'Nowhere,' he said.

'If I find you're lying to me you'll be in deeper shit than you could possibly imagine. What's the Wi-fi password for this dump?'

Richard jotted down a string of letters and numbers, and in return she had handed over her card, one to each of them. 'If you decide to talk,' she said, 'you know where to find me.' She had backed out of the room without taking her narrowed eyes off Richard.

'She seems nice,' said Ayanna.

Richard said nothing.

'You still fancy her, don't you?'

'I can truthfully say that I don't.' He looked at the card. 'No surname, just *Mara*. This isn't her real name, anyway. At least it wasn't her name when I knew her.'

It was hard to know what to say about all this, and Ayanna took the opportunity to disappear to the bathroom. When at last she emerged, she had done something unexpected and amazing with her hair.

Mr and Mrs Bell hosted an evening meal for everybody in the house, as well as the parson and Wilberforce Selfram, who by this point had regained the use of most of his body. At eight o'clock they assembled in the dining room of Parsonage Cottage. Mrs Bell had planned it all to the last detail. Ayanna had let them know ahead of time that she was a vegetarian, and she had been well catered for. The whole meal was meat-free, and made with such skill that even the most strident omnivores among them couldn't have found cause to complain. Before long, everybody had a big plate of tasty-looking food in front of them, apart from Wilberforce Selfram.

'We've got something extra-special for you, Mr Selfram,' said Mrs Bell. Mr Bell appeared, carrying a white ceramic tureen which he placed before their guest. 'Do you remember yesterday, when you were telling us all about how you can't imagine ever going back to normal food because you love eating slugs so much? Well, David's been out in the garden all afternoon collecting some for you.'

Wilberforce Selfram lifted the tureen's lid, and looked inside. There he saw a mass of live, writhing molluscs. 'How thoughtful,' he said. He recognised the young woman with the blonde bob as a journalist. They had appeared on the same edition of *Newsnight* not long before, and knowing he had a reputation to maintain as a devoted follower of Beoffrey of Biddenden, he picked out a medium-sized slug, put it in his mouth, and swallowed it. 'Yum,' he said, 'or *kjempegod*, as our Norse cousins would say.' He didn't chew, it just went straight down. He soon regretted this, as he felt the slug moving inside him, thrashing around as it tried to escape its fate in the darkness of his gullet.

'Glad you like them,' said Mr Bell. 'It's a funny thing, I always seem to be seeing the little buggers when I'm not looking for them, but when I was out there today, they were all in hiding. Still, I got there in the end. I thought about trying one, just to see what all the fuss was about, but then I thought that if you eat a slug whole, you would also be eating all the poo that's inside it, waiting to come out. No offence to you Mr Selfram, but I draw the line at that.'

Wilberforce Selfram had spent the preceding days trying not to think about the raw faeces that was still inside the slugs he ate, but as he looked at his meal, he could think of nothing else.

Doing their best not to dwell on the contents of the tureen, everybody else tucked into their food. Mrs Bell hadn't made an issue of the mask coming off, but she kept stealing glances at Richard and Ayanna, who were getting along very well. Mara was silent, observing through narrowed eyes.

At the other end of the table, in between slugs, Wilberforce Selfram was holding forth on the subject of his views on the best way to pepper normal conversation with long words. He was explaining how he was prepared to countenance the use of shorter words if they were less commonplace than a longer word. He used the example of favouring *inexistant* over *non-existent*. 'The latter, though longer, is often employed by the commonplace citizenry; the former, however, is in scant usage and is therefore the preferred choice of the public intellectual, such as oneself. Likewise, when making reference to the contents of one's scrotal sac, one's preference is to employ *testes* over *testicles*.' He also explained that it helped to use foreign words as much as possible, particularly Latin, and he advocated the lengthening of existing verbs by giving them prefixes or suffixes. He shared the beginners' strategy of using the prefix *en*. '*One shall enbrush one's teeth* and *one shall entie one's shoelace* being the textbook examples,' he droned. The parson had volunteered to sit next to him and be the one to absorb the brunt of the inevitable monologue, thus allowing people at the other end of the table to chat freely among themselves. He saw it, he had explained, as his Christian duty.

At the other end of the table Mrs Bell, wanting to make Mara feel welcome, drew her into the conversation. 'So, Mara,' she said. 'I hear you're writing about the book festival for the *Guardian*.'

'I am,' she said, 'and I'll be placing it firmly within its geocultural context. When I was walking up your garden path today an old woman leapt out from the bushes, waved her feather duster at me, and told me to *beware the white face*.'

'Ah, yes, that would be Mrs Chapman. She did the same to Ayanna. I'm afraid she's had a very trying couple of days, and her nerves are a little frayed.'

'Frayed nerves or otherwise, there are certainly enough white faces to choose from around here. It's enough to make a BAME person such as myself wonder whether they are even welcome here.'

Ayanna winced. She was uncomfortable about the BAME label. It had appeared overnight, like the Berlin Wall, and she felt it was as if white people had herded everybody else into a pen and labelled them *That Lot*. And besides, Mara *was* white. She was lily white. What was she even on about?

'Sorry, a *what* person?' asked Mrs Bell.

'BAME,' said Mara. 'Black, Asian & Minority Ethnic.'

'Yes, I thought that was what you said.'

'I am BAME,' she huffed. 'I get this all the time; we need to have an urgent national conversation about the non-visual BAME community. My great-grandfather was Chinese Singaporean, and I take my cultural heritage very seriously. Obviously *she's* black, or half-black, I can't quite tell which,' she said, pointing to Ayanna with her knife. Ayanna needed all her self-control not to grab Wilberforce Selfram's tureen and empty it over Mara's head. 'She's one of the lucky ones, because, unlike me, you can tell just by looking at her. And anyway, she's not from here, she came in for the festival. Other than that, this area is pretty much a whitescape, and,' she sighed, 'I'm not sure how comfortable I am.'

'I'm sorry you feel that way,' said Mrs Bell. 'But I think you'll find people around here are very friendly, and you're certainly welcome in our home. You know, our daughter's going to be marrying a black man in a few weeks' time, and we're ever so fond of him. I'm very much hoping we'll have some little BAME grandchildren before too long.' She glanced at Ayanna, and wondered whether there would be even more to hope for, and then she realised that the hoping had already begun.

Mara changed the subject. 'How can I get in touch with the LGBTQIA+ community around here?' she asked. 'I'm pansexual. I expect that's shocked you.'

'I'm afraid I'm not quite sure what it means.'

'That doesn't surprise me. There's so much ignorance about my sexuality; this is exactly why we need there to be an urgent national conversation on the subject. It means that I'm open to attraction to anyone, regardless of gender. Mostly my relationships have been with men, but I once got off with a girl at a student party. I remember it well.' She looked, for a moment, almost wistful. 'Republica were playing on the hi-fi, and all the boys were watching.'

'Didn't that used to be called bisexual?'

'It's completely different from being bisexual. You need to be educated on the matter; I'll send you some links. Anyway, this places me firmly on the LGBTQIA+ spectrum, and I feel quite isolated here.'

'I'm so sorry to hear that, Mara,' said Mrs Bell. 'Darling,' she called across the table to Mr Bell, who, to his dismay, had fallen into conversation with the parson and Wilberforce Selfram, or rather had found himself hypnotised by the baritone drone of Wilberforce Selfram's monologue as he explained in great detail how the pages of the thesaurus had begun to pass out of his system. 'I'm sorry to interrupt, but Mara's pansexual, and she's wanting to meet some of the LGBT gang. Who should we put her on to?'

'Now then,' said Mr Bell. 'There's Simon and Jeremy, we could start with them. Or Ruth and Elaine. And there's always Rochelle; she used to be called Rodney.'

'That's plenty for starters. They're all lovely. We'll ring round, and hopefully you'll be able to meet up with some of them tonight.'

'No, really, I...'

Mrs Bell raised a hand to stop her. 'We can't have you feeling isolated, and it's the least we can do. We'll tell them you're here and, I'm sure they'll all rally round.'

Mara fumed at this hospitality. The journey-into-the-racist-and-homophobic-heart-of-England angle that she was planning for her article was slipping away from her. Mr Bell left the room, and she could hear him on the phone. A few words made it through to the dining table: '...potsexual, I think it was... Ah, yes, *pan*sexual, that's it.' He returned with the news that several members of the local LGBT community had enthusiastically agreed to meet her at the White Horse at nine thirty.

'I'll walk you there,' said Mr Bell.

'I can find my own way,' she said, planning to get lost.

'No no, I insist. I'll introduce you to everyone and stay for one quick drink as you get settled in.'

'I know your *one quick drink* with that crowd on a Friday night,' said Mrs Bell, laughing. 'Last time, you were good for nothing the next day.'

'I'll be on my best behaviour tonight, darling,' he said.

Mrs Bell looked amused and unconvinced as Mr Bell retook his seat, and Wilberforce Selfram continued his account of the movement of his bowels. He informed them that when he had looked into the lavatory pan to check on the result, he could see through the water that some of the words from the thesaurus were still legible on it. '*Peripatetic* was one,' he said, 'and *confabulation*. Additionally, somewhat unfortunately, *nice*.' He went on to explain that he had only inspected the surface of the faeces, but had he scooped it out of the water and set about it with a stick, many more words would have been revealed. 'One has taken to using this technique when working on one's fiction,' he told them. 'One engorges oneself with a lexicon, excretes it into a chamber pot or comparable receptacle, and as one makes one's way through the waste one makes a note of all the surviving wordage. One has written a number of one's recent novels using this technique;

one eschews the vulgar tropes of character, plot, *et cetera*, and simply lists the words in the order in which they are revealed. Needless to say, one prefers to employ more expansive lexica than a humble Roget's. It's a frightfully Modernist method, which one intends to impart to students on an extensive tour of university creative writing courses. One shall offer the wide-eyed scholars live demonstrations of one's working practices, and by the end of one's tour one will have amassed enough material for one's next novel, thereby endoubling one's remuneration.'

He was cut off by Mrs Bell's announcement that it was time for dessert. 'We're all having crème brûlée,' she said, to general delight. 'Apart from you, Mr Selfram – you're having even more slugs.'

'Yum,' he said. 'Or *Oloyinmọmọ*, as our Yorubaphone brethren would ejaculate.'

Chapter 27

*Friday comes to an end with a big night at the White Horse
that is enjoyed by almost everybody*

Richard's family had kept quiet about his return to
the village. He hadn't wanted people knowing he
was staying with them, and they had respected that;
only the parson had been let in on the secret. When he
walked into the White Horse he was greeted warmly,
as any familiar face would be when they had come
back after having been away for whatever reason.
There was no fuss, but a lot of friendly back-slapping
and shoulder-squeezing, as well as a few winks as he
made his way through the happy crowd with Ayanna
following in his wake.

They found seats at a small round table in the
corner of the bar, underneath a stuffed pike. Richard
went to buy their drinks, a twenty-pound note woven
through his fingers. Ayanna had started to wonder

how he paid his way, but she'd found out that in spite of appearances he wasn't unemployed, that he took on freelance jobs to get by – mainly troubleshooting insanely complicated software glitches.

While she waited, she observed the pub's clientele, which was a mixture of Friday-night regulars and book-festival people. After dinner she and Richard had gone back to his room and spent a while there, and by this point in the evening everybody seemed well-oiled and up for a good time. Everybody, that is, except for Mara, who looked like a thundercloud as she sat surrounded by members of the LGBT community that she had not expected to find. The rest of her group was lively, including Mr Bell. He had taken Bevis with him, and they both seemed to be having a good time – Mr Bell was clearly stretching the definition of *one quick drink*, and the Labrador had found a rich source of dropped crisps on the floor.

'There's something not quite right about her,' said Richard, when he had returned with two pints of lager and two packets of salt and vinegar peanuts.

'You don't say. BAME my arse.' Ayanna had gone to a rough school and had, every day, found herself on the front line of racial conflict. In her adult life too, her skin colour had been a relentless issue. Her dad's side of the family had shut her out, which suited her, but this didn't stop them from presenting her as proof that they weren't bigots when defending their St George-flag-festooned social media accounts: *how can i be a racist when ive got a halfcast neice*? Ayanna had stopped counting the ways. Only her uncle had stood apart from them, and he did what he could to compensate.

'I'm sorry about that lot,' he would say. Over the years she had built up certain views and opinions, and she knew she had earned them, and was continuing to earn them all the time. She had a strong feeling that Mara didn't struggle to find a flat share, or have people mutter at her at the bus stop, or feel suspicious eyes following her when she browsed in shops, or... Her opinion of Mara had started low, and gone downhill from there.

'It's not just that,' he said. 'There's the whole *pansexual* thing. You remember that story she told about getting off with a girl?'

'Vaguely.'

'Something doesn't ring true about it. She said it was a student party, and Republica were on the hi-fi.'

'I'm not sure what that means.'

'Neither was I, but I looked it up. It means they were listening to music by a group called Republica, who were from years ago. They're for old people – the over-forty crowd. Why would people her age, and she's supposedly not that much older than us, be listening to them at a party?'

'Maybe it had a retro theme.'

'Possibly. But also possibly not. They were from the nineties, and I don't think anybody ever holds nineties retro parties. I mean, why would anybody want to put their guests through that? I'm starting to wonder whether she's quite as millennial as she wants us to think she is. She called us spods, and I'm sure that's a nineties thing to do. Look at her; her style's got something of the nineties about it too.'

'You've spent too long in that white mask. You don't

have to make a conspiracy theory out of everything.'

'You're right,' he said, 'I'm getting carried away.' He looked into Ayanna's eyes, and tried not to think about her leaving on Sunday morning, and how all this was probably just a fling to her. For now, though, he took her hand and they kissed, right there in the corner of the pub as if nobody else was around. Other people were around though, and after a while they became aware of somebody standing above them, clearing his throat. Richard looked up.

'I'm going home now. Any later and I'll be rolling-pinned. Have you got your key?'

It had been so long since he had last left the house that Richard had indeed forgotten he would need a key to get back in. 'Er, no Dad.'

'It's OK, David, I've got mine,' smiled Ayanna.

'You two have a good night,' he said, and Ayanna noticed a catch in his voice. It obviously meant a lot to him to see his boy out and about, and enjoying himself. She felt a lump in her throat too. Richard and Ayanna watched as man and dog left the pub.

'That was, er…' he said.

Ayanna squeezed his hand. 'They've taken good care of you,' she said.

He nodded. He had needed a lot of looking after; he was only now beginning to realise quite how much.

Each of them had a lot on their mind, and there was a minute in which neither spoke. Then Richard said, 'What do you think about hacking?'

Ayanna had given this a lot of thought, and she didn't hold back. 'I can't stand it,' she said.

'Why not?'

'It's such a cliché. I read a lot of books, a *lot*, and in the last few years there's been this epidemic of hackers. You never used to get them, but now they're everywhere. It really pisses me off. It's just so lazy – whenever an author writes themselves into a hole, one of the main characters just happens to find a nearby hacker, and suddenly everything's moving again. They might as well have them conjure up a genie – dramatically there's no difference. It's the same with TV dramas – when things get complicated a character pops up with a computer, and suddenly there's all this white code going up a black screen, and of course they can understand it all straightaway, and everyone knows exactly what the bad guys are up to. It's bollocks.'

'Yes, that is bollocks. It winds me up too – if it was real, the hackers would be there for weeks, living on Doritos and Monster Energy drinks, and spending almost all their time getting absolutely nowhere. So you don't think people should write about hackers, even though hackers are a real thing?'

'No, I don't think that, but they should write about them a lot less. It's almost as bad as writing books about writers; if I read another novel set at a literary festival I won't be held responsible for my actions. Have some originality. Maybe there should be a quota, and authors should only be allowed to write about things like that every once in a while. If they're on their tenth book, say, they could be awarded a hacking and book-festival token.'

'You should propose that at the next meeting of the council of publishers.'

'I will do. I'll burst in and start shouting. That

always goes down well,' she said, remembering the episode with *Out of the Strong Came Forth Sweetness*. She had written her fan letter to its author, but had explained that it was no more than that, that she was very junior, and people weren't ready to listen to her. At trade nights out, she would try to pitch it to people from other houses if they seemed OK, but they always glazed over as she told them it was about a father and daughter team from Burton-on-Trent who made a living by following rubbish trucks around and cleaning wheelie bins with a high-pressure hose. Even telling them that it was one of the best books she had ever read wouldn't wake them up. They couldn't see the angle that would sell it. *We tried something like that once*, they would say, *and it didn't fly*.

They would then go on to tell her about a forthcoming novel that they were excited by, and it would usually have something to do with a lawyer couple from London who, in spite of their superficially perfect life, were in fact having marital difficulties. She wished she could impress on them that, as with any book, what it was about was irrelevant. What mattered was whether or not it was any good, and this one was brilliant. The author had written back to thank her for her note, and to tell her she had lost heart with it all and wasn't expecting anything to come of it. Ayanna had written back, urging her to keep trying, and suggesting she send it to some independent publishers from outside London because they seemed to be more open-minded.

'But where does all this leave Roderick Ho?' asked Richard, snapping her out of it. They had already bonded over their devotion to the Slough House spy novels, all of which would have struggled to reach a conclusion without their resident hacker pulling rabbits from his PC.

'I don't know. I suppose we'll have to make an exception for Roddy.'

'You've not thought this through, have you?'

'Believe it or not...no,' she laughed.

'I sort of agree, though; it is overdone. It's like a character being dosed with truth serum. That said, I don't think there are any writers left who are shameless enough to use truth serum. But what I meant was, books and telly aside, what do you think about the ethics of it in real life? What if we were to do a little bit of hacking ourselves? Maybe we could find out some more about our self-styled millennial pal Mara.'

'Don't tell me you haven't already looked her up?'

He turned red. 'Well, maybe once or twice, but I never went deep. She had a different name back then. I always found it weird that I could hardly find anything about her on the Internet. Maybe I still won't, but it's worth a try isn't it?'

'Ethically,' said Ayanna, 'it's bang out of order.' She did her trick of raising a single eyebrow. Richard hadn't seen this before, and his mind was blown. 'But these are extraordinary circumstances. Count me in.'

'We'll get on to it straightaway.'

'Straight away? How about in the morning?'

'Fair enough.'

*

Unexpected things can happen when book festivals are in town, and something unexpected happened at the White Horse that night. Earlier in the evening a well-known Danish music star from the nineties had made an appearance in the function room of the Little Bottom cricket club, promoting *Sunday Morning*, her memoir about the highs and lows of her time in the Europop world. The event had gone well, and she had returned to the White Horse, where she and a number of the other authors, among them a visibly blootered Morag MacLochness, had been billeted in the attic rooms. Morag MacLochness, on a high from having sold four hundred books and raised a thousand pounds for her good cause, had snuck over to the jukebox and put on the singer's big hit single. At first the star had demurred, but then, carried away by the jovial atmosphere, she stood up and started to lip-sync her most famous song. The dance that went with it had survived the intervening years, and soon everyone had started to join in. Ayanna took to her feet and Richard followed, copying the moves as best he could, mainly half a beat behind. Next on the jukebox came 'Brimful Of Asha', and as the dancing continued, he conceded that maybe there was something to be said for nineties retro theme-nights after all. Ayanna was right; he had spent too long in his white mask, and he was going to have to work hard to readjust to the outside world. But he was ready.

They sat down, and for a moment he felt overwhelmed by the knowledge of how low he had sunk, and he saw with intense clarity that he had been suffering from a long and profound mental collapse.

There were times when his mum and dad had gently tried to get him to see the doctor; he had always refused, and they hadn't made an issue of that, but he could now see that they were right and he really should have booked an appointment. That morning he had been alone in his room, a broken young man in a mask, but now here he was, dancing along with a real-life pop star, beside a woman who had felled him with her fists and whom he had subsequently come to consider the most wonderful person he had ever met. And as he had danced, the person who had torn him to shreds had been there on the other side of the room, and it hadn't bothered him at all. He had caught occasional glimpses of her; she had been the only one in the pub who hadn't at least tried to do the dance. He couldn't shake the feeling that she would have known the moves, that it was from her era.

Everyone was going back to their tables, sweaty and elated, and he no longer felt overwhelmed; he just felt happy. He saw that Mara was getting up to leave. 'I suppose we'd better see her home,' he said.

'She'll love that,' said Ayanna.

They walked across the village green. None of them spoke. The festival was over for the day, and all was quiet. Ayanna noticed that a light was on in a part of the big marquee, and she idly watched three silhouettes that had been projected on to the canvas. One of them seemed quite squat, and reminded her of Florence Peters. The other two were taller, and looked like the dreadlocked, patchwork-dungareed people from the Happy Smile Energy Company, who had been running the site and distributing free drinks all day. She had watched them at work from Richard's window, and had plans to sample their wares before she left the village. She didn't think much about it, but then something odd happened: one of the taller figures seemed to take their hair off, throw it in the air, and catch it.

She told herself it must have been a trick of the light, and she didn't say anything as they carried on back to the house. She wondered whether she heard a champagne cork pop, too.

Ayanna had only briefly been in the room that had been allotted to her, to drop off her bag and to dip in and out to get things from it. Now it was established that she wouldn't be sleeping there, she went back in to retrieve her stuff. She had a look around. The room was Richard's sister's, and she must still have used it when she came back to stay. There was a framed photograph of her and her fiancé by the bedside. She looked at it for a while. She liked them. She liked the whole family. She told herself, firmly, that she wasn't to think that way, that she was on the rebound, and this was just a sudden and fleeting romance. Strictly speaking it wasn't a holiday romance because she wasn't on holiday, but really that was what it was, and she would be a bit misguided if she started thinking it might last.

Back in Richard's room – toothbrushed and wearing the enormous T-shirt that she used as a nightdress – she curled up beside him in his single bed. It had been quite a day, and soon they were both asleep.

Saturday

Chapter 28

Much toast is eaten, and we learn of the
passing of another unfortunate animal

Mrs Bruschini had spent her Friday evening being ferried from venue to venue, making her inspections and ensuring that everything was running smoothly across the festival. She hadn't joined in any of the late-night merrymaking, and when all the events were over she had returned to Honeysuckle Nook in the company of her young treasurer and two bottles of sherry. Thus she had missed out on witnessing the dancing authors in the White Horse, and was also unaware of the scenes in another corner of The Bottoms, where a group of three supposedly promising debut authors had celebrated the relative success of their shared event (twelve in attendance, four books sold) by heading to a different village pub for an attempt at a quiet evening that had ended with two of them embarking upon a torrid romance while the other vomited into a municipal shrubbery. They woke on the Saturday morning with churning guts, diabolical heads and crushing feelings of regret, but all this was tempered by a comforting sense that important traditions had been upheld.

There was no such comfort for the treasurer. After a fitful sleep, he had woken before dawn and lain there, looking at the ceiling as his mind went over and over what had happened in London. He knew he couldn't go on like this. He needed to talk to somebody, and he tried to work out who, and how. Sedated by her sherry, Mrs Bruschini slept on beside him as if nothing was untoward.

Among the many things of which Mrs Bruschini was unaware in her slumber was how Wilberforce Selfram had kept himself entertained the night before. She was not alone in this. After finishing his pudding of slugs at the Bells' house, he had headed out into the night, and his movements from that point on were unclear.

As Saturday morning established itself, a lot of people across the area began to unpick the tangle of the night before. In Market Horten there were recollections of a tall and unfamiliar figure in a Hawaiian shirt and backwards baseball cap who had appeared in The Wheatsheaf and gone around introducing himself as W-Dog. He had ordered *soda pop* from the bar, and assured everybody he met that it *sure was swell* to meet them, all the while dropping words like *faucet*, and *cilantro*, and *specialty* into the conversation. He had put his name down for karaoke, choosing 'Me, Myself And I' by De La Soul, but when his slot came up, he changed the lyrics to 'One, Oneself And One'. His performance was widely considered to be exemplary, and the ovation he received was so loud that the pub's manager, Michael Cartwright, reported that it had shaken the building and woken his baby in the flat upstairs. Calls for an encore had been rewarded with a second number, this time a rendition of Bobby Brown's 'My Prerogative'. He had renamed it 'One's Prerogative', and with the audience helping out on backing vocals, he had delivered it with a faultless re-creation of the original artist's dance moves. Once again, the crowd went wild, though when they looked for W-Dog afterwards, to offer him drinks and slap him on the back in congratulation, he was nowhere to be found.

Also from Market Horten came reports of a tall, solemn-looking character lurking in the street behind the railway station, not involving himself at all, just standing in the shadows and observing with still, glassy eyes. There were also those who recalled a lengthy stranger at the counter of the Kwong Yick on Water Street, offering to write bespoke Modernist aphorisms for their fortune cookies in lieu of conventional payment. Throughout the negotiations, which had ultimately failed, he had appeared to be propped up by some kind of stick.

In the village of Long Bottom, several people were woken in the small hours by the sound of bells coming from the green. Curtains were peered through, and for years to come the tale would be told of how on nights when the sky is clear and the moon is full, an elongated and inhumanly grey-visaged figure in full Morris-dancing regalia will sometimes appear there alone, waving its hankies as it works its way through an impeccable 'Under The Old Myrtle Tree' before disappearing as quickly as it had arrived.

But no matter how Wilberforce Selfram had spent his Friday night, by nine o'clock on Saturday morning he was once again at the breakfast table in the parsonage, piling up slices of toast, smothering them with marmalade, and gorging himself before anybody had a chance to bring him any more slugs.

Something else had happened late on the Friday night and into the early hours of Saturday, this time in London, beneath the offices of the ancient publishing house of HarperCollins. Regarded throughout the industry as the darkest of all the ancient houses, it is often whispered that below its headquarters there runs a maze of cells, a windowless, strip-lit purgatory, where those who fall foul of the company's top brass are sent to work until their sanity is stretched to its limit and they leave the building for the last time, trembling, and sometimes screaming, without even stopping at HR to negotiate a severance package. There is much truth behind these whispers, but what is never whispered about, because those few who know would not dare, is how of all these cells, number 44 is always left empty. It has never been used to house these wretched souls, in case they were to discover its secret. To look at it through the bars of the small window in the door, it looks much like any other, with its fluorescent tube, its uncomfortable chair, and the standard-issue bust of Shakespeare that is to be found on every desk within the HarperCollins headquarters, a ubiquitous reminder of their devotion to quality literature above all things. In Cell 44, however, the head of the bust can be grasped by the pate and tilted back, revealing a switch that opens the far wall, through which it is then possible to pass into a large vaulted chamber which, for this night of the full moon, had been decked out with flaming torches. Robed figures stood around an altar in the centre of the room, chanting as they passed a chalice from hand to hand. When everybody had drunk their share of blood, the meeting was called to order with three rings of the low bell. Their host, the jovial Lord Collins, spoke.

'Welcome, welcome,' he said, 'to our humble underground chamber. Uncle Rupert sends apologies for his absence, but has asked me to let you know that he wishes you all well, and that he is here in spirit.'

All hail Uncle Rupert, they chanted. *All hail him.*

'And as you have seen,' Lord Collins continued, 'he has kindly provided us with a juvenile okapi from his own herd.' The animal lay still on the altar. 'I must admit I had never drunk the blood of an okapi before, and I found it most palatable; vibrant yet loamy, and with notes of, perhaps, blackcurrant.' This was met with a murmur of agreement. He then led some chanting, the usual stuff about destroying those who would challenge them, before handing the meeting over to the President. It had been widely remarked upon that

Lord Barnstable had groomed his beard in such a way that he had begun to resemble Tsar Nicholas II more than he did George V. Either way, his presence and his authority were absolute, and the room fell silent as the hooded figures waited to be addressed.

The President told them about various foes who had been vanquished, as well as those who were about to be vanquished, then he provided them with an update on *Sour Grapes*, the forthcoming novel by the ageing troublemaker, Dan Rhodes. 'He is up to Chapter 28,' he explained. 'We believe this to be somewhere around the two-thirds mark, as the plot, if indeed it can be called a plot, appears to be inching towards a tipping point. Since I last updated you there have been some more toilet jokes and a little light romance, as well as a sequence of increasingly exhausting and indistinguishable set pieces at author events. There have also been further references to shadowy forces within British publishing. The similarities to our discreet little get-togethers are quite remarkable; mention has even been made of Cell 44.' This was met with gasps. 'The author is giving no indication of calming down – in his fury and confusion he puts me in mind of Charlton Heston at the end of *Planet of the Apes*. His deportment is most indecorous. We shall, however, continue with our plan to place this book at the top of the bestseller lists for the reasons previously stated.'

The President, though visibly exasperated, stayed

on the subject. 'The Scots are unaware of our plan, yet they are restless. This author's former publisher has heard of the auction we have been staging, believing it to be the real thing, and has somehow learned of his own, not entirely flattering, appearance in the story. As many of you will know, he has been visiting us one by one, dressed in a velvet suit with lace collar and cuffs, and sporting what appears to be a uniquely unbecoming periwig. He is very keen for us to know that this author is difficult, and has been hinting rather heavily that we abandon our bidding war.' Lord Barnstable smiled coldly. 'This debacle is their doing, and they are in no position to ask for solidarity from us. The author had to go in like Uncle Vanya to get the payments he was due – if they had done the sensible thing when the missing money was found, and engaged an impartial external auditor to go through all the relevant figures, he wouldn't have subsequently gone rogue and, in his bitterness and fury, threatened to expose the workings of the entire industry. It would have cost them, but sometimes you have to clear up your own mess. They could have kept it all behind closed doors, and given everybody the opportunity to put the episode behind them and move on with their lives, but instead they insisted, rather weakly I must say, that they had the credibility to police themselves. In so doing they instigated a war of attrition that is continuing to this day, and which is causing untold collateral damage to our business. Their short-sightedness is dumbfounding.'

There were cries of 'Down with Scotland, up with England.'

'Quite,' continued Lord Barnstable. 'The publisher is insistent that he is not really Scottish; he believes himself to be one of us. He tells us he has filled the company's senior positions with old Harrovians and so forth, and that even the Scots he has been obliged to retain for the sake of appearances aren't the sort to have that ghastly, grating accent. Even if this is the case, they must be treated with extreme caution. His operation falls under the Brotherhood of Darkness (Scottish Publishing Division), and you will all know that we have been at loggerheads with them ever since the incident with the turkey, the toothbrush and the parachute.' There was a collective shudder at the recollection of this episode. 'Yet he seems to assume we will close ranks with him.'

This was greeted with a snigger.

'We grandees of the London publishing trade should not have had to face this intolerable exposure. It is, as you know, our duty to ensure – with, of course, the dogged cooperation of our allies and enablers within the Brotherhood of Darkness (Literary Agency Division) – that the industry is institutionally unfair to authors, to see that they only ever receive the scraps under the table; so when they find that even these scraps have not been reaching them, their ire is not only inevitable but also, to a degree, understandable.'

His audience wondered whether he had started to go soft, and he seemed to sense this. 'We're still going to have him killed, though,' he explained. 'We can't have our writers finding out how our finances really work, and this one has got too close for comfort.' This was met with palpable relief.

'On a lighter note,' continued Lord Barnstable, 'you will be pleased to hear that as a punishment for the Scots' impertinence, the Fifty-ninth Earl of Doubleday has signed up their flagship author, leaving them quite critically impoverished, certainly as a credible cultural force, and perhaps commercially too.' This was met with a round of applause, which the Fifty-ninth Earl of Doubleday accepted with his customary nonchalance.

After some rather more humdrum business it was time to let go of formality and hear the announcement of the results of Common People Bingo. The Duchess of Bloomsbury waited, sure that her entry would glide to an easy victory. When the time came, though, Ayanna only managed to limp home in third place, winning her publisher just a small tin of biscuits. The silver medallist, winning her publisher a medium-sized tin of biscuits, was a school dropout from Middlesbrough who had worked in a Little Chef, and the winner – picking up a large tin of biscuits – was the publisher who had recruited a single mother from Stourbridge, who had come straight from the night shift at Birmingham Mail Centre. When Stourbridge was mentioned there was a snigger throughout the room, as well as a number of attempts at mocking the West Midlands accent, and the Duchess of Bloomsbury knew then that her girl from Croydon had never stood a chance. She felt humiliated, and was furious that she had indulged her rebellious ways and wasted all that money paying her wages.

There followed a brief check that, in spite of their new scheme, they were all predominantly continuing to employ one another's godchildren, and nieces and nephews, as well as the offspring of various co-directors on their many boards. After this, they let their robes fall to the stone floor before going back to the okapi, which had been bound by its hind legs, hoisted up, and decapitated. A puddle of blood had formed on the altar, and they smeared it over their naked bodies.

The Duchess of Bloomsbury fell into a group with, among others, the evening's host Lord Collins, who was cheerily expounding upon his continuing incredulity about the way in which authors were attracted to his house. 'I honestly don't understand it,' he chuckled. 'They're forever campaigning for this worthy cause or that, and you'd have thought they would have refused to sign a contract with a company owned by Uncle Rupert, but no. They come like moths, even those you would least expect, the ones who spend most of their lives complaining about Fox News, or the *New York Post*. Incorrigible *Guardian* readers, a lot of them; they wouldn't be seen dead with a copy of *The Sun*. It's as if they don't realise it's the same company, but they are intelligent people so they *must* know. It's the funniest thing – they have the power to bring down a huge chunk of the Murdoch empire by taking their books elsewhere, but they won't do it. It baffles me, but of course I'm not complaining.'

The Duchess of Bloomsbury peeled herself away, and collared Lord Barnstable beside the body of the okapi. As they coated themselves with a fresh layer of blood she asked again when she was going to be rid of either Selfram or Johannes.

'You must be patient,' said the President. 'The break has to appear natural. Rest assured they will see to it that you are accommodated.'

'Good.' She looked at him from the corners of her eyes. 'I remember you saying that MI7 would be happy to do me a favour.'

'Absolutely, after all you've done for them. I'll let my contact know to anticipate a request. I wonder what you have in mind.'

She just smiled in reply. She had something very specific in mind. *Third place*, she was thinking, as the harmonium started up. She had been head girl at Roedean, and Roedean head girls don't come third. They all stood to attention for the national anthem. *Third place and a small tin of biscuits.* She couldn't shake the sense of humiliation. Croydon-features was finished, and not just in publishing. She was dead.

Chapter 29

*Richard does some hacking,
and Mara demands a lemon*

Knowing she would have to drive the van the following day, Ayanna had kept to a glass of wine with her meal and a single pint of lager in the pub. Though she woke up fresh at half past eight, it took her a moment to work out where she was, and why she was there. She was alone in bed, but Richard was up and about already. She watched his back view as he tapped away at his computer keyboard. 'Morning,' she said, and he turned around. His face was white, and smooth, and expressionless.

The mask was back on.

Oh great, she thought. *So that's the end of that.*

*

In the room across the landing, Mara was also awake. She too was typing, the glow from her skinny laptop lighting up her angry face. Everything she wrote, she deleted.

Ayanna took a bundle of clothes through to the shower room, where she got dressed, and cursed herself for having allowed herself to become fond of her holiday fling. Maybe she'd misjudged him completely. Maybe he really was a weirdo and a sex case. She went back to Richard's bedroom. She started to gather her bits and pieces, and stuff them into her bag, ready to take them to his sister's room, where she would remain for the rest of her stay.

'Are you OK?' asked Richard, from behind his mask.

'I'm fine.'

'You don't seem fine. What's wrong?'

'Have a guess.'

The face stared blankly back at her. There was a long silence then he said, 'Oh shit, I'm so sorry. It's just what I've been doing every day for years, I just reached for it without thinking, and…' He tore the mask off, dropped it on the floor, and trod on it with a bare foot. It bent and split. He opened a drawer in his desk, pulled out a handful of identical masks, and gave them the same treatment before stuffing the bits into his bin.

She smiled and shook her head. His mortification was real enough, but she took the episode as a warning. He had a long way to go before he could be considered serious boyfriend material. She wasn't looking for a project.

'That was embarrassing,' he said, and she could tell he was truly ashamed. 'I'll get us some coffee.' He lowered his voice. 'I've got quite a lot to tell you about...you know who.'

They sat together with their coffee, and looked at the monitor. Richard navigated to the website of a carpet remnant wholesaler from Whitehaven. 'Look,' he said, pointing to a line at the bottom of the screen that told them it had last been updated in 2005. This matched the dated look of the site; its layout and font were very much of that time.

'OK. So we most likely won't be ordering any offcuts of carpet from them today.'

'They don't seem to be trading any more, so anyone who stumbles into this little corner of the Internet will just move on.'

'Unless they're perverts for bankrupt carpet company websites. Like you.'

'Exactly. And if you're a *real* carpet dogger, you might click here, on sisal roll ends...'

This brought up a small blank box, which Richard filled with complicated text. Suddenly everything changed. The layout was modern now, even futuristic. The screen was filled with a silver whirlwind, which after a few seconds morphed into mercury-like lettering, spelling out:

MI7
Securing YOUR Future!

'MI7,' said Richard. 'Have you heard of them?'

'Loads. If someone's writing about spies but they're too chicken to mention MI5 or MI6 in case it gets them into trouble, they say they're from MI7. It's corny. It's not real, Richard.' To her relief and disappointment, the magic faded further still.

'Sometimes corny things can be real though – like villages with *Bottom* in their name; as pathetic as it might seem, it does actually happen. I thought MI7 was a bad joke too, until last week. I've been here a lot in the last few days, and it's the real deal. It's the most secretive British intelligence agency going. It used to be a wartime propaganda arm, mainly keeping the press on-side. It was disbanded after World War II, but they quietly revived it in the nineties. These days, rather than existing for the sake of national security, it's used for one reason only – meddling on behalf of the establishment to make sure politics always leans in their favour. There are no public references to it anywhere, and the more I read about it, the more I realise why.'

'If you and your Incognito pals know about it, it can't be that hush-hush.'

'That lot don't know about it. I didn't tell them. If they had their hands on this information, they would get over-excited. It's very sensitive, and there's so much information I've barely scratched the surface. I don't know what to do about it yet. What I do know, though, is this.' He typed in *Mara*, and she appeared on the screen, a rotating 3D figure. Beside her was a brief biography:

NAME: Mara
AGE: 25
JOB: Journalist/Activist/Millennial
MISSION: Operation Polarisation
SEXUALITY: Pansexual
ETHNICITY: White/12.5% Chinese Singaporean
STATUS: Active

'So at least her age checks out. And I guess that must be her real name.'

'And I suppose she is a bit mixed race,' said Ayanna. 'Hang on...' She'd spotted something, and pointed to the very bottom of the screen, to where it said, in very small letters, CLICK HERE FOR REAL BIOGRAPHY.

'Well spotted,' said Richard, and he clicked. The picture remained the same but the text changed.

NAME: Rachel Lewis
AGE: 43
CURRENT MISSION: Operation Polarisation
PAST MISSIONS: Bristol DSI project/Operation Own Worst Enemy/Operations Wild Side & Lord High Executioner
SEXUALITY: Hetero/fleeting lesbian experimentation in student days
ETHNICITY: White/12.5% Chinese Singaporean

FIELD NAME: Mara (Hindu Goddess of destruction). No surname.
STATUS: Active

'Forty-three! I've got to admit she doesn't look it,' said Ayanna.

'It's probably her Chinese genes,' said Richard. 'East Asian women tend to look younger than they are.'

'Making racial generalisations now, are we?'

'Maybe a bit, but I don't think we're going to see Asian women marching in the streets complaining about how people think they look younger than their years.'

'Don't be so sure. We'll discuss this later, in great depth.' She poked him in the ribs. 'But for now…what's she doing? What's her mission? Why is she here?'

'I don't know… I've got some ideas, but you'd probably just say I was being a conspiracy theorist. I need to dig a little deeper. Give me a few minutes.'

Ayanna watched him at work. The screen turned black, and filled with fast-moving white code. His brow furrowed. He clearly knew what he was doing. She knew that it was well-established that seeing somebody do something at which they are very talented can make them extraordinarily attractive, but until that moment she never would have thought that this would have applied to working a computer. Her thoughts of moving to the other room had evaporated, and she wondered whether she might be in the market for a project after all. Apart from poking him in the ribs she hadn't touched him yet that day, but now she put her arms around him, and rested her head on his shoulder as he attacked his keyboard. A moment later he gave a jolt, spotting something amid the scrolling text. 'Jesus Christ,' he said.

Ayanna looked at the screen to see what he had found. It was just more screeds of code. He went back to work and she toyed with the curls at the nape of his neck. Her last boyfriend had been bald, and so had the one before that. It made a change to have some locks to fiddle with. She thought some more about her last boyfriend, the one with whom she had parted company just a few days before. He hadn't even had a bookshelf to scrutinise, and had had a habit of firing rubber bands at her when she was trying to read. She wondered how he had lasted so long, and then she remembered. It hadn't been a total waste of four months of her life.

'Fucking hell,' said Richard, knocking her back to the present. He carried on typing, and decoding the code.

The door opened. It was Mara, or whatever her name was. She hadn't knocked.

'I need a lemon,' she said. 'Get me a lemon.'

Ayanna wasn't sure how he had done it so quickly, but at the first sound of the door opening, Richard had made a video game pop on to the screen. He had casually played on for a bit, before pausing it and telling her he would go to the kitchen and get her a lemon, and that he would come back with some coffee and croissants too. He told Ayanna and Mara to stay where they were while he got on with it, then he put on some music, a bit too loud, and left the room.

For a long while they didn't say a word, then Ayanna began to think she ought to say something, so as not to appear suspiciously silent. 'So what's the lemon for?'

'What?'

Ayanna raised her voice over the music. 'What's the lemon for? Are you fighting off scurvy?'

'I'm writing an opinion piece for the *Guardian*,' she sighed, 'and I find they go a lot better if I suck a lemon while I'm doing it. It helps me to find the appropriate pitch of indignation.'

'Right.' Ayanna didn't have much to say to this. 'So are you going to any of the events today?'

'I suppose I'd better go to one or two so I can at least try and string an article together. I might try the Selfram one.'

'He talked you into it, did he?'

'Not really, it's just I know him a bit from the outside world; we were on *Newsnight* together a couple of weeks ago. I was talking about important millennial issues, like which dating apps to use, and he was droning on about old-people stuff, like the economy or something. I wasn't really listening; you don't at my age.'

Ayanna bit her tongue.

'Where's your boyfriend got to with my lemon?' huffed Mara.

Ayanna was going to correct Mara, telling her that they weren't really a couple, but she stopped herself. Let her think what she wanted to think. Besides, it was too much effort to talk over the music. It was coming from the computer, and she had no idea how to control the volume, so they both gave up.

After a few minutes, which seemed like hours and which Ayanna spent cursing Richard, he returned with a tray on which were three coffees, a plate full of croissants, and Mara's lemon sliced into quarters. He turned the music off, and distributed his bounty. Mara took a coffee, a croissant and her lemons, and went back to her room.

'I'm glad you took ages,' said Ayanna. 'It gave me and her a chance to really get to know each other.'

Richard shrank the video game and went back to his hacking. It seemed to be going well, as he kept shaking his head in disbelief, and swearing under his breath. 'This is... I'll tell you all about it in a few minutes.' They heard the door across the landing open. 'Or maybe I won't. Here she is, right on cue. I'll get her to tell you.'

Ayanna wondered what he was talking about, then Mara came into the room. She was smiling. 'Hi kids,' she said. 'Can I hang out with you two for a while?'

'Of course you can Mara,' said Richard. 'Or should I say...?'

'Rachel,' she said. 'Rachel Lewis.'

'Tell us a little bit about yourself, Rachel,' said Richard, in a credible impersonation of a gameshow host.

'Let's see,' she smiled. 'I'm forty-three, I'm Capricorn, I'm a level seven psychopath, and I'm fluent in nine languages.'

'And what do you do for a living, Rachel?'

'I suppose you could call me an agent provocateur.'

Chapter 30

The parson receives an unexpected visitor

It wasn't only the HarperCollins offices that boasted busts of Shakespeare. Wilberforce Selfram, his belly full of toast and marmalade, spotted one on a shelf of the dresser in The Parsonage's kitchen. 'One observes you revere the Bard of Avon.'

'I do. I can't get enough of him – I even put in a turn at the annual amateur dramatics production. Never a big role, but I do enjoy it. This year we did *A Midsummer Night's Dream*; I played Egeus.'

'One has also appeared in said play in one's schooldays,' said Wilberforce Selfram. The parson willed him to say it, and he obliged: 'You should have seen one's bottom.'

'Ah, so you played the man with the donkey's head.'

Wilberforce Selfram looked nonplussed. 'Negative.

That was a lower-case *b*. One was cast as merely a background sprite, yet in solidarity with one's homosexual brethren one performed one's role clad below the waist in nothing but a pair of leather cowboy chaps. Every time one presented one's back view to the audience, they were greeted with an unimpeded view of one's fundament.'

'Oh,' said Reverend Jacobs, wondering what else he could possibly have said to this.

'One supposes you do not share one's support for the Friends of Dorothy.'

'On the contrary, I'm part of the local LGBT outreach committee, and I'm forever lobbying the synod to do more to welcome gay people into the church. So how about you? Are you a Shakespeare fan?'

'One admires much about him: the readiness to pilfer from pre-existing works; the long and obscure words; the extended passages that baffle the laity. He is not, however, in the same league as JG Ballard or, though one says so oneself, oneself.'

The parson merely smiled at this.

Wilberforce Selfram looked glassily at him. 'One finds you rather a blank character, parson,' he said. 'Were this a work of fiction, this fractured isle's most forward-thinking intellectual staying in the home of a simple country clergyman would have led to debate, conflict and drama. However, this is not a novel.' He went on to explain his reasoning as to why this could not possibly be a novel.

'I suppose I must just prefer the quiet life, Mr Selfram.' Reverend Jacobs chose not to tell Wilberforce Selfram that in anticipation of his visit he had tried to read a couple of his guest's books, and found they hadn't really been up his street. Consequently, he didn't really want to talk about them. He was more at ease making sure his visitor had a clean towel and plenty of toast than he was in engaging in verbal fireworks. He had, though, quite enjoyed having him around, with his slugs and his monologues. The parsonage often felt quite empty, and the days a little too alike. Having him there made a change.

'Upon reflection one begins to wonder whether your lack of dramatic purpose could be considered to some extent Beckettian,' said Wilberforce Selfram. 'Either way, one is grateful for your hospitality.'

'Thank you,' said the parson. This pleasantry hadn't come as a surprise to him. He had been observing his visitor quite closely, and had started to notice something about him. He accepted that he could of course be wrong, but ever since his reaction to the throwaway comment about killing hedgehogs with cricket bats, he had started to wonder whether underneath it all, and in spite of his best efforts, Wilberforce Selfram was, in his own peculiar way, not quite as awful as all that. He had even grown quite fond of him.

'One shall ascend to one's eyrie and commence the scription of one's walk hither, aping the bygone footsteps of Beoffrey.'

'Do you have everything you need?' asked the parson.

'Affirmative.' And with that he was gone.

As the parson cleared up the breakfast things, he was interrupted by a ring at the doorbell. This was not an uncommon event, and he went to answer it. Standing there was a local young man whom he recognised as Mrs Bruschini's driver. *My treasurer*, she would call him. 'Vicar,' he said. 'Can I come in?'

The parson was quite used to being called a vicar. Often people would ask him what the difference was, and sometimes he would tell them, and they would look blank and nod, saying, 'I see,' even though they hadn't seen at all, but had given up their interest in finding out the answer. More often he told them that it was basically the same thing, which was fine because it was. He sometimes wondered whether the only reason the Church didn't change his title was because they wanted to avoid the expense of changing the wooden sign outside his house from *The Parsonage* to *The Vicarage*.

The young man was shown through to the kitchen, where he stood nervously before being gestured to take a seat at the table.

'What can I do for you?'

'I need to give confession,' he said.

'Ah, there's a slight problem there, I'm afraid. It's the other lot who do that – the Catholics.'

'But I really need to do this.' His eyes were haunted.

'You can talk to me in confidence.'

'But I mustn't see your face. I want to do it like in Mafia films, where they're in a sort of box thing.'

The parson thought quickly. 'You could go in the cupboard.' He emptied a few bits and pieces out of the cleaning cupboard until he could fit a dining chair in there, and the treasurer went in and sat down. There was no light, so when the door closed he was in the dark.

'Bless me father, for I have sinned,' he said.

'Pardon?' said the parson.

The treasurer repeated himself, to no avail, and the parson came up with the idea of opening the door a crack so they could at least hear each other. This was better.

The treasurer began again. 'Bless me Father, for I have sinned.'

Quite enjoying himself, the parson said, 'Unburden yourself, my child.'

The treasurer did just this, and the parson continued enjoying himself as he heard about what the young man had been up to with Mrs Bruschini. He hadn't expected that at all. Then he stopped enjoying himself. When the confession was over, he opened the door and saw the treasurer sitting there with his head in his hands.

'How many Hail Marys, father?'

'I'm afraid we don't do Hail Marys. You're going to have to call the police.'

Chapter 31

A proctor's reputation takes a tumble,
and Mara receives a phone call that makes her giddy

'What were we just talking about?' asked Mara, her eyes steely again. 'And why am I here, wasting my time with you spods?'

'You probably need to get back to your article,' suggested Richard.

'I will. I'll get back to it right now.' She backed out of the room, eyeing both of them suspiciously. When she was gone, Richard switched off the recording function on his phone.

'What just happened?' asked Ayanna.

'I managed to get a look at a list of her kit on the MI7 website, and it turns out she always travels with a few doses of truth serum. I put the music on annoyingly loud so she wouldn't hear me sneaking over to her room to get it. I didn't know if I would find it, but fortunately it was in a phial marked *TRUTH SERUM*. Then I laced the lemon quarters with it. I was quite busy, that's why I was so long.'

'Please stop doing this,' said Ayanna.

'Stop doing what?'

'Making me think you're a bit of a dick, then having me find you're really not quite as bad as all that.'

Richard was pleased to know for sure that she liked him, or at least that she didn't always think he was a dick. He hoped he was in with a chance of holding on to her, but now was not the time for a tender moment; they had just uncovered an extraordinary plot to foment social division. It turned out Wilberforce Selfram was right; this really was a fractured isle, and now they knew just how things had got so bad. Before they had a chance to make full sense of what they had just learned, a perky Mara came back into the room. She must have sucked another lemon.

As well as giving the dosed party a propensity to tell the truth, this particular serum also makes them want to please the people around them, temporarily overriding even level seven psychopathy, and for twenty minutes Mara happily answered all the questions that were put to her, before once again returning to her old self. Richard had read that this particular truth serum puts its users into a dreamlike state, and when they come out of it, they're not quite sure what has happened. Again she stormed out, backwards, and returned to her room, and again she reappeared, smiling, a few minutes later.

When the final quarter of lemon was sucked she came back to Richard's room, just as perky as the previous three times, and just as desperate for them to like her. They were dazed by all the information she had offered up, and had run out of questions. Instead, Mara began to ask questions of her own.

'So Ayanna,' she said, 'How is Selfram's event selling?'

Earlier, Ayanna had called in to the box office, and been given the latest figures. 'He's up to about forty tickets.' *About forty* was a slight exaggeration; the figure had been closer to thirty, and she wasn't sure how many of those had been bought for children.

'It's not enough, is it? I know, I'll do you a favour and cancel whoever's on the main stage at the same time, so everyone who was going to that will go to his talk instead.'

'There's no need,' said Ayanna.

Mara picked up a copy of the running order, and looked to see who he clashed with. 'Ah, it's Eric Finlayson. Right…'

'Really,' said Ayanna, 'I would rather you didn't. And anyway, how can you cancel an event?'

'I'm not talking about cancelling his event,' she said, 'so much as cancelling *him*. The event will just be collateral damage. I could set up a bomb scare or something, but this way is a lot more straightforward.'

'Please don't,' said Ayanna.

'No, really,' said Mara, 'It's no trouble at all.' She opened her laptop, and navigated to the now-familiar MI7 website, where she soon found a file on Finlayson.

'Eric Finlayson has a file at MI7?' asked Richard.

'We keep files on pretty much everyone who has any kind of profile, in case they need cancelling at a moment's notice.' She scrolled for a while. 'Ah, here we are... Poor old Eric,' she said, smiling as she typed away.

Ayanna watched her as she went about her business. She was seeming to take real joy from doing what she thought was a favour. Her eyes were bright, and her smile revealed previously unseen dimples. Perhaps this was the face she had shown to Richard. For the first time she could understand him taking a shine to her, and asking her to join him for a sausage-on-a-stick. They would have made an attractive couple.

As Mara typed on, Ayanna tried to work out what she could do to stop her, short of grabbing her computer and throwing it out of the window. 'Whatever you're doing...please don't,' she said.

Mara didn't seem to hear. 'Poor old Eric,' she said.

Eric Finlayson had catapulted to national fame in late middle age, just a few years earlier. Until then he had been leading a low-key life, working as a proctor. All the while, though, he had been filling notebooks with his thoughts and experiences, and after a proctoring accident had left him temporarily bedbound with two broken legs and a hairline fracture to his skull, he had gone back through his writings and turned them into a book based on his career. *Trust Me, I'm a Proctor* had come out eighteen months later, and had taken the bestseller lists by storm. Its follow-up, *Is There a Proctor in the House?* had done equally well, and a third volume, *The Proctor Will See You Now*, had cemented his status as the nation's favourite proctor. The books were currently being adapted into a Sunday-night television drama, and there was much excitement about this among people who were interested in that sort of thing. A few murmurs of discontent had happened around the publication of his most recent book because its title, *It Shouldn't Happen to a Proctor*, didn't work as a pun. This minor furore had passed though, and the book had sold in enormous quantities, and he was still considered to be the People's Proctor. But here was Mara, upstairs at Parsonage Cottage, tearing him down.

'You can't cancel Eric Finlayson,' said Ayanna. 'He's lovely.' She had read all his books, and had found them to be warm and amusing. She'd met him a few months earlier, and he had signed a book for her mum, who was a big fan.

'Too late. He's cancelled.'

'Already?'

'I don't hang about.'

'What have you done?' Ayanna felt cold. She wished she had thrown Mara's laptop out of the window after all, before she'd had a chance to go through with it.

'It was easy. His archive has just been preserved for the nation at University of Tipton, and our people have been through it to see what we can use against him. It turns out that in 1973 he said the wrong thing about lesbians.'

'But that was ages ago, and he'd only have been

about...' She tried to work it out.

'He was nineteen. And who cares how long ago it was?' She smiled, coldly now. 'This is publicly available information, and I've let people know about it on Twitter.'

'So you've asked everyone to cancel him?'

'No, I've just called for dialogue.' She read out her tweet. '*Such a pity that Eric Finlayson has been found to have said the wrong thing about lesbians in 1973. We need to have an urgent national conversation about his place in the culture.* I'll leave the calls for cancelling to everyone else.'

'So the lesbians are up in arms about it?' asked Richard.

She looked at her computer. 'No, they don't seem particularly bothered one way or the other, but the people who stick up for lesbians have gone ballistic.'

'Of course,' muttered Richard. 'I was forgetting that was how it worked.' He and his Incognito comrades had spent a lot of time discussing the way in which online unrest is orchestrated, and they had even started some themselves from time to time, but it still felt bizarre to have a front-row seat at the government-sanctioned inception of a storm.

'Look,' said Mara, pointing at the screen, 'he's already trending. And here's a film of someone setting fire to a pile of his books. It's not even been a minute – that might be a record.'

'But this is horrible. Can't you uncancel him? Selfram won't mind having a small crowd; he's used to it. He's bound to have a few fans in, anyway.' This was true. Wherever she had toured with him there had always been, among the more general book festival demographic, a core turnout of around half a dozen usually very pale people in their thirties and forties, always dressed in dark clothing, the men in black jeans, polo necks and suit jackets, and the women in black dresses, with bright red lips and scraped-back hair. They always came alone, and they never acknowledged one another. She knew that, with his style of writing, he was mistaken ever to have expected a wide readership, and that there was something hopeless about the way he harked back to a non-existent, or as he would say *inexistent*, Golden Age when his books would have sold by the truckload. She knew that his selective appeal had nothing to do with a broad cultural malaise, or the death of the novel; books still sold well – difficult books – some of them. His work was not without its admirers, though. These predominantly ghostly people were his real readers, the ones who could tune into his wavelength. There just weren't very many of them, that was all.

'It's too late,' said Mara. 'He's never coming back from this. Oh look, here's a tweet from the sponsor. *Our statement on Eric Finlayson.*' Below this they had posted a letter:

> *We at Happy Smile Energy are saddened by the news that Eric Finlayson said the wrong thing about lesbians in 1973. Saying the wrong thing about lesbians is contrary to everything that Happy Smile Energy stands for. With this in mind we feel we can no longer endorse his appearance at the All Bottoms*

Book Festival this afternoon, and we confirm that it will no longer be going ahead.

'There we are,' said Mara, or Rachel; to Ayanna it was hard to discern where one ended and the other began. She and Richard had agreed to regard her as Mara for the most part though, to avoid suspicion and confusion when the serum was not in effect. 'He's over. Not just his talk, but the man himself. It really is that easy.'

'But what did he say that was so terrible?'

'That's the funny thing – I've not even told anybody what he said, and they've still come in behind me anyway. No detail, no context, nothing. All I had to do was click my fingers. If you must know, it was in a letter to a friend that had found its way into the archive. He'd written it from a rented cottage in Dorset on a family holiday.' She referred back to it: *'I get the feeling there's a bit of the old Sapphism going on in the cottage next to ours. Attractive girls, too; I might nip round later and see if I can peek through a gap in the curtains!* I'll quote it in my article, and we'll keep the momentum going that way. I'll say it's reprehensible voyeurism, and he's objectifying lesbians as if they only exist for the titillation of men.'

'Or you could say it was just a light-hearted comment in a private exchange,' said Ayanna. 'I doubt he was really going to spy on them.'

'You know who else used to make light-hearted comments in private exchanges? Hitler, that's who. If you want to align yourself with him, that's up to you.'

'So you're trying to set things up so that people feel that if they come out against the cancellation of Eric

Finlayson, it means they're pro-Hitler?'

'Exactly. Everyone will have to pick a side. Personally, I'm quite ambivalent about Hitler – I think he had a lot of good ideas. The Mara character's against him, though. Even without him, it comes down to the same thing: you're either for lesbians or you're against them. So which are you? For or against?'

'I'm for them, obviously, because I'm not a horrible weirdo, but I'm against what you've done.'

'You can't have it both ways.'

Here were MI7's Operation Polarisation tactics in action: just as Mara had told them, she was toxifying debate by pushing it to two extremes, and shutting out anything in between. She knew that the newspapers would look at social media, and as ever would pick out only the shrillest contributions, presenting them as if this was where a consensus lay, and consolidating a battle line behind which many people who were broadly on that side of the debate would find themselves corralled, even if, in their hearts, they would much rather not have gone to that extreme. Anyone who didn't entirely cross this line would be snapped at as though they were a mortal enemy. In turning well-meaning people into attack dogs, they were tricking the left wing into eating itself alive; the broader ambition of creating a fairer world was lost as they bickered, carped, mounted their high horses, and tore one another to shreds, turning themselves into an unattractive prospect to the casual observer, and stultifying a lot of people who may otherwise have become politically engaged, ensuring their support remained at a level that didn't threaten their opponents. A lot of observers would even be catapulted to the opposite end of the divide, where a similar battle line will have been drawn, this one more robust in its simplicity.

This was what Mara had chosen as her vocation, and they had to concede that she seemed to be good at it.

With Eric Finlayson's life in ruins, neither Richard nor Ayanna knew what to say. The three of them sat in silence for a moment, then Mara's phone vibrated. She smiled when she saw who it was, and she answered. 'Hey big boy,' she said, then she moved to a foreign language for the rest of the conversation, which clearly consisted of a lot of flirting and giggling. When it was over, she hung up and sighed.

'Your boyfriend?' asked Ayanna.

'I wouldn't say he was my boyfriend,' said Mara, trying to sound cool, but unable to disguise her giddiness, 'but we hang out.' Then her expression changed. She was angry again, and she stared at Richard. 'I remember you now,' she said. 'You're that spod who ruined the Declaration of Sexual Interest project at Bristol Gerard Langley University. It was going so well; we were on the verge of rolling it out nationally, and gifting it to the feminism-has-gone-too-far movement, as well as fatally discrediting all student politics by making it seem oppressively self-righteous and nightmarishly proscriptive. That was mainly what I did back then,' she explained, 'providing content for the you-couldn't-make-it-up columnists on the tabloids. Normally they do just make it up, but sometimes – to do a favour for a friend, and bolster their morale – we'll work with them to set up a verifiable project that they can complain about; usually we'll misrepresent something that the bleeding hearts think is a force for good. With your one, we set out to make it look as if feminism is all about equating old-fashioned courtship with sexual harassment, and bringing down decent, normal men.'

'Which it isn't,' put in Ayanna. 'I know because I read a book about it once.'

'Perhaps not,' said Mara, apparently impervious to sardonicism, 'but with a bit of creativity it can be made to look that way. Anyway, your boyfriend started getting all sorts of sympathy – people were whispering, *Oooh, he only asked her out,* and *Oooh, it's not as if he's a sex case,* and *Oooh, isn't he dishy?* There was such an undercurrent of quiet support that there was a possibility of it going public. We couldn't get the feminism fangirls completely on board, and in the end we lost traction, and had to drop it; I wouldn't say I wasted a year's work because of you, because we did still spread a good amount of toxicity, and did our bit to make progress in gender equality look like a silly sideshow to the casual observer, but it should have gone a lot bigger than it did.'

'Wow,' said Ayanna, aghast. 'I suppose that's one way of trivialising awful things and setting women's rights back. What a result for the sisterhood.' She had often wondered who these people were, the kind who would devote their lives to spotting emerging fairness and doing all they could to hobble it. She hadn't expected to meet one of them in a quiet village in the middle of the English countryside.

'There is no sisterhood,' said Mara, with a condescending smile. 'They were good days; I can see why undermining the right-on brigade has caught on as a national pastime – I was in there from the start, and I can't think of anything more satisfying. Now, what was I doing?' She looked confused. 'Hang on, did I dream it, or did I just cancel Eric Finlayson?'

'I'm afraid you did,' said Ayanna, sadly.

She looked pleased. 'Well done me. My boss, Agent X, will be pleased; tearing down someone as well-liked as Finlayson always results in a swing to the right. So that's my article sorted. I was struggling to find something worth writing about in this dismal backwater, but thanks to you spods I've got my story – five hundred words on the downfall of Eric Finlayson: millennial dispatches from the front line of high-profile homophobia.'

She started backing out of the room, her eyes ablaze, then she stopped. She had spotted something. She walked over to the bin and picked out one of Richard's cracked masks. She placed it over her own face. 'Not so incognito now, are you?' She threw it across the room. 'You'd better start sleeping with one eye open.' She completed her backwards exit.

Ayanna thought Richard would be feeling relieved to hear that there were more people on his side than he had thought, who hadn't been convinced by Mara's cynical divisiveness, but instead he looked petrified. It was a while before he could compose himself and speak. 'Did you see whose picture came up on her screen when her phone rang?'

'No. I could see there was a big pink heart with a man's face in it, but I couldn't make it out. Who was it?'

'Vladimir Putin.'

'But if she's working for MI7…?'

'I think she has two jobs.'

'Oh shit. Is there a lock on this door?'

Chapter 32

The treasurer plants a tree

It had been an accident, Mrs Bruschini had told the treasurer. A year earlier, two days before she had arrived in Broad Bottom, Mr Bruschini had been telling her all about the place he had found for her in the countryside, and had handed her the keys, and thanked her for twenty-eight wonderful years. 'It's a pity you decided to go to bed with the milkman,' he had said, 'but it is what it is, and I'm sure we can both be very civilised about it all.' As she felt everything slip away from her – the visits to Glyndebourne, Sadler's Wells, Vienna and Berlin, not to mention their box at the Coliseum – she had picked up a kitchen knife. She insisted she had only meant to cut herself a slice of cheese, but had somehow stumbled and mistakenly stabbed her husband through the heart.

The treasurer had told the police all this, even though he no longer believed the part about it being an accident. He moved on to an account of his trip to London. He had been told what to expect: a body wrapped in cling film lying on the Welsh slate flagstones of their spacious kitchen. She told him she had kept the air conditioning on full blast to prevent putrefaction. As he had journeyed by train, and then taxi, to their mews house, he had pictured the body hermetically sealed in its plastic wrapping, but when he opened the door to the kitchen he was hit by the stench. It turned out that air conditioning was no match for a chest freezer, and the cling film, though several sheets thick, had not been able to keep everything contained – the corpse lay in a dried puddle of ooze. Mr Bruschini's eyes were open, and what was left of them stared at him through the plastic. The treasurer told himself that the mouldering remains of his face looked kind, as if the corpse understood the situation he was in, and had forgiven him.

'All you have to do,' Mrs Bruschini had told him, 'is pretend to be a gardener, dig a deep hole in the middle of the lawn, drag the body in, and plant a tree on top. I think a weeping cherry would go well. I do so adore cherry blossom.'

High walls surrounded the garden, and the lawn was not overlooked by the neighbours. The grass had grown high, and his first job was to mow it. Then he had measured and marked the centre of the lawn, and dug his hole. He hadn't got far when he hit a layer of rubble, so the hole was nowhere near as deep as he had hoped. As night fell on his third day in the house, he dragged the heavy body, inch by inch, through the patio doors and pushed it in to the hole. He covered it with a layer of soil, and the next morning he went out and bought a young cherry tree, and planted it, fanning the roots over the shape of the still-wrapped corpse, then filling in the earth around it. Mr Bruschini had been quite short, but other than that he had not been a small man, so there was quite a mound around the base of the tree. Then the treasurer scrubbed the kitchen floor as best he could, and took the train back to Market Horten. His bag was full of the mail that had accumulated on the doormat over the preceding year. Mrs Bruschini had asked him to bring it back so she could make sure nobody had noticed anything amiss. 'It's frightfully important that we make it look as if he's still alive,' she had said. 'He would have hated me to miss out on his pension payments, and as long as they keep popping into the joint account all will be well.'

The detective was a world-weary-looking man with dishevelled grey hair and a drinker's nose. The treasurer knew him as Brian, having lived in the house opposite his for his entire life. Brian licked the lead of his pencil, and made some notes. 'And where would the lady in question be at this present moment in time?'

The treasurer's first call after his confession hadn't been to the police, but to Dave the taxi driver. Telling him he had been unavoidably detained, he had asked him to pick up Mrs Bruschini and drive her around. Dave was on standby to buzz around the festival all day anyway, so he had no reason to think that anything was untoward. 'She'll be somewhere in The Bottoms. Look for Dave's taxi and she won't be far away.'

'You'd better stay here for now,' said Brian. 'Safest place for you, with a killer on the loose. Now, I've got some calls to make, not least to our friends at Scotland Yard. I'll tell them to dust off their shovels and get digging.' He left the room. The treasurer was alone, turning over what he had done, and wishing he had learned to say no. He also wished he had tried a little harder to convince the secretary to go out with him. She was the one he really wanted, and he knew now that he had only allowed himself to become enamoured of Mrs Bruschini to fill the void.

Now he had no chance of going out with her. Brian had been sympathetic to his plight, but had told him there was only so much he could do to help. His cooperation would count for a good deal, but there was no getting away from it – you don't get caught burying the body of a murder victim without going to jail for quite some time.

Chapter 33

We discover a little more about The Selfram Project, and Richard and
Ayanna are shocked when they find out what is on his hard drive

Using his technical wizardry, Richard had managed
to transfer the entire contents of the MI7 website to
his computer. He and Ayanna were unable to resist
snooping around it. There was a lot to go through, and
something caught Ayanna's eye. 'Scroll back up,' she
said. Richard did as he was asked, and there it was,
almost buried in a long list: **The Selfram Project**.

He clicked, and they read all about it.

'Poor Selfram,' she said. Through familiarity, and in
spite of herself, she had grown fond of him, in the
same way an owner will grow fond of an irritating
dog. She had got to know him quite well as she had

travelled around with him and his dictionaries. 'He'll be gutted if he ever finds out.' Having read his file she was relieved that he wasn't in any mortal danger. Even so, what she had discovered had not been great. She had sometimes wondered how an author of such arcane books had managed to get himself as high a profile as he had, and now she knew.

Some years earlier, fearing a modern equivalent of the Paris student riots of the 1960s, in which academic-minded youths clutching slim volumes by influential thinkers had risen up and directly challenged the government, the powers that oversaw the running of the United Kingdom had become uneasy. The possibility of a movement of young and highly literate alternative brainboxes was too much of a threat for them to countenance, so they had set out to hobble it before it had the opportunity to gain significant momentum. In the early nineties, MI7 had been tasked with the mission of ensuring that swathes of people who might go down this route were put off, and they had anointed Wilberforce Selfram as the nation's leading alternative public intellectual. They had used their network of high-level contacts to ensure he was provided with television punditry slots, acres of review coverage in broadsheet newspapers, and guarantees of big magazine interviews accompanied by full-page photographs. With him positioned in this way, the potential future left-leaning eggheads of Britain had accepted his status. The problems began when they tried to read his novels. They hadn't been sure what they had been expecting, but it hadn't been this. They investigated further, and the man fell apart before their eyes. *What is he?* they asked themselves, and the answer inevitably came that he was a fancily educated restaurant critic, *Evening Standard* columnist, and occasional novelist, who had styled himself as a Bad Boy, and seemed to think that plucking long words out of a thesaurus made him clever. They also had a nagging feeling that with his overdeveloped sense of superiority and his incessant sighing about how those around him couldn't satisfy his intellect, he was also something of a snob. They quietly rejected him and his work, and in many cases these intelligent young people were so dismayed that they never again attempted to read a book. The threat of a highly literate opposition had been substantially dampened.

Ayanna read that the Duchess of Bloomsbury had accepted large subsidies in order to cover his advances. Her name was highlighted, and she clicked on it. A biography popped up: boarding school, Oxford, etc., then her MI7 missions were listed. Just below The Selfram Project was **Operation Own Worst Enemy (Johannes)**. *Oh, bloody hell*, thought Ayanna. *Not him as well?* She was back to being the owner of a dog that was wretchedly annoying, but was still *her* dog, and somehow, she felt she should be on its side.

She was aware of Harry Johannes's ignominious history – making up quotes, being forced to return awards, and disguising his identity in order to relentlessly vandalise his rivals' Wikipedia pages. It was a squalid list, and she had often wondered how he had been able to so swiftly resume his career after it had all come out. She was soft enough to believe he should be allowed a second chance in life, but not so soft that she thought this second chance should involve him going anywhere near the written word. She could never understand why he had been given a book deal by the Duchess of Bloomsbury, or why his efforts were given so much oxygen on publication, rather than being distrusted and ignored into oblivion, their places in the catalogues being taken by consistently reliable writers.

Now she knew. MI7 had their reasons – someone with his chequered history remaining an active member of the left-leaning journalism community, which had granted him clemency, cast a shadow of doubt over all of them and helped them towards their goal of keeping the country's politics pointing to the right. Though he struggled to place his work in newspapers, MI7 had arranged for the Duchess of Bloomsbury to provide him with a high-profile outlet. As long as Johannes was around, the left-wing press, which was already on the margins, was damaging itself further still; they had been fed just enough rope, and were unwittingly propping up the ancient power structures that they believed themselves to be challenging.

So that was what she had been doing for the last few months of her life – oiling the wheels of MI7 as they did all they could to weaken the establishment's potential opponents, bolster the right wing, and maintain the status quo. She felt sorry for poor, oblivious, Selfram and, to a lesser extent, Johannes, but above all she felt sorry for herself. She'd had enough. She would drive the van back to London, and that was that. She wasn't going back to work.

*

Mara had written her article, and it had already been posted. There she was, in her pursed-lips by-line photo, looking coldly into the camera; underneath, her piece matched her expression. She had included the quote from the letter. *I thought we had come so far,* she sighed, and *Knowing this man has been revered as a National Treasure is another heartbreak for we of the LGBTQIA+ community,* and *His silence speaks volumes,* and *His youth at the time of the outrage is no excuse; bigotry has no sell-by date.* She concluded by declaring the cultural landscape to be a little more hopeful with the removal of Eric Finlayson, and expressing her heartfelt sympathy for the objectified couple. Ayanna wasn't impressed. 'She comes across so sanctimonious, as if she's never had an off-colour thought in her life. If her readers knew what a big phoney she was…'

Richard smiled. 'That can be arranged.' Using the real biographical details they had found on the MI7 website, they did a bit of digging, and almost straightaway they found something that, using her own logic, would bring her down. They spent the next half-hour piecing together their own exposé, and getting it ready to post. Using computer trickery, Richard had hidden their identities so they couldn't ever be traced as the originators of the piece, not even by Russian intelligence.

They sat back and looked at their handiwork. They were going to tell the world that she wasn't who she claimed to be. And not only that, they had found a mention of her in a clipping from a local newspaper: *It was pistols at dawn at Sunny Lane C of E Primary School last week, when they held a Cowboys & Indians fun day to mark the last day of term. Rachel Lewis, 9, came dressed as a Red Indian Squaw.* And there she was, culturally insensitive feathers and all. Her own followers, pumped up on their own indignation, would turn on her and eat her for breakfast.

They didn't post it. They agreed that it had been fun to put together, but when it came to it, they didn't want to sow even more discord and division. And besides, she had looked so sweet in the photograph; just an innocent little girl enjoying herself. Ayanna even began to wonder whether there had been something in Richard's abandoned theory that once, a long time ago, she had been a nice person.

Richard felt he should do something though, and started to wonder about sending an anonymous message to MI7 to let them know about her Russian connections. They probably knew already; maybe they'd even set it all up. The Russians were everywhere, after all. Still, he supposed it wouldn't hurt to drop them a line.

While Ayanna carried on scrolling through the MI7 material, Richard was on one of his other computers, from where he found that Wilberforce Selfram was using next door's Wi-Fi. Almost without thinking, he used his hacking skills, and soon he had access to all the writer's files. He looked around to see if he had any inkling of The Selfram Project. He wondered whether he knew of their work and was going along with it, or whether he was truly oblivious, as Ayanna believed he was. He scrolled around until he got to a folder that was named *Top Secret!* He clicked on it, but found he needed a password. He could have found a back door, but that would have taken a while, so he tried an easier way. Casually, he asked Ayanna, 'What do you think Selfram's favourite word is?'

She answered without missing a beat: 'It's *Pneumonoultramicroscopicsilicovolcanoconiosis.* It's some sort of lung condition. Every time he hears someone clearing their throat he'll tell them to consult a physician in case they have an acute case of it. It's just another excuse for him to show off about knowing a long word.'

He duly typed it in, and it was rejected. Realising Selfram had probably included a number and a symbol or other special character too, he then typed *Pneumonoultramicroscopicsilicovolcanoconiosis1!* He was in. He started to think about how well he and Ayanna worked as a team, and how much he wanted to spend the rest of his life with her, but this train of thought was quickly derailed. 'Oh no,' he said. 'This is horrible.'

'What is it?'

'Don't get angry, but I've just been having a little shufty around Selfram's hard drive.'

'That is completely out of order,' she said. 'It's private. It's none of your business.'

'I know. I'm sorry. I shouldn't have done it. And I kind of wish I hadn't now. I've found something...a folder full of images...'

Ayanna knew she shouldn't look because it would

make her complicit in Richard's wrongdoing, but she couldn't help herself. She put a hand to her mouth. 'Oh shit… What…? Why…?'

'It gets worse,' he said. 'These weren't downloaded on to his computer. They were created on it.'

Chapter 34

We find out the truth about the noisy ice machine

With all the drama that had been unfolding that day, Ayanna had almost forgotten that she had work to do, and was due to set up Wilberforce Selfram's talk. She and Richard had been snapped out of their adventure by a call from downstairs. Mrs Bell was telling them it was nearly time to go next door to the parsonage for their pre-event lunch. It was only then that Ayanna realised she hadn't yet brushed her teeth. She began to understand why hackers had such a reputation for poor personal hygiene.

'I haven't had a chance to find you any slugs, Mr Selfram,' said the parson, 'so I'm afraid you're going to have to eat normal food. I hope you won't mind too much.'

'One shall endure the multifarious horrors of contemporary rural comestibles with stoicism,' Selfram replied, noting the presence of the *Guardian* contributor, and feeling the need to protect his brand by reiterating his love of raw Dark Ages cuisine. This lunch saw the same guest list as dinner the night before, with one addition: a squat woman in tweeds, her silver hair tied in a scrappy bun, who had been introduced as Florence Peters, the book festival impresario. Ayanna recognised her, and Wilberforce Selfram had clearly encountered her before on the circuit, but she was a stranger to the others. There was also an empty place at the table – Mrs Bruschini had been invited, but had not arrived. She was the one who had asked for Florence Peters to be accommodated. The parson supposed Mrs Bruschini had been arrested for murder by this point, but he had set a place for her anyway, for the sake of appearances.

Mrs Chapman had insisted on coming over to help the poor, widowed parson prepare the meal. As she began to bring the plates to the table, the doorbell rang. The parson answered it, and there on his doorstep was the murderer. 'Mrs Bruschini,' he said, gulping a little. 'Do come in.' As she swept past him, he felt a chill.

She took her place at the table, and glared at Mara. 'I read your nasty little article,' she said.

'People like Finlayson are a poison in our society,' retorted Mara, calmly. 'We members of the LGBTQIA+ community will sleep easier tonight knowing he's been wiped from the culture.'

'Oh, you mustn't have heard,' said Mrs Bruschini. 'He's been uncancelled.'

'No. That can't be.' Mara reached for her phone, and as she scrolled she looked furious.

'That's right,' Mrs Bruschini announced to the table. 'Everyone's very fond of him, and apart from some fringe elements on the Internet there was no great hunger to send him to Coventry for something so petty. Even the National Council of Lesbians poured cold water on your efforts. They said that it wasn't the sort of thing they would ever concern themselves with, because there were far more pressing issues than hounding people who hadn't really done anything wrong. The couple he had been talking about have come forward too; it turns out they had ended up spending a lot of time with him on that holiday, and had got along well, and they are still in touch all these years later. He had even been a guest at their wedding, and when they were told about his letter, they thought it was hilarious. They also pointed out that they didn't need any sympathy, heartfelt or otherwise, from newspaper columnists.'

'Foiled again by residual affection,' snarled Mara. 'But what about Finlayson himself? Surely he immediately issued a grovelling apology for all the pain he's caused? They always do that.'

'He won't know anything about it; I'm told he's very old-fashioned, and doesn't even carry a mobile phone. He's on the train up at the moment, and has probably slept right through it.'

Richard and Ayanna had phones though, and they immediately looked up the latest mentions of the episode. There was another post from the Happy Smile Energy Company. *A second statement on Eric Finlayson.* Below this was another letter:

> *Contrary to our earlier statement, in which we expressed our dismay about Eric Finlayson, following discussions with our many friends in the LGBT+ community, we now realise that our response was disproportionate, and we would like to offer our apologies to Mr Finlayson. All our staff will be undertaking an extensive course of sensitivity recalibration in the near future, and we hope that such misunderstandings will not arise again. We are glad to confirm that his event will be taking place as advertised.*

Mara was fuming, and Richard and Ayanna wondered whether she would get into trouble with her bosses at MI7 for messing this up. 'Hang on,' whispered Ayanna. 'Look at this.' She pointed to some almost microscopic small print at the bottom of the statement: Happy Smile Energy is a subsidiary of Klaxxon Fracking, Inc.

'You're good at spotting small print,' he said, squinting at it. He fiddled with his phone, ignoring his mother's disapproving glares. She hated phones at the table. 'It's all coming together,' he said.

The parson couldn't help watching Mrs Bruschini as she handled her steak knife. He would have to be careful not to offend her in any way. She was holding court, and singing the praises of Florence Peters, whom she saw, and this was very rare for her, as an equal. She told them all that she looked forward to a long and fruitful relationship with the Book Festival People. 'She found us our sponsor, you know.'

'That's a very loud ice machine they've got,' said Richard.

'Yes,' said Florence Peters, in her small voice, 'they've been kept ever so busy giving out all those free drinks.'

'I've got a seismograph app on my phone,' he said, 'and some of the vibrations have been sending the dial over two on the Richter scale.'

'As I said,' continued Florence Peters, 'they have been very busy making all those lovely free cocktails. Everyone's been very thirsty because of all this sunshine. Haven't we been lucky with the weather?'

There was general agreement about this, but Richard persisted. 'They may have an ice machine, but that's not what's been making all the noise, is it?'

'Darling,' said Mrs Bell. 'Not now.'

'You've been test-drilling for shale gas, haven't you? Happy Smile Energy is just a front for Klaxxon Fracking.'

'Test-drilling for shale gas!' Florence Peters chuckled. 'Mrs Bell, I'm afraid that son of yours must be a little funny in the head.'

Mrs Bell's lips turned thin at this, and she was about to say something when Ayanna beat her to it: 'Don't talk about Richard like that.'

Mrs Bell was delighted by Ayanna's defence of her boy, and she had a tear in her eye at the thought of love in bloom, but then she remembered that Florence Peters needed taking down yet another peg or two. 'If

Richard says you've been test-drilling,' she said, in her calm voice, 'then you've been test-drilling. So what do you have to say about it?'

Florence Peters cracked. It didn't matter now, anyway. 'So what if we have?' she said defiantly, in a voice none of them had heard before. 'It's a free country. And you know what? Yesterday we found hard evidence of the presence of shale gas. Corks were popped. Wigs were thrown in the air. We've struck gold, right under your feet. One year from now, this village will have been knocked to the ground and replaced with England's most profitable fracking site. All this will be gone – the church, this house, the village green, everything. You'll wave placards, and sit in trees, but it won't do you any good. All that easy money – the government's hardly going to let it go to waste because of a few sentimental villagers.'

Eyes were not so much on Florence Peters as they were on Mrs Bruschini, who was the one who had brought her into The Bottoms.

'I thought they sounded nice. Happy Smile... It sounds so...nice.'

'I'm afraid all the big companies do that,' said Richard. 'They set up a green operation that they can point at whenever they're accused of being environmentally irresponsible, but really the bulk of their business just carries on as usual.'

'He's right,' said Florence Peters. 'It's a bog-standard greenwash.' She pointed a thumb at Mrs Bruschini. 'It wasn't her fault. She never had a clue – she was just a patsy; we saw her coming from a mile off. You know what we called her? *Target Number One*. This whole book festival was set up so we could put up that tent and get drilling without all the tiresome attention that sort of thing usually brings.'

'Don't you need all sorts of permits to do that?' asked the parson.

Florence Peters laughed, and untied her bun, letting her hair fall loose. 'There may be a minor regulation or two, but there's always a way around that sort of thing if you know the right people. Laws are invaluable, of course. Rules, on the other hand, are adapted to the circumstance.'

'That,' said Mr Bell, 'is unmitigated gobbledegook.' Ayanna noticed a steeliness to him that he had kept well-hidden until now. 'I am a semi-retired solicitor, Ms Peters, and Susan is also a semi-retired solicitor. Put us together and you have a whole solicitor with an awful lot of time on their hands. Semi-retired solicitors are ten a penny in The Bottoms – throw a stone, and there's a very high chance you'll hit one.'

Mrs Bell's steel was no less tempered. 'We won't be going down without giving you the fight of your life.'

Ayanna was impressed with their spirit, but knowing what she now did about powerful forces, she was doubtful about the likelihood of stopping the government machine.

There was a silence while they all tried to make sense of everything they had just heard. Only Wilberforce Selfram wasn't engaging in the episode; he was so lost in his world of normal food that he seemed not to have noticed anything unusual happening around him. His eyes stared straight ahead.

Mrs Bell was the first to speak. 'So you mean that

after all the hard work we volunteers have put into it, and with all these authors travelling all this way, the festival has just been an excuse to line the pockets of a small number of people who don't think twice about ruining lives and tearing the countryside to pieces?'

'That's one way of looking at it, but let's not be too cynical. Hasn't everyone had a super time along the way? Lots of nice drinks, and talks from people off the telly. Your problem is not uncommon: so many people seem to misunderstand the nature of arts funding.' With a wag of her finger, and a condescending smile, Florence Peters said, 'You mustn't be so naïve. Without corporate sponsorship, how could there ever be art? There would be no books, no paintings, nothing; no exchange of ideas. It is absolutely necessary for the nation's cultural life. Admittedly we usually make sure that any social or environmental havoc our sponsors wreak is out of view of the festival itself; in the Arctic circle, perhaps, or somewhere in sub-Saharan Africa, but I have a living to make, and this was too good an opportunity to turn down.'

Again, eyes turned to Mrs Bruschini. Not because they were looking for someone to blame, but because she was making an unusual sound. Her face was buried in her hands, and she was sobbing.

'Never mind her,' said Florence Peters. 'She'll get over it. The compulsory purchase orders will be signed in a few weeks' time. And don't worry, to compensate for the inconvenience you'll all be getting a full two per cent over the market value for your houses. You start packing, and we'll start fracking.' She threw her head back and laughed. Then, as if nothing unusual had happened, she said to Mrs Chapman, 'These potatoes are delicious. You must tell me your secret – I can never get mine this fluffy on the inside.'

Mrs Chapman didn't tell her the secret of her potatoes. Instead she emptied the gravy boat over Florence Peters' head. 'Nobody,' she said, 'threatens my village.' Then, not content with this, she raised the empty gravy boat and smashed it down on to Florence Peters' head. 'I'm sorry about your gravy boat, Reverend Jacobs,' she said, 'but there comes a point.' The gravy had cooled just enough for it not to be at a scalding temperature when it had landed, but the crockery had made its mark, and a trickle of blood ran down her forehead, merging with the brown.

Stunned by Mrs Chapman's outburst, nobody noticed Mrs Bruschini taking an unusually strong grip on her steak knife. It was only when she raised it and aimed it with great force at Florence Peters' heart that their attention was caught, and everything went into slow motion. The tip of the blade grazed the edge of Florence Peters' tweed lapel, and went into her blouse, and just as it began to pierce her body, Wilberforce Selfram's hand shot out with the speed of a lizard's tongue, and grabbed the assailant by the wrist. The knife, having left only a scratch on the victim's skin, fell to the floor.

Wilberforce Selfram returned to his meal.

Chapter 35

Wilberforce Selfram tries, without success, to introduce sugar-crazed youngsters to eighteenth-century German philosophy

One end of the Upper Bottom village hall was a hive of activity. Lots of people had bought tickets on the door, and the turnout was more than double the numbers the organisers had been expecting. Children in costume were running around, brandishing broomsticks and cuddly owls while their parents watched from the sidelines. The inflatable Hogwarts was a great hit, and there were other obliquely supernatural activities – apple bobbing, face painting, and spooky crafts – to keep them entertained when they weren't busy bouncing. The tombola prizes had gone, and the cake table had been stripped. Mrs Bruschini was satisfied as she surveyed the raucous scene.

After her attempt to kill Florence Peters, the parson had said a prayer and persuaded everyone that it would be best to put it all behind them, to consider it one of those unfortunate incidents that happen in the heat of the moment. His main motivation for this was to make sure that Mrs Chapman wasn't arrested for aggravated assault with a gravy boat. When Florence Peters had at last gone back to her B&B though, to shower off all the gravy and dress her wounds, and to change into an unstabbed outfit, the parson was straight on the phone to Brian at the police station, to check that the treasurer had been in touch with him about Mrs Bruschini.

Brian assured him that it was all in hand. 'It's a very complex business, a murder investigation,' he said. 'I'm not really supposed to tell you anything about it, but since you're a parson I'm sure it'll be OK. We've got our London lads – and ladies, let's not forget the ladies – digging up the garden as we speak. As soon as they verify the presence of a cadaver, we'll be off to have a little chat with our friend Mrs Bruschini. You say our suspect is proceeding in a northerly direction?'

'Yes,' said the parson. 'To Upper Bottom village hall in Dave's taxi.'

Mrs Bruschini had been accompanied by Mr and Mrs Bell, who were on hand to restrain her if she was to go for anyone again. The parson had taken Mrs Bell aside and given her a very quick outline of the allegations, also assuring her that he would be in touch with Brian. Ayanna and Richard were following along in the van, with Wilberforce Selfram wedged in between them. It felt odd to have him there, knowing what they did about the images they had seen on his hard drive. Now they had found out about them, and also how he had been responsible for distributing them far and wide, it had changed everything they thought they had known about him. Neither of them knew what to say. They couldn't raise the subject, because he would know what they had been up to, and with so much going on, it was hard to work out a strategy for dealing with it. There was always the possibility of doing nothing at all, and keeping the secret to the grave. That would certainly be the easiest course of action; after all, it was something they should never have known about in the first place.

They were both a little nervous as they made their way along the country roads, Ayanna because there was a knife-wielding madwoman on the loose, and Richard because it was the first time he had seen his new girlfriend driving her van, and a particular law of biology was in full force – the one where if you find somebody attractive, they become even more attractive when you see them behind the wheel of a large vehicle. The last twenty-four hours had been very strange, with so many ups and downs, and he was afraid of there being another down, and losing her. He was beginning to brace himself for it.

Amid all the drama there had been some good news at lunch, and everyone was still on a high about it. The village was saved.

After the prayer, as Florence Peters had sat at

the table, covered in gravy and bleeding from her head and her chest, she looked disconsolately at her remaining food, which was inedible due to all the porcelain shards from the shattered gravy boat. She had hoped that their Christian charity would extend to offering her a fresh plate, but there was no sign of this happening. Her phone rang, and she answered it. The earpiece volume was high enough for everyone to be able to hear the person at the other end.

'Is that the Silver Eagle?' said the voice.

'The very same.'

'Slight setback when it comes to the old fracking, I'm afraid.'

'Go on.'

'We've had the detailed analysis back from the lab, and it turns out those chemicals weren't evidence of shale gas after all; we'd actually struck a seam of fossilised mammoth urine. Apparently, they have a very similar atomic structure, or something.'

'Fossilised mammoth urine? Is there any value in it?'

'Only curiosity value I'm afraid, Silver Eagle.'

'Rats' cocks.'

'Quite. It turns out we're not alone – all the other sites are reporting the same. There doesn't seem to be any shale gas under the entire country, just lots and lots of mammoth urine. According to the geologists, they used to wee so much it would find its way through cracks in the rocks and collect in vast underground reservoirs, which solidified over time.'

'I never did like mammoths – if you ask me, they were just hairy elephants. But what about all this amazing shale gas detecting equipment we had? The government told us it was world-beating.'

'Unfortunately, their official line is that Britain is the best country at everything, so instead of using tried and tested technology invented by Johnny Foreigner, they decided that all domestic exploratory fracking should be done with their own shale gas detectors, invented from scratch by their British friends in various tax shelters around the world.'

'A noble idea. If only their shale gas detectors had been able to detect shale gas.'

'It feels rather unpatriotic to say so, but the abject failure of the equipment has been something of a setback.'

'But at least I'll get my bonus for setting up this ridiculous festival.'

'I'm afraid not. Klaxxon have unloaded Happy Smile, and three minutes ago they went into liquidation. None of us are getting a penny. The festival's OK because they were paid up-front, but the rest of us are royally screwed.'

'Rats' cocks,' she said again.

'If it's any consolation, every potential fracking site in the country will be shutting down.'

'How's the government going to spin that?'

'They're keeping the mammoth angle under wraps and announcing a moratorium on fracking for environmental reasons. They'll pick up a few green points and save a bit of face, but really this whole episode has been an expensive national disgrace.'

'Business as usual then.' She sighed. 'And it's always the little guy who loses out.'

'You may be short, but I wouldn't describe you as

little.'

She finished the call.

'You have your village back,' she said. 'And I suppose I'll have to return to the day job.' She glared at Mrs Bruschini. 'Just because you stabbed me, don't think you won't be receiving an invoice.'

'Our payment is already prepared,' sniffed Mrs Bruschini. 'I've even signed the cheque myself, for a hundred pounds.'

Florence Peters had forgotten that she had been expecting such a deluge of money to come in from the fracking side of things that she had effectively waived her normal fee in order to smooth things along. A hundred pounds would barely cover her petrol. 'Rats' cocks,' she said, for the final time, and without another word – not even to thank Wilberforce Selfram for saving her life – she left the parsonage.

While all the mayhem was happening at the children's end of the village hall, the other end, where the stage was, looked like the unhappiest bingo hall in the world.

Ayanna had set up the trestle tables and the complete set of dictionaries and thesauruses, and in the midst of them was Wilberforce Selfram, sitting behind a microphone and being watched intently by half a dozen serious-looking black-and-grey-clad people in stackable plastic chairs. They poised their pens on their notebooks as he began his talk. He had decided to warm up his audience with a selection of long words picked from the books. He would choose a volume, open it at a random page, and read the longest word that caught his eye. There would be no definition given, and once each word was spoken, he put the lexicon back in its place and moved on to another. His readers wrote each word down, intending to look them up later. After ten minutes of this, and thirty of these words, he moved his talk to its next phase.

Knowing that he would be facing a youthful demographic, and wishing to maintain the momentum from the previous day's triumph at Lower Bottom Primary School, Wilberforce Selfram had decided that the next segment of his event would take the form of a children's introduction to one of his favourite philosophers, Immanuel Kant.

As he took to his feet and extended his arms, he resembled a basking cormorant. 'May one have your attention please,' he monotoned into the microphone. His end of the hall had been completely disregarded by the children, but some of the parents had glanced over and wondered what was going on. They now supposed that this was all part of the entertainment, and these odd-looking people were perhaps a cabaret troupe about to perform for them – their dark costumes and cadaverous complexions were certainly in keeping with the event. The room fell quiet while their audience waited for them to break into a dance.

No dance came. 'Come hither, infants,' said the man who appeared to be their leader, beckoning with his long, grey fingers, 'and one shall tell you all about

Kant.' There was no movement towards the stage, so he tried again. 'Kant, Kant, Kant,' he said. 'Roll up for Kant, children.'

The next thing he knew, Mrs Bruschini was on stage beside him. 'Mr Selfram,' she said, 'I hardly think this is appropriate.'

Recalling the earlier episode with the steak knife, and bearing in mind the absence of any takers for his short course in Junior Transcendental Idealism, he decided not to make an issue of it, and to move straight on to the third phase of his event, in which he planned simply to talk about some of his books. Slightly mystified by what had just happened, but reassured that it seemed to be in hand, the people at the other end of the room resumed their activities.

Richard and Ayanna sat at the side of the hall. They noticed that Mara had found her way there too, presumably on her motorbike, and was working intently at her skinny laptop. Morag MacLochness had slept through her alarm and missed her plane back to Scotland, and had hopped on a Book Bus to the event to give herself something to do. She had bought herself a blue Slush Puppie to drink, but after a few sips she had fallen asleep under a fire extinguisher. The background noise was such that nobody noticed her snores, or the sound of an incoming helicopter as it flew overhead and towards the nearby recreation ground.

'One was contracted to enwrite a novel,' explained Wilberforce Selfram to his six listeners, 'yet one had been so preoccupied with psychogeography that one did not have in one's possession a single idea for such an undertaking. One arranged an audience with the Duchess of Bloomsbury and inquired, indeed enquired, whether she would accept instead a new version of one of one's short stories, only much, much longer. She said, and one shall always remember these words, "For God's sake, Selfram, do what you want." Such is her trust in one's ability to produce work of only the finest quality. One duly enwrote the book, and it was published to much press coverage and modest sales. Its failure to dominate the bestseller lists was symptomatic of a br...' He was interrupted at this point by a commotion at the other end of the hall.

A tightly clustered group of four people, two men and two women, entered through the main door, all of them unusually tall and wide-shouldered, and wearing suits and dark glasses. They dispersed from their cluster and formed a line to reveal that at their centre had been a fifth member of the party: a woman, dwarfed by her companions, who was also in dark glasses, and who seemed somehow familiar. A hush fell over the room, and everybody stared. The woman reached up, and took off her dark glasses. Suddenly, she became very familiar indeed.

'Oh look,' said Mrs Bell. 'It's that nice Harry Potter lady.'

Chapter 36

The treasurer receives a visitor to his cell

The treasurer had watched enough TV crime dramas to know that he was entitled to make a phone call from the police station. He also knew that the sensible thing to do under these circumstances was to use it to arrange legal advice. He decided instead to call the secretary. He didn't want her to find out about his incarceration through the rumour mill; he wanted to be able to tell her everything, and let her know that it had all happened because he had been thwarted in his pursuit of her. He didn't expect to ever see her again, and he wanted to say goodbye. He hoped she would be flattered. The phone rang, and she answered.

'Hello.'

'Hello. It's the treasurer.'

'Oh. Right.'

'Yes. I wonder if we could have a meeting.'

'I suppose so. When?'

'Are you free now?'

She sighed. 'Not right now. Maybe a bit later. Where?'

'It'll have to be at Market Horten police station. I'm in the cells.'

'In the cells?'

'Yes, I've been arrested. Not formally, but as good as.'

'What for?'

'Assisting a murderer and preventing the lawful burial of a body.'

'I like the sound of that,' she said. Her voice seemed to have developed a purr. 'Are you guilty?'

'Yes.'

'I'll be right over.'

Because the treasurer hadn't yet been arrested or charged, the policewoman on duty let the secretary join him in his cell. 'Did you ever hear the name Mad Charlie O'Higgins?' she asked as she sat beside him on the hard bed.

'What, that nutter who tore those people's heads off?' He had seen photos of him in newspapers, a barely human lump of gristle.

'That's the one. I'm his widow.'

'What?'

'Have you heard about women who find prisoners really sexy, and write them letters in the hope of forging a relationship?'

'Er…yes?'

'I'm one of them. Before Mad Charlie I was married to Mad Lenny Crump, who used to nail people to the ceiling. I was only eighteen at the time. Anyway, they're both dead now. I'd only been married to poor Mad Lenny for a few months when his cellmate stabbed him in the throat with a shiv made out of a sharpened toothbrush, and last year poor Mad Charlie's cellmate stabbed him in the throat with a shiv made out of a sharpened carrot. I've been single ever since, but maybe it's time to move on.'

The treasurer wasn't sure what to say. Suddenly this reserved young woman seemed terrifying. 'You don't strike me as the type,' he gulped.

'Oh, I'm the type all right,' she said. 'I may be a bit quiet,' she said, 'and maybe I don't always stick up for myself, but when it comes to men it's different. I know exactly what I want, and I get what I want: prisoners. I would send them pictures, like this.' She tapped her phone, and there she was, in a number of provocative poses. There wasn't a cardigan in sight; no wonder Mad Lenny and Mad Charlie wrote back. Terrifying or not, he wanted her more than ever.

'I always thought you were a bit dull,' she said, 'but I'm seeing you in a new light. Tell me everything. I mean *everything*. Don't leave out a single detail.'

As he told his story, she hung on his every word and moved incrementally closer until their bodies were touching. 'So if it hadn't been for you,' he said, 'I would never have got involved.'

'I love it. I've driven you to a life of crime. We're like Bonnie and Clyde.'

'Brian says I'll definitely be going to jail,' he said. 'But he thinks they'll let me out on bail before the trial.'

'Out on bail,' she sighed. 'Just think of the opportunities. Sometimes Mad Lenny and Mad Charlie would be allowed out on conjugal visits. The times we had...' she sighed. 'My mum and dad hated having them in the house, pounding away at me in my bedroom and only ever coming out to eat loads of meat with their hands.'

Her lips were a hair's breadth from his by this point, and he kissed her. She made little moans and sighs as he guided her down on to the hard bed, where their bodies fused.

'We'll get engaged now, and get married when you're inside,' she said, in between moans. 'I love a nice prison wedding.'

The treasurer gazed at his fiancée. Everything was worth it – the boring committee meetings; the affair with Mrs Bruschini; digging the hole; dragging the body across the lawn. It all made sense now because, albeit in a rather quirky way, he had got his girl. He wondered whether Richard Curtis would be interested in buying the film rights to their story. He would write to him from his cell.

'I hope they give you a nickname,' she said. 'Maybe they'll call you Mad...' She realised that until that day he had made so little impression on her that she was completely unable to bring his name to mind, and at the same time he realised he didn't know her name either. Still, formal introductions could wait for another time; for now, they had each other's bodies to explore.

*

Brian entered the cell. 'Break it up, lovebirds,' he said, 'they've dug him up. She'd wrapped him in thirty layers of cling film. Thirty! Can you imagine?' He looked at the treasurer, and shook his head. 'You don't half know how to pick 'em, son.' The local law enforcement was clearly aware of the secretary's matrimonial history. 'It's high time we started observing the protocols. I am arresting you in the name of Her Majesty the Queen. You have the right to remain silent…'

The secretary stood behind Brian, smouldering, licking her lips, and running her hands across her body.

'Sorry Brian,' said the treasurer, when the policeman had finished. 'Would you mind repeating all that? I got a bit distracted.'

Chapter 37

Everyone was delighted that the Harry Potter lady had turned up, and they waited to hear what she was going to say. She looked around, and didn't appear to be impressed with what she saw. She pointed at the bouncy castle, and said to one of the very tall men, 'Pop that.'

Everyone gasped. The children had been having such a nice time on it.

One of the very tall women whispered something in her ear.

'What do you mean we're not allowed to pop it? It's clearly a violation of my intellectual property rights.'

'It isn't though, is it?' said the woman, giving up on whispering. She pointed at the large lettering at the top of the castle. 'It doesn't say *Hogwarts*, it says *Wizard*

School.'

'It's the same thing.'

'We've been through this - you didn't invent wizard schools. As your senior legal adviser, I must remind you that a number of other auth...' She was stopped by a raised hand.

'Enough. Look how they described it in the promotional materials.' She guided her team across the room to the noticeboard. There were a number of pieces of A4 pinned up, advertising Women's Institute events, Pilates classes, and amateur dramatics auditions. There were also two small posters relating to the book festival – one asking people to search the backs of their cupboards for unopened bottles to present to the authors, and the other advertising this event. 'You can see it right here, just as my network of informants told me. They've used my intellectual property, without my permission, to lure people in. And does muggins here get a cut of the takings? No, she does not. Once again my livelihood is undermined.'

The senior legal adviser wasn't so sure. 'They've put *Bouncy 'Hogwarts' Castle*. It's in inverted commas, so it's something of a grey area. The best we could do, realistically, is send a cease-and-desist to whoever owns the castle, to make sure anyone who hires it doesn't use the word *Hogwarts* in their promo materials. It's hardly worth the bother though.'

'Hardly worth the bother? *Hardly worth the bother*? Just listen to yourself. Sometimes I wonder why I give up my weekends to fly around in a helicopter suing people when all I get is *Oooh, we can't take him to court,* or *Oooh, we can't take out an injunction against her.* I'm not leaving this hall until we find someone to take legal action against.'

Somebody started to cry, but as they attempted to suppress a sob it came out like a snigger. She couldn't work out who it was, so she addressed the whole room. 'I suppose you all find this funny, watching somebody doing nothing more than protecting their property. Well let me tell you what happened to the last person who made a joke about me being litigious: I sued them. Let that be a warning to you. There will be no laughter.'

Something in her eyes made them think that they should do as they were told. She clearly meant business. The room was silent, apart from the snores coming from Morag MacLochness in her position under the fire extinguisher. Even though she had somehow managed to spill her Slush Puppie all over her face, she remained comatose.

JK Rowling walked over to the cake table, where the volunteers were relieved that all the Hogwarts house-themed cakes had been eaten. She looked in the apple barrel for possible infractions, and found none. Then she reached the craft table. Some children were there, part way through drawing pictures. One little girl had almost finished a rudimentary felt-tip portrait that was just about identifiable as a female figure. Underneath, she had written HERMYONE.

'This,' said JK Rowling, snatching the picture and holding it up for all to see, 'is an unacceptable breach of my copyright. I am confiscating it, and commandeering it, and it shall be taken from here unto a place of incineration, and there it shall be burned until it be nothing but ash.'

*

JK Rowling had truly intended to carry out her threat of destroying the drawing, but she had chosen the wrong target. This little girl of six years old came from a local family which, every generation, produced a single child with such large and limpid eyes that everyone who came into contact with them was immediately, and completely, disarmed by their gaze. The latest inheritee of these extraordinary eyes looked up at the angry grown-up, and the angry grown-up made the mistake of looking down at her. She stopped waving the picture when she noticed the big eyes moisten as a tear began to form. The sight awoke something buried deep within her.

She put the picture back in front of the child. 'That,' she said, addressing the whole room, 'was what a baddie would say. But I'm not a baddie. So instead, I say this to you all – who would like to hear a story?'

A great sense of relief was felt throughout the room, and a big cheer went up.

'Gather round,' she said, and she perched herself on the edge of the bouncy castle as the children sat beside her, and cross-legged on the floor below her, while the adults stood around the edge of the group. Richard and Ayanna joined them. Mara, however, carried on working at her computer. She was absorbed in something.

'Who here likes Harry Potter?' asked JK Rowling, and another big cheer went up. Even Morag MacLochness had woken up and started to take an interest. 'Well, I'm going to give you a little treat, and read a story from the Harry Potter world that isn't in the books.'

There was a collective delighted gasp, then a droning voice came over the microphone. 'Genre nonsense,' it said.

'I'm sorry, Ms Rowling,' said Mrs Bell. 'I'll switch the speakers off while you read your story.' She found the plug and flicked the switch.

JK Rowling carried on. 'Who remembers the character Perkin Ellmister from Hufflepuff?' Lots of hands went up. 'Some of you may have noticed that quite often Perkin will look very sadly to the left, and then to the right.' Many little voices told her they had noticed this. 'So who can tell me why that is?' This was met with quiet. 'You won't know, because I don't tell you why in the books. Even Perkin himself doesn't know why he does it. Today though, you are going to be the first people to find out.'

Wilberforce Selfram sat behind a dead microphone at Vratislav Effenberger's wallpapering table, and stared straight ahead. His six readers sat in place, but then one of them broke ranks and went over to the bouncy castle to listen to the story. They were followed by another, and another, and then there were none.

He sat very still. He was quite a long way away from the centre of the action, and he didn't want to move because he didn't want his clothes to rustle and drown out the Harry Potter lady's voice. He was determined that nobody would ever find out, but in spite of his open derision of what was happening at the other end of the room, there was part of him that desperately wanted to know why Perkin Ellmister would sometimes look very sadly to the left, and then to the right.

Chapter 38

We hear more about Perkin Ellmister, and Wilberforce Selfram's
greatest fear comes to pass when his secret is made public

Wilberforce Selfram did his best not to let a tear
roll down his cheek. It was no good. He could feel
it coming, and pretending to look for a pen he
disappeared behind his pile of books as the drop made
its salty way down his pale grey face. He needn't have
bothered hiding though, because nobody was paying
him any attention, and besides, with the exception of
Mara, everybody else in the room was crying tears of
their own. Richard was comforting a sobbing Ayanna,
who was in turn comforting a snuffling Richard.
Adults and children alike had quite dissolved. Closely
watched by a quivering Mrs Bell, just in case she was
to go on a rampage, Mrs Bruschini dabbed her eyes
with a handkerchief. The story of Perkin Ellmister had
hit them right in their hearts.

Perkin, they discovered, had always felt an indefinable sense of loss, which came from him having been born in the middle of a row of identical conjoined sextuplets: Gherkin, Jerkin, Firkin, Perkin, Popkin and Pipkin. The boys were joined together like paper dolls, and their desperate parents had taken them to a rogue wizard in the hope of separating them, but the magic had gone wrong, and all but one of the siblings had perished. With only Perkin surviving, Gherkin's right arm had been salvaged and grafted on to him, as had Pipkin's left arm. And so his brothers had become a part of him. Nobody who knew this secret could ever bring themselves to tell Perkin why he felt this constant melancholy, but everybody who had heard the story at Upper Bottom village hall now knew that whenever he looked very sadly to the left, and then to the right, it was all because of the faintest trace of an intangible babyhood memory of the brothers he would never know.

'And that,' said JK Rowling, 'is the end of the story.' The audience applauded as they wept, and when the applause died down, she addressed them. 'I do hope you enjoyed that. If you did, please consider giving a little money to a wonderful organisation called Castle Dwellers for Social Justice, which has just made me a Companion of Honour. My bodyguards will pass among you now, collecting any coins you may have to give. As I'm sure many of you know, there are few things closer to my heart than social justice – I said as much to Johnny Depp when I was buying his yacht off him, and he enthusiastically agreed.'

An extremely tall man and an extremely tall woman

moved among them, collecting coins in silk pouches. As they did, a small child took the opportunity to approach the author and ask her whether she would mind answering a question.

'I would be glad to, little boy.'

'Actually, I'm a little girl.'

'I'll be the judge of that. Either way, what would you like to know?'

'I was wondering, why do you always write "hiccough" instead of "hiccup"? My dad's been reading the books to me at bedtime, and he says it drives him mad.'

As if a switch had been flicked, her eyes once again became wild with rage. '"Hiccough" is the correct word. Anybody who uses "hiccup" is wrong. Wrong, do you hear me?'

Wilberforce Selfram certainly heard her, and he couldn't help but be impressed. He too preferred hiccough to hiccup, on account of it being both profoundly unpopular and containing more letters.

Furiously, JK Rowling stood up. 'To the helicopter,' she bellowed to her entourage. 'I've had news of a ninth birthday party in Corbridge where they are using unlicensed Harry Potter balloons purchased from the Internet. We'll soon put a stop to that. Pins at the ready.' And with a new mission to pursue, they re-formed into their huddle, and left the way they had come in.

For a moment, with the Harry Potter lady gone, people were at a loss as to what to do. It was the children who

got things moving again, by returning to the bouncy
castle, or the craft table, or buzzing around on their
broomsticks. Wilberforce Selfram's readers, a little
shamefaced now, returned to their chairs, and Mrs Bell
switched the PA system back on. Wilberforce Selfram
supposed he should continue from where he had left
off.

'...oad cultural malaise, which tragically persists to
this day. Should you wish to find out what happens
at the end,' he said, recalling the line he had been so
impressed with the day before, 'yous'll huv to buy the
book to find oot.'

Morag MacLochness had once again fallen asleep
under the fire extinguisher, but the sound of somebody
else appropriating her trademark sales pitch penetrated
her subconscious, and roused her from her slumber.
Slowly she opened her eyes, and the world came into
focus.

Wilberforce Selfram carried on. 'Were you to
purchase the aforementioned volume, it would be...'
He broke off to pick up a huge tome, and leaf through
it. 'One shall utilise one's most elephantine thesaurus
in order to find an obscure synonym for the rather
commonplace *wonderful*.' He flipped back and forth
between a couple of pages until he found what he
was looking for. 'Ah, yes, this is perfect. Were you to
purchase the aforementioned volume it would be...
fandabidozi.'

This was too much for Morag MacLochness, who
took to her feet. Her hair was dishevelled, and the
colouring in the Slush Puppie had left broad streaks of
vivid blue down her face. 'Selfram,' she said, 'Ah'll no

stand to huv ma native tongue offendit. *Fandabidozi* is the greatest word ever uttered by human being, living or deid, and Ah'll no huv ye calling it an "obscure synonym". Shang-a-lang, Selfram – any mair of this and Ah'll snap yer heid aff.'

Wilberforce Selfram was quite taken aback, and wasn't sure what to say. Luckily for him, two things happened to help him. Firstly, Morag MacLochness lay down again and went back to sleep, and then, moments later, there was another commotion by the main entrance. This time it was two new groups of people arriving in quick succession: first the press, and then the police.

A substantial proportion of the authors in the area at that point were journalists with books out, so when Mara had let them know that JK Rowling had put in an appearance in Upper Bottom, they had raced over in the hope of a story. They had arrived too late, but that hadn't bothered Mara. She had only used the Harry Potter event as a useful bait; the presence of a big star had made it easier than she had anticipated to build up a live audience for her exposé. MI7 had called her that morning, and told her the time had come for her to end the Selfram Project, to kill him off as a cultural presence. They had given her six weeks to achieve this, but she thought she might as well get it over and done with straight away. This time she knew that underlying affection would not stand in her way.

The Eric Finlayson episode hadn't been quite

the failure it seemed. It had further toxified public debate, which was an end in itself, and even though his cancellation had been cancelled, he would, from now on, always have a **Controversy** paragraph on his Wikipedia page. She still felt it could have gone better though, with his complete destruction, which made her all the more determined for this mission to work. Richard wasn't the only hacker in town, and he and Ayanna hadn't been the only ones who had rummaged around Wilberforce Selfram's hard drive and found a way into the folder marked *Top Secret!* All the time she had been at the village hall she had been collating the material she had found there into a Powerpoint presentation.

The representatives of the press had entered first, waving their passes and looking around for JK Rowling. Moments later the police burst in, led by Brian, who was furiously blowing his whistle. 'That's her,' he said, pointing, and a group of heavily armoured officers made a beeline for Mrs Bruschini. Like lightning she reached into her bag, pulled out her gavel, and set about them. She landed a few solid blows, but before long she had been disarmed, handcuffed, and read her rights.

'My husband shall hear of this,' she cried. 'He's very high up, you know.'

'That's funny,' said Brian. 'When we found him, he was very low down, in a hole in the ground as a matter of fact, and wrapped in thirty sheets of cling film. Thirty!' She was bundled out of the building, towards the waiting Black Mariah.

'It wasn't me,' cried Mrs Bruschini, 'it was my

treasurer. Check for fingerprints.'

The press were so busy looking for JK Rowling that they barely noticed this happening. They were inclined to leave that sort of thing to the crime desks, anyway; their line of journalism tended more towards the what-I-had-for-breakfast end of the market.

Had the journalists been real reporters, on finding their quarry absent they would have gone out to look for her, and they would have found her on the nearby recreation ground, standing beside a stalled helicopter with her hands on her hips. 'Get its spinner thing going,' she bellowed at her hapless mechanic. 'You can't fly a 'copter without its spinner.' She tapped her watch. 'Those balloons aren't going to pop themselves.' For a moment longer she watched the mechanic at work, before losing patience and elbowing him aside. 'Why do I always have to do everything myself?' she huffed. She grabbed a spanner, fiddled around for a few minutes, and said, 'Try it now.' The blade began to rotate. 'Finally, we're getting somewhere.'

Mara knew that village halls in reasonably affluent areas tended to have been awarded National Lottery funding to buy state-of-the-art projectors, and Upper Bottom's was no exception. She had hacked into it without difficulty, and had also set things up so her presentation of the darkest corners of Wilberforce

Selfram's computer would be live-streamed through numerous hijacked accounts on thirty-six different social media networks. None of it could be traced back to her, and if anybody was to catch a glimpse of her laptop screen it would look for all the world as if she was playing solitaire.

She moved the four of hearts around until the house lights dimmed, then the screen at the back of the stage, behind Wilberforce Selfram, lit up. His seated figure could be seen in silhouette as the room fell quiet and everyone's attention moved to Mara's presentation.

WILBERFORCE SELFRAM, read the text. **You may know him as a mid-profile restaurant critic, radio essayist, newspaper columnist, current affairs pundit, and occasional novelist. You are about to learn something else about him.**

Wilberforce Selfram pivoted around in his chair, and his silhouette was now in profile as he read the text. An image from the secret folder on his hard drive flashed up on the screen, and he knew then that all was lost.

Chapter 39

Wilberforce Selfram returns,
disconsolate, to the parsonage

Over at the main stage, Eric Finlayson's event was coming to an end. It had been a great success. He was apparently oblivious to his removal from the culture and his swift reinstatement, and nobody had raised the subject. There had been much laughter at his anecdotes, and even some tears, and with a few minutes left to run he had opened up to questions from the audience.

A number of expectant hands went up, and Eric Finlayson picked, at random, Mr Goslyn, a popular local dry cleaner.

'I must say, Mr Finlayson,' said Mr Goslyn, 'how much my wife and I enjoy your books. We buy them as soon as they come out, and we always have a bit of an argument about whose turn it is to go first. We think they're terrific.'

'Thank you,' said Eric Finlayson. 'I'm so glad you enjoy them.'

'There's only one question I would like to ask,' Mr Goslyn continued, 'and I ask it on behalf of my wife as well.' Mrs Goslyn sat beside him, looking excited and bashful at the same time. 'What we would like to know is, what exactly is a proctor?'

There was a rumble of approval for this question, as people turned to one another and said *Oooh, I'm glad someone asked that, because I'd been wondering too.*

Had Mrs Bruschini been there, she would have been delighted by Eric Finlayson's gracious manner as he began his answer. 'I think the best way to describe a proctor is as someone who...' The rest of his answer was drowned out. Instead of standing in the wings while she approved of his manner, Mrs Bruschini was in the back of an armoured van, en route to a police station in London, where she was to be questioned by the very toughest detectives at Scotland Yard. The van happened to be passing through Green Bottom at just that moment, and its siren's wail rendered the author inaudible. When it had died away, Mr Goslyn explained to Eric Finlayson that because of the siren he hadn't quite caught the answer, and asked whether he would mind repeating it.

'Certainly,' said the author, graciously, and he began his answer again. 'I think the best way to describe a proctor is as someone who...' This time it was submerged beneath the sound of a helicopter flying low over the tent. JK Rowling had fixed the rotor blade, but not quickly enough for them to be able to get to Corbridge in time to pop the child's balloons. Instead, they made their way back to her private helidrome in silence. It had not been the most successful of days.

This time Mr Goslyn didn't ask Eric Finlayson to repeat his answer. He decided instead to look up the word in his dictionary when he got home.

There was another sound from outside the tent, this one far less intrusive – the hum of Dave's taxi pulling up outside The Parsonage. Mr and Mrs Bell got out of the back doors, and Mr Bell opened the passenger door, from which emerged the long legs of Wilberforce Selfram.

The journey had been a difficult one. Dave had been relieved that Wilberforce Selfram hadn't returned to the subject of his book about a taxi driver by the name of Dave, but on the other hand he had been disconcerted by his demeanour. He didn't know what had gone wrong at the village hall, and he thought he would be better off staying out of it as Mrs Bell tried to reassure the author from the back seat, saying things like, *I'm sure everything will be fine in the long run*, and *Get a good night's sleep and it won't seem so bad in the morning*. Nothing she said seemed to reassure him. He just stared ahead, his face more deathly than ever.

He slowly rose from the car and, hunched over, made his way back to the parsonage, where he went straight to his room and lay on the bed, staring at the ceiling.

*

Richard and Ayanna loaded the books into the van, and returned to the stage to fold away the trestle tables. Ayanna felt melancholy. She had known this was going to be her last time doing an event with Wilberforce Selfram, but she hadn't known it would be his last event as well. She couldn't see a way for him to come back now that his deepest secret was public knowledge and his reputation was in ruins. 'I know he's brought it on himself,' she said, 'but I can't help feeling sorry for him.' Unsure of what to say, Richard put a comforting arm around her shoulder. 'I even quite like him,' she admitted.

The hall was emptying now. There were a few volunteers tidying up, and while most of the children had gone home, some whose parents were volunteers still charged around on their broomsticks. The bouncy castle had been deflated and was being packed away.

Without having said a word about it, Richard and Ayanna both knew that Mara was behind the hacking of the projector. They looked around for her, but she wasn't there. They heard the roar of a large motorbike fading into the distance.

Sunday Morning

Chapter 40

We find out, at long last, what Wilberforce Selfram
was hiding on his computer

The original plan had been for Wilberforce Selfram to remain in The Bottoms after his event, undertaking a little rural psychogeography before being driven back to London late on the Sunday morning. Ayanna had been expecting to drop him beside a dual carriageway somewhere on the outskirts of the city, from where he would walk home, inspecting various slip roads, bankrupt mattress warehouses, and unloved stretches of canal along the way. His intention had been to turn this into an essay about his return to an urban environment after so much time in the countryside, seeing the cityscape anew, as if through Beoffrey's eyes. He had been confident that he would be able to place it with a leading journal for a substantial fee, but who would commission it now? All Wilberforce Selfram wanted was for Ayanna to deliver him, defeated, to his home.

She had risen early and gone around to the parsonage to check up on him. The parson was going through his notes for his sermon, and had let her in. She went upstairs, and knocked on Wilberforce Selfram's door. After hearing a feeble '*Enter*,' she had found him still in bed, in his nightgown and nightcap, staring at the ceiling. In a faint voice he had asked her to go and get all the Sunday papers and meet him in the kitchen in a few minutes' time.

Wilberforce Selfram was still within his slumberwear at the kitchen table as Ayanna dropped her armful of papers in front of him. When she had picked them up at the village shop she had seen that he was mentioned on the cover of several of them. There was no getting away from it; everything had changed. On top of the pile was *The Observer*, which had made him their second story and carried a picture of him on the front page. He looked at it with something that might once have been pride, and unable to let go of the verbosity that had stood him in such good stead for so many years, he said, 'One's visage is no *étranger* to the rotogravure.' There was a deep sadness to his monotone, though. The headline confirmed his fears: *Keep Calm and Be Nice*.

Wilberforce Selfram had answered the phone only once the previous evening, and that had been to speak to *The Observer* in order to present his side of the story. He had placed a lot of work with them over the years, and had hoped they would at least give him a fair hearing. He read the story they had written, and supposed they were about as kind as they were ever realistically going to be.

Wilberforce Selfram's readers, they explained, had been left reeling over the revelation that images found on his hard drive had shown that he was responsible for upwards of ninety per cent of the *Keep Calm and Carry On* phenomenon. Operating from an industrial unit on the outskirts of Stroud, his company had spent much of the preceding decade cornering the market in mugs, place mats, fridge magnets, T-shirts, flags, cushions, tea towels, tote bags, clocks, aprons, and more or less anything else that could conceivably be printed on. As well as adopting the famous wartime slogan *Keep Calm and Carry On*, he had adapted it to accommodate anything for which there was a demand: *Keep Calm and Have a Cuppa* tea cosies; *Keep Calm and Bake Cakes* oven gloves; *Keep Calm and Drink Gin* tumblers; *Keep Calm and Go Fishing* thermos flasks... The list was as extensive as it was twee.

His supporters, they explained, had turned away from him, unable to align themselves with somebody who had done something as un-Modernist as flood the nation with unironically saccharine mottoes. The membership of the National Psychogeography Fan Club had united to announce that they were no longer tergiversating between him and Iain Sinclair for the position of Pre-eminent Extant Psychogeographer, and all six of them were now openly putting their weight behind Sinclair alone. They then apologised for having used the word *tergiversating*, when *vacillating* would have worked just as well, perhaps even better. They explained that they just couldn't help themselves.

The newspaper also reported that he had parted company with his publisher. This was not news to Wilberforce Selfram, as the call from the Duchess of Bloomsbury had come in while he was still on stage with the screen behind him, and his readers, one by one, were getting up from their stackable chairs and leaving the hall in dismay. He wouldn't normally have answered his phone on stage, but these were unusual times. 'Oh, hello Selfram,' she had said. 'I'm just calling to thank you for your years of service, and to wish you all the very best in your future endeavours.' The moment the Powerpoint presentation had gone live, MI7 had contacted her with the news that he was no longer her responsibility. With these revelations dulling his reputation as a great alternative thinker he had outlived his usefulness, and The Selfram Project, which had lasted a lot longer than any of them had expected, was deemed to have served its purpose.

He was quoted in the article a number of times, and was obliged to accept that they had used his words fairly. He had told them that he had been having a struggle within himself for years. He had found that the older he got the more forgiving he had become of things of which he had previously been aggressively dismissive. He went on to say that he now knew he had been so dismissive of these things because all along he had been afraid of the warmth he felt towards them, a warmth which, if embraced, would have undermined his self-image – and public reputation – as an outsider, so instead he had pushed them away. He admitted that he liked watercolours of countryside scenes, and romantic comedies and, above all, he had begun to have extraordinarily fond feelings towards hedgehogs. He explained that he genuinely found the *Keep Calm and Carry On* slogan to be charming, and its variants lightly amusing. Poignantly, he said that he wasn't sure who he was any more. While he remained as keen on long words as ever, and still considered himself to be a keeper of the Modernist flame, he couldn't deny that there was another side to him, and that he could no longer keep it hidden. 'After years of inner conflict,' he said, 'one is coming to terms with the fact that there is a substantial part of one that is, to an extent, quite normal, and even rather nice.'

Some of the other papers, the ones he hadn't spoken to, were harsher in their treatment of him, and they tore him down with glee, almost as if they had been waiting for this moment for a long time. They had mainly used the modern journalistic technique of substituting reporting with lists of things that people had said on social media, and much of it was viciously amusing. The *Sunday Mirror*, though, had a gentler take on the story, and Ayanna made sure he read their piece all the way through, because it gave him a little credit, and even a bit of hope. They had made some effort, and had contacted his employees who, while never having known who their ultimate boss was, told of good pay and conditions. They had also dug into the financial side of things and found that Wilberforce Selfram himself was not the owner of the enterprise, that it was the property of a charitable trust he had established, called The Fretful Porpentine Foundation, which supported the protection of hedgehogs. Wilberforce Selfram had never taken a penny of the profit; it had all gone to the hedgehogs, providing them with a national network of state-of-the-art hospitals and rehabilitation centres, and buying up swathes of land where they could safely thrive. They concluded by saying that behind his carefully cultivated Bad Boy image he was quite the softie. There was even a suggestion that this could be the start of a new chapter for him.

'Think about it,' said Ayanna. 'Now people can see you're not quite as much of a dick as they'd thought, it could open doors for you. What about all that Beoffrey stuff? It's much more likely that BBC2 will go for your ideas now. You're not the long-words show-off any more, you're the nice hedgehog man.'

'Child, perhaps there is some veracity in that which you speak,' he said. His face became a shade less pale. 'Find one the *Sunday Times*.' He had just remembered that his *Why One Intends to Walk in the Footsteps of Beoffrey* piece was due to be in their travel supplement.

Ayanna dug it out. The travel section was always one of the first to be put to bed, and consequently it had been printed as planned, before the scandal had broken. She noticed that the news pages seemed to have tactfully ignored the *Keep Calm and Carry On* story, perhaps not wishing to draw their readers' attention to them having given a double-page spread to someone who was in the process of being roundly discredited.

He sighed to see himself leaning against the *Welcome to Biddenden* village sign, and sighed again when he saw they had changed the title from *Why One Intends...* to *Why I Intend...* 'One despairs of contemporary subeditorial standards,' he droned.

This moment of respite was short-lived. Ayanna looked at the *Sunday People*, and there he was again, staring out from the front page. Their story, though, was not about the contents of his hard drive. The headline gave her a chill, and she tried to hide it from him, fearing it might all be a bit too much for one day. She was too slow though, and he saw it. The small amount of colour that had returned to his face drained away. He read the story.

EXCLUSIVE: Beoffrey of Biddenden revealed as a hoax!

Top history eggheads were in shock last night as the prof behind the renowned Beoffrey Papers admitted he had written them himself! Hailed as a major insight into Medieval life, the papers had recently been published to enormous interest around the world. However, lab tests revealed that the supposedly ancient parchment was in fact modern writing paper that had been soaked in tea and dried out on a radiator before being scorched around the edges over a candle. The team of scientists also discovered that when they held these papers up to the light they all had a Basildon Bond watermark. Rutland University history boffin John Dumbleton, 36, broke down as he told our reporter that he was guilty as charged. 'I mainly set it up to trick Wilberforce Selfram into eating slugs,' sobbed the married father-of-one, 'and it got a bit out of hand. From what I've heard it worked, though.'

He immediately tendered his resignation, but it was refused by the Chancellor, who said that he was prepared to write it off as one-of-those-things. When news of his slug-cess reached the student body, Dumbleton was carried shoulder-high around the campus and treated to a boozy Saturday night in the union bar. Notorious windbag Selfram, whose catchphrases include 'symptomatic of a broad cultural malaise' and 'one' was unavailable for comment. (Turn to page 7)

'One would very much prefer not to turn to page 7,' he said. At that moment his phone rang. 'One supposes it will be Her Majesty's Press,' he sighed. 'One wonders what they want of one.' Too weak to lift it to his ear, he pressed the speakerphone button, and Ayanna was able to listen in.

'Wilberforce Selfram speaking.'

'Hello Mr Selfram,' came the voice. 'It's the *Guardian* here. We're running a series of live masterclasses and we were wondering whether you might like to present one for us?'

His eyes widened. 'Tell one more.'

'We're wanting you and Harry Johannes to come in and give a talk on the theme of *Coping with Disgrace*. What do you think?'

He removed his nightcap. 'Pray enlighten one as to the nature of the remuneration.'

She told him. It was the *Guardian* so it wasn't much, but it was something.

'Very well,' he replied. 'Very well.'

They ended the call, and immediately the phone rang again. Invigorated, he picked it up. '*Celebrity Sewage Farm*, you say? Channel 5, you say? Jeff Brazier, you say?' Ayanna found a scrap of paper and furiously noted down the details.

That call over, Wilberforce Selfram's phone pinged again. This time it was an email. 'From one's agent. One cannot bear to read it.' He passed it over to Ayanna, who read it out to him.

'"Funniest thing, Selfram,"' she read. '"I was just about to drop you as a client when the email below came in. On a Sunday morning as well! Turns out you may not be quite as far down the drain as all that. Get back to me right away. Pip pip."' Ayanna scrolled down and read the forwarded message. It was from a TV producer. She carried on: '"We're in deep shit. We're due to start shooting a new show for daytime TV tomorrow, called *All Things Nice with Anneka Rice*. Trouble is, Anneka's sprained her ankle and has been ordered to rest up. We need an urgent replacement - I read about your Selfram's image change in the *Sunday Mirror*, and thought he might be up for it. We could change the name to *Wilberforce's World of Whimsy* – basically him going around the country admiring glass figurines and cooing over puppies. None of his silly words – this is daytime telly."' He moved on to the fee. It was the BBC so it wasn't a fortune, but it was something. '"We'll need him on set at seven tomorrow morning – we're shooting at a holiday park for Muscovy ducks, so it should be up his street. Let me know within thirty minutes, or I'll have to start ringing round."'

'One should be marble, but one is clay,' he whimpered. 'Accept their offer, would you?'

Ayanna wrote back, making sure they knew he would be unavailable for the last two weeks of November because he was already committed to *Celebrity Sewage Farm*.

'One shall, of course, put a Modernist spin on it all,' he said, barely making any effort to convince himself that this was what he would really do.

'Of course you will, Selfram,' she said, with a comparably transparent lack of conviction.

'It appears one is going to be rather busy,' he said. 'One wonders whether you would consider becoming one's personal assistant, driver, bodyguard and amanuensis?'

'Oh fuck it,' she said. 'Why not? I draw the line at amanuensis, but as long as you give me a decent pay rise I'll do the other stuff.'

He told her what her salary would be, and she fired off an email to her ally in HR, telling her she had finally broken free.

Chapter 41

The Duchess of Bloomsbury visits the headquarters of MI7
to arrange Ayanna's assassination

The main control room of MI7 looked much as would be expected – the brilliant white walls were lined with vast screens displaying satellite images, maps, covert surveillance footage, and extreme close-ups of eyes. In the centre hovered a hologram of a shifty-looking character, his face partly hidden behind an open copy of the *Morning Star*. 'Please don't be put off by all this,' said the genial silver-haired man known only as Agent X – his title denoting the highest rank in the organisation – as he cordially welcomed the Duchess of Bloomsbury. 'I'm afraid the interior designers went a little overboard.'

'I rather like it,' she said. 'It's giving me ideas for our riverside penthouse.'

He waved the compliment aside. 'Congratulations

on The Selfram Project,' he said. 'We'll be sad to see it go, but it's done a wonderful job. I really do believe that those cock-awful books of his have done their bit to protect the nation from a radical swing to the left. Thank you so much for your invaluable help.'

'I'm glad to have been of service to our fine nation,' said the Duchess of Bloomsbury, before getting to the point. 'Lord Barnstable said you would be ready to do me a small favour in return.'

'Of course we will, my dear Duchess of Bloomsbury; it's the least we can do after everything you've done for us. What did you have in mind?'

The Duchess of Bloomsbury reached into her bag and pulled out a C4 envelope. She opened it and handed him a slim sheaf of papers, including four prints of photographs that she had taken without her subject knowing. 'Take a look at this woman.'

He took the photographs, appraised them, and lay them on a table, where they were quickly scanned by an android and fed to the hologram projector, which replaced the furtive left-winger with a life-size and very realistic image of Ayanna. She rotated in 3D before them.

'There she is,' said Agent X. 'Now, what would you like us to do?'

'This young lady has been working as an assistant at my company for a few months now, and...' She paused. She had never arranged an assassination before, and her heart was thumping. 'I would like her to be taken out.'

Agent X thought for a moment. He pressed a code into a keypad, and some sliding doors opened. A young man entered the room, and saluted. 'Agent 3498Z reporting, sir.'

'Agent 3498Z, you see this hologram?'

'Yes, sir.'

'I would like you to take this young woman out.'

'Very good, sir. Where does she live?'

Agent X looked through the papers. 'Croydon.'

'That's handy,' the young man said. 'I live in South Norwood, so quite close. There's even a direct bus from the end of my street. Do we know if she likes pizza?'

Agent X looked through the notes. 'It doesn't say, but I expect she does. Who doesn't?'

'I was thinking Pizza Express might be nice.'

'A good choice, 3498Z. You always know where you stand with Pizza Express. They're good for special diets too, so if she has any preferences or intolerances I'm sure she'll be well catered for. And if you pay a bit extra, they do these really big thin ones.'

'Oh yes, I like them, sir.'

'I always ask for extra artichokes.'

'I'm an extra-sweetcorn man myself.'

'I've never been able to get along with sweetcorn on pizza, but each to their own, I say. I think this is just what you need, 3498Z. You've been moping ever since you split up with…what was her name?'

'Kazumi, sir.'

'Oh yes, Kazumi. She was a lovely girl, but it's over now. It's time to move on, and a date with…' he looked at the file to remind himself, '…Ayanna – I do hope I pronounced that correctly – will be just the tonic you need. Don't expect anything from it, just relax and have a good time. Think of it as dipping your toe back in the water. If there's no chemistry, at least you'll have had a nice pizza together. And if there *is* chemistry… well, those days are far behind me now, but I always used to think that the best way to get over a broken heart was to embark upon a new romance.'

'Quite so, sir.'

Agent X turned to the Duchess of Bloomsbury. 'So there we are. We're a tight knit unit at MI7, and 3498Z is like a nephew to me; I can unequivocally vouch for his character. Your assistant is in the safest of hands. There's no time like the present,' he said, 'so let's see if we can arrange this for tonight. I do hope they hit it off,' he said. 'It would do 3498Z a world of good.'

'Are you sure this young agent has what it takes to…' again her heart began to thump, '…rub her out?'

Agent X's eyes widened. 'My dear Duchess of Bloomsbury, Agent 3498Z has some experience in these matters, but let's not get ahead of ourselves; it's only a first date, after all. We'll have to see if they hit it off before he tries to…' he had turned a little pink, '…do that thing you said. As I was saying to Agent 3498Z, we're somewhat at the mercy of chemistry. Let's start with the pizza, and take it from there.'

'Just a minute,' said the Duchess of Bloomsbury. 'Please reassure me that you're talking in code.'

'Code, your grace?'

'Yes, all that stuff about extra artichokes. What were you *really* talking about?'

He looked at her, wide-eyed. 'Extra artichokes,' he spluttered. 'I'm afraid I don't quite understand; I thought you wanted us to take her to dinner or a film or something. I assumed she was feeling a little lonely.'

'I didn't mean take her out on a date. I meant…you know…*take her out.*'

He looked at her quizzically.

'Bump her off,' she tried.

The penny dropped. 'Oh, *rub her out* in that sense. I thought you meant you wanted him to…never mind. So just to be clear, you want us to kill her?'

'Yes.'

Agent X chuckled. 'I'm awfully sorry. We've been talking at cross purposes. I'm sorry to you too, 3498Z, for raising your hopes like that.'

The young agent looked disconsolate. 'I was looking forward to meeting her,' he said.

'It's a real shame. You know what, though? Even though you never got to eat pizza with her, she's still played a big part in your life.'

'How do you mean, boss?'

'Think about it. You were excited about going to dinner with her, which means you're ready to get over Kazumi and move on. Ayanna may not be the one, but by Jove, as of right this moment you are back in the game.' He playfully punched the young agent on the shoulder.

He smiled. 'You're right, sir, I hadn't thought of it like that. I'll always be grateful to her.'

Agent X looked vacant for a moment. 'Now where were we? Oh yes, you wanted us to kill her.'

'That's right.'

'But why?'

The Duchess of Bloomsbury told him about her disappointment at coming third at Common People Bingo, and how Ayanna had been cheeky around the office. 'I also heard that she was making unacceptable suggestions.'

'That sounds serious. What were these suggestions?'

'She had this ridiculous idea that the industry worked too slowly, and that the traditional year-long gap between the completion of a book and its publication means that novels are losing ground as a vital force, and lagging behind other media. What rot. If she had her way, fifty percent of novels would be fast-tracked and published a few weeks after being completed. We in the Brotherhood of Darkness (Publishing Division) don't work that way, Agent X, and we have no intention of doing so. And don't get me started on her views about the industry adopting Japanese production standards. If it was left to her, first editions would no longer be traditional, clumping great British hardbacks, but *exquisite objects,* all high-grade paper and glossy covers with striking artwork. It doesn't bear thinking about. And besides, I just don't like the girl.'

'And it was Lord Barnstable who assured you we would do this?'

'Yes. Well, he said he was sure you would do me a favour. I assumed he knew what I meant.'

'How did you think we would go about it?'

'Oh, I don't know. With a ray gun, maybe, or a poisoned apple.'

'I see. I'm sorry to say it's out of the question. We can't just go around killing people with ray guns because they've been a bit lively at work and aren't amusingly proletarian enough to win you quite as many biscuits as you'd hoped for. I must admit I rather like the sound of this girl. She seems spirited.' He sighed. 'I'm frightfully sorry about the mix-up, Duchess of Bloomsbury, but normally when somebody asks for a favour they just want to come in and have a nose around the office. Sometimes they ask us to pull up a few files on old enemies from school, or have a look at the shark tank, that sort of thing.'

'You have a shark tank?'

'Yes we do; we believe it's the biggest secret-service shark tank outside China. I'll tell you what, since you've come all this way – on a Sunday morning too – why don't I give you a little tour? Follow me.'

There was a circular walkway around the edge of the vast tank, and the Duchess of Bloomsbury felt a frisson as she looked at the great whites circling in the water below.

'Aren't they beautiful?' said Agent X. 'They're peckish, too, we've made sure of it. It may seem a little corny,' he said, 'but this really is a very efficient way to dispose of a body.' He checked his watch. 'It's feeding time any minute now.'

As if on cue, two broad-shouldered security guards bundled a small female figure through a door and on to a platform that jutted out over the water. She was in a harness, and they clipped her to a rope and winched her into the air, high above the dead centre of the tank.

'Her name is Rachel Lewis,' said Agent X. 'Also known as Mara. She was one of ours – an effective agent, too. She used to run the campaigns to ban Lou

Reed and The Mikado, and she did very well; she annoyed so many people that she added an estimated fifth of a percent to the Conservative vote, and drove a comparable amount of potential left-wingers away from politics altogether, because they felt that if getting involved meant that they would have to stand alongside the same people who tried to blacklist "Walk On The Wild Side" then they'd rather not bother. The trouble is, she'd been sent here by the Russians, and was running errands for them. She was basically doing what we've always done, but on their orders, and under her own initiative, she was taking it too far. Rather than tilting things to the right just enough to let us live our lives in peace, she and those like her have been emboldening the brutish end of the market, blurring the boundaries between us and them, and that's the last thing we need. We had a tip-off last night that she was somehow directly involved with Vladimir Putin. We followed it up, and sadly it all fell into place. I'm not sure why we'd not spotted it ourselves, quite honestly. I can't say I'll miss her.'

The woman struggled on her rope, crying, and begging for her life to be spared. 'Where am I?' she sobbed. 'Who are you people? Why do I have *I* ❤ *Vlad* tattooed on my arm?' None of this was having any effect on her captors. Her desperate pleas echoed uselessly around the enormous room.

'I recognise her,' said the Duchess of Bloomsbury, 'she's that newspaper columnist. I don't like her.'

'Then I'm going to give you a very special treat, and I hope it'll make up for your little disappointment earlier. Come with me.'

She followed him around the walkway until they got to a control panel.

'You see this red button here?' he said. 'This releases the clip that's holding our poor traitor on to the rope. Once it's pressed, she will very quickly begin her descent. I wonder, would you care to do the honours?'

The Duchess of Bloomsbury's face lit up. 'Oh yes please, Agent X.'

'Here we are then. Finger at the ready. After three: one…two…three…'

The Duchess of Bloomsbury pressed the button, and with a scream Mara plunged into the water. It seemed a little anti-climactic at first as she managed to stay afloat, frantically swimming in small circles, but soon the sharks began to take an interest, and she was dragged under. The water churned, and a plume of blood turned it red, and then pink, and when it cleared the sharks were still there, but the woman was not.

'How super,' said the Duchess of Bloomsbury, forgetting Ayanna altogether. 'Thank you, Agent X.'

'Not at all, your grace. Just remember not to tell a soul. I wouldn't want to have to send *you* for a swim.'

The canteen at MI7's headquarters was less showy than the main control room, and resembled something that might be found at a service station off a dual carriageway. Agent X sat with Agent 3498Z, and as they drank their coffee and ate their doughnuts they talked over their morning's work.

'I don't understand these publishers, 3498Z,' said

Agent X, adding a sugar lump to his coffee, and stirring. 'They're forever launching schemes to increase inclusivity, but when the people they recruit turn up for work, the top brass expect them to fall in line and behave exactly as they would if they had come to them via the usual channels – boarding school, Oxford, and all that. If they act a little differently, rather than embrace the change, the head honchos come here and try to get us to kill them with apples. The way she was described, that young lady seemed like a breath of fresh air. They should have listened to her ideas; I've been to a bookshop in Japan, and it was like visiting an art gallery. I bet the retail side of the trade would be delighted to move in that direction.'

'I thought she was lovely,' said a glum Agent 3498Z. 'I'm glad we didn't kill her. I don't think I've ever felt that way about a hologram before.'

'Agent 3498Z, one day you'll find true love. Take some comfort in the knowledge that it'll all be over for the Brotherhood of Darkness (Publishing Division) before too long anyway.'

'How so, boss?'

'The world is changing, and token gestures aside, they aren't changing with it. I don't see them being of much use to us for a great deal longer. All their animal sacrifice and chanting is a little passé, wouldn't you say? And you know that book that's being written about them?'

'I've heard about it. Apparently it's very good.'

'It's superb, Agent 3498Z, and it's going to be an unstoppable hit. The author's up to Chapter 41 now, and seems to be wrapping things up. The publishers think that if they cheer it on to the bestseller lists, people will assume their little guild couldn't possibly exist. I'm not convinced, though. Times have moved on, and I think this will be the end of them; it just rings a little too true. We shall certainly be withdrawing our patronage. We'll let them get away with killing the author – I've already promised them the police will hit a brick wall in their investigation – but that will be the end of our association. I'll break the news to Barnstable next time we have a top secret meeting on a bench in St. James's Park. Without us in the picture I can't see them continuing as much more than a social club, and with no direct link to the Palace they'll start to wonder why they're taking their clothes off and smearing themselves with blood. It's fizzling out anyway – Uncle Rupert always used to be the first to get his robe off, but these days he just sends excuses and endangered animals.'

'Good riddance to them. If they would even think about doing that to Ayanna...' He shook his head. 'Speaking of women I find attractive,' he said, 'it's a shame about Mara. Was she at peace in her final moments?'

'Not particularly, no, but not to worry.' Agent X had started to worry a little, though. The more he thought back to the way she had pleaded, the more her anguish rang true. She really had seemed to be mystified by it all, and terrified. Normally when people were suspended over the sharks they were resigned to their fate; some of them had even been known to say *Hey-ho* as they fell. He wondered whether the rumours he had been hearing were true, that the Russians really had found a way to implant appalling personalities, and even level seven psychopathy, into previously normal, decent people. He did his best to shake off this feeling.

'Do you think anyone will notice she's not around any more?' asked Agent 3498Z.

'We've already wiped every trace of her from the archives. One or two of her fans may wonder where she's gone, but I don't suppose they'll be turning every stone to find her. Most people will be relieved to see the back of her. I'm told even Vlad's not too bothered that she's stopped returning his calls. Her character was ripe for retirement, anyway – millennials are becoming rather old hat. People have become accustomed to them, and in some cases they're even starting to feel sympathy for them; you've probably read that recent study which concluded that the average millennial is now widely considered to be forty per cent less exasperating than they were five years ago. They've been confronted with the practicalities of life – things like arranging boiler maintenance, and trying to fathom the Key Stage 2 literacy curriculum – and it's humbled them. They're just not as full of themselves as they used to be, and as far as our operation goes they're being put out to grass. To make sure the next generation gap is a real schism, the Palace is insisting we replace Mara with a new columnist, a genuine Generation Z-er called Kgmaxionu 7. This one's far more up to date – impossible to gender, from Bristol of course, and with a worldview that is completely incomprehensible to anybody more than three years older than they are. They've not reached the stage of life where they have to put up shelves, or deal with plumbing emergencies, so they have all the time in the world to scroll through their phone, judging others and finding them wanting. To help things along, they won't even know they're working for us. We've just set up their column, and we'll leave them to it. It's far more straightforward than sending in our own people. Cheaper, too. This way we give them enough rope, and away they go. Their column starts next weekend. It's called *OK Millennial.*'

'I'll miss Mara though.'

'She was an absolute horror, that girl. Take all the work she did on the DSI project. She deliberately made something that was, in my view, a leap forward – giving sex pests a haul across the coals – and fabricated a tableau to try and make it look as if it was nothing more than political correctness gone mad. She was too talented an operator, and I should never have given her free rein. That's the trouble with the Russians; our brief from the throne is to keep the country dressing just a little to the right, enough to make sure socialism and republicanism don't gain too strong a foothold in the nation, but that lot always take things too far. We've ended up in a situation where people who until recently would have been dismissed as the work bore, or the loony on the bus, are megaphoned by the media, and allowed to shape the national agenda. It's all very tiresome. I'm not sure what we can do about the Russians now, though. For all her successes, Mara was only a small player, and they'll take her loss in their stride. They've got everyone in their pocket, right up to the very top of government, so much so that we might even get our wrists slapped for feeding her to the sharks. Time will tell. Oh, those Russians,' he sighed. 'I'm starting to think it might all be a little beyond me these days, you know. They say you get more right-wing the older you get, but if anything I'm starting to go the other way; I'm even thinking about voting for the Liberal Democrats at the next election. Perhaps it's time for me to stand aside and let a younger agent grasp the tiller.'

He noticed that Agent 3498Z had stopped listening, and was staring into space. He told himself off for having drifted into one of his soliloquies. He assumed agent 3498Z was thinking about Mara, and Ayanna, and Kazumi, but he was mistaken. Agent 3498Z was remembering something odd about his journey to work that morning. A stony-faced man wearing a big fur hat had boarded the almost empty train carriage, and sat opposite him. From a breast pocket he had taken a shiny gold watch on a chain, and had gently swung it from side to side. The next thing Agent 3498Z knew, he was waking up having missed his stop, and the man had gone. It had all been quite strange, but he told himself it was nothing. As Agent X droned on, he tuned out, and a mist began to clear in his mind. He remembered an urgent and top secret task he had been given. It was something to do with some blueprints, and microfilm, and a bench in St. James's Park. He also felt an unstoppable need to set up a few dozen pseudonymous social media accounts and tell the world that if NHS nurses had wanted enough money to be able to afford food, they shouldn't have become NHS nurses in the first place.

Agent X smiled indulgently, and as he finished his

doughnut he idly tried to work out how the author of *Sour Grapes* had found out about the shark tank, and the hologram projector, and even the smaller details, like the doughnuts, and Agent 3498Z staring into space. He supposed they must have been lucky guesses.

Chapter 42

Ayanna and Wilberforce Selfram
say goodbye to the village

Mrs Bell had a lot on. With Mrs Bruschini and the treasurer in police custody, and the secretary having abandoned her post, apparently in a state of uncontrollable erotic ecstasy, it was down to the rank-and-file committee members to see the festival through its final day. With her reputation for calmness and clear thinking, it was only natural that they would all look to Mrs Bell to step up as *de facto* leader. She looked through the programme and saw that the grand finale – *Children's Choir, John Banville & Gymnastics Display* – was due to finish at eight in the evening, and only when that was over would she be able to relax. There would still be authors to shepherd on and off rail replacement buses, but at least the festival itself would be in the past, never to return. Knowing that the game was up, the Happy Smile Energy contingent had taken off their wigs, packed away their drill, and left the area. Florence Peters had gone too, driving away at high speed in a furiously backfiring Triumph Spitfire.

Mrs Bell had been up since six o'clock, making lists and sending text messages. At last she was sure that there were volunteers in place for all the events, and she just about had time for a cup of tea before heading off to church. Ayanna was back from next door, and had gone upstairs to pack before joining them for the service. When it was over, it would be time for her and Wilberforce Selfram to drive back to London.

Richard had a confession to make. 'I really like you,' he said.

'Thanks,' said Ayanna, as she struggled to zip her bag. 'I really like you too.'

'No, what I'm trying to say is…I really like you.'

The night before they had been out for a pub meal, and there seemed to be an unspoken agreement that neither of them would bring up the subject of what was going to happen after this weekend. It had been a successful strategy, and they had had a very enjoyable time. It felt as if they had known one another for years, and Richard hadn't smiled so much in a long while.

Neither of them had wanted to have this conversation, but time was running out, and here it was.

'I've had a very strange but excellent weekend,' said Ayanna, 'and I'll always remember it.'

That didn't sound encouraging. He carried on

anyway. 'You know when we first met, and you punched me to the floor, and we ended up kissing?'

'Mmmm.'

'Everything changed. I could feel it happening; I knew I was leaving a lot of bad things behind. And there was something I did while you were in the shower.'

'Are you sure you want to tell me this?'

This broke the tension, and he laughed. 'I had a lecturer who told me that when I was through with my Incognito phase I should call him and he would sort me out with a job. He said...well it doesn't matter.'

'No, what did he say?'

'He said that I had one of the best minds of any of his students, and that people would be falling over themselves to offer me work. Anyway, I called him. He said he knew I would one day. The upshot is that by the time you'd towelled yourself down I'd got myself an interview in London for next week. Apparently it's just a formality. It's more to see if I want the job than if they want to employ me.'

'Congratulations.' She felt really happy for him.

'So I was thinking, since I'm going to be in London, maybe we could meet up?'

Ayanna still couldn't get her bag's zip to fully close. She put all her strength into it, and compressed the contents until at last she got it shut. She remembered everything she had told herself. 'Maybe,' she said, quietly and in a tone of voice that made him very sad.

She felt sorry for him, but she knew it was for the best. There was no way this was going to last, and she didn't want to dangle false hope in front of him.

*

The service had been very different from the ones she went to with her mum most Sundays, and she had enjoyed it. Just being in such an excellent village church had been enough to make it worth the effort, and the parson had made a good impression on her from the pulpit. Her travels had seen her dip into a number of village churches, and she found country vicars tended to pander to the locals who came in from the big houses in their Jaguars and BMWs, glossing over the obvious disparity between the gospels and their lifestyles. She was happy to find that Reverend Jacobs turned out to be, in his amiable way, something of a socialist firebrand, and his congregation looked progressively sheepish as his sermon went on. She recognised a few faces; for one, Mrs Chapman had been singing in the choir. Her scratches had faded, and she was looking so holy that it was hard to believe she was the same person who had smashed a gravy boat over Florence Peters' head the day before. Ayanna sat with the Bells. Richard had tagged along too – for the first time in years, according to his mother. Wilberforce Selfram had been invited, but had declined, saying he had some urgent psychogeography to be getting on with. She knew that he was really staring at his phone, waiting to see whether any more offers came in.

And then it was over, and they were outside, in the churchyard, and it was time to say goodbye.

Mr Bell awkwardly shook Ayanna's hand and told her very sincerely that it had been nice to meet her, and Mrs Bell gave her a warm embrace. 'Good luck with the last day,' said Ayanna. 'I would stay and help, but I've got to get back. I'm up at five tomorrow.'

'I do hope we'll see you again,' said Mrs Bell.

Ayanna didn't know what to say. Then it was Richard's turn. He stood there looking awkward, so Ayanna helped him out. She wrapped her arms around him and put her head on his shoulder. 'Goodbye Richard,' she said.

Wilberforce Selfram sat in the passenger seat, staring straight ahead as Ayanna pulled out of the Bells' driveway and made her way along the narrow lane out of the village. She turned into another narrow lane, and then another, and after a few minutes it became clear to Wilberforce Selfram that they had circled back to Green Bottom. There was the pub, and the marquee, and the church.

'One is beginning to have misgivings about having employed you as one's driver,' he monotoned.

'I'm not lost, Selfram,' she said. 'Not any more. Just give me a minute.'

She pulled up outside Parsonage Cottage, and got out of the van. Wilberforce Selfram watched as she walked up the path, rang the bell, and waited. It was Mr Bell who answered, Bevis by his side. Mr Bell went back in, but Bevis stayed put, and Ayanna made a fuss of him. A minute later, Richard appeared, looking a little dazed. Wilberforce Selfram couldn't hear what they were saying, but their conversation went on for quite some time, until they stopped talking and just looked at one another, each sporting a silly grin. Then Richard gently put his hands on her face, and fiddled with her ears a bit, and she fiddled with his ears in return, and they kissed.

Wilberforce Selfram wiped away a sentimental tear and then, with a long grey finger, he reached over and beeped the horn. It was time to get going. He had a TV show to present.

A Year Later

Chapter 43

Following the successful publication of Sour Grapes,
the TV adaptation premieres

Richard had discovered that being some sort of computer genius didn't necessarily make you wealthy by London standards. On being told his salary he had pictured himself in a warehouse conversion with a balcony overlooking the Thames, but the flat he had ended up renting was on a main road lined with takeaways and phone repair shops, and what little view it had was barely visible through the impossible-to-clean windows. It was just one room, with an ageing micro-kitchen in the corner, and an awkwardly proportioned en suite shower room with a door that didn't quite shut, but it felt like home. Though firmly established as an attached gentleman, he was still a bachelor with dominion over his own territory, and he had observed the convention of choosing a television that was far too big for the room, and had managed to squeeze in a sofa for two.

He had only been home for a few minutes when Ayanna came in. She had her own key, so she hadn't had to buzz. 'Five minutes,' she said, giving him a kiss, and settling into what had become her side of the sofa. She switched on the enormous screen, found the CBeebies channel, and wondered what on earth was going on as some eerie puppets danced around a half-real-half-cartoon woodland. Richard prized the caps from a couple of bottles of beer, and sat on his side of the sofa. They leaned into each other, and waited.

There was some gentle, twinkly music, and suddenly a familiar figure appeared, accepting the honour of reading a bedtime story to the nation's children. 'Hello,' he said. 'I'm Wilberforce, and I'm going to read you one of my favourite stories. It's called *Samuel Spaniel*, and it's by a writer called Mr Fish.'

'See how he didn't say *One's given name, indeed forename, is Wilberforce, and one shall proceed to enread you a narrative...?*' said Ayanna, whose impersonation of him was pretty much perfect – at least her impersonation of the old him; lately his voice had become less of a drone, and his eyes were not as glassy as before. 'I really think he's grown up these last few months.'

He's not the only one, thought Richard, as he considered how his life had changed since meeting Ayanna. In the getting-to-know-each-other phase they had honoured the ritual of separating and reuniting a few times, and every time they had bounced back stronger, with lessons – always his – learned. He had left the wilderness behind. 'They probably wouldn't have broadcast it if he hadn't followed the script.'

'Maybe not. But still.'

The story, which didn't contain a single long word, reached its conclusion as Samuel Spaniel was forgiven for his cheeky antics. 'Goodnight,' said Wilberforce Selfram. 'Sleep tight.'

'I was expecting that to be the stuff of nightmares,' said Richard, 'but he did a pretty decent job.'

'Apparently it's quite a big deal to be offered that gig,' said Ayanna. 'They say it cements your status. He's been shitting bricks about it, anyway.' She fired off a message: *Nice one, Selfram*. He had told her he would be spending the evening sitting in the dark and staring straight ahead as he listened to Bulgarian soundscapes on Radio 3, but she knew he wouldn't be able to resist switching on the TV to see how things were going.

This was only the beginning of a Friday evening packed with Wilberforce Selfram-related programming. Ayanna quickly changed the channel to BBC1. The run of *Wilberforce's World of Whimsy* had been a great success, but with the recovery of Anneka Rice's ankle, *All Things Nice* had been revived. Wanting to keep hold of their popular new signing, the BBC had offered him frequent roving reporter slots on the early-evening family magazine programme *The One Show*, which was about to start. His contribution was to be a pre-recorded segment, to which she had driven him three weeks earlier. It had been her first visit to the flatlands of eastern England, and the landscape had blown her away; it had been like visiting another country. She had always known that she wouldn't be doing this job forever, but she was enjoying it, and days like that made it truly worthwhile. She had even dragged Richard out that way the following weekend, and they had sat drinking wine on the veranda of their Air B&B, looking out at fields that went on forever. Without either of them actually proposing, they had somehow established that they were going to be getting married before too long, but there would be no big white dress and no marquee, just a short service at her mum's church, followed by a meal in a room above a pub.

Ayanna had quite a lot of downtime from her Wilberforce Selfram-related duties, and had managed to fit in a part-time job working for Malwod Editions, a small press based outside London. She had met the publisher some time before, while doing her rounds with Wilberforce Selfram, and they had fallen into conversation; the extensive overlap on their reading Venn diagram saw to it that they clicked extraordinarily well. They had exchanged details, and one day she had contacted Ayanna and offered her a job. They didn't have much money, or many hours, but they let her fit her work around her other commitments, and she sometimes took the train out to meet up with them. She liked them a lot, and was particularly impressed with their determination to keep coherent and reliable accounts.

She had been brought in to do bits of reading and editing, and naturally her first mission was to lobby for *Out of the Strong Came Forth Sweetness*. To her delight, the others loved it as much as she did. Mystified, yet unsurprised, by London's indifference towards a book that was clearly a masterpiece, they had taken it on. It had been Ayanna's job to call the author and tell her. That had been the best shift of her life.

'And now,' said the presenter, 'it's over to Wilberforce Selfram, who's been to Bardney in Lincolnshire to visit a particularly impressive array of ceramic thimbles.'

The VT played, and showed Wilberforce Selfram flying into raptures over various ornamental finger protectors from the collection of an ancient woman who had been amassing them all her life, and now had over forty thousand on display in her bungalow. He singled out one with a picture of a hay wagon on it for particular praise, and another commemorating the end of British rule in Hong Kong. The segment ended with him presenting the delighted collector with her very own unique *One Show* thimble. He addressed the camera: 'If you've been inspired today, why not start your own collection? It really is as thimble as that.'

The programme returned to the studio. 'Wilberforce Selfram there,' chuckled the show's host. 'He's thimbly the best – a true National Treasure.' There it was again: National Treasure. It was a phrase Ayanna had been hearing a lot. It seemed that apart from a few snooty arts correspondents and literary extremists, very few people thought badly of him for his *Keep Calm and Carry On* work; if anything they had warmed to him, and as news of the hedgehog angle became more widely known, the broader populace took him to their bosom. It was winning *Celebrity Sewage Farm* that had really put him on the map, though. It had been a great boost to his bankability, and had even resulted in his forthcoming pantomime debut as Alderman Fitzwarren in *Dick Whittington* at the Wyvern Theatre in Swindon; Ayanna was helping him learn his lines and practise his dance steps. She hadn't seen him dance before, and had been pleasantly surprised by the fluidity of his movements. She had noticed a profound difference in him. He seemed happy in a way he never had before, and it had even been months since he had last complained about anything being symptomatic of a broad cultural malaise. She had a feeling that all he had ever really wanted was to be liked, but he had always gone about it the wrong way. Now it was finally happening to him.

At Mrs Bruschini's trial, a count of attempted murder had been added to the charge sheet, and Wilberforce Selfram's popularity reached fever pitch when the world learned how he had saved Florence Peters' life, bravely disarming a knife-wielding madwoman in the nick of time. After her brush with death, Florence Peters had taken some time to reflect, and had joined the Salvation Army in the hope of atoning for her past misdemeanours. When she turned up in court to give evidence she was dressed in her uniform, and in the courtroom drawings she looked quite angelic, which only added to the glow surrounding Wilberforce Selfram's actions that day. Ayanna had been there when the offer of the Queen's Gallantry Medal had come in, and she had felt proud of him when he had stuck to his principles and politely declined it.

He was still having difficulties in Scotland, though; his apparent belittling of their national word had made the front pages of their tabloids, and even after all this time anger was still simmering. The First Minister had stepped in and done a capable job of calming tensions though, and apart from a few potential flashpoints in the Central Belt, things were easing off. Even so, the Scottish Secret Service had advised him not to travel north of the border for some time to come, just in case. This had not stopped him from being anointed a National Treasure in all other territories, and it had stood him in good stead. He had even got himself a new book deal on the back of it – Viscount Penguin had called him personally and told him he was free to write whatever he wanted, because his new status meant that coverage was guaranteed. They told him they wouldn't even check it over before sending it to the printers, and that they weren't too bothered about sales because there was an odd kind of prestige attached to having him on their roster. So even without state subsidy, The Selfram Project continued under its own momentum.

In spite of all the other changes in his life, he had refused to compromise his fiction by making it in any way readable to his new fans, and had stuck to the technique that he had developed, to which he had added the twist of taking out all the spaces; his next novel was to consist of just one überword, stretched over five hundred pages. Ayanna had learned to stay out of his way when he was working on it. She had once made the mistake of going round to his office to do some paperwork while he was in full flow, but the stench was too much to bear and she had quickly bailed out. Since then she had just made sure he always had a good supply of prunes, and left him alone with his chamber pot and his stick. The first two hundred pages of this work had been circulated around the film industry, and the rights had been snapped up by the director Sam Mendes, who had released a press statement announcing that the book was right up his street, that it reminded him of *On Chesil Beach* and the recent James Bond scripts, and that he had already recruited Saoirse Ronan and Mark Rylance for the leading roles.

'Next up on *The One Show*,' said the presenter, 'we're hitting the catwalk as some of our models demonstrate the trend that's sweeping the nation. Yes, you've guessed it – it's the wimple. Everybody seems to be wearing one right now, and here to tell us all about them is the author of the popular book *No-nonsense Wimples*, Enid Halcrow. Welcome, Enid.' Her publisher had talked her out of her proposed title, *Sblomtamgungulous Wimples,* and it had swiftly become the biggest-selling sewing book of all time. She stood there in the studio, looking proudly on as a stream of models passed by, each wearing one of her designs.

Because they were relatively young, Richard and Ayanna thought nothing of ordering food by tapping a telephone. A jovial man with a big beard delivered it, and they sat on the sofa eating from cardboard cartons as they waited for the biggest event of the evening: the premiere of the highly anticipated TV series *Sour Grapes*, based on the novel that had been written about the events surrounding Wilberforce Selfram's visit to The Bottoms.

Previews of the show had been ecstatic, and Edward Tudor-Pole had been tipped for every award going for his glassy-eyed portrayal of Wilberforce Selfram. Only Kgmaxionu 7 had swum against the critical tide, furiously declaring the show to be offensive to at least four of the six emerging genders, and explaining that even though they hadn't seen it, it was clearly intolerant and was consequently not to be tolerated. Their followers on social media, who hadn't seen it either, raged against it, called for its broadcast to be pulled, and vowed to boycott it, all the while secretly planning on tuning in because they had heard it was going to be good. There were a lot of takers for the programme, in line with MI7's long-standing theory that when told not to do something by a peevish teenager from Bristol, most people will immediately want to do it, no matter what it is. Ayanna noticed that the usually relentless traffic noise from outside had stopped as people hurried indoors to switch on their televisions and see what all the fuss was about.

Richard and Ayanna had seen the trailers, and were impressed with the way Edward Tudor-Pole was in black and white while the world around him was in colour. Most of all, though, they were curious to see how they had been portrayed. They weren't sure whether they would find out tonight, because in the novel Ayanna hadn't appeared until chapter ten, and though Richard was in chapter two he was only glimpsed as a spectral face at a window, and hadn't come back in until around the halfway mark. They wondered whether the producers would have given the story a more conventional structure, and introduced the principal romantic players earlier on. They knew they hadn't been written out though, because they had been told who would be playing them. They had both enjoyed the book, and found it had painted a fairly accurate picture of their own experiences. It had been published as fiction, and the sections detailing the Brotherhood of Darkness (Publishing Division) and MI7 had been dismissed by reviewers as flights of fancy. Even so, there were plenty of readers who had sensed a ring of truth about them, and journalists – real reporters rather than arts correspondents – had been investigating to see whether the author had somehow gained access to forbidden knowledge. One particularly dogged freelancer had even found a secret entrance to the sewers around London Bridge, and after months of searching had found what appeared to be the femur of a juvenile okapi.

When the novel was released, the nation's publishing mandarins, remembering Lord Barnstable's words, forced their faces into rictus grins, and declared on their various social media accounts that they found the depiction of their industry in *Sour Grapes* to be rather delightful. 'The author's description of the upper echelons of publishing is so imaginative,' they dictated to their secretaries, 'that it could only ever be read as rather top-notch entertainment. Publishing boardrooms are, of course, bastions of social diversity.

Notwithstanding its myriad factual inaccuracies, we cannot recommend this charming and light-hearted novel highly enough.'

They became quite animated as they fulfilled their brief, and their responses, all notably similar in tone, were seized upon. Until this point the book had garnered very little attention, and shops had been ordering it in unremarkable quantities, but when this unexpected wave of enthusiasm appeared, people began to take an interest in it. A debate was sparked, as holes were picked in the publishers' assertion that their industry was an egalitarian wonderland. Anecdotal evidence to the contrary piled up, with dozens of past and present book-trade workers offering their own takes on the matter, successfully wresting the narrative from the increasingly panic-stricken grandees. When someone pitched in with a well-received observation that the senior publishers' world was 'basically a cross between a hedge fund managers' convention and a Sloane Rangers' tea party', the backlash hit the news pages.

Well-known authors were wheeled out to defend the publishers, to let it be known that they didn't recognise Rhodes' depiction of their industry. This strategy backfired when it was pointed out, quite reasonably, that, as cash cows, they had been cosseted and consequently had only a narrow viewpoint to draw on. This bickering resulted in a good amount of people feeling they ought to buy a copy of the book in order to help them form their own opinion of the matter, and sales soon gathered their own momentum.

Along with the publishers, not all the well-known

people depicted in the book had taken it well. A handful of them had unwittingly assisted the author's publicity drive by writing an open letter to *Harper's* magazine, in which they argued that while they accepted that the lampoonery of public figures was established as being quite normal in newspaper cartoons, animated cartoons, television sketch shows, radio spoofs, foul-mouthed operas, student revues, Welsh raps, Geordie adult comics, visual art, television puppet shows, big-screen puppet shows, Internet collages, satirical fortnightlies, novelty singles and stand-up comedy, it should never be permitted in fiction. 'Don't ask us why novels are different,' they concluded, 'they just are.'

Another group, though, had been vocal in their support of the author; Eric Finlayson and Alexander Armstrong had even joined forces to offer a substantial contribution to a fighting fund should anybody take offence and try to get the book withdrawn from circulation. On Alexander Armstrong's insistence, they referred to the proffered money as 'an amazing jackpot'.

Even though Richard and Ayanna were private citizens, and consequently had more to be aggrieved about than a lot of the other real people in the story, they had joined the chorus of support. It was light entertainment after all, and people were enjoying it; they weren't going to be party poopers.

The closest the author came to facing legal action had been after his former publisher had read the work and immediately announced a press conference to address the matter. Due to an administrative misunderstanding, it had been held in the yard of a suburban gardening company, Gleneagles Total Landscaping, and as the publisher stood surrounded by water features, ceramic gnomes, and piles of paving slabs, all the while desperately pretending that this had been his preferred location all along, he announced his intention to have the book removed from the shelves for having misrepresented events at his company. Dan Rhodes had got wind of this though, and had furnished the press with a dossier of correspondence, as exhaustive as it was chilling, and the publisher had quickly crumbled under cross-examination. He was obliged to admit that large sums had indeed gone missing, that the author had chased this money for years, and even following its recovery, coherent and convincing explanations had been hard to come by. They had even struggled to agree among themselves on exactly how much of his money they had lost. Reams of pertinent questions, he conceded, remained unanswered. He also had no choice but to publicly accept that the author had discovered an edition under their marque that he had never been told about, and the existence of which they had never explained. This hadn't even been mentioned in the book, and until this press conference it had not been widely known. 'It's hardly a publisher's job to tell their authors every minor detail,' he huffed. 'If we were to spend all our time making double sure that we've paid them correctly, and telling them when something as trivial as a distinct, rejacketed edition of their work is published, we wouldn't have time for any of the important things that publishers do, like...well, I can't think of anything on the spot, but I can assure you we are very busy people.'

The publisher began to splutter something about how the gentlemen and women of the press would benefit from reading the latest celebrity-fronted self-help title from their catalogue in order to achieve the wisdom they were so clearly lacking. At this, his legal team started to pack their folders back into their briefcases, and make the universal *let's go to the pub* signal to one another. When asked what exactly were the grounds he had for claiming misrepresentation and demanding the book be pulped, the publisher, by now literally clutching at straws from the pile of hay bales that had been set up as a makeshift lectern, said that he had never worn a velvet suit trimmed with lace, that the suit was in fact moleskin. 'I'm wearing it right now,' he cried, as the lawyers and the members of the press started to make their way out of the yard. 'You are invited to approach and inspect the weft.' There were no takers. A button from the famous suit chose this moment to come adrift, and his trousers fell down, revealing enormous boxer shorts – pink with large yellow spots. He hadn't seemed to notice this happen, though a departing photographer had, and a picture was taken that was to grace the front pages of all the national newspapers the following day. This photo, together with the accompanying news story, was credited with propelling the book's domestic sales through the seven-figure barrier. Soon the publisher was standing alone at his upturned bale. 'It's all in the weft,' he shouted, to nobody but the garden gnomes. He pointed at one of the sleeves. 'Feel the weft.'

*

Amid all this, a cloud of mystery remained around the true identity of the Wilberforce Selfram character. A number of possible candidates had been put forward by newspaper commentators, and social media was abuzz with theories as to whom the mid-profile restaurant critic, radio essayist and occasional novelist might have been based upon. No matter the differences between the theories that people came up with, they all agreed that the author had done an extraordinary job of blurring facts just enough to disguise his protagonist's identity: a little misdirection here, an inspired stroke of the quill there.

A small industry grew up in the mystery's wake, with the slogan *One is Wilberforce* appearing on T-shirts, badges, baseball caps and baby grows. Dan Rhodes himself refused to be drawn on the subject, giving only two evasive promotional interviews before giving up in exasperation when it became clear that the only thing the journalists wanted was the big scoop: the author unmasking the hero.

Ayanna knew who he was, though, and she also knew that very few facts had been changed to turn the story into fiction, but she had never raised the subject with the real Wilberforce Selfram. The book had become the cultural event of the year, and she supposed he must have known about it. Though his name had been mentioned among the lists of possible templates for the character, he had remained silent on the matter.

*

In one of his two interviews, the author had spoken about how surprised he was when Chatsworthy Editions had come in with an offer, and he had given them credit for their boldness. Though Lady Chatsworthy had tried to distance herself from the publication by making it appear to have been undertaken by a small press based in the shires, the secret quickly leaked. She had only reluctantly printed the book on Lord Barnstable's orders, and had been surprised by the positive publicity that had come her way. She was happy to bask in the unexpected kudos, and found her supposed courage rewarded when a number of well-known novelists left their own houses and moved over to hers, seeing her as a trailblazer for authorial freedom. She had shown up at the next meeting of The Brotherhood of Darkness (Publishing Division), below the offices of Haynes Manuals, with the intention of grandstanding, but she had found it quite a dismal affair, and not conducive to showing off.

The meeting's host, the Marquess of Haynes, had never particularly liked his title because he thought it made him sound like a woman. In his younger days he had led, without success, a campaign to have himself, and those of his rank, given the title of *Marchion*. Many Marquesses before him, their masculine pride similarly bruised, had gone out of their way to engage in stereotypically manly pursuits in order to redress the balance; one had famously hung around the outside of boxing rings, shouting instructions to burly young men as they thumped one another. The current Marquess of Haynes had decided at an early age to assert his manliness by covering himself in oil and fixing cars, and thus had an empire of motor manuals begun. He had forgotten that he was supposed to be hosting the latest meeting of the Brotherhood of Darkness (Publishing Division) until the last minute, and in a state of panic he had grabbed his daughter's gerbil from its cage and put it in a jam jar, before making his way over to his central London office to open up their underground garage.

All but four other publishers had cried off with feeble excuses, and those who turned up found themselves surrounded by a broad range of vehicles in various states of dismantlement. In lieu of flaming torches, the Marquess of Haynes had switched on the hazard lights of a nearby Austin Allegro. There was no bell to ring, so he had begun proceedings by hitting a hubcap with a tyre iron, after which he beheaded the gerbil with a Stanley knife, using a battery from a Bedford van as a makeshift altar. He had neglected to punch air holes in the lid of the jam jar, and the rodent had died in transit; by the time of the meeting it had already begun to stiffen. He made a mental note to visit a pet shop and buy a lookalike before his daughter had a chance to notice her pet was missing. As she was already eight years old, she was away at boarding school and wouldn't be home for several months, so there would be no particular hurry. The assembled publishers took small sips of what little blood they could squeeze out of it, and half-heartedly chanted about destroying their enemies, before moving straight on to disrobing. The only incident of note had been when Lord Orion had followed his announcement that this would be his final meeting before retirement by slipping on an oily rag and falling into an inspection pit, where he had flailed for quite some time. It was considered to be something of a sorry end to what had otherwise been quite a respectable career.

Lord Barnstable had seemed distant throughout. Just that afternoon he had met Agent X on a bench in St. James's Park, and been given the news that their group's ties to MI7 and the Palace had been cut. He wondered how long the industry would be able to hang on to its old ways without their patronage; perhaps the change they had feared, and had fought so hard against, had arrived. Maybe social mobility was an unstoppable force, and the industry would have no choice but to open its doors to those of ignoble birth. As he dabbed his naked torso with the raw neck of the decapitated rodent, and tried not to sigh as he made disappointing marks like tiny potato prints, Lady Chatsworthy approached him and asked whether he would let Dan Rhodes stay alive a little longer so he could write another bestseller or two. She had, foolishly it was now clear, wriggled out of her obligation to publish his back catalogue, but having had a taste of success she wanted more. Lord Barnstable had told her that the die was cast. The killer's blood had risen, he explained, and there would now be no hope of reining him in.

The Marquess of Haynes had, of course, neglected

to set up the harmonium, so the assembled publishers had to make do with an *a cappella* rendition of the National Anthem. They started it too high, and when they got to *Send her victorious,* it all fell apart.

'Oh, that'll do,' said Lord Barnstable. The room smelled heavily of stale exhaust fumes, and they were all impatient to leave. He had hoped there would still be a spark of life to cling to, but there was none. He didn't feel the need to announce the dissolution of the Brotherhood of Darkness (Publishing Division); there was no getting away from the cloying sense of an ending as they got dressed, gathered their belongings, and went away.

Though Lord Barnstable had been able to secure blanket coverage for the novel, he had not been able to exercise editorial control, and it had landed on the desk of each paper's most stony-faced critic. In a review that was later to be highly commended in the Astute Observations category at the Royal Literary Critics' Guild's annual black-tie awards ceremony and dinner dance, *The Times'* correspondent had concluded that the titular sour grapes were the author's own, and that at many points he was so intent on settling scores that he seemed to forget that he had a story to tell; the *Guardian* said that the burlesque tale of a mid-profile gasbag staying with a country clergyman was so close to the premise of the author's preceding novel, and so many lines were egregiously repeated, that anyone who had bought the earlier book should have been offered a money-off voucher for the new one; the *Express* called it, 'A pointless, childish, overstretched and wholly unsuccessful undertaking in which an irredeemably rancorous author takes aim at anyone who is doing better than him,' before going on to declare that it had brought shame on everybody involved; and the *Sunday Telegraph* ran just a two-word review: 'Shit grapes.'

The reading public seemed to pay them no attention though and, as if in defiance, the book had been widely enjoyed. Even Rhodes' complete lack of interest in promotional activities hadn't stood in its way as it charged to the top of the bestseller lists. Everybody, even its writer, had thought it was too parochial ever to make an impact internationally, but it turned out that Wilberforce Selfram was a type, and that every nation has one. Seeing its domestic success, the best translators were mobilised all over the world, some choosing to transfer the action to their own countries, and sales had exploded globally. Prior to this upsurge in his popularity, Ayanna and her colleagues at Malwod Editions had, for a peppercorn advance, secured the rights to most of the author's old titles, and they were now selling thousands of copies every week as people clamoured to read more of his work. That afternoon she had received a call telling her that thanks to this, Malwod finally had the budget to offer her full-time work, and she had accepted straightaway. She felt a little guilty at the prospect of leaving Wilberforce Selfram, but she was confident that he would get by without her. A few months earlier, handing in her notice would have seemed like abandoning a new-born baby in the desert, but now it felt more like leaving a new-born baby on the steps of a hospital. He had his TV work, his book deal and his lucrative personal appearances, and his album of classic love songs, *Let's Caress*, had gone straight into the charts at number one. He would be OK.

She felt melancholy about the fate of Dan Rhodes, though, particularly since his work had precipitated this great leap forward in her life. She had met him just once, to discuss Malwod's plans for reviving his backlist. She had read all his books, and loved them, and had long wondered why they hadn't found a wider audience. She particularly felt that *This is Life* should have been a big hit, and was delighted to have the opportunity to relaunch it, alongside the others. She had met him for a pint of lager and a packet of salt and vinegar flavour peanuts in a pub near his Derbyshire home. After she had finished telling him off for mispronouncing her name, he had told her about his visit to the headquarters of Chatsworthy Editions. When he was writing it, he had thought that *Sour Grapes'* appeal was somewhat niche, and wouldn't extend beyond his existing readers; consequently, he had been expecting it to be released by a small press, or maybe even from his own kitchen table, so he had been amazed when a big-money offer had come in. He had felt uneasy about signing with a major label, but with a family to feed he felt he ought to endure it. When the paperwork had been finalised, he had been called in to their penthouse office on Trafalgar Square, but when he got there they hadn't offered him a cup of tea, or even a seat. Lady Chatsworthy had just swept in, put the contract in front of him, and said, 'Sign this.' Once he had done so, she had swept away again, leaving him nose to nose with Nelson. He told Ayanna he had been refreshed by Lady Chatsworthy's overt awfulness, having found that senior publishers normally at least tried to hide their black hearts behind an air of faux bonhomie.

Ayanna had read an advance copy of *Sour Grapes* by this point, and he told her how in early drafts he had killed off her character on the final page, with MI7 successfully poisoning her with an apple, but had decided to change it because it felt too similar to the ending of one of his earlier novels, in which a decent and likeable character is killed while the perpetrator blithely carries on with life. He had chosen instead to go down the fantasy route, and offer an ending where the villains had some kind of comeuppance and the world became, in a small way, a fairer place. He explained that while he knew that such a conclusion blunted the novel a little, it meant he wasn't repeating himself too much, and he also hoped it would help him to stave off legal complications; suggesting the possibility of anything more than superficial change at the top of the publishing industry would bolster his defence that this was clearly a work of extremely fanciful comic fiction, and was not to be taken seriously.

Ayanna had been relieved to hear that she had survived a brush with death, but the enduring tragedy was that though the author had saved her, he had not been able to save himself. Just a few weeks after *Sour Grapes'* publication, he had died in the countryside. The police had said that the only potential clue left at the scene had been the paw print of what they believed to have been a golden retriever. Though the cause of death remained unknown, they were insistent that there was no evidence to suggest foul play.

This was no time to think too deeply about all that though, because the TV show was starting. There was a lingering shot of the village green, and the church, and the parsonage, then Mrs Chapman was there, cleaning the attic bedroom. She didn't look too much like the real Mrs Chapman, but her mannerisms were perfect. Her vacuum cleaner's battery ran out, and humming a hymn, 'Praise For The Fountain Opened', she went downstairs. Looking a little uneasy, she walked through the hall, and opened the kitchen door.

Acknowledgements

You've made it through. Well done. I know how hard it is to find the time. I hope you enjoyed it.

I'm impatient to acknowledge my debt to the following people and things, real and imagined, for one reason or another: everybody (well, almost everybody) thanked in the 'When the Prof' paperback, plus Mr Thwaites of the Rosamund Tea Rooms, Rambling Sid Rumpo, John Keats, John 'Hannibal' Smith, John Shuttleworth, John Betjeman, Boney M, 'The New Men' by C.P. Snow, Mazza's 24/7 wren consultancy service, Mrs Sagir, Colin, Claire, Sabrina the Teenage Witch (the proper one, not the reboot), the peerless Blue Aeroplanes and their inexhaustible surname mine, Penelope Boothby, my compadres at the DO, Pseuds Corner, the librarians of Ōtautahi, Cummings Your Way (do yourself a favour and visit their Youtube channel – start with Buxton or Lincoln and go in from there. It's a gold mine), Mary Webb, 'Cards of Identity' by Nigel Dennis (I passionately recommend you track down a copy), the real Morag, and Cleopatra. Repeat mentions must go to Spinal Tap and South Park, as well as Francis Plug – if you've not read the Plug books yet, you know what to do. Also, my GP tells me that Viz comic is in my blood – Tinribs, The Modern Parents, Fru 'T' Bun, Mr Logic and Half-Ton Hanrahan are heroes to me. So are all the others when it comes down to it. And since you ask, yes it is still going and it is still funny. The same can be said of Goldie Lookin' Chain, whose 'Fear of a Welsh Planet' LP is a high watermark in the history of recorded sound. I listened to almost nothing else while writing this.

Big thanks to all the good people who came in with support during my latest scrap with the biz (which – one despairs – is ongoing). You'd think that writing *Sour Grapes* would have got it all out of my system, but it hasn't. If anything I'm more riled up than ever. Watch out.

It will be clear to you by now that this book is a ludicrous folly that should never have been written. I hadn't expected it to come out, at least not properly, but it has, and I have Scott, Dan, Simon, Clio, Hugh and Begoña at the Eye/Lightning skyscraper to thank for that. They also got it out into the world a lot faster than the lumbering dinosaurs of the capital cities would have done. Have a look at their catalogue – the interesting stuff really does happen in the provinces.

I'd been longing for an Andrea Joseph book jacket ever since seeing her Strictly Ballpoint exhibition at Buxton Museum ten years ago. She rules. Dreams can come true, kids.

My three people remain marvels. That I've ended up with such excellent housemates is a constant source of wonder.

I know I said this earlier, but not everyone (I'm talking

lawyers, senior publishers, etc.) is as quick on the uptake as you are, so please forgive the repetition: it's all made up*. The well-known people didn't really do those things.

No slugs were harmed in the writing of this book.

Thanks for reading.

*Apart from, etc etc…

If you have enjoyed *Sour Grapes*, do please help us spread the word – by putting a review on Amazon (you don't need to have bought the book there) or Goodreads; by posting something on social media; or in the old-fashioned way by simply telling your friends or family about it.

Book publishing is a very competitive business these days, in a saturated market, and small independent publishers such as ourselves are often crowded out by the big houses. Support from readers like you can make all the difference to a book's success.

Many thanks.
Dan Hiscocks
Publisher
Lightning Books